PROLOGUE TO MURDER

Addie hopped out of the car, and her eyes were immediately drawn to a reflection on the chair beside the front door. She frowned, narrowed her gaze, and made a direct line toward it. When she reached the bottom porch step, she froze.

Simon, following close behind, bumped into her and sent her stumbling forward. He grabbed her in mid-motion and righted her before she crashed onto the steps. "Whoa, what just happened?"

"Look—that box on the chair."

He dashed up the stairs toward it.

"What are you doing? Don't touch it! Call the police."

"Because of a gift someone left you? Don't be silly." He picked up the box and shook it, still wearing his leather driving gloves. "It's not ticking and definitely not heavy enough to be a bomb. Aren't you curious?"

"No, I'm not."

He slid the silver ribbon from around the tall red foil box.

"Stop, don't open it. It's not a gift—"

Simon pulled off the lid. His eyes widened. "If it is, someone's pretty warped. . . ."

Books by Lauren Elliott

MURDER BY THE BOOK

PROLOGUE TO MURDER

Published by Kensington Publishing Corporation

PROLOGUE
TO
MURDER

Lauren Elliott

KENSINGTON BOOKS
KENSINGTON PUBLISHING CORP.
www.kensingtonbooks.com

KENSINGTON BOOKS are published by

Kensington Publishing Corp.
119 West 40th Street
New York, NY 10018

All Kensington titles, imprints, and distributed lines are available at special quantity discounts for bulk purchases for sales promotion, premiums, fund-raising, educational, or institutional use.

Special book excerpts or customized printings can also be created to fit specific needs. For details, write or phone the office of the Kensington Sales Manager: Attn.: Sales Department. Kensington Publishing Corp., 119 West 40th Street, New York, NY 10018. Phone: 1-800-221-2647.

Kensington and the K logo Reg. U.S. Pat. & TM Off.

First Printing: May 2019
ISBN-13: 978-1-4967-2020-7
ISBN-10: 1-4967-2020-2

ISBN-13: 978-1-4967-2023-8 (eBook)
ISBN-10: 1-4967-2023-7 (eBook)

10 9 8 7 6 5 4 3 2 1

Printed in the United States of America

Chapter One

A smile played on Addison Greyborne's lips when windswept sea-salt kisses danced across them. As she stepped inside the back entrance of Beyond the Page, her book and curio shop, she was struck by the combination of aromas. She took a deep breath. The briny tang of the sea air mixed with the delicate scent of spring flowers outside, and the heady scents of old books and leather chairs inside. These were fragrances she knew she'd never tire of. She hummed a popular tune as she zigzagged through the narrow aisles of bookcases and around the carved wooden pillars, straightening books on the shelves on her way to the front entrance. She flipped the door sign to "Open" and placed the advertising sandwich board on the sidewalk, holding it steady when an unexpected gust of wind threatened to send it tumbling into the road.

As she double-checked its security, her line of vision drifted up to the bay windows on either side of the glazed entrance. She stood back, admiring the new Founder's Day displays she'd created to commemorate the day in the seventeen hundreds that her forefather had declared Greyborne Harbor the site of a new town. A smile tugged at her lips. Yes, it was going to be another good day. Business had picked up since she was cleared of any wrongdoing in the Greyborne Harbor murder case of the century, and she had become more accepted in her new town. What could go wrong?

Back inside, she paused to adjust the fishnet backdrop in one of the windows to give it a more billowing appearance, straightened the starfish, adjusted the pirate galleon in the sand-and-sea diorama, grinned, placed a pod in the coffee machine, and waited. The aroma of a fresh brewed cup soon filled the air, taunting her nose. The doorbell chimed behind her, and she turned to see a petite, fiery redhead at the corner of a bookshelf.

"Serena, good morning. Do you want a cup?"

Her best friend and the local tea merchant stood unmoving except for one finger coiling a lock of her long, curly hair.

"Are you okay?" Addie glanced at Serena sideways and stirred cream into her coffee. "You seem a bit foggy this morning, and you look as though you need coffee more than I do." She offered Serena the cup of fresh brew.

Serena accepted the offer. Her hand trembling, she brought the cup to her lips. The hot contents dribbled down her chin. She cringed and quickly handed it back to Addie.

"Okay . . . ? Is everything all right?" Addie's brow furrowed. "You don't look well. Did something happen?"

Serena's hand still wobbly, she pulled a newspaper from under her arm and then stood wringing it in both hands, the color draining from her usually rosy cheeks.

Addie's eyes narrowed. She set the cup down. "What's this?" She snatched the paper from Serena's slender hand.

Her eyes scanned the front page of the *Greyborne Harbor Daily News*. She turned the page and searched the next, then the next, and the next, and stopped. Her fingers clutched the edges of the paper. Her bottom lip quivered, and she leaned against the counter.

"I thought you might need some company when you read this." Serena's usually silvery voice tightened.

Addie stared down at the article. "How could they?"

The Greyborne Harbor Daily News . . . Page 6
Continued from Page 5—Around Town

Finally, Miss Newsy asks the question on everyone's mind today: was it an alien abduction, which is the theory of some, or is the mysterious disappearance of local librarian June Winslow something far more sinister? Many Greyborne Harbor residents are asking that very question today; I know I am. What is really behind her disappearance, and who would have the most to gain by her sudden departure from the Harbor?

Reports were made by Mrs. Winslow's daughter of shaking ground and strange, flashing lights when she began searching for her mother, who failed to return home from a book club meeting. The report of unusual seismic activity in the area at the time in question was confirmed by Dr. Peterson, a seismology expert at Boston University. He is quoted as saying, "These disturbances did not warrant strong enough seismic activity to have opened up the ground and swallow anyone."

The local utility department also confirmed that a minor power surge did occur at the time in question. However, there was no lightning bolt activity, and the fleeting surge caused no reported damage to infrastructure and posed no threat to citizens.

So, what really is behind this sudden departure of a much-loved and respected member of our community? Who would have the most to gain? Perhaps Addison Greyborne can tell us.

It's rumored that Miss Greyborne, owner of Beyond the Page—Books & Curios, may have more answers than she's letting on. Being a librarian herself and the operator of an allegedly failing local business, she is most likely the one who could shed some light on the reason why there is currently an opening for head librarian at our beloved Harbor Library.

"What? How could they publish something like this?" Addie stared wide mouthed at Serena. "No proof, no evidence—they have nothing to substantiate the claim that I would know anything about her disappearance." She shook the paper in Serena's face. "Besides, I wasn't even a librarian. I was in research. Something that reporter had better learn how to do." She crumpled the newspaper.

"I know, I know." Serena grasped the paper from Addie's white knuckles and tossed it on the counter. "I think you need to sit down. I'll make you a nice, hot, fresh coffee since I took yours."

"I don't want a cup of coffee." Addie smacked her fist on the counter. "I want answers."

"I know you do." Serena took Addie's vibrating shoulders and ushered her onto a counter stool. "Please sit, and I'll try to explain something about the *Greyborne Harbor Daily News*."

"You shouldn't be explaining. They need to. I'm going over to the newspaper office right now." Addie sprang to her feet.

Serena placed her hands on Addie's shoulders and pressed her back onto the stool. "Not a good idea with you in this state. First sit and listen."

Addie raked her hands through her long hair.

"Take a deep breath." Serena's fingers pressed firmly on Addie's shoulders. "Count to ten. Let me make you a cup of coffee and we'll talk."

Addie nodded reluctantly.

"Promise me that if I turn my back on you, you won't bolt out the door and do something rash."

Addie clenched her teeth.

"I'll take that to mean that yes, you will behave." Serena slowly released her grip on Addie and backed toward the coffee maker at the end of the ornately carved Victorian bar Addie used for a cash and coffee counter.

Addie let out a deep breath and bit her quivering bottom lip. "I thought all this speculation about me being one of the bad guys was over, but now this?" Her hand brushed across the newspaper, sending it fluttering to the floor.

Serena sighed and placed a steaming cup on the counter in front of her. "And it should have ended any talk of you being part of or trying to evade some Boston crime ring, but . . ."

"But what? Did it just fuel the flames for some very small-minded people around this town? And who on earth is this Miss Newsy?"

"Miss Nosy is more like it," snickered Serena.

"Exactly! And how in heaven's name can she get away with printing something as libelous as this about me? I'm going to sue." Addie huffed into her cup, then set it down. "Really, I don't get it. When did unsubstantiated reporting become acceptable?" She shook her head and picked up her cup, taking a large gulp.

Serena cringed. "That's still hot."

Addie flinched, and the cup slipped from her fingers. She

leapt to her feet as hot coffee poured in all directions and ran down the counter edges toward her lap. Serena jumped up and raced toward a roll of paper towels behind the counter. Addie started to laugh, then cry, then laugh again. Tears streamed down her cheeks. Soon Serena, too, doubled over, holding her stomach and gasping between fits of laughter. A voice boomed behind Addie. She spun around, coming face-to-face with the chief of police, Marc Chandler. She gasped, lost her footing, and stumbled toward him.

He grabbed her mid-collision and righted her before she head-butted his chest. "This isn't quite the scene I envisioned walking into." A broad smile swept across his face. "But glad you girls can see the humor in it."

Addie glared up at him.

His smile crumbled.

"Humor in this?" she snapped.

"But I just thought . . ." Marc's face turned ashen. "I mean, you were—"

"Were what?" Addie planted her feet firmly, swept a strand of honey-brown hair from her eyes, and straightened her shoulders. "Actually, you're just the person I want to talk to, *Chief*."

Marc took a step back. "Okay . . . Miss Greyborne, how can the Harbor Police Department be of assistance today?" He looked warily from Addie to Serena, who had slid up beside her friend. Addie spun around, snatched up the newspaper from the floor, and thrust it at Marc.

"This, this . . ." Addie's voice vibrated, "this piece of trash that was printed about me." Her finger stabbed at the page.

Marc clutched the brim of his police cap in his hands and rocked back on his heels. "Well, Miss Greyborne." He cleared his throat. "I can take your statement . . . I guess. But"—he sucked in a deep breath—"I must caution you. That article was published in the gossip column of the paper and doesn't have to be factual to be printed." Addie's eyes flashed. He glanced sideways at his sister, Serena, his dark brown eyes pleading for help.

"That's what I wanted to tell you, Addie," Serena crooned from a safe distance. "Come on, let's sit down and I'll try to explain how this newspaper works. It's probably nothing like the big papers you're used to in Boston, London, or New York."

"No, it's not. They report the news. They don't run a gossip column where anyone can print anything they like, true or not! I've never heard of something like this." She threw the newspaper to the floor and stomped on it on her way to the counter stool.

"Good, that's right. Sit down, and I'll make you another cup of coffee," Serena chirped, heading to the coffee maker. "It's a tradition that's been followed since the paper was first printed in the early seventeen hundreds. It was a way for people to find out the goings-on in town for such things as bazaars, deaths and births, who was new to town, and stuff like that." She called over her shoulder as she stirred cream into Addie's coffee, "Here, this will help." She grinned and then looked at Marc, who was still standing stiffly by the doorway. Her head motioned toward the stool beside Addie, and he plopped down beside her, laying his hat on the still-damp countertop.

Addie turned, lifted it up, and placed it back in his hand. "Don't ask," she muttered and turned back to Serena. "Go on, this is fascinating," she said between gritted teeth.

Serena looked briefly at Marc, took a gulp, and continued. "Well, like I was saying—it's always been a harmless piece in the paper that just kept the townsfolk in touch with what wasn't headline news but was little things that helped connect them."

"Yes," Marc piped in, "like when Old Man Watterson broke his leg a few years ago and couldn't get out to grocery shop or shovel the snow from his sidewalk. It brought the whole town together to help him until he recovered."

Addie looked from Marc to Serena, her cheeks flushed.

Marc reached over and patted Addie's hand. "I know it doesn't help you today to see the good in what that column brings, but it's important to the people in this town."

She snatched her hand away. "'Good'? You call this 'good'? How would you feel if you were accu—" A face in the window caught Addie's eye, and she leapt to her feet. "Here we go again." There was no mistaking Martha's pudgy face and bakery-flour-stained hands shielding her eyes from the sunlight as she pressed her face against the glass. "She's probably waiting for you to cuff me and haul me away, and I'm sure she'll be more than willing to substantiate the gossip and keep it going." Addie collapsed back into her seat, her head in her hands. "From day one, she never liked me." She groaned. "This will fuel that even more, and I haven't done anything to deserve it. Have I?" She glanced from Serena to Marc.

"Don't be silly. It's like I told you before; it's jealousy. You are a direct descendant of the founding family of Greyborne Harbor and new in town, and people are just, well . . . they're just—"

"Leery," Marc jumped in. "They only need to get to know you better, and then they'll accept you." His eyes softened, and a slight smile curved the corner of his lips.

Addie shook her head and turned toward the window. "Do you really think *they* will ever give me a chance?" She pointed to the now three faces pushed up against the windowpane. Two other town merchants Addie recognized from her travels around the Harbor had joined Martha. "It looks like this gossip has made me a suspect—*again*."

Marc stood up, adjusted his police cap on his head, placed his hands on his hips, and turned toward the window. The women dispersed. He took his cap off and sat back down. "They won't be bothering you again for a while." He sipped on the coffee Serena had given him.

Serena crossed her arms and leaned her back against the counter. "I just don't get it. Miss Alice wrote that column for what, fifty years? And she never published something as inflammatory as this."

Marc nodded in affirmation.

Addie sat upright. "So who is this Miss Newsy, then?"

Marc shrugged and set his cup down. "She must be the new replacement. Miss Alice passed away about two months ago—she was ninety-two and not well—but the town was in such an uproar that they weren't getting their daily dose of 'what's what' that Max Hunter, the editor in chief, was desperate to replace her. I guess he did."

"But he didn't do a very good job of training this replacement, did he?" Addie shook her head and pushed the paper away. "Didn't he make it clear to this new person that libel is an offense? I'm certain the long-standing goodwill portrayed by the previous columnist is not being adhered to now."

Marc rubbed his neck. "Look, it's a gossip column, it was referred to as a rumor, and you weren't actually accused of anything, so the standard rules and laws don't apply here. There is no actual legal violation."

"Just a moral one that implies I had something to do with her disappearance." Addie fumed, tapping her fingers on the counter.

"She's right, Marc." Serena scowled. "This does cross the line. We need to find out who this Miss Newsy is and stop her before she does any more damage."

"Okay, okay, against my better judgment, I'll stop in and see Max now and try and get a retraction printed, but don't count on it, as it wasn't front-page news and is just gossip, and there's no law against that."

"Yes." Serena cleared her throat. "Or Martha and her posse would be in prison for life by now."

Addie nodded.

"Don't worry, Addie." He stood and placed his cap on his head, adjusting it so the chestnut-brown waves falling across his forehead were securely tucked under the brim. "We won't let this go any further than it has, and I'll try to find out what's behind it."

"Just remind Max that even implying that I had something to do with June Winslow's disappearance, without a shred of evidence, isn't a bit of harmless town gossip and isn't exactly in keeping with the long history of his newspaper." Her jaw tightened.

"That's right," Serena shouted as Marc disappeared out the door. "Besides," she said, pursing her mouth and looking at Addie, "it was a relative of yours who printed the first edition of that newspaper, and Max better remember that before he goes messing with your family's good name."

Addie jumped at a sharp *thwack* against the window. She spun around and darted toward it, peering out in time to see an older model green and white pickup speed off down the road. She looked at the two splatter marks on the glass and groaned at the sight of the thick, oozing drizzle running down the pane.

Serena stared at the innards of raw eggs running down the glass. "I'll get the window cleaner and a mop."

Chapter Two

Addie went through the motions of the day. She smiled and nodded at her customers, but it wasn't heartfelt. What she really wanted to do was shut the doors, sit down, and cry. So much for believing that her name was cleared. Today, it was as if she were reliving her first days in Greyborne Harbor, when only nosy gawkers popped in in order to see the newcomer and heiress to the Greyborne family fortune. She assumed they came in now just to get a closer look at the woman reported as being the person behind June's disappearance.

With the last snooping browser leaving, she closed up shop, walked out the front door into the crisp, spring evening air, and sucked in a deep, cleansing breath. She clasped her jacket tight around her neck, fending off an icy Atlantic Ocean windblast, and strode next door to SerenaTEA.

The lights were out and the door was latched. Addie's heart sank. It had been a long day, and dinner with Serena would have eased her troubled spirit. "Oh well, guess you're on your own tonight, girl," she mumbled and turned back toward Main Street, her thoughts now focused on treating herself to a wonderful Italian meal at Mario's Ristorante.

She passed by the window, noting it wasn't too busy,

which was a relief, as she hadn't made a reservation, but stopped short when she eyed Serena seated at a window table, her freckled face lit up with laughter. Her head bobbed up and down as she hung on every word her blond table companion spoke.

Stealth-like, Addie skirted past the window and turned to see who Serena was engaged in such an enthralling conversation with. It was no one she recognized, but the woman was really quite stunning in a Hollywood-type way, with her hair cascading in a waterfall of golden waves. Addie crept backward, her eyes fixed on the mysterious woman, and then a familiar chestnut-brown head appeared at the table, leaned toward the blond woman, and gave her a fleeting kiss on the cheek.

"Marc?"

Addie gasped when the blond-haired woman threw her arms around his neck and pulled him close for a kiss, a passionate kiss . . . on the lips. A tight fist clenched around Addie's heart as she remembered the last kiss she and Marc had shared, just days before. The memory sent her stumbling backward, bumping directly into the door and accidentally thrusting it open.

"Ah, *Signorina* Greyborne, how *fantastico* to see you again," cried Mario, rushing to grab hold of her as she teetered, arms pinwheeling into the foyer as she headed directly toward the floor fountain basin.

"Hi, Mario." She gazed up into his dark eyes, noting his flawless olive complexion, Romanesque nose, and sharp cheekbones. She flushed, steadied herself, and straightened her shoulders. "Table for one, but not by the window, please."

"Most certainly; anywhere you like." He nodded, his lips twitching a slight smile, and led her to a table close to the entrance.

The main room of the restaurant used short room dividers

topped with potted plants to establish smaller dining areas and create a sense of intimacy. The table Mario indicated as hers was separated from the front desk by a divider crowned with lush, leafy plants. "Is this acceptable?"

She eyed the height of the divider shielding her from the main entrance and looked down at the chair. She then took a seat, making certain she could also see past the planters defining her six-table dining area and still watch Marc's table without being obvious. "Yes, this will do just fine, thank you." She smiled at him and took the menu he held out for her. "I'll just need a minute."

"Veal Parmesan is the special tonight. If you're not pleased, no charge, but I guarantee you will love it. *Magnifico.*" He brought his fingers to his lips and blew a kiss.

She laughed and closed her menu. "That sounds perfect. And a glass of white wine, thank you."

He clicked his heels and turned toward the kitchen.

Addie settled back in her chair as a server filled her water goblet. "Thank you." She smiled at the server and took a sip as she eyed her target. The blonde wrapped her arms around Marc's shoulder and drew him toward her, gazing into his eyes. Her finger stroked the outline of his jaw. Addie choked and sputtered a mouthful of water down her chin. She grabbed the napkin, wiped her face, and blotted at the water stains on her dark pink tunic blouse and gray boyfriend jacket collar.

She shifted in her seat for a better look. Marc's cheeks were clearly flushed. He answered his phone, flung his napkin on the table, and stood up. He nodded at Serena, glanced at the woman, made a helpless gesture, and marched toward the front entrance. A grim look spread across his face. Addie slunk down in her chair, but his eyes were set straight ahead as he bolted out the door behind her. Addie sat back, gnawing on her lip. She swerved in her seat to try to see past a pale blue blur that obstructed her view of the two women still at the table and looked up into a familiar beaming face.

"Oh, Catherine, hello. How are you this evening?"

"Better than you, by the look of things." Catherine Lewis' gaze rested on Addie's soaking wet blouse. "Are you all right, dear?"

"Yes, I'm fine." She looked back at Catherine and smiled at the woman who had played such an important part in her father's life when Addie was a baby and toddler. Catherine had been friends with Addie's great-aunt, whose estate Addie had inherited when she passed away. "Forgive me. I've just had a stressful day, and I'm tired."

Catherine took a seat and pushed stray strands of her dark shoulder-length hair from her taut face. "Yes, I well imagine, after that bombshell in the newspaper this morning. I meant to stop by today and talk to you about it, but . . ." She shrugged. "I got busy, and the time just flew by, so I'm pleased to run into you."

The server placed a glass of wine on the table in front of Addie. She nodded at her, replaced her water goblet with the wineglass, and took a large gulp.

Catherine watched her. "Are you sure you're okay?"

"Yes, yes, I'm fine," she said, taking another mouthful and setting her glass down, smiling. "So are you dining alone this evening?"

"No, I'm here with friends." Catherine motioned with her head back over her shoulder.

She scanned the room behind Catherine and saw five smiling faces looking at her. She waved, and they all waved back. "I gather that group of women is them?"

Catherine turned around and chuckled. "Yes, that's the girls, and you can see that they're all pleased as punch to see you out and about."

"I don't recognize any of them. Should I know them?"

Addie took a crispy roll from the basket, broke it in half, and offered a piece to Catherine.

Catherine shook her head and placed her hands flat on the table, her petite shoulders stiff as she leaned toward Addie. "We have a favor to ask of you," she whispered.

"Me? What could I possibly do for you? Or"—she leaned toward Catherine and whispered—"is there someone you want me to make disappear?" She sat back and took another gulp of wine. "After all, you read the newspaper." She motioned to the server for a refill of her now-empty wineglass.

"*Phfft*, that bit of silliness." Catherine waved her hand. "That's what I wanted to tell you earlier today. It doesn't mean a thing. It's just some old busybody trying to stir things up. None of us believes it. Why would you let it worry you?"

Addie searched the faces of the diners close by. They quickly averted their eyes when she looked at them. "Gee, Catherine, I don't know, but maybe because some people do believe it." She took her refilled glass from the server and downed a gulp.

Catherine shook her head. "I get the feeling there's more going on here than some gossip columnist rant in the paper. What is it, my dear?" She reached for Addie's hand. "You can tell me."

Addie shifted in her seat and glanced toward Serena's table. Both women were staring out the window, then stood quickly, gathered their coats and handbags, and hurried toward the door. Addie ducked and hoped the plants would protect her from detection, but the women were heavily immersed in conversation and didn't hesitate as they passed her table. She frowned and looked back at the window.

"What is it?" Catherine glanced over her shoulder.

"Umm . . . nothing . . . I think. I don't know. I just thought I saw something."

"Well, I should get back to my book club, but I just have to ask you . . ."

"Okay." Addie reached for her wineglass, stopped, and picked up her water goblet instead. "What's on your mind?"

Catherine took a deep breath. "Will you please do us the honor of chairing our book club?"

"Your book club? Chair it?"

Catherine nodded.

"Does a book club need a chair? I always thought they were just groups of people who read the same book, then get together to discuss it?"

"True, for the most part, but, well, except for this month and the Founder's Day weekend approaching, our preference, when left to us on our own, is sizzling romance novels." She giggled. She reached her hand out to Addie and clasped her fingers. "We really need a leader who can steer a group of lonely women into exploring a wider scope of novels. We hoped that with your background at the Boston library and all, well . . . you could guide us toward more varied reading than"—her voice dropped—"very, very steamy romance novels." Her face flushed, and she looked away.

"Catherine," Addie giggled, "I never thought you of all people would have—"

"Shush!" Catherine placed her red-tipped nails over her lips, arched a sly brow, and grinned.

"Sizzling romance novels you say, well then. I'd be happy to chair your book club," Addie said, her eyes holding a glint of impishness. "It sounds like a group I'd enjoy spending time with."

"Good." Catherine squeezed her hand. "Well, I've kept you from your dinner long enough. I'll drop by your shop tomorrow and give you the details."

Addie nodded, but a strobe of blue and red flashing lights streaking past the window caught her eye. Catherine turned around, her gaze following Addie's.

"What on earth?" Catherine rose to her feet as the other diners in the restaurant moved toward the window to catch a glimpse of what was happening outside.

"I have to go." Addie grabbed her jacket and purse, threw a fifty-dollar bill on the table, and headed out into the chilly night air.

Chapter Three

A frigid blast of evening wind slapped Addie's face. She clutched her jacket tighter, put her head down, and marched across the street toward the scene of the red and blue flashing lights in the park behind the library. She scanned the forming crowd as she approached the yellow police tape and recognized many fellow merchants from shops along Main Street. She stood up on tiptoes, trying to catch sight of Marc. He was around the back side of the police barricade. She skirted around the taped-off area and hurried toward him, then stopped short. He was talking to Serena and the blond woman.

Serena spotted her. "Addie," she squealed, darting toward her. "Can you believe this?"

"Umm, I'm not really sure what's going on. I just saw all the police lights and came over."

"You haven't heard?"

"What?"

"It's June Winslow. They found her body in the utility shed."

"No." Her throat went dry. "I hadn't heard."

"Well, I'm sure Marc will tell you all about it later." She flipped around and, as she pointed to where he'd been standing, struck the blond woman in the face. "Oops, sorry, an accident."

The woman tossed her long golden locks back and laughed. "Don't worry about it, Serena. My fault for not announcing my arrival to this cozy little gathering. And who is this?" Her narrowed gaze scanned Addie from head down to her black Italian leather booties. "Aren't you the woman I saw watching us from the street earlier?"

Heat crept up Addie's collar to her now-burning cheeks as she stared at the willowy woman beside her. Addie judged her height to be somewhere between her five nine and Marc's six three as the blonde peered down her all-too-perfect nose at her.

Serena looked at Addie questioningly.

"I . . . I . . ." Addie choked. "I was just trying to decide if I wanted Italian food or not."

"I see." The blonde's collagen-plumped, ruby lips twisted into a half smile. She turned to Serena. "Well, are you going to introduce us? After all, she did spend most of the evening watching our table." She fleetingly glanced at Addie over her shoulder and flashed a bright white toothy grin that didn't quite reach her cold eyes. "Of course," she said, looking back at Serena, "that was after she decided on Italian and made such a grand entrance into the restaurant." She turned to Addie. "I'm so glad Mario caught you before you landed in the fountain."

Serena's eyes widened as she looked back and forth between the woman's smug expression and Addie's paling face.

The lanky woman offered her limp hand toward Addie. "Since our little Serena appears to be at a loss for words, I'm Lacey." Addie shook her outstretched, cold, flaccid fingers. "An old friend of Serena and, of course"—she leaned closer to Addie and whispered in a breathy voice—"Marc."

The hairs on the back of Addie's neck prickled. She

dropped Lacey's hand. "I'm Addie Greyborne. Pleased to meet you." Her eyes held fast on Lacey's ice-blue gaze.

Serena coughed. "I don't know about you two, but I'm freezing. Why don't we all go grab a cup of coffee?" She beamed, glancing from Addie to Lacey.

"Excellent idea, Serena." Addie smiled at Lacey, or at least, she hoped it was a smile, and not a grimace. "It'll give us all a better chance to get acquainted."

Lacey straightened her shoulders and looked at Serena. "Yes, an excellent idea. I'd *love* to get to know more about the infamous Addison Greyborne." Her tone of voice sent tiny shivers up Addie's spine. Lacey blew Marc a kiss and turned back to Addie, her smile so saccharine-sweet that Addie tongued her teeth to check for instant cavities. "Well, where should we go?"

"It's Serena's idea. Let her decide."

"I know, why don't we head down to the coffee shop in the harbor—"

"No," snapped Lacey. "I'd like to stay close to the action and see what unfolds here. You understand, don't you? Old habits die hard and all."

Addie blinked. "Old habits?"

"Yes, you know, Marc and I, well, we were . . ." Lacey licked her red lips and feigned a smile.

"Okay . . . well, let's go to my shop. The tea is on the house, and it's warm." Serena took Addie's arm in hers and gave it a gentle squeeze.

"Wait." Marc's voice rang out from behind them. Addie spun around as he trotted toward the small group. "Wait, please," he called breathlessly.

"I'll wait as long as you want," cooed Lacey, arching toward him, her eyelashes fluttering. Marc stared at her, his jaw clenched. He glanced at Addie, and a fleeting look of apology crossed his face. Addie could feel the knives of Lacey's glare in her back.

Marc pulled a twenty-dollar bill out of his wallet and locked eyes with Serena. "It looks like I'm going to be here awhile. Do you think you could run to the coffee shop and pick up"—he glanced over his shoulder, his lips twitching as he counted—"umm, about seven cups and grab some cream and sugar—"

"Chief," hollered one of the officers from an area behind the library, "I got something here you should see."

Marc waved back at him. "Okay, I gotta go." He shoved the money into Serena's hand.

Lacey snatched the bill from her and spun on her heel. "Come on, Serena," she said as she turned and blew Marc a kiss over her shoulder. "Be back soon, darling." Her honey-dripped voice sent lethal sugar rushes shooting through Addie. Lacey flipped her hair and was off, Serena chasing her like a baby duck after its mother.

Marc heaved out a deep breath and looked down at Addie. "Don't let her get under your skin. I grew up with her, and she can be, well, shall we say, overly dramatic most of the time."

She pursed her lips and nodded, rolling a small stone under her foot.

"I mean it." He placed his hands on her shoulders. "Don't let her get to you."

"It's not Lacey. I grew up with girls like her." She bit her lip and looked up at him. "It's just that, after everything that was printed about me in the paper, is it true that June was murdered?"

"Murdered?" He stepped back, frowning. "I don't know . . . that's still to be determined."

"Why the crime scene tape, then?"

"Because any unexplained death is considered suspicious until proven otherwise, and this one . . . well, let's just say this one has left me with a few questions."

Her eyes widened. "Need any help?"

"No." He rolled his eyes. "I do not, and you'd better promise not to go poking around in this."

"But we make such a good team, right, partner?" She grinned, giving him a quick hip-check.

"Addie, I'm warning you. Stay away from this. Too many fingers have been pointed at you already, and if you go nosing around, you never know where else it will lead."

She crinkled up her nose.

"Promise me?"

Her bottom lip quivered; the tone of his voice cut through her, and she weakly nodded.

"Good." A smile dangled at the corner of his lips. "But I do have to run, they're waiting for me. See you later?" He brushed strands of windswept hair from her eyes. She shrugged and gave him a tight-lipped smile. He exhaled a sharp breath, shook his head, and ducked under the yellow police tape, heading toward the young officer waiting for him.

Addie tapped her foot and glanced in the direction that Serena and Lacey had gone, and there Lacey was, standing beside Serena's Jeep, her dagger-filled eyes staring back at Addie. Her arms were crossed, her long, slender legs planted firmly. She reminded Addie of a Norse warrior who was ready to do battle. Addie looked over at Marc, who was now talking with two more officers. When she glanced back toward the Jeep, it was gone, and all Addie saw were the taillights heading down Main Street.

She shifted her weight onto one hip and, surveying the taped area around this section of the park, noted that the open door of the shed appeared to be left unattended by officers. Slowly, she made her way through the crowd of onlookers to get as close as she could. She needed to get a peek inside. Thanks to *Miss Nosy*, this whole mystery seemed to involve her now, at least in the eyes of the townspeople. So, regardless of what she'd just implied, but not actually said, to Marc, she couldn't let it go. After all, it was her reputation on the line, not his, and one quick look inside couldn't hurt, could it?

Her eyes darted from one officer to the other as they swept the surrounding grounds with flashlights and metal detectors. She sucked in a deep breath, lifted the tape, and stopped. Jerry, one of the police officers, appeared in the shed doorway, his crime scene kit in hand. Addie drew back, her eyes locked on him. He glanced at his watch, wrote something in a notepad, and turned toward Marc, who was standing on the far side of the shed. "I'm all done in there, Chief," he called, walking toward him. "I think we can let the utility company guys in now to check for damage."

"Good work, Jerry. You can run what you have there over to the lab."

Jerry nodded and headed toward the police station on the other side of the library.

That was all Addie needed to hear: it was no longer an active crime scene—at least that's what she told herself as she ducked under the tape and sprinted through the open shed door. She screeched to a halt and grabbed the steel railing at the top of the small concrete catwalk inside the door. Her foot teetered over the edge of an opening to a set of stairs that looked more like a ladder, considering the angle of descent. She shuffled backward, gripping the handrail, and peered over the edge to the utility chamber twenty feet below. She sucked in a sharp breath, turned backward, and made her way down the industrial ladder to the bottom.

When her wobbly foot landed on cement, she turned around and realized that she was standing inside a chalk body outline. "Yuck," she gasped, struggling to fill her air-deprived lungs. She bent over, hands on knees, and drew in deep, calming breaths.

"What are you doing in here?" Marc's voice bellowed from above.

She gulped and looked up to the top of the stairs. "Hi."

She waved her fingers. "I, umm, well . . ." She stood upright, wincing. "It's kind of a funny story."

"You'd better start talking now." He glided down the ladder like a firefighter might and stood in front of her, arms crossed, eyes blazing.

She shuffled from one foot to the other, avoiding eye contact with him because she knew exactly what his eyes would be telling her. "I heard Jerry tell you he was done in here and . . . well, it's not really an active crime scene now, so I thought there would be no harm if I took a quick peek." She cringed and looked up at him.

His feet planted firmly, he shook his head, his mouth taut. "You're incorrigible, do you know that?"

She gulped.

"This is still off-limits until I clear it, do I make myself *clear*?" His guttural voice reverberated through the small chamber.

She blew out a breath that she wasn't even aware she'd been holding and nodded. The whole thing started to feel a lot like when her father used to catch her with her hand in the cookie jar or reading under her blanket with a flashlight well after bedtime. Except she knew this might be a tad more serious, based on the tone of Marc's voice.

"You promised me, Addie."

She shuffled her feet and gazed down at the chalk outline. "Well, not really." She bit her lip as she looked up into his fiery eyes. "I didn't actually *say* I would stay away from this."

His eyes flew wide open; his jaw snapped closed.

"Look, half the town accused me of knowing something about her disappearance, and how could I have? I never even knew this place existed." She glanced around the chamber. "Where exactly are we?"

Marc blew out a deep breath. "This bunker is the entrance to the underground tunnels that allow access to the water, utility, and communication lines for all the essential services' buildings. You know, for the police station, the hospital—and the library, too, since it was built on the site first."

"I didn't know that." She craned her neck to see down a secondary opening.

"Not everyone does. It's not something we want made public—fear of terrorism you know."

Her brow furrowed. "Well, obviously June knew about it, and came in for some reason." She rubbed her neck, looking down at the chalk markings. "She disappeared a couple of days ago. Was she here all this time? Why didn't anyone know before now?"

"Because there was no reason to come in here until to-night, when a power surge issue was reported. Otherwise, the utility company follows a state mandated routine maintenance schedule."

"Why wasn't it searched when she was reported missing?"

"The investigation team at the time tried the door and it was locked. They had no reason to believe that it might not have been earlier. No one except the utility company employees have a key. The entire area is kept pretty secure."

"Not secure enough, I'd say." She frowned looking down at the chalk drawing. "Who found the body?"

"One of the utility workers, when he came to check the power output."

She shook her head, clicking her tongue. "I guess he found more than he'd planned on."

Marc nodded.

"If it's kept so secure, are you thinking it was employee error that that led to her death, or"—she gulped—"that an employee murdered her?"

He scoured his fingers through his thick hair. "We've thought of that, but they are vetted pretty thoroughly, since it is a vulnerable area."

"Did someone maybe lose a key?"

"Anything is possible at this point. A couple of officers are at the station interviewing all the utility company employees right now. We're hoping to find out if someone forgot to lock up after they worked down there or if anyone lost their key and was afraid to report it or something." He threw his hands up. "Let's hope one of them admits to it though."

"Yeah, if she did find a key, and then someone came back and locked the door, not checking to see if there was anyone inside first, their mistake may have caused someone to lose their life."

"Exactly, because it would have been dark in here, and at first glance, it looks like she took a fall off the platform and fell down the ladder opening."

"Yeah, I know how easily that could have happened, even with the lights on." She shuddered. "But what would ever have possessed her to come in here in the first place?" Addie chewed on her bottom lip, scanning the chamber.

Marc's brow creased. He studied her face for a moment and then turned back into RoboCop. "You've had your history lesson. Now can we go, before I get into trouble?"

"With whom, the *chief*?" She smirked, walking toward the tunnel entrance.

"Stop right there," he snarled.

She spun around and glared at him. "Do not speak to me like I'm a child, thank you."

"Then stop acting like one."

"Look, it's my reputation at stake here. Miss Newsy has already implicated me in June's disappearance, so Lord knows what she'll try and do with all this." She waved her hand wildly in the air and pointed to the chalk outline.

His lips set in a tight line.

"Marc, I'm pleading with you. Since I'm already here, the least you could do is let me have a quick look around and ask a few questions. Unless, of course," she said, crossing her arms and tapping her foot, "you plan on handcuffing me and carrying me up that ladder."

His jaw tightened. He fumbled in the pocket inside his police-issue jacket and pulled out two paper shoe coverings and a pair of rubber gloves. "At least put these on." He thrust them toward her.

Chapter Four

Marc stood over the chalk drawing, staring at it, and then looked up at the concrete platform, and then back at the body outline. Addie paced around the small utility tunnel access area, chewing on her bottom lip.

"You're too quiet, and you're doing that lip-chewy thing again," he said. "What's on your mind?"

She walked over and stood beside him, sighing heavily. "It's just that . . . it doesn't make sense, does it?"

He glanced sideways at her. "What are you thinking?"

"I'm not sure, but so many things seem off about this whole scene." She ignored his narrowed gaze. "Like, for example, why was the body removed so quickly? That's not normal, is it? At least not in the murder movies I've seen."

"Because I was supposed to have the night off and left orders not to be disturbed unless it was imperative. So I wasn't called until Sam Bolton, one of the district medical examiners, insisted on removing the body as soon as he arrived on the scene."

"But, but . . ."

"Just listen." To the rhythm of her tapping foot, he continued. "He said it was obviously an accidental fall and that he was in the middle of his retirement party but was the only coroner available, so he wasn't pleased about being called in and let everyone know it. He said he wanted to get back to his party so he could kiss this thankless job where the sun don't shine and leave it behind."

"So?"

"So, that's when they called me. They couldn't reason with him and hoped as chief that I'd have better luck."

"Then why didn't you stop him?"

"He and the body were gone by the time I got here. The team had been here awhile already examining the scene and dusting for prints—you saw Jerry finishing up, didn't you?"

She nodded. "I guess that makes sense, but you did tell me once that as chief, you were always on duty. Shouldn't they have called you as soon as the body was discovered? Isn't that kind of an imperative reason to disturb you?"

He shook his head. "I'm not indispensable. Initial investigations *can* be conducted without me on scene."

"I know, but—"

He placed his finger gently over her lips. "Shush. It's the best explanation I can offer. My team is thorough. You know that. They wouldn't have left any evidence unexamined."

"You're right. So, what did they say about the angle of the body? Broken neck, back, bruises, head injury, the distance of the body from the ladder and where it landed, what? Have you got anything?"

"All I know right now is this is where the body was discovered." He pointed to the chalk outline. "She was face-down. Lots of facial bone damage from the impact, I assume, but we won't know for sure until the coroner's report. Her purse, containing her keys, was lying beside her. No cell phone was found and there's been no other obvious evidence uncovered so far, and we won't know anything else before the lab finishes running tests, and before you ask, the access door was locked."

Addie turned. Her eyes focused on the concrete tunnel

leading off the small room. "There has to be access to the utility corridors from the library, hospital, and police station, right?"

"All access points have been checked. They were all secured, from the *inside*."

"Where does the tunnel end?"

"At the far side of the hospital. Why?"

"Is it a concrete wall? Brick? What?"

"What are you thinking?"

"Could anyone have tunneled in from the other side? A hidden door to a passageway maybe?"

"You and your hidden doors and passageways," he snickered.

"Hey, as you discovered, they're more popular than you thought they were."

"Come on, I think we've seen all there is to see here tonight. Let's go back to the station and grab some hot coffee. I want to see if any of the preliminary reports are in yet."

"Sounds good. I'd kill for a cup of coffee right now." She made her way cautiously up the ladder.

"Somehow, saying you'd kill for something while in the middle of a crime scene isn't really appropriate," he said with a chuckle, climbing up behind her.

"You're right. All I need is for what's-her-name to hear that." She giggled and flung the shed door open, then came face-to-face with a set of steel-blue eyes.

"Well, well, Chief, what have we got here?"

"Lacey," Marc roared, "how did you get past the police tape?"

"Don't fret, Marc. I'm here on legitimate business." She flashed a press pass.

"Press? You? Here? Why on earth would your viewers in Los Angles be interested in an East Coast small-town crime scene?"

"Oh, didn't I tell you?" she cooed. "I'm now a reporter for the *Greyborne Harbor Daily News*." She smirked at Addie.

Marc's face dropped, his neck veins throbbing. He took a step toward her. Through clenched teeth, he hissed, "Miss Davenport, the other side of the police tape, now"—he pointed—"and stay there."

"Yes, sir." She saluted him, smirking. "But rest assured, I'll get my story somehow, Chief. You can't stop the news."

Marc grabbed Addie's elbow and led her toward his patrol car in the library lot. "Damn that woman," he muttered.

Addie winced. "Do you want to talk about it?"

"No," he snarled. "Sorry, no, I don't. I thought I was rid of that she-devil for good, but now?" His hand slammed the hood of his car. "Darn it. I opened one little door to try to be just a teeny bit friendly to keep Serena happy, and now she thinks . . . God only knows what she thinks."

Addie took a deep breath, and her heart dropped to the pit of her stomach when she saw the soulful pain in his eyes. She cupped his face in her hands. "Sometimes we have to face the demons from our past to make them vanish completely," she whispered.

"You're right." He inhaled sharply. "And my demon will have to wait for now." He glared back at Lacey, who was standing beyond the yellow police tape, fluttering her fingers at him in a waving motion. He turned toward Addie. "Time to get to work. I have a mystery to solve."

Marc placed a steaming cup in front of her as she took her seat facing his desk. "Nothing's back from the lab yet, and I don't imagine Sam will get to the autopsy for a day or two anyway, especially if he is partying tonight." He slumped into his leather desk chair.

"If he even bothers to do it, now that he's officially retired," she muttered as she sipped her coffee. "Mmmm, this is exactly what I needed, thank you."

"Cheers." Marc held up his cup and toasted. "Don't worry, if Sam refuses to perform it, the DA will assign another coroner."

"Can they do that? Assign someone who wasn't at the scene?"

"Yup, Sam will have submitted his initial findings and it will all be on record, so the autopsy part can be conducted by any of the other coroners."

She set her cup on the desk. "I hope he wasn't in too much of a rush to do a proper visual inspection first, and it wasn't just a matter of scoop and run."

"Why would you say that?" Marc's eyes narrowed and he set his coffee down. "Sam's been with the county for over forty years. He's as professional as they come."

"I'm not questioning that. I just meant if he was partying— never mind, I'm just tired and cold, I guess."

His lips tightened. "Well, I won't know anything until we get some test results and the autopsy report, anyway." He sighed. "Are you warmer now? Want me to take you home? It looks like it'll be hours until the preliminary reports are ready."

She sat back and stretched out her neck. "I guess so, but my car's parked behind my store. You can give me a lift there if you don't mind."

"Sure. Finish up, and we'll go."

She smiled at him. "You know, this feels good."

"What does?" He took a swig of his coffee.

"You know, you and me sitting in your office, talking about a case, like old times." She laughed.

He choked. "Well, don't get too comfortable. It was only a short lapse of judgment on my part, because that woman got me so riled up. She's a reporter here now, too. That spells trouble, I fear." He drummed his fingers on the desktop.

Addie started to reply, but sipped her coffee instead.

He stared over his cup rim at her, his brow cocked.

She turned up her nose and grimaced.

"I know that look. What's on your mind?"

"Nothing . . . well . . . no." She finished her coffee and set the cup down. "Ready? I could use a hot bath when I get home. I'm chilled to the bone." She stood up. "I assume Serena told you about my shop being egged?"

"Yes, she did, and I knew right away who drives that truck she described."

"And?"

"And it was just some local kids who thought it would be funny. I've spoken to them and their parents and warned them that any future incidents would come with more than a warning. You should be egg-free in the future."

"Good. It takes forever to get that goo off. Although I'm sure Martha enjoyed watching my pain."

He grabbed his cap from the coatrack, placed his hand on the small of her back, and ushered her out the back door. The swirling wind sucked at Addie's breath. She put her head down and marched right into an unmoving, dark blur.

"Ah," she gasped, her head shooting up. "Lacey?"

"Being escorted out of the station?"

Marc appeared beside Addie.

"Chief, do you have a comment for the good people of Greyborne Harbor regarding any suspects in this murder case?" She glanced at Addie.

"No, I do not," he all but growled. "And it has not been ruled a murder as of yet, Miss Davenport. Now kindly move and let us pass."

She straightened her shoulders, and although her pen tapped on the notebook in her hand, her gaze never wavered from Marc's hand at the small of Addie's back. "Very well, then." She stepped aside and let them move toward Marc's car. "Remember, Chief," Lacey shouted over the wind, "I get an exclusive when it does come out that this is a murder and when it becomes clear *who* committed it."

Addie felt all the venom of Lacey's glare as Marc got into the car, and they sped out of the parking lot.

Chapter Five

The aroma of fresh coffee welcomed Addie to the start of her business day when she stepped through the door of her bookstore. "Welcome back, Paige," she called from the front door to her young part-time shop assistant. "I hope you had a nice day off yesterday?" She came around the end of a bookshelf and paused when she spotted Catherine seated at the far end of the counter. "I didn't know we were meeting this morning, or I'd have been here sooner." Addie handed her blond, curly-headed assistant her coat to put behind the counter and dropped a coffee pod into the machine.

"That's okay. I was just at the library to pick up June's copy of the book that the club is reviewing now and thought I'd better drop it off to you on my way home." Catherine pulled a book from her oversized handbag and placed it on the counter.

Addie peered over her shoulder. "*The Ghosts and Mysteries of Greyborne Harbor*? Never heard of it. Fiction or nonfiction?" She stirred her coffee and sat down on a stool beside her.

"It's a historical account, actually, a mix of local legend, myths, and facts. It makes excellent reading, especially around Founder's Day."

Addie picked it up and stared at the black-and-white cover. "The photo definitely has an eerie quality about it—must be because of the reference made to ghosts in the title." She glanced at Catherine, then back at the book. "The author is June Winslow? I had no idea she was a writer, too."

"She used to be president of the historical society, and she spent years researching and documenting the history of Greyborne Harbor. When she stepped down from that role a few years ago, she decided to put all her findings into a book." Catherine's hand caressed the cover, her eyes moist. "It's been a local best-seller since it was published two years ago."

Out of the corner of her eye, Addie glimpsed a movement as Paige slid a copy of the *Daily News* under the countertop. "What's that?" She snatched at the paper.

"Nothing, I'm just tidying up." Paige's blue eyes darkened at the same speed as her usually pale cheeks turned bright pink.

"Let's have a look." Addie tugged it out of Paige's trembling hand and scanned what she had been reading. She slammed the newspaper on the counter. "I can't believe it," she cried. "The nerve."

Paige cringed and shuffled backward. "I guess you hadn't seen it yet?"

Catherine patted her arm. "Now, now, Addie, it's a gossip piece, not fact, remember." She reached for the paper. "No need to upset yourself so early in the day."

"No, she has to answer for this." Addie kept her death grip on the paper. "Miss *Nosy* has gone too far." Her hand trembled as she fished her cell phone out of her jacket pocket, fumbled it, and sent it crashing to the floor. She bent down to retrieve it, but a loud cry pierced the air behind her. Her head flew up and smacked the counter ledge. "Darn it!" She spun around, rubbing the back of her head.

Serena stood in the doorway, her face contorted and tears in her eyes. "I can't believe it." She crushed Addie to her in a bear hug. "That, that woman. How dare she?"

"I just hope she has a good lawyer," Addie grabbed the paper off the counter and poked at it with her finger. "This is libel, undisputably. Now we'll see what Marc has to say."

Serena gently took the cell phone from her hand. "Calm down first. He won't take it seriously if you're mad and yelling at him."

Addie slumped onto a stool. "You're right. But now to say this—" Her finger stabbed at the latest report in the gossip column.

"It says here that you were at the station with Marc last night," said Serena, pointing to a line in the column. "Is that true?"

"Yes, but it's taken completely out of context. I wasn't arrested."

Serena continued to read it aloud for Addie's benefit. "I have it on good authority that Miss Addison Greyborne was led away last night by Chief Chandler from the crime scene where June Winslow's body was discovered. She was detained at the police station for an extended period of time. She was already considered by many the main suspect in June's disappearance. Have the Harbor police discovered that she's the number one suspect in her most mysterious death now, too?"

"The only good authority could be Lacey," Addie said. "She was there when Marc and I left the station, after having an *innocent* coffee when we went back to see if the preliminary lab results were in yet." She glanced at Serena.

Serena shook her head. "No, I've known Lacey most of my life. She's a real reporter. She would never give false or misleading information to Miss Nosy."

"Well, someone did, and I doubt it was anyone from inside the police station."

"We've all known Lacey her whole life," piped in Catherine.

"Yes, she used to babysit me," Paige added.

"She's really a good person." Catherine patted Addie's hand. "A bit headstrong and driven, but that's how she ended up cohosting the morning news in Los Angeles. She would never share information that wasn't true. Her reputation and credibility would be ruined."

"Okay, okay, so you're all members of the Lacey Davenport fan club." If Addie had even a wee bit less maturity, she would have stuck her tongue out, but she was a grown woman, and grown women didn't do such childish things, no matter how strong the urge. "If she's such a great reporter, why is she working now at the *Greyborne Harbor Daily News*? That's pretty far away from the bright lights of a morning show in LA." She looked from Paige, to Catherine, her eyes coming to rest on Serena.

Serena's eyes filled with tears. "Because her mother's dying, so she came home."

"I didn't know."

"That's probably why she seemed so unpleasant toward you last night. She's hurt and upset, and taking it out on everyone, even me. You heard her snap at me, too." Serena pursed her lips and sat down beside Addie. "Someone else must have seen you leave with Marc and said something to Miss Newsy."

"But why would this person implicate me in her disappearance in the first place, and now call me out as a suspect in a death—which we both know means a murder suspect?"

"Yes, but there's no evidence. Only gossip and speculations from some unknown source," Serena said.

"But it's the same thing that Lacey implied last night when she ambushed me and Marc on the back stairs of the police station." Addie frowned. "She asked him if he had any suspects, then looked at me. Who else would have given Miss Nosy Newsy the information?"

"I don't know." Serena shook her head. "But it doesn't mean she was accusing you. Maybe she was just hoping one of you might answer. The information could have come from anyone, even harmlessly."

"Exactly," chimed in Catherine. "Miss Newsy might have overheard an innocent conversation at a coffee shop between two officers who were there and jumped to conclusions."

Paige and Serena nodded.

"Listen to us, Addie," pleaded Catherine, "Lacey isn't the source. She's a good person. Why would she and Marc have been engaged for so long if she weren't?" Her eyes widened and her mouth snapped shut.

Serena choked and looked sideways at Addie.

Addie felt as though her body would slip through the cracks of the floor. She pinned Catherine with a stare as the poor woman edged toward the door, only to bump right into Marc. "Speak of the devil," Addie murmured under her breath.

His lingering gaze scanned the faces of the four silent women. "What have I missed?"

"Umm, we were just . . ." Catherine looked at Marc, then to Addie. "The club meets tonight here at seven. See you then." She skirted past Marc and headed out the door.

Marc looked from Paige to Serena, then at Addie.

"I'll be in the back sorting the new shipment of books." Paige darted to the storage room.

"I'd better be off too and open my shop." Serena slid past Marc and out the door.

Marc plopped a pod into the machine. "Sorry, I didn't mean to interrupt anything. Mind if I grab a coffee?"

"Nope," Addie crooned sweetly. Could sugar shock maim somebody? She sure hoped so. "Help yourself." She stood up and ordered her knees not to wobble. "I'd better get to work anyway." She looked out the window, trying to dispel images of Marc and Lacey as a couple.

"Is everything okay?" Marc moved up behind her, his hands resting on her shoulders. "Did something happen? You seem shaken."

She jerked away from his touch and scooted around the counter. "You haven't read the morning news, then?"

"No, I haven't had time."

She swung around and looked at him, a smile pasted across her face. "Well, then drink your coffee and have a read." She pointed to the newspaper on the counter and began totaling yesterday's receipts.

Addie watched him out of the corner of her eye as he read the article. He raked his fingers through his hair and shook his head. His hand scrubbed across his cheek. "God, Addie, I had no idea."

"Yeah, one of the many shocks I've had this morning." She snapped the receipt book closed.

His brow creased. "What else happened?"

The door chimes rang. Addie looked up and fought an involuntary eye roll. "Lacey? Good morning." She didn't bother with a fake smile. "Shopping or browsing today?" Addie shot Marc a piercing glance as she made her way around the desk.

"Actually, neither," Lacey drawled. Addie's hand itched to slap that smug look off her face. "I've come to have a private word with Marc."

Marc's jaw tensed, and he spun around on his stool. "I have no further information regarding the case at this time." He turned back to his coffee and stirred in a sugar packet.

Lacey glided up behind him and placed her hands on his shoulders. "This is private. Not work-related." Her lips brushed his cheek, but her eyes were on Addie's with a Cheshire cat gleam.

Marc stiffened, pushed his coffee away, and rose to his feet. "Fine," he mumbled and headed out the door.

Lacey chased after him, and Addie went to the window. Marc had stopped on the sidewalk, his back to her. Lacey grabbed his arm, spinning him toward her, and said something to him. He stepped back. Martha appeared on the sidewalk, broom in hand. Lacey greeted her with a warm embrace. Over Lacey's shoulder, Martha glanced at Addie in the window and smiled smugly.

Chapter Six

The shop was church-mouse quiet. Paige had worked noiselessly rearranging the storage room all morning, and not one customer had come in. Had it been any other day, Addie might have been concerned, but today it was a relief. No nosy townsfolk coming in to gawk, wasting her time, and it gave her the opportunity to review the book she'd be expected to discuss at this evening's book club meeting. Today, she'd accept anything that distracted her from thoughts of Marc and Lacey's past engagement.

She wasn't sure why it bothered her so much. After all, she had a past, too, with David. But Lacey? She shuddered and refocused, scanning a paper she'd found on the Internet that June had written before she compiled her book. None of the information contained in it was in the book, as far as she remembered, which she found rather curious. Her stomach growled, and she looked at the clock on her computer.

"Paige, I'm going out to pick up some lunch. Do you want anything?" The only response was the ticking of the clock on the wall behind her. "Paige? Are you there?" She got up and headed back to the storeroom. "I'm guessing you have your earbuds in and can't hear me?" She laughed and peered into the empty back room. "Paige?" She tapped on the bathroom door. "Are you there?" She jiggled the handle, and it opened. Scratching her head, she noted the back door was propped open with a book.

Addie flung the door open. The blinding sunlight stung her eyes. When they'd adjusted, she spotted Paige standing beside Martha's Dumpster speaking with a woman. She looked familiar, but Addie couldn't make out her features. She shielded her eyes and squinted. "Paige, do you want me to pick you up anything for lunch?"

Both women started.

"Umm, no, that's fine. When you come back, I'll grab something from next door." Paige looked from Addie to the woman she had been speaking with. "Addie, this is Jeanie Winslow, June's daughter."

Addie walked toward them and extended her hand. "It's so nice to meet you." Jeanie recoiled. Addie slid her hand back into her pocket. "I'm so sorry for your loss."

Jeanie stiffened. "I've been asking Paige for her opinion of you."

"In what way?"

"Jeanie just wanted to know if I thought you were . . ." Her round blue eyes beseeched Addie's for mercy.

"The kind of person who could have had anything to do with my mother's death?" Jeanie bit out the words. Addie made a mental note to check for bite marks later.

A snicker came from behind Addie, and she spun around in time to see Martha's pudgy, flour-covered face peeking out of the bakery's back door. The door shut, and Addie looked back at Jeanie, whose eyes hadn't wavered from her. Addie took a step back and gestured toward the door. "Come inside, Jeanie. Let me try and put your mind to rest."

Jeanie faltered, but slid past Addie into the storeroom. Now Addie could see why she had looked so familiar. Jeanie was a younger version of the photograph of her mother in the newspaper. Addie wasn't a great judge of age, but as she looked down at Jeanie, she guessed her to be only about ten years older than she was, which would place her in her early to maybe midforties?

"You, too, Paige," she called to her clerk, who seemed to be stuck in limbo by the Dumpster.

Addie scanned the storefront to make sure no one had come into the shop while they were out back, then motioned to a couple of crates. "Please sit, so we can talk."

Jeanie plopped down onto a box. Paige stood, fidgeting with a loose string on her shirt. "I think I'll just keep an eye on the front," she said and disappeared into the shop.

Addie sat on a box facing Jeanie and met her deep brown-eyed gaze. "Please let me express my condolences. I hear your mother was a lovely person and much loved in the community."

Jeanie nodded, her dark, straight, bobbed hair swinging freely.

"And please know, regardless of what you read in the paper, I had nothing to do with either her disappearance or her death." Addie looked down at her damp hands in her lap. "I've never even met her."

"But, but I thought since you owned a bookshop, and she was the librarian . . . you used to be a librarian, right?" Her eyes narrowed.

"No, I was a researcher, but I did work at the Boston Public Library. I was in acquisitions and—"

"But I was told"—Jeanie shifted on the crate—"that you were after my mother's job, because the shop isn't doing well and your criminal Boston friends were trying to make sure you got a job there for some reason." She hung her head, and then straightened up. "I guess I should have learned by now not to believe the gossip in this town."

Addie's lips tightened, and she slowly nodded.

"I'm sorry, really I am. I hope you can understand. If it were your mother who disappeared out of the blue, you'd be

inclined to let your mind run through every crazy scenario."
She sniffed. "I'm just grasping for answers, I guess."

Addie handed her a balled-up tissue from her pocket.
"Don't worry, it's clean." She waited for Jeanie to compose
herself. "My mother passed when I was very young, but I do
understand. When my father was killed last year, I went
through the same thing." She took Jeanie's hand in hers,
gave it a light squeeze, and smiled. "Now, let's start fresh.
I'm Addison Greyborne, and it's very nice to meet you, Jeanie
Winslow."

"Will you forgive me? I've just heard so much lately from
so many different people that my head's ready to explode,
and I don't know what to believe anymore."

"Of course I can, but there's nothing to forgive. It's just
been a really bad time for you, and people like to stir things
up—and sometimes enjoy making everything worse."

"Yes, I see that now." Jeanie dropped her tensed shoulders. "I'm just so confused. I don't know if it was a horrible
accident or if someone, like it suggested in the newspaper,
killed her. She was a good person; everyone liked her. She . . .
she . . ." Jeanie covered her face with the tissue and sobbed.

Addie placed her hand on the shaking woman's shoulder,
trying not to relive her own grief.

"I am sorry about doubting you based on gossip." Jeanie
dabbed her reddened nose.

"We all, including that reporter, have to wait to see what
the autopsy shows and stop jumping to conclusions."

Jeanie nodded and sniffled. "But why did the paper report
you were taken in for questioning then?"

"I wasn't." Addie shifted. "Marc and I are just friends."
The word "just" burned in her throat. "We crossed paths in
another investigation."

"I remember hearing about that."

"Yes, and last night he only wanted my opinion on something, and, well, I just happened to be there. Nothing more."

Her mind raced to an image of Lacey, and her heart sank at that apparent truth.

"Well," Jeanie said as she stood up, "if I can answer any questions for you, please give me a call." Jeanie held out her hand. "And again, please forgive me." She turned toward the storeroom doorway. "I better go. I have some arrangements for my mother to make this afternoon."

"Jeanie, wait."

Jeanie stopped and turned back.

"Did your mother carry a cell phone?"

"Yes, always. I even gave her an expensive case on her birthday." Her eyes dropped. "But the police said it wasn't with her, and I can't figure out where it would be." She looked at Addie, her eyes filled with renewed tears. "She loved that case. It was a pink pearl tortoiseshell design. I bought it for her in New York City." She dabbed the tissue to her eyes.

"I'm sorry." Addie stood up, rubbing her hand up and down her arm. She bit her lip. "There is one more question."

"Sure, what?" she sniffled.

"I found an article on the Internet that your mother wrote some years ago. It was about a tunnel system built during the sixteen hundreds to eighteen hundreds under what is now the Greyborne Harbor town site, but I don't remember seeing that information mentioned, at least in detail, in her published book. Do you know anything about it?"

Jeanie shook her head. "Not really. I do remember when she first wrote the book she was spitting mad one night after a town council meeting because they had objected to some of the facts she had in her original manuscript and forbade her to publish them. I remember her ranting on about censorship, but that's all. She didn't mention anything specific."

"Why would she have shared her unpublished work with the town council?"

"They had given her a grant to write it—something about boosting tourism or something? I don't really remember."

Addie tapped her finger on her chin. "Okay, sorry to keep you. I was just thinking out loud." Addie smiled as Jeanie turned to leave. "If you do think of anything else, please let me know."

"I will." She called back as she made her way through the shop. The door chimes rang, and Jeanie was gone.

Addie scowled and raced to her computer on the front desk and clicked open the article. She reread it, jotted down some notes, pressed print, and grabbed June's book from under the counter. Her eyes widened as she flipped through the pages.

"Is everything all right?" Paige glanced over at Addie from the bookshelf she was organizing. "You look like you've just seen a ghost or something."

Addie shut the book and her gaping mouth. "Not a ghost, but . . . I think I did find something. I need you to watch the shop for a few more minutes before you go for lunch." She grabbed her purse and jacket. "I won't be long," she called back as she headed out the door to share her findings with one of the few people she could trust.

Chapter Seven

Addie flung the door open and stopped. Serena's shop was the busiest she had ever seen it. There were tables and chairs cramming most of the floor space typically reserved for the sale racks, teapots, various tea strainers, and cup displays. Which were now neatly arranged in the wall cubbies alongside the silver tea bags of SerenaTEA's most popular blends.

The buzz of conversation ceased when all eyes in the shop came to rest on her standing in the doorway. She nodded and smiled as she passed many familiar faces, and the ones she recognized as being her loyal daily coffee group averted their eyes as she made her way toward Serena at the back counter. "I see business has picked up."

Serena spun around, splashing tea over the tray she was preparing. "Yes, I'm swamped today. Can you believe this?"

"What happened? Are you holding a fire sale or something?" Addie laughed, looking around the tea shop. "This is wonderful. Whatever made you decide to add tables?"

"Actually, it was—"

"Hello, Addie." Lacey appeared in the doorway to the back room, drying her hands on a kitchen towel. "Come to congratulate Serena on her very successful grand reopening?"

"Her reopening?" Addie looked questioningly at Serena.

"Didn't you see the announcement in the paper this morning?"

"I must have missed it." She met Lacey's icy smile with a frosty one of her own.

"I'm not surprised, given that piece in the column today," said Serena, resetting her tea tray. "I've been meaning to pop in all day, but as you can see . . ." She shrugged and headed toward a table.

"Serena, there's a few other orders for you to take back there in the corner." Lacey turned on her heel and headed back through the storeroom door beside the counter.

Addie moved closer to the door and peered in. Lacey drew up a chair, took a sip of tea, pulled a newspaper off a crate, and began thumbing through it.

She slowly looked up, her waxed brows cocked at an odd angle. Or maybe they were penciled on. Addie could only hope they were. "Is there something I can do for you, Addie?"

"No thanks, I was going to grab an apron and give Serena a hand out here, but I see she has plenty of help already." She looked over her shoulder at Serena hopping from table to table, her face damp and flushed.

"Yes, she does." Lacey sipped from her steaming cup. "You should probably hurry along back"—her hand made a shooing gesture—"to your shop now. I'm sure *you're* swamped, too." She chuckled and kept reading the newspaper.

"Did I just overhear that you're crazy busy today, too?" Serena chirped behind her.

Addie pulled Serena toward the front door. "Is she your new partner or boss?"

"Oh no, but none of this would have been possible without her. Just yesterday, she came up with the idea for me to add the tables, and then she immediately put the ad in the paper. She's been such a big support today. She even dropped off these tables and chairs for me to set up this morning. I really couldn't have done it without her."

"I can see just how much support she is." Addie glared at the storeroom doorway. "You say she only came up with the idea yesterday?"

"Yes, she said the idea just came to her, and she thought this would be the perfect time to relaunch my shop." A new customer waved Serena to a table. "I'd better go, but I must say I've missed her and her big-city ideas. She was right, just look at this place. I can't keep up." Serena turned and dashed over to the new party of four.

"Too bad she's not helping with the increased work, too," mumbled Addie as she headed out the door. The hushed whispers that had fallen over the room when she entered returned to a normal din of conversation at her exit. She sighed and headed back to her empty bookshop.

"You're back already?" Paige glanced up from the desk.

"Yes, not a good time."

"Did you at least pick up something to eat?"

"No, I'm not feeling very hungry at the moment. But you go ahead, my treat," Addie said, withdrawing a ten-dollar bill from her wallet.

A few minutes later, Paige returned with a sandwich bag in her hand. Addie retrieved her laptop from the counter and headed to the back room, "I have some work to do. Holler if you need me."

She placed her laptop on the small writing desk she'd retrieved from her aunt's cellar and stared up at the blackboard she had used to keep track of previous events and suspects. She pulled down the drop cloth covering it from prying eyes, picked up a piece of chalk, and wrote, *Lacey Davenport*, then stood back and stroked her chin.

It was no use. Nothing about Lacey came to mind, except the facts that Addie didn't like her and her gut told her not to trust her, but that hardly made her a suspect in anything.

She chewed her bottom lip and paced in front of the board. It was no use; there was no proof of Lacey's involvement with feeding Miss Newsy false and misleading information, and no one would listen to her based on a hunch. She needed evidence to support her gut feeling.

She opened her laptop and searched *Lacey Davenport, Los Angeles morning television news*. It didn't take long for over ten pages of related items to appear in the search results. She clicked through one after the other. They all expounded the talent of the rising young news reporter from the East Coast who had taken Hollywood by storm. Result after result held glowing reports of her journalism prowess, many calling her the next Diane Sawyer. Except for one report, found buried on page eight. The word "Fraud" in the headline popped out at Addie, and her finger twitched with excitement.

"Why are you researching Lacey?"

She jumped and spun around. "Marc, I didn't hear you come in."

"I can see that." He leaned over her shoulder, the sleeve of his police jacket grazing her ear as he eyed the web article.

She snapped her laptop closed and kept her mouth shut, too.

"What's up, Addie?" He stood back. His gaze went to the board, where Lacey's name was written, then back to her. "Do you think Lacey really is a suspect in the disappearance and death of June?"

"No, no." She jumped to her feet. "I was only trying to find some background information. After all, she grew up here and I wanted to know more about—"

"I can tell you anything about her you need to know." His eyes fixed on hers. "And, I assure you, there is nothing you need to know, because it's not important." He turned toward the door and stopped. "Trust me, Addie, you don't need to worry about her—past demons, remember." His lips curved into a shy smile. "I just dropped in to give you a fresh cinnamon roll from the bakery in the harbor. I thought you might need a pick-me-up today." His face reddened as he set a cling-wrapped paper plate on the desk, turned, and left.

"Thank you," she called, but there was no reply. She looked at the cinnamon roll he'd thought to bring to her and smiled, then looked up at the name scrawled across the blackboard. "Crap." Addie sighed and leaned against the desk. "He thinks I'm investigating her because of him. Men." She shook her head. "Well, it is because of him, but just a little bit, I suppose." More than she liked to admit. She opened her laptop, returned to reading the article about Lacey, and sank her teeth into the roll.

When she had finished reading, she wiped her hands on a napkin and leaned back. Her fingers interlocked behind her head. "Well, well, Miss Davenport, most interesting." She stood up and wrote on the board:

1. *Started as a host on a small-market morning television show*

2. *Did series of investigative news stories*

3. *Based on those stories was offered AND accepted a coanchor position with a MAJOR network*

4. *Before she left the morning show, her fabrication of the news stories broke*

5. *Was dismissed from the morning show*

6. *Offer was withdrawn when proved to have used fictitious stories as a leg up in her career*

She stabbed her chalk piece to make the period. "As Dad always told me—when in doubt, follow your gut."

And her gut sure doubted.

Chapter Eight

Addie checked the time and dashed to the front of the shop as Paige unplugged the nautical lights around the Founder's Day window displays. "Addie, you startled me." She chuckled, patting her chest. "Are you done? I didn't want to disturb you but didn't think you'd mind closing a few minutes early." She shrugged her shoulders. "No one's been in all afternoon."

"No. Go on and head home. I should get ready for to-night's book club anyway. Not sure what's expected of me as hostess, but I'd better run out and get some snacks at least."

"That reminds me." Paige went over to the counter and handed her a note. "Catherine Lewis called about an hour ago. She told me not to interrupt, but to have you call her as soon as you were available."

Addie looked at the scrawled phone number and nodded. "Thanks, I'll do that right now. Have a good evening. See you tomorrow." She hoped there would be a tomorrow. If shoppers and her regulars avoided her store much longer, she might have to let Paige go.

Addie dialed the number Catherine had left. The phone went directly to voice mail, but the message voice sounded eerily like Lacey's. Addie stared at the phone and rechecked the number she had dialed and tried again. This time there was an answer, and it left no doubt in Addie's mind when Lacey's voice cooed over her speaker. "Hello."

"Umm, hello? This is Addie. Is Catherine Lewis there?"

Lacey's yogurt-smooth voice curdled to sour milk. "Of course. Just a sec."

The phone crackled, and something clunked against the receiver. "Addie, so glad you got my message." Another clunk; the sound echoed through Addie, and she held the phone at arm's length, frowning. "So sorry, dear, these earrings aren't meant for phone conversations."

"That's okay." Addie flipped off the reverberating speaker and pressed her ear against the phone to hear. "Oh . . . Sure, I understand . . . Yes, a bad time . . . Thanks for letting me know . . ." She pressed the phone closer to her ear. "Sorry, I couldn't hear that, the background laughter . . . Yes, yes, of course . . . Thanks, chat soon, bye."

Addie bit on her lip, tapping her phone on the counter. She jumped at a knock on the door and peeked out to see Marc holding a tray of cling-wrapped pastries.

"What's this?" She opened the door, looking at the tray and back up at him.

"I knew you wouldn't have much time to run out to buy anything, and all the nearest shops are closing now, so I thought I'd drop it off for your meeting tonight." He swung past her, placing the silver tray on the counter.

"Thank you. Wow, that's a very nice thought, but unfortunately I won't need it tonight."

His smile vanished. "What happened?"

"Oh, nothing much," she said, pausing to upright a fallen book on a shelf. "But it seems that the meeting has been postponed until after June's memorial service. *Apparently*, Lacey thought it in poor taste to rush ahead with it under the circumstances."

"What does Lacey have to do with the book club?" He slid onto a stool.

"That's what I'm wondering." Addie shrugged, taking the stool beside him. "If the suggestion had come from Jeanie or the group members, it would make sense, but Lacey?" She shook her head and frowned.

"This is all my fault."

"How on earth is this your fault?"

He scoured his hands over his face. "Because . . . I might have let on to her that"—he took a deep breath—"you and I are a couple."

"You did?" A mutinous part of her heart did a flip. "I guess that answers the questions I had about why she appears to want to discredit me." She frowned. "Why would you tell her we're a couple? We're just friends." A flush crawled up her neck onto her cheeks. "Aren't we?" She scrubbed at a random stain on the countertop. At least she wasn't gazing at Marc like she knew he was at her.

"Yes, of course we are. I may have embellished a bit because I was a coward, I admit it. When she got back to town and came on so strong, making it clear she wanted to pick up where we'd left off, I thought if she thought I'd moved on she'd . . . Well, and honestly, I kind of thought you and I . . . Never mind."

"Looks like that scheme backfired." Addie tore her eyes off the stain in time to see Marc duck his head and study his shiny shoes. A small smile skipped onto her lips. "Well, now that I know I'm just dealing with a petty, jealous woman and not some bigger conspiracy, I can handle it. David had his fair share of groupies over the years, too." She touched his knee. His hand covered hers, and for a second, just a split second, time stopped. A car backfired on the street, and time began ticking again. Clearing her throat, she slid her hand off his knee.

His hand captured hers. "So are you comparing what we have to something similar to what you had with David?"

She looked up into his dark, smoldering eyes, started to stand up, and wavered when her knees refused to work correctly. "No, not at all, it's just that . . ." Why couldn't she think around him? She pulled her hand from his, severing the electric surge his mere touch brought her. Forcing an easy smile, she leaned against the counter. "Maybe it's time you did fill me on Miss Lacey Davenport, as it seems she has recruited my few friends into her camp. I distinctly heard Serena laughing in the background when I was talking to Catherine." If he noticed her change of topic, he didn't say, but his eyes dimmed, and he broke his gaze away from hers.

"What do you want to know?"

"Nothing personal. I mean, only if you want to, and I don't need . . . want the gory details." Where was a handy hole when one wanted to slide into it and oblivion?

He chuckled. "Good, because I may have been a coward, but I don't kiss and tell. I am still a gentleman."

"It's just that now she thinks . . . Never mind what she thinks. She has me in her sights."

"Trust me." He took her hand and rubbed his thumb over the top. "I never thought that would happen, or I wouldn't have implied anything."

Her chest fluttered at his touch. She could only nod.

"I would never do anything to hurt you. Ever."

Her hand felt warm, safely tucked in his. "I guess I can see why you implied what you did seemed like a good plan at first. She is a strong personality."

Marc laughed and released her hand.

"What's so funny? It's true, isn't it?"

"You have no idea how true that is. She can be a piranha when she sets her mind on something, and she did that with me more than once."

"I just thought if you could give me some backgr—"

"What is it you want to know? How she hunted and stalked me most of my life, trapped me, led me on, and then abruptly left me cold, practically standing at the altar?" He reached for her hand again, but dropped his own into his lap.

Addie's fluttering heart dropped to the pit of her stomach. "No," she whispered. "Not the demons, just . . . I don't know, but this isn't just about you, even though you think it is." She ignored his twitching lips. "I found something else about her online." She glanced at him. He appeared to be sulking, and she guessed it was about the comment she'd made about this not all being about him. "I guess . . . I'm wondering if she's the type of person who would do what they say she did."

Marc straightened his back. "I'd have to read it to tell you."

"My laptop's in the back room."

"Let's go." He swung his long legs to the floor and stood up, his eyes searching her face. "And . . . don't worry about her befriending Serena. That's a weapon she's used most of my life. Befriend the little sister to stay close to the target."

"And I'm a target now, too, but in the seek-and-destroy category." Addie headed toward the back room. "Have you talked to Serena about her?"

"Many times, but Lacey is good. Even after she left town abruptly without so much as a goodbye to Serena, which really tore her up, I might add. Serena could never stay angry with her for long. I guess Lacey cast a spell over her at a very young, impressionable age, and Serena would always forgive her, no matter what Lacey did to her."

"That's unfortunate. I thought Serena was wiser than that."

"She is in most everything else, but she's blinded to Lacey because she made her an idol at a very young age, and Lacey's used that to easily manipulate her ever since."

"Yes, I think I saw a bit of that earlier today."

"So, what are we looking at?" Marc leaned closer to the

screen. His phone pinged with a text notification. He pulled it out, looked at it, and put his phone back in his pocket.

"You tell me." Addie sat back and waited until he finished reading.

He stood up and shook his head. "Yup, sounds like her— especially the last part, using it as a stepping stone. She's always used people with her flashing bleached smile, saying the right things and being ever so charming. People tend to fall easily into her trap."

"Is that what happened to you?" She looked up at him.

"And everyone in town. She uses people, then casts them aside when she's done. I'm glad someone called her out on it." His phone rang. He tugged it out of his jacket pocket, checked the caller ID, and put it away again.

She searched his face, but it was blank. She shrugged and looked back at the screen. "I just don't understand why something this newsworthy is buried so far back in the search."

"The major network referred to probably didn't want it to get out they had been duped."

"That makes sense, I guess. The reporter who broke the story was at the UCLA student newspaper at the time, so it was probably easy enough to kill it."

He rubbed his hands over his face. "Enough of Lacey— she's not worth it. I was hoping you had some theories on June's death." He looked at the blackboard. "But I see where your focus has been today."

"I was only trying to figure out why Lacey was so bent on making my life miserable. Then that last gossip bit printed, and I was trying to find out if she would have fed Miss Newsy the information about me being at the police station." She ran her hand down his jacket sleeve. "Honestly, I wasn't prying into your private life."

"Actually, you make a good point." He rocked back on his heels, all cop-like again.

"I do?"

"Yes." He sat on the edge of the desk and stared at the board. "I wonder after reading that article how far Lacey would really go to destroy your reputation in town." He scratched his neck.

"But why—just to win you back?"

"Yeah, even that seems too far out. After all, this isn't high school anymore."

"I hope she knows that," Addie mumbled, looking at the computer screen. "Maybe there's another motive?"

"The only thing I can think of is . . . No, she wouldn't. Would she?" He looked at Addie.

"What?"

"Search 'Greyborne-Davenport feud.'"

"What?"

"Just enter it and see what comes up." He walked around behind her as she typed.

"Oh my God," she whispered. "What's this?" Addie sat back and took a deep breath. "Wow, this part"—she pointed to the screen—"is a piece of town history I had no idea about." She continued reading. "It says a British navy warship swooped down on the whole village in the early seventeen hundreds to crush the piracy that ran rampant in the area."

"Yes, prior to Gerald Greyborne making it a permanent settlement of the Crown. It had already been used by both pirates and legitimate sailors for well over two hundred years as a safe harbor from the sometimes severe Atlantic storms. The way the rock peninsula shelters the area, made it an ideal location for a thriving pirate haven which eventually developed into a small village."

"It says here that it was a tip from Gerald Greyborne that ultimately led to Henry Davenport's arrest for committing acts of treason by being in collusion with the pirates. He was tried and then hanged, along with a number of others accused of piracy." She looked back up at him, her eyes wide. "The hangings took place in the old main square of the Harbor?"

"Yeah, it was devastating to the settlement at the time. The scandal tore the village apart. Some were pro piracy—it made them a lot of money—and others, like Gerald Greyborne, an upstanding sea merchant captain, were not, as it cut into their legitimate business dealings."

"But would Lacey carry on a grudge that happened three hundred years ago?"

"I don't like to think so, but"—he shrugged—"you never know. Those wounds ran deep, and the two families were never the same. Some people around here have long memories."

"Surely," she said, looking up at him, "not today, though. It's been a few hundred years." He bent over her shoulder. His warm breath wafting across the back of her head didn't go unnoticed by her, and she smiled to herself.

He straightened up. A pang of disappointment struck her. "I've often wondered," he said, "if that's why Lacey was so headstrong and bent on being successful, having to have the best of everything. You know, to try to alter her family legacy?"

"And you were the best, and she wanted you, too." She chuckled, minimizing the screen and turning toward him.

"She had big plans for me. Politics."

"Really?"

"Yup, but when I joined the police force instead . . . she decided a patrol officer wasn't good enough for her. She then set her sights on me becoming chief immediately, and when that didn't happen, she left for Los Angeles."

"And now you are chief and she's back."

"I know that look—what are you thinking?"

"Nothing, really, I'm just trying to figure out how someone could be so shallow and heartless." She touched his arm, fighting the tears that burned behind her eyes.

"I'm fine, really." He stroked the back of her hand. "Now, enough of all that. What else did you find?"

"Well," she said as she turned back to her laptop and maximized another screen, "after reading the story about the feud and the piracy, this makes more sense to me. It's a paper June published years ago, but I couldn't find reference to it in her book, *The Ghosts and Mysteries of Greyborne Harbor*, the one the book club is reviewing now."

Marc leaned over her shoulder and read. "What does this have to do with anything?"

"Maybe a lot."

"Come on, you can give me your theories over dinner. I'm starving, and we can't live off pastries."

"Sounds good. I'll put them in the fridge. We can take my car out back. It's less conspicuous than your cruiser," she said with a laugh and went to retrieve the pastry platter from the front counter.

"If you're trying to hide from prying eyes tonight, I know the perfect out-of-the-way place, and you'll love it, especially after reading about the town's history of piracy."

Pastries tucked in the fridge, she grabbed her coat. "Where's that?"

"It's out on Smuggler's Road." He helped her put on her jacket, his fingers lightly brushing the back of her neck and coming to rest on her shoulders.

Her neck still tingling from his touch, a quiver of excitement raced down her arms. "You've got to be kidding?"

His hands didn't release the gentle hold he had on her. "No." His warm breath wafted across her cheek, and she closed her eyes. "It's called the Smuggler's Den, and it's allegedly built on the same site as an original smuggler's haven. They even used some of the old bricks and timbers in the restoration."

"Really? I can't wait to see it." She braced her legs to stop the wobble in her knees and turned around to face him.

"Well, there appears to be no shortage of mystery in this town, so all we're missing from June's book is the ghosts." She smiled, but her gaze went not to his eyes, but to his lips, so close to hers.

His thumb stroked the outline of her jaw. "Then you are in for a treat come Founder's Day Eve."

"What's happening then?"

"A wonderful tradition in the village. I think you'll enjoy it."

"Give me a hint as to what to expect." His touch lingered, and she leaned into his hand.

"Better yet, I'll show you myself." He brushed his lips against hers in a whisper-light kiss.

Breathless, she broke the magnetic pull of his lips, her heart beating wildly. "Did you just ask me out on a real date?"

His fingertip lifted her chin, and his lip curled up at the corner. "I guess I did."

Chapter Nine

"Why haven't I heard about this place before? I love it." The rum barrels stacked around the perimeters of the room, the ornately carved bar and counter, the brick archways and floor all oozed history of the illegal activity that once went on inside these walls. She made herself comfortable in a chair repurposed from an old oak barrel and continued scanning the large dining room and bar camouflaging an original pirate's lair.

"I thought you'd like it," he grinned at her over his wooden-plank menu, "especially after reading that bit about the important role that piracy played in Greyborne Harbor history."

"Like it? I love it. This has officially become my new favorite place in the world. It feels so real, it makes me wish I had a parrot."

He smirked. "The food's not too bad either. Have you decided what you want yet?"

"I haven't even looked." She scrutinized the plates of the customers seated close by. "I don't know. It all looks so good. What do you suggest?"

A waiter dressed in high boots and breeches and looking every inch a swashbuckling pirate swept past her and placed a platter on the table across the aisle from theirs. Addie's eyes widened. She waved at the waiter as he turned to leave. "What is that?" Addie motioned toward the lone diner's plate.

"That, madam, is our rum-n-beer barbecue beef rib, fresh grilled asparagus, and baked potato special. May I tempt you with an order?"

"A beef rib? It looks more like a dinosaur rib." She held her hand over her rumbling stomach. "Yes, that's what I'll have." She smiled at the salt-and-pepper-haired man hovering over his newly delivered meal. He returned a rather surly glare and began stripping the rib meat from the bone.

"And for you, sir?" The server turned to Marc.

Marc's cell rang again. He checked the caller, switched it off, and handed the waiter their menus. "Yes, I'll have the same, thank you."

The waiter swept into a low bow and left, leaving the surly man open to observation. He set his fork down on the platter, wiped his mouth, and turned his glacial gaze on Addie's. She shuddered. Marc tapped her foot with his under the table. She jerked and looked at him. He shook his head. She shrugged and began sipping her water. Out of the corner of her eye, she saw the man pick up his fork and begin to eat his meal again.

"Sorry," she whispered. "I'm just so hungry I wasn't aware I was being rude."

He muttered something Addie couldn't make out. She feigned kicking him under the table. He flinched and clutched his leg. She playfully swatted at his hand.

"Okay, okay, you win." His eyes twinkled in jest, but his foot against hers felt very serious indeed. "You said you had a theory, and now that I've brought you to the most inspiring ghost tale environment that there is in the Harbor, let your story begin. I can't wait to hear what it is."

"Don't laugh." She pouted. "This might be something worth considering."

"Hit me with it." He grinned at her over the top of his water glass.

"Well . . ." she said as she shifted in her seat, careful not to dislodge her foot from the comfort of his, "as you know, I was asked to chair the romance book club."

"I didn't realize it was a romance book club?" He gently grasped her hand, stroking the back of it with his thumb.

"And as you know"—her gaze met his, rendering her breathless—"the book they're reviewing this month is *The Ghosts and Mysteries of Greyborne Harbor*."

His eyes held fast on hers. "It's not exactly a romance novel, is it?" His thumb trailed small circles over the back of her hand. "Unless, of course, there's a ghostly buxom wench embracing a handsome pirate on the cover." He winked.

"You only wish." She smirked and shook her head. "But, from the short conversation I had with Catherine, I believe they are looking to expand their reading interests, and I guess since June was the author and chair and it's close to Founder's Day, it seemed like the perfect choice."

"I see. And so what is this theory of yours, and how could this book be connected to June's death?"

"Not the book. But maybe something she found out researching it that the town council forbade her to include in the book."

"What? This is news to me. They actually edited her book?"

"According to Jeanie, there were originally sections in it comprised of the research she had done for years as president of the historical society that they forbade her to include in the finished draft."

"Can they do that?"

"I guess since they were giving her a grant to write the book, they felt they could. It was something to do with tourism and the good name of the community. Maybe they didn't want any skeletons exposed."

Marc shook his head. "This doesn't make sense, but I'm

going to look into it. Censorship from any government agency, no matter what level, isn't right." His brow furrowed. "What was the information they demanded to be removed?"

"I had found an article she wrote some years ago posted in the Boston Public Library's archives. It was about—"

"Wait, you still have access to the Boston Public Library's archives?"

"They haven't deleted my access code yet." She slid her hand from his and fidgeted with her napkin.

He raised his glass in a salute. "No wonder you can find out all the information you come up with. Most of it isn't available on the public Internet."

"Anyway," she said, grinning at him and clinking her glass to his, "her research was based on the stories of tunnel systems that were constructed during the sixteen hundreds to as late as the eighteen hundreds, underneath what is now the Greyborne Harbor town site."

"I've heard rumors about those my whole life, but I thought they were only legends or myths. Isn't most of her book based on that, legend and myths?"

"Something I found out as a researcher was that there is usually some reality base to most legends. Some appear to be simply myths because there has never been any hard evidence discovered to prove them true."

"So you think that June may have found the proof and the town council wanted to suppress it? But why? If it's true, it's an important part of local history."

Addie nodded and glanced at the man seated across from them. He was slowly chewing his meal and staring directly ahead. His eyes flickered sideways. He dropped his head, focusing on his scantly touched food. She frowned and looked back at Marc.

"Well," he said, "why would the town council want to leave those facts out?"

She glanced back at the man and shifted in her chair. "I'm not really sure. I haven't read through all her findings yet"—her voice dropped—"but there was a link to a map."

Marc's eyes widened, and he took a sip of water.

"Maybe," she said, still whispering, "they were afraid that tourists and residents would start digging up the streets to find the tunnels."

"That's ridiculous," he said, placing his glass on the table. "Surely it would be a historical find that would put them on every tourist map, and you'd think they'd want just that to boost the economy. Dig them out and do tours and stuff, you know, make it part of the ghost walk for Founder's Day weekend celebrations. It brings in lots of tourism money."

"A ghost walk? Is that the mysterious date you have in mind?"

He bit his lower lip. "Maybe."

"Well then," she said, "I'll need a big, strong escort. Do you know anyone who fits that bill? Jerry, perhaps?" She gave him a cocky wink. Marc's face flushed, and Addie laughed, glancing at the man across from them. His sideways gaze quickly diverted back to his meal. She sat back, and then leaned forward, whispering from behind her raised water glass. "Maybe there's more to it than just tunnels?" She looked fleetingly at the man, who now appeared to be inclined toward them but staring straight ahead.

Marc glanced sideways and dropped his voice. "Like what? Buried treasure?"

She shielded her mouth and whispered, "I don't know. I'll take a look at what she discovered later tonight and let you know what I find out, but there has to be more to it."

Marc leaned forward on his elbows, his voice barely audible. "There was an archeological find made back in the late eighteen hundreds. At least, I think that's when it was."

She leaned closer to hear him.

"A group of kids playing down on the rocks at the base of the cliff, just down the hill from here, actually, found a large cave and began exploring. Apparently it didn't lead anywhere though, no tunnels or anything, but the back wall did look like it had been blasted, because they found cannonball artifacts in there. It was considered a major discovery at the time, because it also contained some old daggers, swords, and a few other pirate-type relics."

"Interesting. Is it still there?"

"Not really. Access was blocked years ago. It had become too dangerous. There were a series of minor collapses, so officials closed it."

"Makes sense—if it was blasted, it would have become geologically unsound. The article about the Greyborne-Davenport feud said the British had imprisoned Henry Davenport, so they probably blew up the cave to lessen the chances of any future smuggling operations, and that would have weakened its physical integrity."

"But what does this have to do with June's book?"

"Maybe nothing, but it is worth us looking into, isn't it? She was killed for a reason, and—"

"Wait right there. The autopsy report isn't in yet, so we still don't know if she was pushed or just had an unfortunate accident."

"You're right, but maybe she was onto something or had some information someone wanted, and that's why she was in the utility shed to begin with."

"Is that the reason you asked about other accesses to the utility tunnels and about any signs of digging through the back wall when we were down there? You knew about her research and you didn't tell me then?"

"I didn't even know about June's book when we were down there—it was just a wild guess. Tunnels always lead somewhere and I just wondered where that one led and what was at the end of it. Now, after reading her book and doing some research, my question makes even more sense. Doesn't it?"

"It's just that how many times do I have to tell you that *I'm* the cop here, and you have to tell me any and all information that is relevant to an ongoing case?" He sucked in a deep breath. "I just worry so much about you getting in over your head, and there is some information I do need to know first."

"But you are the first to know. I haven't told anyone about any of this. I swear." She crossed her heart.

"I know, I know. Just promise me that you won't go off exploring on your own, not at the cave site, or following some clues or a map you find of June's or—"

The waiter appeared at their table and flashed her a sizzling smile. Serena would love a smile from this pirate. She glanced at another server not far away. Actually, from any of these pirates. She chuckled inwardly, mentally noting to bring her friend here one evening. He placed their platters on the table, poured them each glass of wine, bowed, clicked his heels, and left.

She raised her glass to meet Marc's in a toast and glanced to the table beside them. The man was gone, his meal barely touched.

Chapter Ten

Addie settled on the antique sofa in her living room, flipped her laptop open, and dug in to the archives of the Boston Public Library. It didn't take long to pull up the map June had referred to in her research papers. It depicted a footprint of the village back in the early eighteen hundreds. Since she was still a newcomer and not familiar with the local landmarks, her brow knit in concentration as she tried to make sense of it. She did manage to make out the shoreline and a scribble that looked like a rough opening to a cave. Her eyes followed the faint dotted line leading from that spot to what she supposed was the current site of the Smuggler's Den restaurant, but from there she was lost.

She jumped at a knock at the door and eyed the grandfather clock ticking softly. Nine. She glanced out the large lead-paned window before she opened the door.

"Serena, what a nice surprise."

Serena gave her a hug, a box wedged between them.

"What's this? You come bearing gifts." Taking the silver box from Serena's outstretched hand, she fingered the blue, silk ribbon that tied it closed.

"No, it's not from me. I found it sitting on your doorstep."

Addie looked at the box and frowned. "I haven't been

home long, and I'm certain it wasn't there when I got home. But please come in. It's great to see you." She stood aside and let Serena enter the foyer, setting the gift box on the marble side table.

"I know. It feels like ages since we spent time together," Serena said, hanging her jacket on the coatrack. "Where were you tonight anyway? I've been calling for hours, and it kept going directly to voice mail."

"Really?" Addie retrieved her phone from her pocket, leading the way into the living room. "Sorry, the battery's dead." She pointed to the walnut liquor cart. "Want a nightcap?"

"Sounds perfect." Serena settled on the overstuffed sofa. "Did you do something fun tonight? It must have been such a relief not to have had to go to the stuffy old book club meeting." She took her drink from Addie, who settled down on the opposite end of the couch.

"I went out for dinner with a friend."

"A male friend?" Serena's eyes dropped, and her fingertip circled the rim of her wineglass. "I couldn't get ahold of Marc either, so I assume . . . ?"

"Never you mind." Addie playfully swatted at her. "It was only dinner." She inwardly cursed her warming cheeks.

"Okay, if you insist."

Addie tried to forget the feeling of his foot against hers and the security she had found in that small gesture. "Yes, I do insist." Addie took a sip of wine. "So, no outing with Lacey tonight?"

"No, she got into a real mood."

"What's up with that?"

"Not sure—I'd just be guessing. But after you talked with Catherine, she suggested that she, Lacey, and me should go out for dinner since the book club was off. Lacey said I should call Marc and have him meet us. I texted him, then she called him twice, I think, but when we couldn't get ahold of him, she went very quiet." She looked questioningly at Addie. "Her mood got even worse as we tried to decide where to go. So I feigned a headache and left her and Catherine to figure it out. I wanted to talk to you before—"

"Well, I'm glad you dropped by. I've missed you." Addie clinked her glass against Serena's.

Serena's gaze traveled to the laptop sitting open on the table. She leaned forward and picked it up. "What are you working on?" She scanned the screen.

"Just some research I was doing on June's book." Addie reached out to take the computer from her and paused. "Actually, maybe you are just the perfect person to help me decipher this."

Serena studied the screen. "It's an old map of Greyborne Harbor. What do you need this for?"

"Well, I don't need it. I was trying to understand her book better. You know, for the book club meeting. So I was just looking into the history of the Harbor and found this old map pretty interesting." Addie glanced sideways at Serena. "After all, it's my history now, too, I guess."

"You're right." Serena shrugged, glancing back at the map. "What do you want to know?"

Addie shuffled closer to her and pointed to the landmarks named on the map. "These. I don't know the town that well, and I'm curious as to where they are in relationship to today's topography."

Serena squinted and brought the screen closer to her eyes. "Well, this gnarled tree is on the edge of what I assume is the small rock cliff south of town, and it's where the fork into town leads from Smuggler's Road."

"I see." Addie slid closer, pointing to a sketch of a rock closer inland.

"That boulder used to sit on the site of the current Main Street and Municipal Park, but it was removed about ten years ago to make way for the hospital expansion and the new loading dock."

"Hmmm." Addie leaned closer. "And what about this line"—her finger trailed across the screen—"leading to the hill at what looks like might be my street?"

"It ends just before the road up the hill to where your house would be, just there, at the bottom where the playground and park are." She pointed.

"Okay, I think I get it now. But going back to the boulder, what about these other lines leading here and here?'"

"Umm, not sure. There's been a lot of development over the years, and it's hard to say what these are now, but this one . . . yes . . . I'm pretty sure it's running from the hospital site to where the police station and the library are now and across the street to Fielding's Department Store. See, they meet up with the line going to your street here." She stabbed the screen with her finger.

"So this map shows how all the future important buildings in town are connected?"

"Maybe it was a planning map—you know, what the village wanted to do with future development."

"Yes, that's probably it." Addie tapped her fingers on her knee. She wasn't certain she was ready to share with Serena. Given the distance that had grown between them since Lacey's homecoming, she suspected the lines might actually represent tunnels. "Want another drink?" She got up and headed to the cart.

"Sure, I'll have one more, then I have to run. If I get as slammed at the shop tomorrow as I did today, I'll need my wits about me in the morning." She chuckled.

"Yes, it was nice to see you so busy today." Addie poured two more glasses of wine.

"I hope it had a trickle-down effect on your shop." Serena took her glass from Addie's fingers.

"Not really. It was pretty quiet today—dead, actually."

Serena frowned. "I hope it wasn't because of my reopening."

"Don't be silly. I'm sure it was because that gossip columnist suggested I was a suspect in June's death in this morning's edition. So don't worry. It had nothing to do with your reopening." Addie stared down into her glass. "Although it is funny how that latest gossip article appeared today, and you said Lacey only had the reopening inspiration yesterday."

"Are you suggesting Lacey had something to do with leaking that information to Miss Newsy? What, so my store would get all the business today?" Serena placed her glass on the table. "Just a coincidence, I'm sure," she snapped. "I've known Lacey most of my life, and she wouldn't have done that. And if she did do it, then why?" She pinned Addie with a glare.

"I'm not saying she had anything to do with it. It's just a funny coincidence, that's all. Sorry, I was only thinking out loud, I guess." Addie gulped her wine.

"Come on, Addie." Serena clasped her hand. "You and Lacey are my two best friends in the world. Once you get to know her, you'll love her as much as everyone else does. Besides, she was going to be my sister-in-law at one time. Give her a chance, please."

Addie couldn't resist her friend's puppy dog face. "All right, for you, I'll give her a chance."

Serena's brown eyes brightened.

"On one condition though. You tell her to do the same for me. I know she and Marc have a history, but it's in the past." Addie rolled her eyes at Serena's pained look. "It is, isn't it?"

"Well . . ." Serena's gaze dropped. "I think Lacey is hoping to relight that flame. That's what I came over to talk to you about." She swirled the wine in her glass. "I know Marc told her that he was with you now, but he's just confused, I think. After all, you're new in town and exciting. Maybe he was a bit lonely because there really hasn't been anyone since her. So I'm sure if you made it clear that you and he are just friends, then everything would be okay, and we could all be friends." Serena stared down at the glass in her hand.

"So," Addie said as she swung her feet to the floor and stood up, "we're back in high school, are we?"

"No." Serena jumped up. "But you have to remember they were in love once. So maybe you'd better just cool things with Marc for a while and let what happens happen."

"This advice"—Addie tossed her head back, chuckling—"coming from the same woman who just a short time ago was throwing me at her brother, despite my protests and my telling her *I* wasn't ready, since it hasn't even been two years since David died."

Serena grabbed her arm and spun Addie toward her. "But things have changed since then. Please, I don't want to have to make a choice between you and Lacey. I want us all to be friends. You both mean so much to me." Her eyes filled with tears.

Addie's hand was drawn to her lips where Marc's kiss still lingered, her eyes narrowed. "I think you'd better check with him before you start playing Cupid anymore, because this isn't high school. It's the real world, and he has his own feelings about all this."

"What are you saying? Has Marc said he doesn't care about her anymore?" Serena's usual rosy face paled. "They were so in love. They were going to get married."

"Look, Serena, I really don't want to talk about this anymore, and besides, it's none of my business. Just remember," she said, placing her hands on Serena's shoulders, "he's your brother, and you should want the best for *him*—no one else, just him."

Serena nodded and flopped onto the sofa. "You're right," she whispered.

Addie took a deep breath and sat down beside her, silence enveloping them until Serena leapt to her feet.

"We forgot all about the box on your porch. Aren't you curious to see who your secret admirer is?" She giggled and retrieved it from the foyer table.

Addie took it reluctantly from her outstretched hands, fearing it was from Marc, which she knew would set Serena off again. "If you insist, I'll open it now." She slowly untied the blue ribbon and lifted the lid.

Serena shrieked and jumped back.

Addie's breath caught in her throat, and she tossed the box on the floor and jumped up on the sofa. "Who on earth?" she screamed. "A dead rat?"

"Better than a live one, I guess." Serena edged backward, stretched out her shaking arm, and pointed to the box. "What, what does that piece of paper on the top of it say?"

Addie peeked over the side of the sofa and cringed at the sight of the box's contents. She squeezed her eyes shut, counted . . . seven . . . eight . . . nine . . . ten, and slowly opened one eye, then the other. *BACK OFF OR ELSE.* The bold words next to the rat's prone body made bile rise in her throat. It sounded too much like a promise.

Chapter Eleven

Marc's authoritarian stance in the center of Addie's living room should have comforted her, but Addie found his dead-pan face and tone disconcerting. He made no personal comments as he scribbled in his notebook. She hated that she wanted a kind word, a comforting glance, his warm hand on hers. But the only one getting words was Serena, who, from her apparent waspish behavior, wasn't appreciating her brother's line of questioning.

Marc tapped his pen on his notebook. "Jerry, please escort Miss Greyborne into the foyer so I can question Miss Chandler."

Addie tried to hide her surprise, but her body betrayed her with a sudden jerk. She had forgotten that Jerry was even in the room, bagging the evidence and taking his own notes.

"Miss Greyborne, please." She followed the forgotten officer to the foyer; from there, he led her still farther down the hall and into the dining room.

"Now what?" Addie croaked. "Do you start asking the same questions to see if our stories match up?"

Jerry tapped his pen on the spiral binding of his notebook. "No, ma'am. I don't have any questions for you. I think the chief covered it all."

"Then what's this all about? Why separate us?"

"Just routine."

Addie blew out a breath and leaned against the wall beside him. "Okay, if you say so."

They stood in silence except for the continual pinging sound of Jerry's pen tapping on the metal binding of his notepad. She placed her hand on his pen and shook her head.

He chuckled. "Sorry, not sure what to do now."

Serena's shrill voice rang out from the living room, and they both turned to look at the door. Marc's stern voice over-powered hers, and then all went quiet. Addie looked at Jerry, her brows raised.

"Families, hey?" Jerry shrugged his broad shoulders.

Addie nodded and leaned back against the wall, tapping her foot. Jerry sighed heavily.

"Something on your mind, Officer?"

He shook his head.

"Yes there is. What is it?"

"Nothing, really." He glanced sideways at her. "Well, just thinking that this used to be such a peaceful, quiet town, but since you moved here, there's no end to the excitement." He stifled a chuckle.

"Are you saying this is all my fault?" She spun toward him.

"No, no, it's fun, actually."

"Fun?"

"You know, not as boring." He turned to her. "Actually, since your arrival, the chief—"

"Serena, come back here. We're not finished," Marc's voice bellowed from the living room.

Serena's voice could have frozen ice. "Yes, we are. I won't listen to another word of this." The sound of the slamming door acted as an exclamation point.

Marc appeared in the dining room, his face flushed. "We can leave now, Jerry. I have everything I need." He tipped his hat. "Thank you, Miss Greyborne, I'll let you know of any future developments." He hardly looked at her as he whisked out the door. Jerry grabbed his evidence case from the floor beside him and followed close on his heels.

Addie's mouth gaped open when the door shut. "I guess that's that." Spinning on her heel, she headed for the kitchen. She plopped a pod in her coffee maker and leaned against the counter, gasping for air. She straightened her shoulders, shook her head, and paced back and forth as she waited for the brewer to stop. "Darn you, Marc Chandler, how could you be so freaking cold?" She slumped onto a counter stool, sobbing as the coffee maker hissed and puffed.

Addie couldn't move her arms without pain shooting up her neck. She stretched out her stiff shoulders and winced, opening one eye and then quickly snapping it closed. The sunlight was more than she could take right now. Sunlight? Her head snapped up from the counter. "Oh my God." She glanced at the wall clock—ten a.m.—a whole hour late in opening. She dashed upstairs, quickly showered, and bolted out the door. In her rush, she dropped her keys, bent over to grab them, smacked her head on the doorknob, and cursed all the way to her car.

She sped to her shop, reproaching Marc the entire way. If it hadn't been for his boorish behavior last night, she wouldn't have wept herself to sleep on the kitchen counter. She rushed through the back door and stumbled into the front of the shop, straightened herself, and walked calmly to the front counter, where Paige was hunched over the desk reading the newspaper.

"Good morning. How are you today?"

Paige jerked and slid the paper under the counter.

"What's that you're reading?"

"Nothing—well, nothing interesting. Sorry I wasn't working, but no one's been in yet this morning, so I decided to take a break from sorting." She looked down, her usual pale complexion flushed.

Addie smiled. "Don't worry about it. I keep reminding you that you *are* permitted to take breaks. I'm not a slave driver. I myself, apparently, needed a bit of a break this morning, too, and overslept."

Paige walked around the counter. "Well, I should probably get back to sorting through those new boxes you brought in last week from your attic collection."

"Sounds good." Addie nodded and began rearranging the knickknacks in the display case by the counter.

"Oh, I forgot. There was a call for you. The message is beside the cash register," Paige called back from the storeroom.

Addie reached for the slip of paper, scanned it, and pushed it away from her. "Another canceled book consignment appointment. What's next?" she muttered, tapping her fingers on the countertop as the doorbells chimed behind her. She straightened her shoulders, smiled, and turned around to greet her first customer in two days.

"Jeanie, how nice to see you. Come in. Can I make you a cup of coffee?" She motioned to a counter stool.

"Actually, that sounds wonderful." Sliding onto a stool, Jeanie placed a letter-paper-sized file box on the countertop. "I've been running errands around town since dawn, and I'm exhausted."

Addie noted her haggard, pinched face. "I hope, you're not overdoing it. You've had quite a shock to your system."

Jeanie shook her head. "I'm fine, really." Her hand shook as she took the steaming cup from Addie. "I just didn't realize how much there was to all this death stuff—the paperwork and arrangements. You know, having lost your father and all."

Addie sat on the stool beside her and clasped her hand. "Yes," she whispered. "It is much more work than most people realize." Jeanie's dull, puffy eyes reddened with unshed tears. "If you need anything, please let me know. I'm here to help in any way I can."

"That's good to hear, because I've come to ask a favor."

"Sure, anything. What can I do to help?"

She removed the lid off the box on the counter. "These."

Addie's eyes narrowed as she inspected the stack of papers. "What are these?" She pulled the top one out.

"Last night I started to clear out my mother's house and found these in a trunk in her bedroom closet. I took a quick look through them, and they appear to be her notes for the articles and the book she wrote."

Addie thumbed through the top few pages. "What can I do with them that will help you?"

"I was hoping you could decipher much of what she has scribbled here. There seem to be a lot of old maps and copies of old documents that I can't make heads or tails of. You said this was your speciality, research." Jeanie tapped the cover of the box. "So I was hoping you might be able to tell me if there's information in here that might be worth something? I mean, you know, that I should keep? Or is it all in her article or book already?"

"Sure." She looked at Jeanie's hopeful face. "I'll take a look through them and see what I can find."

"Wonderful." Jeanie swung her short legs off the stool and stood. "I'll be off, then. I still have about ten more stops to make this morning."

"Well, don't overdo it today. You need to take care of yourself." Addie followed her to the door.

"That's exactly what I'm doing."

Addie shivered at the coldness in her voice, and then smiled. "Yes, I'm sure you are."

"I forgot to mention, Mother's memorial service is tomorrow afternoon at two. I know you said you'd never met her, but thought you might like to know." She flipped her dark head and marched across the street toward a car.

"Thanks for letting me know. Yes, I'll be there," Addie called out to her.

She closed the door and noticed a tall man get out of a black SUV parked behind Jeanie's car. When she opened her car door, he grabbed her elbow, spinning her toward him. Addie gasped and opened the door, stepping out onto the sidewalk, but stopped when it became obvious that the two knew each other. Addie retreated into the shop, her eyes fixed on the couple, who appeared to be in a heated discussion. Jeanie stabbed her finger into the man's chest and shouted something that Addie couldn't make out. He spun around and stomped off toward his SUV. Addie's chest constricted when she saw his face. It was the eavesdropper from the restaurant.

"Is everything all right?" asked Paige when Addie turned back into the store. "My mother didn't do or say anything, did she?"

Addie shook her head and plopped onto a counter stool.

Paige's eyes narrowed. "Are you sure?"

"Yes, everything's fine. I didn't even see your mother." She smiled at her. "I'm just tired I guess." She began fingering through the papers in the box in front of her.

"Okay then, I'll get back to work." Paige retreated to the back room.

Addie skimmed the pages and stopped, grabbing one that caught her eye. It was a map of the town, but more detailed than the one June had published in her article. She examined it, her heart racing.

"Paige, can you come here?" she called.

Paige's blond, curly head appeared from through the back doorway. "Sure, be right there." She dropped the books in her hand on a cart and dashed to the front. "What's up?" She stood breathlessly beside Addie.

"We're going to close the shop for the afternoon, and I'm going to take you out for lunch." Addie retrieved her purse from under the counter. "Plus, we might even have a bit of an adventure while we're at it."

Chapter Twelve

Addie slid her red and white Mini Cooper into a parking space in front of the Smuggler's Den restaurant and jumped out. She scanned the rough clay brick and plank entrance façade, her gaze drifting over it to the turf-covered roof. The salt lick of sea air tingled on her tongue, a taste she'd come to love since living in the Harbor.

"So this was actually built into the hillside?"

Paige nodded. "As far as I know, but I've never been here before, 'cause it's too pricey for my budget."

"It was dark last time I was here." She started to walk to the front door. "I sure have a better idea now of what was involved in the restoration. It's amazing to me what they've done."

A young woman dressed in a seventeenth-century wench's outfit consisting of a long flowing skirt and off-the-shoulder blouse cinched tight with a colorful sash at the waist seated them at a table in the back. When Addie's eyes had adjusted to the dim lighting, she surveyed the faces of the diners and didn't recognize any locals. When she skimmed over the lunch menu, she understood what Paige had said about it being pricey. She felt regret at not noticing the prices when Marc had brought her here. The patrons, she thought, looking around her, must be tourists and perhaps a few of the most elite locals, as the people she knew wouldn't be able to afford this regularly. She turned her menu over and looked at Paige, who was white-faced reading hers.

"This is my treat," Addie said smiling, and took a sip of water from the glass the server had just filled.

Paige smiled hesitantly. "Okay, if you say so. You're the boss. Thank you."

Addie laughed and watched the wide-eyed girl scan her surroundings. "What do you think? Isn't it everything I told you it was? The food is amazing, too." Addie raised her glass in a salute. "To us playing hooky this afternoon."

Paige laughed and clinked her glass with Addie's.

The server returned with notepad and pen in hand, took their orders and bent her knees in a low sweeping curtsy. Both Addie and Paige fought to stifle their giggles as she departed from their table. "I feel like we're royalty." Addie choked out as Paige covered her mouth, nodding furiously.

"So, Paige," Addie said regaining some semblance of control. "How are things going? Have you and your mother come to an understanding about you working for me, or is she still convinced that all the crime in Greyborne Harbor since my arrival is because I have close connections to some crime syndicate?"

Paige shook her head and took a long sip of her water.

Addie shifted on her chair. It was hard not to notice Paige's pasty skin and the dark circles etched under her eyes. The girl hadn't been making this whole getting-to-know-her thing easy, and it didn't look like today would be any different. She really knew very little about Paige aside from the fact that she and her mother, Martha, had a rocky relationship. She was aware, from her job application, that Paige had gone to Brown University, but that was it. Although, according to Serena, she had lived in Boston for a time with one of her professors and was rumored to have had a child with him. However, Paige had never mentioned a child, so she suspected that part must just be gossip.

Addie took a deep breath. "You never told me where you finally found an apartment. Is it nice?"

"It's okay. Small. But it will do for now." A look of relief swept across Paige's face when the server appeared with their meals.

Addie let out a deep breath and studied Paige's face as she dug into her Caesar side salad. She looked so young and vulnerable. She just wanted to hug her and tell her she was there for her, but she was all too aware that Paige was holding a lot back from her. The duration of the salad and clam chowder meal passed in relative silence, broken only by sporadic comments regarding the uniqueness of the restaurant's decor.

The server cleared the table and placed the bill in the center between them. "I'll take that, thanks." Addie scooped it up, smiling at the server. "Also, do you have a pamphlet or a brochure about the restaurant?"

"Yes, we do." She smiled and retrieved one from the bar area. "Here, this gives a bit of the history of the Den, and the town of Greyborne Harbor, too."

"Perfect." Addie tucked it into her purse. "Shall we go, Paige? I'd like to take a walk around for a bit before we head back to the shop."

Paige followed close on her heels. "Thank you for lunch. I really enjoyed going out with you."

"Yes, it was nice." Addie shielded her eyes from the bright sunlight. "Let's go around the back here. When we went in I noticed a walking trail, and I'm dying to see where it leads." She marched toward the railed pathway leading around the bottom of the turf-covered building.

She glanced over her shoulder to see if Paige was keeping step with her quick pace and stopped when her eyes caught the reflection off the windshield of a black SUV. A shiver of déjà vu raced through her.

"Is everything okay?" asked Paige, breathlessly catching up to her.

"Yes, just a little winded. I guess I'd better slow down." She eyed the SUV over Paige's shoulder. "Come on, let's have an adventure."

The women followed the railed pathway behind the earth mound concealing the restaurant and were soon standing on the edge of a rock cliff. The graveled path wound along the sharp cliff edge and led them directly under the earth mound to the rocky beach below. Addie looked up the twenty-foot embankment and surmised that the gnarled tree on June's map had once sat on that cliff top.

"There it is," she cried as she scanned the beach.

"There what is?" Paige looked at her, and then looked in the direction Addie pointed. "That's just an old cave entrance."

"I know it is." Addie set off toward it.

"But you can't go in. It's closed," Paige called behind her.

Addie tripped and stumbled a few times as she made her way over the rock-laden beach and arrived at the blockaded entrance, favoring her right ankle.

"Don't worry. I'm not going in," she called over her shoulder to Paige, who stood unmoving at the base of the pathway that led onto the beach. "I just wanted to see it for myself." She stood back, eyed the partially concealed entrance, and pulled June's map from her handbag. She edged backward on the slippery rocks, moving as close as she dared to the crashing surf breaking behind her, examined the map, and looked up, then back at the map.

"Okay," she called to Paige. "We should get back now." She winced and stumbled back toward her, still favoring the ankle she'd twisted on a slippery stone. Addie took a deep breath, shielded her eyes from the sun so she could gaze up at the long, steep, tree-shrouded path they'd come down, and groaned. "Why does coming down always seem easier than the climb back up?" She shrugged her shoulders. "It'll be a nice bit of exercise for us after that rich meal." She swept past Paige, ignoring her incredulous stare, and began ascending the trail.

As they approached a sharp switchback on the trail, a large rock crashed and bounced across the path immediately in front of them, and then another directly behind them. Paige let out a shrill yelp as debris flew up. Sobbing, she crouched down and began rubbing her ankle, her white stocking now red with oozing blood. Addie's high-alert radar went into overtime as she crouched beside the weeping girl and scanned the slope above them. What dislodged the rocks? Animals, or another sightseer—or was someone deliberately trying to harm them? After examining her injury, she pulled a tissue from her bag and tucked it under Paige's sock to help stop the bleeding.

"Come on. Lean on me. We'd better hurry back," she said, hoping Paige didn't notice the uneasiness in her voice. "This place isn't safe. I'm surprised there aren't any 'Caution: Falling Rocks' warning signs posted." She wrapped Paige's arm around her neck, keeping a vigilant lookout over her shoulder.

The two of them hobbled up the path to the parking lot. As they approached it, a wave of relief swept through Addie. Her own ankle had stopped aching. It was amazing to her what a shot of adrenaline and being forced to stretch the muscles out could do, but she knew Paige hadn't been so lucky and would need medical attention.

"You sit here." She helped Paige onto a bench by the door and handed her the last tissue from the travel package. "I'll see if they have a first aid kit inside."

Addie glanced around the parking lot. There was no sign of the black SUV, but she did note a trail of dust hovering over the gravel road in front of the restaurant. She wondered if the incident was another warning to back off, bit her lip, and darted inside, appearing moments later with the restaurant manager, a first aid kit in tow.

The manager, a pleasant-looking fifty-something fellow, also dressed in pirate regalia, flipped up his black eye patch and took a quick look under Paige's sock. "You should probably have this looked at by a doctor, miss." He looked up at her as he cleaned and dressed the wound. "And I'm actually very shocked to hear that something like this happened. We've never had reports of falling rocks before."

"Really?" Addie's investigative antennae quivered.

"Yeah." He put the final strip of medical tape over the gauze. "I hope you'll come back though. You'll both get a meal on the house."

"Thank you. We will." Addie shook the manager's hand and then guided Paige back to her car.

"I think I'd better take you to the hospital." Addie glanced at her passenger's white face.

"No, just drop me off at my doctor's office. He's just on Second Street, off Main, before the town center."

"Are you sure? Will he be able to see you right away?"

"Yes, he's been my doctor my whole life. It won't be a problem."

"Sure, if you insist."

"I'll be fine." She leaned forward and peeked under her sock. "It's stopped bleeding by the looks of it. It's just throbbing a bit right now. It's right there." She pointed to an office building on the left-hand corner of the side street.

Addie made a sharp right turn and stopped.

"This is good. Thanks again for lunch, Addie."

"You probably shouldn't be walking on it. Let me at least wait and drive you home."

"No, I'm just up the road." She waved her hand. "I'll be fine," she called, limping across the street to the office.

Addie shrugged, made a U-turn on the side street, and headed back on Main toward the town center. She checked her rearview mirror and stiffened. Gripping the wheel tighter, she accelerated. The black SUV behind her did the same. She made a sharp left down Birch Road, but it kept pace. When she hit the brakes and veered left into the alley running to the rear entrance to her shop, the SUV flew past on Birch. She pulled into her parking spot and dropped her forehead on the steering wheel. Her heart pounded against her chest, the sound swooshing through her ears.

Making sure the coast was clear, she hopped out, her eyes skimming the alley as she hurried to the door. She disarmed the alarm, flipped on the lights, threw her jacket on the desk, willed her wobbly knees to the front of the shop, and froze. The fine hairs at the back of her neck prickled. Across the street was the SUV. She edged backward and crashed into a display rack, sending the items on it into freefall. Books flew in all directions, but her eyes never the left the car. Out of the corner of her eye, she glimpsed a police cruiser parking in front of Martha's bakery. Marc jumped out, and a wave of relief flooded through her. She looked back at the SUV as it pulled away and sped off toward Main Street.

She heaved a heavy sigh and smiled, but Marc strode past her door, patted his hand on his gun holster, and without even a sideways glance went into SerenaTEA.

Chapter Thirteen

Addie's shoulders sagged in resignation. Something had obviously changed between them. There was a time when he'd pop in to see her before he stopped in at Serena's, but now? He'd become distant toward her recently, and she wasn't certain why. She took a deep breath and turned her attention to the pirate and American Revolutionary War historical fiction novels she'd arranged for the window displays. Perhaps it was time to make some changes. She glanced at Marc's patrol car and nodded. Yes, changes were exactly what she needed right now. A fresh outlook and . . . Marc led Serena past her window. He flung open the back door of his patrol car and ushered her into the back seat, went around to the driver's side, removed his cap, tossed it on the passenger seat, and drove off.

"No, not again." Addie grabbed her handbag and sprinted out the rear door.

She raced into the police station parking lot and flew up the front stairs, coming to a screeching halt at the sergeant's desk. "Hi. Carolyn, isn't it? We've met before, I'm—"

The desk sergeant jerked and blinked at her. "Yes, Miss Greyborne. Hello."

"Where's Serena Chandler? She was just brought in, right?"

"Umm, yes, the chief's with her now." Her head motioned toward his office door. "You can have a seat over there until they're done, if you like." Carolyn pointed to a row of plastic waiting room chairs.

Addie took a seat and tapped her foot to the rhythm of the clock ticking away the seconds. Over an hour passed before Marc's office door opened. Addie jumped to her feet, but the door abruptly slammed shut. The sergeant looked at Addie and shrugged.

Addie drummed her fingers on the magazine sitting unread on her lap. She glanced toward the clock, then at her phone. Time felt as though it was standing still, and she shifted on her hard chair. The door opened. Serena burst into the waiting room, but stopped when she saw Addie. Her usually soft brown eyes were red and swollen. She began to speak, but no words came out. She spun on her heel and fled out the door.

Marc stood in his doorframe, hands on hips, staring at Addie. He took a deep breath and waved her into the office. Closing the door behind her, he took his place behind the desk. She leaned her back against the door, shaking, tears stinging at her eyes.

"Have a seat in a chair, please, Miss Greyborne." He cleared his throat and motioned opposite him.

Her eyes widened. "Miss Greyborne? Is that what it's come to?" She plopped down, glaring at him. This was *her* chair, not to be referred to as *a* chair. After all the hours she'd spent in it over the past while, she had laid claim to it. No matter what Chief Sour Pants said.

He fumbled with the papers in front of him on the desk, straightened his shoulders, and looked up at her. His brown eyes, cold and dark, bore into hers. "What brings you in today?"

She tried to speak, but snapped her mouth closed and glared at him.

"I'm afraid, Miss Greyborne, that I am very busy. So, if that's all, I'll show you out." He stood up and leaned his hands on the desk.

"No, I'm not leaving until you tell me exactly what is going on," she snapped and rose to her feet.

They stood glowering at each other over the desktop.

Marc's shoulders drooped, and he sat back down. Scrubbing his hands through his thick, chestnut-brown hair, he mumbled, "What is it you want to know?"

"What I want to know," she said, taking her seat, "is why you questioned Serena so harshly last night at my place and why you dragged her in here today?"

He blew out a deep breath into his hands and sighed. "When I saw the box and read the note at your place, I got worried, okay?"

"What does that have to do with Serena, and with why you're suddenly treating me like we're strangers?" She stared blankly at him.

"Because, well, because I've seen that box before."

"You have? Where? What are you talking about?"

He spun around in his chair, his back to her. "I gave a welcome-home gift to Lacey when she first came back, and it was in that same box."

She jumped to her feet but found her knees unwilling to support her. Oozing back into her chair, she bit out every word. "You gave it to Lacey?"

"Ye . . . yes." His voice was barely a whisper as he turned his chair and faced her.

"So the warning is from her?"

"It appears so." His head slumped down onto his chest. He sucked in a heavy breath. "I just couldn't believe I was responsible for what she did. I'm so sorry." His eyes softened as he gazed into hers.

"You? How are you responsible?"

"Because if I hadn't stretched the truth and told her that

you and I were a couple now, none of this would have ever happened. I had no idea just how crazy she's become." He slammed his hand on the desk. "Like I said, she's a piranha."

"So why did you go after Serena the way you did? She had nothing to do with it, did she?"

He shrugged. "Think about it. Knowing what I did about the origin of the gift box and you telling me Serena handed it to you when she came in, it stands to reason that she was Lacey's messenger. I needed to find out if Serena was a willing participant or another victim in Lacey's conniving scheme."

"I see. Yes." She looked down into her lap and wiped her damp palms on her jeans. "But would Lacey have been that careless?"

"What do you mean?"

"If you gave her the box in the first place, and knew she had it, would she use the same box to threaten me with a dead rat? It would automatically make her the number one suspect, wouldn't it?"

"You're right. I hadn't thought of it like that. I was too busy feeling guilty and thinking of ways to avoid you to protect you from her." He rubbed his chin. "But even she's smarter than that."

"Exactly!" Addie clapped. "Now we're getting somewhere. See what a great crime-fighting team we make?" She grinned.

He chuckled and shook his head. "A crime-fighting team, no. But two friends talking, that I can live with." He winked.

She leaned forward. "So, friend," she said, giving him a crooked smile, "now we just have to figure out how someone would have gotten their hands on the box. Has Lacey reported a robbery, anything out of the norm?"

He shook his head.

Addie slumped back in her chair.

"What are you thinking?"

"I was just thinking what I do know about Lacey. She is devious, given what she did in LA, and what she has pulled off here with you in the past, and how she manipulates people like Serena, so—"

Marc leaned forward. "So?"

"So maybe she did send it, knowing full well that you would know where it came from originally, which she's using to actually deflect from her guilt. Because you would automatically think she wouldn't be that careless, and that someone else would have to have sent it. Chances are, now that you have accused Serena of being the messenger, Lacey will try to tell you that she threw it away and that someone must have plucked it out of her garbage."

"First you say Lacey wouldn't have sent it, then you say she did? That's a quite a flip-flop, even for you, isn't it?"

"Never mind," she chuckled. "I'm just thinking out loud."

"That does sound a bit too devious of a plot even for Lacey."

"Well, she has been living in LA." She smiled. "Maybe television and film plots have worked their way into her scheming mind. Who knows, maybe she was dating a screenwriter."

"Yes, maybe," Marc chuckled.

She loved that sound. "You never know." She stood up. "Thanks for telling me about the box and finally why you've been behaving so weirdly. Although, I thought we knew each other well enough that you could have called or texted to tell me that you were avoiding me for my safety."

The corners of his lips turned up in a sheepish smile, and he looked down at his desk. "Sorry," he murmured. "I wasn't thinking clearly I guess, and distancing me from you was my instant reaction in wanting to protect you. Not a well calculated one though it seems." He raised his doleful eyes to hers.

"No. It wasn't as far as I'm concerned. I thought we were closer than that, but today, you have cleared up a lot of questions—doubts that I had, so thank you. In the future, if you want to protect me from something, or someone, please discuss it with me first so we can work it out together, okay?" She gave him a clipped nod, hoping her eyes conveyed her annoyance with him but also her forgiveness of his blunder in judgement, and then she turned and headed toward the door.

Marc rose. "Are you leaving?"

"Yeah, I'd better go talk to Serena."

"Just a warning, Lacey was in her store when I was there."

"Thanks for the heads-up," she said over her shoulder as she headed to the door.

"Speaking of stores, why was yours closed most of the afternoon?"

She spun around, batting her eyelashes. "What, were you checking on me?"

"I drove by a few times, trying to work up the nerve to pick up Serena, and noticed the closed sign."

"Well, if you must know, I took Paige out for lunch to the Smuggler's Den."

His face went ashen. "Why?"

"Because I loved it and wanted to take her there."

"No other reason?"

A warm blush spread up her neck to her cheeks.

"Addie, what have you been up to?"

"Well . . ." She leaned against the door. "I found another old map of June's and just wanted to see the landmarks that she had noted on it for myself."

"Is that all?" He placed his hands on his hips, his eyes focused on hers.

"Yes, but . . ."

"What?"

"When Paige and I were heading back to the car after our walk down to the cave entrance, some rocks tumbled onto the path, and Paige got hurt."

"Is she okay?" His eyes widened.

"She seems fine. I dropped her off at her doctor's office."

"That's good." He sighed. "But I get the feeling you're not telling me everything that happened?"

She looked past him to the window.

"Addie?"

She heaved a deep breath. "No, I'm not."

"Aha, I knew it. Sit back down and tell me what else happened."

She walked to the chair. A sense that she had been sent to the principal's office washed through her as she plopped back down into it.

"I'm waiting." He stood towering over her, arms still crossed.

She took a deep breath. "Unless you plan on paddling me, Principal Chandler, I suggest you quit treating me like a naughty little schoolgirl."

He perched himself on the edge of the desk. "Does this mean you don't role-play?"

"Never you mind. Now, do you remember the man who was seated across from us at the restaurant last night?"

"Vaguely."

"He struck me as odd because he was so unfriendly and aloof."

"You were bothering him, and he was trying to eat."

"I know, I know, but later when we were eating and talking, he seemed to be listening too hard to every word we were saying. Anyway, this morning Jeanie dropped by my shop with a box of old notes her mother had made when she was researching her book, which," she went on quickly, "is where I found the map that was more detailed than the one she had published in her paper."

Marc stroked his chin, his eyes never leaving her face.

"When she left my store, a man in a black SUV was parked behind her car, obviously waiting for her. He got out, they appeared to exchange a few heated words, and she left, but when he turned around . . . well, it was the same man from the restaurant."

"Hmmm."

"Anyway," she said, waving her hand, "I was curious about the papers she had dropped off and began thumbing through them, came across the map, and wanted to go see for myself."

"So you dragged poor Paige along with you?"

She nodded.

"But that's not the end of it, is it?" His eyes narrowed.

She took a deep breath. "After lunch, I wanted to take a walk around the site, and Paige and I headed down the very safe"—she looked up at him reassuringly—"guard-railed pathway behind the restaurant."

His lips tightened.

"That's when I noticed a black SUV in the parking lot."

Marc clutched the side of the desk.

"We went down to the beach. I saw the cave and the rocky outcrop where the gnarled tree once was, and their position in relation to the restaurant, and . . ."

"And what?" He stood up.

"We headed back up the path. That's when the smallish"— she held her index finger and thumb an inch apart—"rock slide happened and a chunk of rock hit Paige in the ankle. When we got back to the parking lot the SUV was gone, but when I got back to my shop, it was parked across the street. Then you pulled up, and it sped away."

"Damn you, Addie. You are supposed to bring me everything you come across and let me assess whether or not it's worth pursuing. You can't keep going off on your own like this, especially after the note you received. Let me do the actual investigating." He leaned toward her.

His breath wafted across her cheek. His closeness confused her. She wanted to slap him and kiss him senseless at the same time, and by the look in his eyes, he was probably thinking the same things about her. Hoping he didn't sense that she was still holding back a few of the minor details, like the bit about that SUV actually following her back to the shop, she innocently gazed into his eyes.

"Then why on earth would you do such a dumb thing? This is still a very much open murder investigation, and we still have no idea what or who is behind it." He flopped into the chair beside her.

"Did you say 'murder investigation'?" She sat upright. "Did the autopsy report come back?"

Marc nodded.

"What did it say?"

"Blunt force trauma to the back of her head. The fatal blow appears to have been delivered by a large, flat object."

"A flat object? Could it be a shovel or a . . . I don't know."

"What on earth would make you think of a shovel?"

"I'm just throwing ideas out there. Maybe one of them will be the right one. After all, her body was found in a chamber leading to a tunnel system, and when I think of tunnels, I think of digging."

Marc sat forward, stroking the back of her hand, which was resting on the arm of the chair. "How can I say this so you're not offended?"

Her heart raced at his touch, but at the look on his face, she pressed her toes to the floor and braced for the worst.

"Let the police do our job, please." His eyes pleaded with her. "It's just a theory. There's no proof of any of that."

She stood up. "If it's proof you want, then drive me to my car and follow me home. I'll show you the proof." She strode toward the door and looked back. "Well, are you coming?"

"Okay." He heaved a heavy sigh and rose, snatching his hat off the desk. "But it's getting late, so you'd better make it worth my while."

"Don't worry." She winked over her shoulder. "Maybe I'll even feed you."

He stifled a laugh. "Scoot. Go," he snickered, pointing to the door.

Chapter Fourteen

Addie bound up her front porch steps. A car door slammed behind her. Boots crunched on the gravel driveway, and a hand tugged at her jacket sleeve. "Whoa, there, missy! I should've pulled you over for careless driving."

"What?" She spun toward Marc. "When?"

"You were going so fast I almost lost you twice."

"Well, I just had some evasive-driving practice earlier, remember?" Her slip of the tongue about her recent occurrence with the black SUV stung in her throat. "Never mind, just joking." She sucked in a deep breath, hoping he wasn't using his cop radar on her right now.

"What? You mean you were trying to lose me?" He shook his head. "What am I going to do with you?" He gently pulled her toward him. Her racing heart jumped to her throat. She gulped and stiffened her uncooperative knees, a common occurrence whenever he touched her or was close. His hand swept strands of hair from her face and tilted it up. She tried to speak, but before she could make a sound, he kissed the tip of her nose and then rested his forehead on hers. His body stiffened. She frowned and looked up at him, but his narrowed gaze looked past her.

"Did you forget to lock the door when you left this morning?" His hands slid to her shoulders, holding them firm.

"I don't think so. Why?" She followed his gaze to her front door, noticing it was open by a crack.

He pushed her behind him. "Get in my car, now." Drawing his gun, he called for backup on his radio and edged the door wide open, pulling his flashlight from his belt and disappearing into the darkened foyer.

Numb, Addie sat in the front seat of his patrol car. It wasn't long before two more police cars arrived and four officers jumped out, guns drawn. Two separated and went in opposite directions around the house. The other two entered the door and disappeared. Their entire arrival on the scene was like watching well-rehearsed stage choreography and was over in seconds. She scrubbed her hands over her face and opened the window, straining to hear any sounds. Time ticked on. She checked her cell and fidgeted with it, dropping it to the floor. She reached down to retrieve it, sat back up, and shrieked. Marc's face was at the window. She patted her pounding chest.

"All clear. You can come in now." He opened the door and pulled her to her feet.

"What happened? Was my house broken into?"

"Not that we can see. Nothing appears out of the ordinary." His softening brown eyes reassured her, but then his fingers tightened on her shoulders. "I think that you may just have forgotten to press the arm button on the alarm and lock the door when you left for work today."

"No, I remember putting in the code."

"The yellow standby light was flashing."

With quick steps, she intersected a group of four officers as she strode into her foyer. It hurt to smile when everything inside her wanted to scream. "Thanks, guys. Sorry, it was a false alarm. My mistake, I guess." Entering the living room, she switched on the table lamp and froze. "Marc!" she shouted. "Marc."

She sensed his presence before he could reply, and she pointed to the coffee table.

He squinted at the table. "What is it I'm looking at?"

"It's what you're not looking at." She scanned the room. "It's gone."

"Care to give me a hint?"

"June's notes. The ones that Jeanie gave me. They were right there in a box, where I left them. Now they're not."

"Are you sure you didn't take them into the kitchen or upstairs or put them in your desk?"

She rummaged through the desk and shook her head. "Nope, I'm positive. I left them there after Serena and I looked at them. I didn't even make it upstairs to bed. I slept . . ."

"Where?"

"It doesn't matter." She shook her head. "But I didn't go upstairs till this morning, and I was running late. The notes were the last thing on my mind, so they have to have still been there this morning."

"Well, you did forget to arm and lock the door."

"That's not fair." She planted her hands on her hips, glaring at him. "So I put in the code and forgot to press arm." She continued to glower at him. "Aha! I do remember now locking the door when I went out, because I dropped my keys and hit my head on the handle when I stood back up. See, I have a bump right here." She pointed to top of her head. "Wanna feel it?"

He chuckled and shook his head. "I would like you to indulge me and satisfy my cop curiosity by checking the rest of the house before we jump to conclusions and I send my officers on another wild goose chase." He took her hand. "Let's check the kitchen first."

They stepped out into the hall. Jerry snapped his notebook shut. "Is there anything else before we go, Chief?"

"Could you dust the coffee table for prints?"

"No problem." He picked up his evidence case.

"And did you dust the door outside and in?"

Jerry nodded. "There were a lot of smeared prints, but I did manage to get a couple of clearer ones. I'll run them when I get back."

"Sounds good," Marc called over his shoulder and followed Addie to the kitchen.

She stopped in the doorway and made a sweeping motion. "See? Not here. It'll be the same thing upstairs." She spun on her heel and went back down the hall to the staircase. She stood at the bottom, waiting for Marc to catch up as he popped his head into the dining room and library on his way past.

"Better to check now than to find a surprise later."

She froze at his tone, but ignored it and headed up the stairs. "See?" She crossed her arms at the top of the staircase. "I told you."

"I guess that's why I'm the cop and you're not." He swept past her down the stairs.

"Excuse me? What does that mean?" She followed close behind.

He spun around at the bottom, catching her off guard, and she teetered into him. He grasped her shoulders. "I need facts and proof, and you—"

"I do what?" She balled her hands into fists at her sides.

"You jump to conclusions based on outlandish theories with no evidence to support them."

"All my theories are based on some sort of proof. You're just too pigheaded to see it." She pushed by him and headed into the living room. "What more proof do you want aside from the fact that the box is missing? And if it's indisputable proof you want regarding what I've been saying about the tunnels"—she fished a paper from her handbag and shoved it at him—"here it is."

"What's this?"

"All I have left from the box. I took the map with me when Paige and I went for lunch today. I guess it was a good thing I did, since most of my other *proof* is gone. Well, except for what's on the Internet. But just take a close look at it. You'll see what I've been talking about—the tunnels, the landmarks. It's all on there."

Marc sagged onto the sofa, his eyes focused on the map he held. Then he looked up at her, his eyes creased at the corners. "But didn't you say that Jeanie dropped the box off this morning?"

"Yes, first thing. Why?"

He leaned back, stroked his chin, and then sat forward. "Sit down."

"Okay, what's up?"

He turned to her and clasped her hands in his, stroking the backs of them with his thumbs.

"Well?" She glanced down at his hands and sucked in a shallow breath.

"Well," he continued, gently stroking her hands, "last night was a late one." He cleared his throat. "I was here, and Serena, and then a whole lot happened today."

"Yes?"

He grasped her hands. "But if Jeanie didn't give you the box until today?"

Her eyes narrowed.

"Then . . . then . . ."

"Then it wasn't ever here in my house."

He nodded, giving her fingers a light squeeze.

"Oh my God." She sat back. "I'm losing my mind."

"No, you aren't." He placed his arm around her shoulder. "There's been a lot happening lately, and if you didn't sleep well last night, and then after today, well, with all that happened, it's just—"

"Just what?"

"Understandable, that's all. You can rest assured the box is safe and sound in your shop tonight."

She nodded, tears spilling down her cheeks. "I just can't believe how stupidly I've been behaving. Insisting it was here and I'd been broken into." She sobbed. "God, I am losing it."

"No, you're not. It makes you human. We all have memory lapses when we're stressed."

"I'm not stressed, darn it."

He chuckled and pulled her closer. "Okay, whatever you say."

She threw her head back against the sofa. "Just great. Your guys are going to find out about my stupidity, and then I'll be known around town, aside from everything else they're already saying, as the crazy book lady."

He kissed her cheek and nestled her head into his neck with his hand. His cell screamed the emergency call ringtone. He looked at it and leapt to his feet. "Not the crazy book lady. If anything, the crazy psychic lady. Let's go."

"Why? What happened?"

"Your shop's just been broken into."

Chapter Fifteen

Addie cringed at the sound of crunching glass under her protective shoe coverings. She stepped gingerly into her shop, but the grating noise in her ears didn't stop there. The entire entrance and storefront lay strewn with shards and beads of glistening crystals that had once been her front door—a good reminder for her that regardless of the extra cost she had incurred having it installed after her last break-in, there really was no such thing as unbreakable glass if someone wanted to get in badly enough.

Jerry's head snapped up from his notebook. "Evening again, Miss Greyborne." He tipped his cap. "Feels like déjà vu, doesn't it?" He smiled, his eyes holding a glimmer of amusement, and then he looked sideways at Marc, who shot him a piercing glance. Jerry's jaw tensed. "Evening, Chief."

"Yes, it does, Jerry." Addie shot an equally stabbing look back at Marc. "It feels like not so long ago that we were all in a similar situation."

Marc walked over and stood in front of Jerry, ignoring her. "What have you got?"

Jerry pushed his cap back. "Well, Chief . . ." he began, his eyes dropping to his notebook, "the alarm came in at ten thirty-three, and myself and Daniels were the first on scene at ten thirty-eight—"

"Wait, it took you five minutes to respond on a quiet night? The station is right down the street."

"Yes, sir. But we were grabbing some coffee at the gas station down in the Harbor district when the call came in."

Marc scowled.

"Anyway," Jerry continued, returning to his notes, "Lewiston and Colburn arrived about thirty seconds later. They're still out searching the street."

Addie turned and peered out the now-glass-free window on her door and spotted one of them rummaging through the garbage can across the road. A beam of light danced in the park behind him. She assumed it was the other officer. They must be the same ones who, only a short time ago, had stood in her foyer, investigating a break-in that hadn't yet occurred. She shivered. Jerry's easy, drawling East Coast accent brought her back to the conversation.

"The perp had less than five minutes in the store before we pulled up. There were no signs then of anyone around. So whoever it was got in and out fast. They knew what they were looking for."

"Notice anything missing?" Marc turned to her.

Her gaze fell onto the countertop, and she nodded.

"The box?"

She sucked in a breath and whispered, "Yes."

"Wait a minute," Jerry said, dropping his notepad to his side, "another box? You had more than one that somebody would commit two break-ins in one day for?"

She looked helplessly at Marc.

"We're not sure," Marc jumped in, and he glanced at Addie, a slight smile creasing the corners of his lips. "Miss Greyborne, as you know, has a high inventory of valuable documents and books in her personal collection. She'll need time to figure out if one or two boxes are in question now."

Jerry nodded and scribbled in his notepad. "Well, I'll take some photos of the rear door to see if they left that way and dust the shop for prints. Anything else, Chief?"

Marc shook his head. "Carry on. I'll lift what I can off the larger glass bits."

"Then if you'll excuse me, miss." He tipped his cap.

She smiled and then looked at Marc. A sense of gratitude and relief swept through her. "Thanks," she whispered. "I didn't want him to know I lost my mind earlier on top of everything else."

"Here, let's have some coffee. It's going to be a while till I'm done, and then I'll drive you home."

She took the steaming cup from his fingers and slid onto a counter stool. Marc went about his business of, well, being a super cop, and she smiled to herself. He might be many things and confusing as heck sometimes, but tonight he helped her save face. A sense of pride and something else she couldn't place raced through her. She gazed at him hunched over the shattered glass shards, probing at them with his pen, and then it hit her, and her chest heaved. She actually had come to care for him. After David's untimely death, she was developing feelings that she had thought she would never have again.

Jerry stuck his head out of the back room door and called, "Chief," and she jumped. Again, she had been focusing only on Marc and had forgotten that Jerry was even there. "Forgot to tell you that when I checked the lock mechanism on the Greyborne house, it did show signs of having been jimmied, and this one back here does, too, although it doesn't look like they were successful. Could be why the perps smashed the front door."

"Well." Marc looked into her strained face. "That puts a whole new spin on things, doesn't it?"

She blew out a deep breath and nodded.

Marc turned back to Jerry. "Did you make a mold of the lock at the house?"

"Yes, Chief. Brewster's working on that now. I'll get this one over to her straightaway. The casting might help us figure out what tool was used on them and lead to where it was purchased anyway."

"Good. Let me know when you hear anything." Marc turned back to the glass shards, then looked up at the door, then back at Addie. "Do you remember anything else being in that box that would be so sought after someone would commit two break-ins in a matter of a few hours?"

She shook her head. "I told you, I only happened to have a map with me. Everything else on quick glance appeared to be her early research notes. I didn't notice anything remarkable, only dates and a few names of locals from that era. I was hoping her original manuscript, the one Jeanie mentioned to me that the town council rejected, would be in there, but it wasn't."

"Hmmm." He chewed his bottom lip.

She stifled a laugh, and he looked at her. "What?"

"I see my lip-biting habit is contagious."

"Spending too much time with you, that's all."

Her face tensed. His voice sounded so matter-of-fact Addie didn't know what to make of his remark. But the pain in her chest told her he had struck a nerve.

"I didn't mean it like that." His lips twitched. "I meant that—"

She waved him off. "Don't worry about it."

He turned back to the evidence on the floor and then glanced over his shoulder at her. A tiny smile touched his lips. She straightened her back and pasted the most detached look she could muster across her face, doing her best to return the smile. She knew she shouldn't take him literally. He was working, and when he worked, he turned into Rambo, cold and calculating. But the memory of his touch on her face, on her lips, burned strong and tugged at her heart, and she had to admit that him saying what he did, even if meant in jest, did come as a jolt.

The hands on the wall clock above the counter slowly ticked forward, but time seemed to have stood still. An ache crawled up the back of Addie's neck and made itself at home at the base of her skull. She laid her forehead on the cool countertop, and then a hand jostled her shoulder. "Addie, wake up," came a soft voice. "I'll drive you home now."

"Marc?" She raised her head and wiped drool from her lips. "Did I fall asleep?" Her eyes flew to the clock hands. "Three a.m.? My God, I've slept for hours." She jumped up, her right foot numb, and she wavered.

"Come on, there you go. Take a minute to wake up." His hands gently rubbed up and down her upper arms as he steadied her.

Her eyes scanned her surroundings. The glass bits had been cleared, there was now a sheet of plywood over the damaged door, and the shop was completely silent, except for the sound of blood rushing through her ears. She looked up at him. Questions filled her eyes.

"You did sleep awhile—and has anyone told you that you do snore a bit?"

"I do not." She slapped his chest.

"Yes, you do. Even with all of Brian's commotion going on securing the door. You didn't even flinch or miss a note." He laughed.

"That's impossible." She scrubbed her hands over her face, willing herself back to consciousness. "Did you finish? Did you find any clues?" Her eyes met his dulled brown ones. "Oh, dear." Her finger traced the dark circles under his eyes. "We'd better get you to bed and soon by the look of it." He leaned his forehead against hers. His breath trailed across her cheek, caressing her face. She felt a flush creep up her neck and tried to pull away, but within seconds, his lips were on hers. She let out a wobbly breath. "Oh, David." His lips froze. She opened her eyes. The look on his face told her everything. Her words hadn't just been in her mind. She'd actually uttered them. He turned on his heel.

"Marc," she cried, "wait." Tears burned her eyes, and she swallowed hard to dismiss the acid taste growing in the back of her throat.

She inhaled, needing to relieve the pressure building inside her chest, but his face had said it all. She knew there were no words that could ever erase that split second. His reply to her was the sound of the back door slamming behind him.

Chapter Sixteen

Addie hovered at the back of the church. She pressed herself hard against the wall, wishing she could disappear through it. Many of the locals frowned when they saw her attending June's service, but worst of all, she knew she'd also see Marc here today. How would she react? Worse, how would he? Her throat tightened when she spotted him edging his way in front of the people sitting in the rear pew of the small chapel. He settled into the last remaining space, directly in front of her, between Lacey and Serena.

Lacey rested her head against his, her shoulders trembling. Marc draped his arm around her and gave her a squeeze. Lacey turned toward him, dabbing her tear-filled eyes with a tissue, and kissed his cheek. Addie thought—no, she hoped—that she saw him flinch when she kissed him.

Organ music filled the overcrowded space, and the pastor moved toward the altar. He removed a red satin shroud from a large portrait that was set on a stand beside it, revealing a picture of June's smiling face. A door opened off to the side of the sanctuary, and Jeanie appeared. The congregation rose to their feet, and Addie's view was blocked. She couldn't make out the person who accompanied her as they made their way to the front row, which was reserved for family.

The pastor moved to the pulpit and opened the memorial service by leading the gathering through an emotion-filled rendition of "Amazing Grace." Addie couldn't see much from where she stood, and she focused on the back of Marc's head. Lacey leaned her curvaceous body against his as she swayed her hips in rhythm to the music. She glanced over her shoulder. Her eyes twinkled when they rested on Addie's. A crooked smile creased the corner of her lip. She flipped her head, looked back to the front, and draped her arm casually around Marc's waist, pulling him toward her.

Addie heaved out a deep breath.

"Sorry," said the man standing beside her. "There isn't much room to maneuver, let alone breathe, is there? But I'll try to move down if I can."

Without looking at him, she nodded her appreciation, but little did he know, her struggle to breathe wasn't due to the fact they were all crammed against the walls like fish in a can. She gripped the handle of her purse, clutched in front of her, took a quieter deep breath to fight back the pressure building in her chest, and scanned the room. She needed to focus on anything other than the Marc and Lacey seduction drama unfolding right before her eyes.

She was startled to see that the service had swelled to the point of people standing two-deep around the perimeters. Her eyes flitted from one tear-stained face to the next. June obviously was a much-loved and well-respected member of the community.

The man next to her coughed, and she glanced at him and then stopped. How could she not have noticed him before? His sea-blue eyes were enough to melt any woman at the knees, but it was the dark curl of hair that swept down over his forehead, the square jaw, and the sharp cheekbones that took her breath away. When he smiled at her, the dimples in his cheeks made his eyes appear to be caressing hers. He was the whole package, and she gulped. Her eyes darted to the back of Marc's head, but the stranger's smile wasn't something she could soon forget. She became all too aware of his arm touching hers during the remainder of the service. A rush of relief swept through her when the pastor led them in a short closing prayer.

The congregation remained seated, much to Addie's angst. She had to fight her flight instinct to stop herself from bolting out the door away from this man and his sea-blue eyes and away from the Marc-and-Lacey show. An usher stood beside the family pew, waiting to escort them back to the side room. A man with black hair was the first to stand up. Addie didn't recognize him, but there was something familiar in the way he carried himself. When he turned to assist Jeanie to her feet, Addie strained to get a closer look. He wore dark-rimmed glasses and had shorter hair today and a goatee, but she was certain it was the salt-and-pepper-haired man from the restaurant and in front of her shop.

She'd have to get a closer look, and as soon as the family room door closed, she pushed her way out through the throng of people exiting and dashed to the front steps of the church in hopes of catching another glimpse of him. She leaned on the railing, tapping her fingers against the cold metal, certain that Jeanie and the man would exit through the side door to the limousine waiting in the parking lot. A shoulder bumped her, and she spun around in time to catch sight of Marc and Lacey heading down the stairs past her. Lacey looked back over her shoulder and winked as she thrust her arm through Marc's.

"I guess my afternoon plans just changed." Serena's abrasive tone tore through Addie's thoughts of quietly jumping on Lacey's back and tearing her golden locks out, one fistful after another.

"Sorry. What did you say?" Addie looked at her friend's flushed, freckled cheeks.

"I was saying that it seems my plans with Lacey have changed. She appears to have made new ones."

Addie watched the couple cross the street and then drive away in Marc's Jeep Cherokee. "Yes, I'd say she has." She put her arm around Serena's shoulders. "Wanna make new ones with me?"

"Yeah, I do. Thanks."

"Good, I've missed you." She squeezed Serena's shoulder as Marc's taillights disappeared from sight. It tore at her how one unguarded utterance could tip the scales of life so drastically.

"Where do you want to go? Lacey and I were planning to head to Mario's for a drink, then dinner. Want to do that?"

"Let's go to the Grey Gull. We haven't been there in a while." Addie looked over Serena's shoulder and spotted the black limousine pulling out of the parking lot. "Can we make one stop first though?"

"Sure, where?"

"I think we need to go and pay our respects to Jeanie. I overheard there's a gathering for friends and family at her mother's house following the service."

The living room was overflowing by the time they arrived. Addie made a quick scan of the packed room for any signs of Marc and Lacey and heaved a sigh of relief. She took the glass of wine presented to her by a young catering server and smiled at Serena. "It looks like she had a lot of friends." Her gaze continuing to assess the room, she determined it must be an early 1950s construction, and by the looks of the furnishings, not much had changed in here since then.

"Did you see the church today?" Serena whispered. "I couldn't believe it. I don't think ten people would attend my memorial service."

"Don't be silly."

"I'm not, but I'd better mingle and try to recruit some more."

"Why, are you planning on leaving us soon?"

Serena quirked an eyebrow and made her way through the throng, nodding and chatting with people as she passed by them, heading toward the buffet set up on the table of the adjoining dining room.

Addie leaned against the side wall and scanned the faces in the room. There was no sign of Jeanie and the man, so she headed down the hallway toward what she hoped was the kitchen. As she passed by a closed door, she heard raised voices, then a crash. Her hand flew to the doorknob, but it opened before she could turn the handle.

Jeanie stared wide-eyed back at her. Her face reddened, and moist beads dripped down her brow. "Addie, hello. Is there something I can do for you?"

The coolness in her voice gave Addie goose bumps, and she took a step back. "No—I thought I heard something crash, so just wanted to make sure everything was okay in here."

"Well," Jeanie said as she smoothed wrinkles from the front of her formfitting black silk dress, "I was trying to rest for a few minutes. It's been such a long day. I'm sure you understand. I just bumped one of Mother's lamps off the bedside table when I got up, and it broke when it hit the floor." She reached behind her, pulling the door closed. Addie peered over her shoulder into the room and thought she spied a lamp intact beside the bed, but the door shut before she could make certain.

Addie clasped Jeanie's hand. "You've already had such a stressful day. I'd hate to think something else had upset you or you were injured or—"

"Don't worry about me." She waved off Addie's remark. "As you can see, I'm fine, just tired."

"But I thought I heard someone yelling, too." Addie looked back at the door.

"Oh, that," she laughed. "I was just startled when the lamp shattered. I must have screeched louder than I thought."

She clasped Addie's elbow and steered her toward the living room. "But thank you for your kind thoughts. I see you have some wine. May I get you anything else?"

"It's I that should be getting you something. You need to rest. Maybe you need to lie down again. Here, let me help you."

"I'm fine, really."

Addie pulled her hand up to brush hair from her face, severing Jeanie's hold on her arm, and lingered in the hallway fixing her hair. She strained, listening for any other sounds, as she was certain there had also been a male voice when she first approached the bedroom.

"Are you coming?" Jeanie stood at the living room entrance with her arm extended, waiting for Addie to follow.

"Sorry, just trying to make myself look presentable. I was meaning to comb it before I arrived and put on some fresh lipstick." She glanced back down the hallway.

"The bathroom is the first door there on the right. That is what you were looking for, isn't it?"

"Ah, that's where I went wrong. Someone just pointed me down the hall, and I must have passed right by it."

"But don't worry. You look lovely as is, my dear." Jeanie placed her hand on Addie's back and all but pushed her into the living room.

Addie stumbled and banged into Serena. "There you are," Serena said, regaining her footing. "I've been looking everywhere for you."

Addie watched Jeanie over Serena's shoulder as she made her way through the crowded room, stopping to receive condolences from everyone she passed.

"Hey, I'm down here." Serena tugged on her wrist.

"Sorry, I was just looking at . . . Never mind. What's so urgent?"

"Have you seen the new guy in town?" Serena swooned. "He's soooo yummy, I just want to—"

"That's great. Can you do me a favor?"

"Umm, sure, but don't you want to hear about him?"

"Yeah, later, but for now I need you to keep Jeanie out here. There's something I have to check out."

"You're not going snooping around, are you? Addie, she's just lost her mother."

"Don't worry, it's okay. I just have to find someone who I think is here, but I haven't seen him yet."

"Marc?"

"No," she said, shaking her head emphatically, "but just promise me you won't let her leave this room."

"Okay, I'll try, but—"

Addie headed for the bedroom, but before she could reach it, the door that Jeanie had come out of was flung open. She grabbed the first door handle she could find, pushed it open, and slid inside. The bathroom, and thank God, it was unoccupied. She leaned her ear against the door and waited to hear the one to the adjacent room click shut. Footsteps padded past her, and she opened the bathroom door and peeked out just in time to see the black-haired man, briefcase in hand, slip out the front door.

She dashed toward the door and slammed right into Mr. Blue Eyes as he stepped out of the living room into the front hall. Addie grunted as she bounced off his chest. She leaned her hands on her knees, gasping for air.

"That's it, breathe slowly. Long, deep breaths." He rubbed her back as she struggled to fill her lungs. "You're just winded. It'll be fine, just breathe."

She nodded and stood up when the burning in her chest had subsided. "Thanks."

"Thanks for helping, or thanks for knocking the wind out of you? I'm so sorry though—didn't expect to find someone running the halls out here."

"I was just . . . Oh, never mind." She rubbed her diaphragm

to try to ease the spasms gripping at her whenever she forced air into her lungs.

"Let me get you a drink. It's medicinal and will help relax the muscle spasms."

"How did you know I was having—"

"Addie, I see you've met the man I was telling you about," Serena chirped from behind her.

"This is him?" Addie croaked.

"Hello," he said, extending his hand. "Simon Emerson."

"*Dr.* Emerson." Serena wedged herself between him and Addie. "He's just moved here from New York City."

Addie extended a trembling, limp hand. "Hello, pleased to meet you." Her eyes met his sparkling, deep sea-blue pools of . . . pure . . . "Delighted to meet you."

"Addie and I were just heading over to the Grey Gull for an early dinner," Serena cooed and fluttered her eyelashes like crazed bat wings. "Would you like to join us?"

Addie stifled a giggle. Serena's attempt at coquettishness and the wing-beating blur of eyelashes made it apparent that she'd spent too much time with Lacey lately. Too bad she hadn't yet mastered the art of dripping honey from silicone lips or the subtle effect of eyelash batting. Then again, maybe she had. They did look remarkably similar giving the same performance. Addie refocused and looked back at her friend. She wanted to take her finger and tip Serena's mouth closed. Her next vision was of her wiping drool from Serena's chin as she waited, mouth gaping open, for Simon's response.

"The inn? Sounds great. I'd love to join you."

"Perfect. Do you know the way, or would—" Then Serena's voice cracked, and she gave a rather unladylike throat clearing. "Or would you like me to be your guide?"

Simon's eyes sparkled, but he was obviously too much of a gentleman to show his amusement with her not-so-subtle and failed attempt at seduction. "Actually, I'm staying there until I find a place. I have a couple of stops to make, so I'll see the two of you"—his eyes flicked to Addie—"in about an hour."

"Perfect." Serena glued her eyes to his back as he headed out the door.

When it closed, Addie grabbed the wall for support; the laughter that had been building up inside her since Serena's mating ritual dance started almost knocked her to her knees.

Chapter Seventeen

Serena laid her head back on the headrest of Addie's car and moaned. "He's coming for dinner. Can you believe it? Wow." She sat straight up. "Lacey won't. I should text her and tell her." She pulled her cell out of her purse.

Addie grabbed it from her fingers. "Hold on there. It's just friends going to dinner with someone new in town."

Serena huffed and looked out the side window, holding her hand out. "Can I have my phone back?"

Addie handed it back to her and started the car. "And, speaking of Lacey . . ."

"Yes?"

"You aren't her, and maybe at dinner, I could suggest a more subtle approach if you want to catch his interest."

"It works for her."

"Well, I guess it does, after the show I watched today," she all but spit out, "but as your friend, maybe just hold back a wee bit. Be yourself."

"Okay, but I saw him first. Hands off."

Addie held the steering wheel with her thumbs and flashed her fingers up in resignation. "Yup, he's all yours. I'm done with men."

"Is that why Marc has renewed his interest in Lacey

again? You thought about what I said and decided they are perfect together and dumped him?"

Addie swallowed hard as she turned into the Grey Gull parking lot and pulled into the first spot she saw. "Yes, something like that."

"Did you tell him last night? He must have been at your shop. I did see the makeshift plywood door and then heard you'd been broken into again."

"Yes, it was last night." Addie grabbed her purse off the back seat and opened her door.

Serena panted, catching up to her across the parking lot. "He called Lacey first thing this morning, so I guess what I said about them still being in love is right. Glad you both finally saw that."

Addie's face burned. She put her head down and marched toward the restaurant door. It was nice to know that he had gone home and slept comfortably in his own bed, that he had already cleared his head of her and moved on to someone else today, after she'd tossed and turned trying to get a few winks while crammed into one of the chairs in her shop. Where he'd left her stranded for the night. She'd hated having to call Paige at seven to pick her up and take her home, and she cursed living in a town without regular taxi service. Well, she could always start her own taxi company, considering both she and Paige might soon be out of jobs, since it looked like her shop was going to be forced to close. When she had spoken with Paige at lunchtime, not one customer had been in, so she had sent Paige home. Marc and Lacey could just go and . . . no. They'd probably already done that, and she was a lady, as she kept reminding herself.

"This is nice. Feels like a long time since we were here. And that delicious waiter is still working." Serena motioned over her shoulder. "I hope we're sitting in his section."

"You're incorrigible. One to-die-for man at dinner isn't enough for you? You want two?" Addie laughed.

"A girl has to hedge her bets." Serena winked.

"There, that's the person I want to see tonight. Not that other ghost of a creature that keeps crawling inside your head."

Serena's harrumph turned into a giggle.

"Speaking of who's been inside your head lately," Addie said, then took a sip of water the busboy had just poured, "I know Marc has asked you in great detail about this, but I'm curious about the box you gave me that evening at my house."

Serena's face paled, and she set down her glass without taking a sip.

"I'm just wondering," Addie said, shifting in her seat, "do you remember seeing it at Lacey's place anytime?"

Serena picked up her glass, glared at Addie over the rim, and took a big gulp of water. "Yes, as I've told my brother, she had one like that, and she gave it to me to take to my shop to use as a decorative package for a customer if one wanted to give an elegant box of tea as a gift." Water slopped over the edge of her glass when she set it down. "Anything else, Counselor?"

"I didn't mean it like that. I'm just trying to figure out how it made its way out of Lacey's possession." She bit her lip. "Why didn't you recognize it when you saw it on my porch?"

"I thought it looked familiar," Serena said, her jaw clenching, "but gift boxes are not uncommon."

"You're right, sorry. I'm just trying to understand what's going on. I didn't mean to come off as accusing you of anything." Addie patted her hand and smiled, hoping to break through the ice field that had just formed between them.

Serena nodded. "I guess you have a right to ask, since you were the target. Sorry, he just grilled me for hours and—"

"I get it." Addie patted her hand. "Sorry, I didn't mean to come on so strong. Still friends?"

"Of course, why wouldn't we be? Well, unless you decide you're going to move in on the good doctor." She tossed her head back and laughed.

"No, I told you, my hands are off. But seriously, getting back to the box. You said you took it to the store. Did you use it as a gift box for anyone?"

"Yeah, a guy came in a few days later and wanted a special blend of tea for his girlfriend, and he loved the idea of the box. I've actually ordered others since then, and they're a hit."

"A guy? Do you remember what he looked like?"

Serena shook her head. "No, Marc asked me that, too, but it was a while ago, and I've had so many customers since then."

Addie sat back and tapped the tabletop with her knife handle.

"But I do remember now that he wanted a very particular blend." Serena leaned forward on her elbows. "Something to help his friend sleep. He said he had some from before that he purchased from a different shop, because she was having problems sleeping. She'd tried it, and it worked like magic, but he'd run out and wanted something similar so he could surprise her. He said it would be the best gift he could give her. I remember that because I found it so romantic that he wanted something that was original to make her happy, not your usual candy and flowers. Now that's true love." She took of a sip of her water.

Addie sat upright. "What kind of special blend? The same kind of *special blend* that other woman wanted a while back, the knockout tea?"

"No, that was completely different. That woman had something else on her mind. This guy only wanted to get a tea blend that would relax her, so she could drift off quietly." Serena shivered. "God. Now that I say it like that, it does sound sort of similar, doesn't it?"

"Do you remember anything else about him—height, weight, hair color, anything?"

"Nope, nothing. Everything else is just a blur."

"I need to see that coroner's report."

"What was that?" Serena looked up from her menu.

"Nothing." Addie waved her off. "Just thinking out loud."

"I hope Simon isn't much longer. I'm starving." Serena glanced toward the door. "There he is." She waved. "Yoo-hoo. Over here."

Addie shook her head. From wannabe femme fatale to Granny Smith in the blink of an eye—now *that* was Serena. She noted her friend had already pulled the empty chair beside her back in anticipation of him sitting there, so she discreetly reached under the table, retrieving her handbag and placing it on the vacant seat beside hers, leaving him no choice. He accepted the ploy and made himself comfortable. Well, as comfortable as he could with Serena shifting her chair as close to his as possible.

"Sorry I'm late, ladies. I got detained at the hospital."

"No problem." Serena's eye flutter returned as she gazed at him, and Addie cringed.

"I don't think I caught your name during our introductions." He turned toward Addie, the deep pools of his sea-blue eyes catching her off guard. She sputtered out her water. Serena looked at her, horror across her face. Addie giggled and wiped her chin with a napkin. Simon's eyes flashed from one to the other. "Did I miss the joke?"

Addie shook her head. "No, no joke. Just me being clumsy."

"Okay?" He looked back at Serena, then at her. "Well, are you going to tell me, or does it remain a mystery?"

"She already said there was no joke."

"I meant her name."

"Oh, right." Serena flipped her hair.

"Sorry, Simon, you know when the girls get together they tend to get silly sometimes." Addie nudged Serena's foot under the table. "I'm Addison Greyborne, but call me Addie, please."

He clasped her extended hand. "I must say, you're not anything like the person I thought you'd be." His face lit up with a smile that exposed a dimple in his left cheek.

He must have held her hand too long for Serena's liking, because she returned Addie's foot nudge with an outright kick. Addie pulled her hand away, breaking his embrace of hers, and glanced at Serena's dagger-filled eyes.

She straightened in her chair and took a sip of water. "And what exactly were you expecting me to be like?"

"You know, the stereotypical shy, withdrawn bookworm type." His lips flashed an amused grin. "I must say, I'm left speechless by the opportunity to be having dinner with the town's most infamous character." His eyes twinkled, capturing hers as he leaned forward, resting on his elbows.

Serena sat back and crossed her arms. Addie didn't have to look at her to feel the lightning bolts shooting at her across the table, and she shrank back into her chair. "So, Dr. Emerson, what brings you to Greyborne Harbor?"

"I'd like to say the scenery," he said, winking at her and picking up his water glass, "but I have to admit it was a job offer."

"Are you at the hospital?" Addie took a gulp of her own water, her eyes nudging Serena.

Serena leaned forward. "What department are you in?" she asked, turning her entire body toward his.

He hesitated as though he had just realized she was there. "I'm a half-time trauma surgeon in the emergency department, like I was in New York, and now also a part-time forensic pathologist."

"You're also a medical examiner—a coroner?" Addie asked.

He laughed. "Yes, I am and board certified, too. It's perfect for me as it's married my two loves in medicine. Why?"

"Oh, no particular reason, I've just had some experience with coroners in the past. That's all."

"Interesting . . . business or pleasure?" He leaned toward her. His eyes never wavered from hers.

There was that kick again. She rubbed her shin. "Actually, dealing with a coroner isn't pleasurable at all." She shot Serena a piercing glance.

"Then you just haven't met the right one." He smiled over his water glass.

Addie let out a quiet breath and counted to ten. "I'd love to talk shop with you sometime, but I don't think this is the time. We're here for a nice *friendly* dinner." She smacked Serena's foot with hers. "So, we should order." She smiled as sweetly as her throbbing shin would allow.

"Well, I for one am fascinated." Serena turned her entire body toward him, her eyelashes flapping at a spastic speed. Addie couldn't stop her eye roll and glanced down at her menu.

When she'd decided on what to order, she looked up to see Simon's hand pressing against the edge of Serena's chair back. His arm was extended to its full length, pushing him away from her. She nearly snorted trying to stifle a laugh. Serena obviously had not taken her earlier advice to heart. She felt sorry for her, but if it was Lacey's footsteps she chose to walk in, so be it.

Addie fidgeted with her napkin, dying to pick Simon's brain about autopsies, but bit her tongue to let Serena continue to hold the spotlight with him. She could speak to him tomorrow, maybe drop by the hospital—a safer environment, where he wouldn't be so keen to overtly display his egotistical charms on her. Then something he said caught her attention, and her self-imposed restraint flew out the window they were sitting beside.

"You took over from Sam Bolton?"

"Yes, sort of. He was with the district and worked out of the Salem office, but there have been so many murders in Greyborne Harbor recently that the DA decided to station a part-time coroner here as well. Why? Did you know him?" His eyes held hers with what appeared to be relief at her reentering the conversation.

"Not really, only by reputation. Did you perform the autopsy on June Winslow, by chance?"

"Yes, as a matter of fact, I did. Actually, that's why I attended her service and went to her house after to pay my respects." His eyes dropped. He scoured his forehead and blew out a deep breath. "After I complete what I do to a body, I need to remind myself they were a living, breathing person before my knife and table."

"That's so beautiful," Serena cooed and folded her hands over her heart.

"Realistically, they weren't living or breathing when they made their way to your autopsy table, or they wouldn't have been there in the first place."

Serena flung another dagger in her direction. "Never mind her, she's just, just . . ."

"No, she's right, Serena. I'm not the reason they aren't living and breathing anymore, but"—he looked at Addie, his eyes steady—"I do need to remind myself they were more than just body parts and tissue samples."

Addie nodded. "You're right. Sorry."

"No need to be sorry. It's just one of the demons I deal with personally in that job, since I work the rest of the time as a trauma surgeon and ER doc trying to keep people off that table." He reached across the dining table, clasped her hand in his, and gently squeezed it. "So don't worry, you haven't offended me." The gesture didn't pass unnoticed by Serena.

Addie released her hand from his and made a "stop" motion. "Wait. There is something I'm confused about."

"You can ask me anything. I'm an open book." He smiled, leaning across the table toward her, his eyes drawing her deep into them.

That darn heat crept up from under her collar again, and she shifted in her seat, breaking his hold over her. "Well, you said you were a trauma surgeon in New York?"

"Correct."

"And yet you accepted a position at our small hospital that barely even qualifies as one, at least by New York standards. I can't imagine that your skills will be fully utilized here."

"Ah." He sat back and crossed his arms. "So you think I came for darker reasons than to practice medicine?"

"Addie, enough," Serena hissed. "You can't look at every person you meet as a potential suspect and start interrogating them."

Simon raised his finger. "Hold on, Serena. She has a point." His eyes took on a hooded look as he whispered, "Remember, I told you that I had two loves."

She wriggled under the spell his eyes and voice cast over her, broke free, and matched his unwavering gaze. "It's just that it would seem so boring after what you're used to. I mean, how many actual traumas would you see here in a day, a week, or a month? After all, even on the worst days, you might only dress a few cuts and attend to a victim of a bicycle-versus-tree mishap."

"Or a head trauma and deadly fall?" He cocked his brow. "As I said, it's an opportunity for me to work as an ER doc and a pathologist slash medical examiner, too, which is something I didn't have the luxury of in the city. I have a good friend at the DA's office, and when Sam Bolton signed his retirement forms, my friend called me and offered me the position. He knew this was exactly the opportunity I had been looking for."

Serena sulked all the way through to dessert and was the first to call an end to the evening. Addie knew she blamed her for ruining her big chance to impress the *doctor*, and the ride home was strained, to say the least. A gnawing lump grew in the back of Addie's throat, and she started to apologize more than once, but bit her tongue. After all, it wasn't her fault Simon wasn't into Serena and had shown it. When she pulled up in front of Serena's building, Serena hopped out without a word and dashed up the sidewalk, but then stopped at the front door and turned back. She came around to Addie's window, tears in her eyes.

"This is so stupid of me. I feel like such a child." She reached in and hugged Addie around the neck. "Friends still?"

"Of course." Addie patted her back. "Forever and always."

"Good." She wiped tears from her cheeks. "Good night, and thanks." She waved as Addie pulled away.

Addie headed home, heart lighter than before, until it all but stopped as she pulled into her driveway. Parked in front of her house was a silver Tesla Roadster. She hit the brakes, grabbed her cell and dialed 911, leaving it open and ready to send if need be, and then slipped it into her pocket. Slowly, she rolled her Mini up beside the car, her eyes glued to its driver's window. The door was flung open, a pair of long-trousered legs emerged, and then there stood Simon, an awkward grin on his face.

Chapter Eighteen

"You're probably wondering why I'm here?"

Addie stared at him over the roof of her car, opening but then snapping her mouth shut. Her eyes narrowed.

"It's just that I wanted to apologize for my behavior at dinner."

"Really?" When had she become snarky?

"Yes, and before you say, *Which part?* let me add, for all of it. Not only for my schoolboyish behavior toward you, but for the way I rudely dismissed Serena. I was a complete jerk."

"So why did you do it? And, better question—how did you know where I live?"

"The second one's easier to answer."

"Then please do tell."

He rubbed the back of his neck. "Well, funny thing about that. My sister works for the Harbor Police and—"

"And she gave you my address?" Addie's eyes flashed.

"No, no, she would never . . . She just mentioned that if I looked on a tourist map and found one of the largest, most historical homes listed in the area, I'd find what I needed."

"Great, I'm on a tourist map. Seems fitting. Home of the local crazy book lady?"

His eyes twinkled with suppressed laughter. "I guess that's what really made me want to take the job and move to Greyborne Harbor in the first place."

"Because of me?"

"No. Because of my sister."

"Oh. So what about the first part of that question? Why?"

"That part's more complicated."

"Try me." She stood back, crossing her arms.

"Look, it's freezing out here. Can we go in and . . . just talk?"

She slid her hand to her jacket pocket and patted her cell phone. "Okay, but—"

"I promise, just talk." He gestured with a scout salute. "I got the feeling you wanted to talk to me at dinner anyway, so here's your chance."

She stopped at the door and turned back to him. "I do, but not in the way I think you took it at dinner."

"Well, I'm here now, so you can tell me what's on your mind. You can trust me, I'm a doctor." His eyes held a glint of amusement.

Addie rolled her eyes. He chuckled and followed her into the foyer. She tapped her cell phone once more for reassurance and led the way into the living room. "Have a seat." She pointed to a chair at far end of the sofa as she sat on the end closest to the door.

He looked at where she sat, and where she indicated for him to sit, shrugged, and sat down in the chair. "Really, I know my showing up out of the blue might contradict this, but I'm not a fiend."

"So, now the answer to the part of my original question that required us to come inside?" She hoped her eyes could still maintain the cool aloofness she was attempting to portray as she inadvertently swam right into his deep pools of sea-blue.

"Ah, yes," he said his lips arching into a sly smile but his eyes holding steadfast on hers. "Well, it's rather *anticlimactic*, if I must say."

Her mind raced for a witty comeback but stopped, knowing that would only encourage him further. "Try. And remember, my question was 'Why did you behave like such an ass and create friction between myself and my best friend?'"

"Yes, yes, I was. Without sounding conceited, any more than I already do, it has been a problem I've had for years." Addie snorted, and his brow furrowed. "I'm just not good at this—explaining or sharing my feelings. Give me a chance, because I feel I owe it to you."

"That's fair."

"Okay, then." He took a deep breath. "Being a single doctor, I have access to a great number of women." Addie couldn't contain her eye roll. "Staff I work with, patients, their friends and families, people I meet outside of work. And there are always the ones who tune in only to the fact that I'm a doctor and I'm single, and they strike like rattle-snakes."

Addie yawned and leaned forward, feigning interest.

"To be honest," he said, mirroring her posture, "it's brought me a lot of heartache over the years. To discover that they don't care about me as a person or anything other than to try and snag a future husband, a doctor. I'm not sure why." He shrugged. "We work crazy hours, and most of the married doctors I know have pretty rocky relationships, but it seems to be a status thing with some women, and a few men I've met, too." He sat back. "So that's it. Serena came on like one of them. You didn't, actually quite the opposite, so I focused on you. Plus, I've heard a lot about you and was—am—intrigued."

Addie leaned back on the sofa. Her eyes never wavered from his. "You certainly have an overinflated ego, don't you?

Because what I'm hearing from you is that women fall at your feet, women are shallow, and that's what gave you permission to be so rude to Serena? Have I got that right?"

He stood up. "Look, Addie, my heart's been torn out of me more times than I can say by women I thought really cared about me and wanted to build a future together, only to discover it was the social status they were after and I was their route to their envisioned lifestyle."

"Well, driving around in a high-end Tesla Roadster probably doesn't help either." She bit her lip. "Sorry, I don't mean to be so dismissive, but I can't buy that as a reason for rudeness. You never took the time to get to know her, and you immediately made a judgment based on nothing, except that she appeared to like you. But don't worry, I think that ship sailed tonight. I doubt she'll join your groupie gang again in the future."

"See?" He threw his hands up. "What's the point in explaining myself? It makes no difference. And remember, you're the one who wanted to know why."

"I guess I just figured that the explanation would go something like *I'm sorry, I was tired* or *not in a good mood* or any other one of a thousand simple explanations." She rose to her feet and glared at him. "Do you want to know what the difference between an explanation and an apology is? A real apology requires no explanation except *I'm sorry, I was an ass*. Not some sob story about how women fall all over you because maybe they want a Tesla, too. Boo-hoo. Suck it up, Doc, and get real."

His eyes widened. "I was being as real as I can with you."

Her head snapped up at the tone in his voice. "Why? Did you think that story would melt my heart and I'd fall over you because I felt sorry for you?"

He stepped closer. "No, but think about it. When I introduced myself to you in the hallway, what was the first thing Serena said?"

Addie shook her head. "I don't remember."

"'*Dr.* Emerson.'"

"You're right. Maybe it's been a problem for you, one that isn't part of my world, anyway, but I don't understand how that excuses rudeness."

"You're absolutely right, it doesn't, which is why I'm here to apologize. I'm sick and tired of it, too, and tired of living like that. I thought Greyborne Harbor might be different, like you seem to be different. You were intrigued by my profession, but it didn't come across as being in the same way." He stood in front of her. "More like a professional interest, not personal. Am I wrong?"

"No, you're not wrong."

"Too bad for me, then," he chuckled. "But I hope it's not because you're sick, and you need my medical services?" Concern filled his eyes as he studied her face.

"No." She pulled away, walked toward the window, and turned around. "But I do have some medical questions."

"For a friend?" The corner of one lip twitched with a half smile.

"Not really. They're about a case."

"My sister, Carolyn, told me about your involvement with the police department in the past. I should have guessed it's my brain you're interested in, isn't it?"

"Better than your social status."

"True, true." He sat down on the sofa. "So what is it you want to know?"

She eyed him sitting in her spot and looked at the far end of the sofa, where she would have to sit. "Would you like some coffee?"

"Sounds great."

"Be back in a minute. Cream and sugar?" she asked over her shoulder as she headed toward the kitchen.

"Just black, thanks," he called.

She returned in a few minutes, two steaming cups in

hand. Simon was standing at her desk, toying with a small figurine. "Do you like it?" She set the cups on the coffee table, placing hers at the end of the sofa nearest the door. It wasn't that she didn't trust his motives, but, well, she didn't.

He returned to the sofa, looked at where she'd placed the black coffee, shrugged, and took his seat back in the chair in front of the fireplace. "You have some wonderful pieces here. This place is a collector's delight, like that Louis the Fourteenth cherub."

"You know your antiques." She sipped her coffee.

"I was raised with them. My mother owns—owned—a shop in upstate New York."

"Did she sell it?"

"She's passed away."

"I'm sorry to hear that. What about your father? What does he do?"

"He was a surgeon." His eyes dropped. "He's passed away now, too."

"I'm sorry. Both my parents have also passed." She took a deep breath. "It's hard, isn't it?"

"Yes, Carolyn and I only have each other now. Well, aside from her husband, three kids, a dog, two cats, a bird, and I think a goldfish."

"Sounds like a busy house. I can see why you opted to stay at the Grey Gull until you find a place."

"You have a good memory for details." He took a tentative sip of his coffee. "So, enough about me. You have a medical question?" His eyes drew her into their cavernous pools.

"Yes." Her hand trembled as she set her cup down. She bit the inside of her cheek to stop the wave of whatever it was that rushed through her whenever he focused on her. "I was told that the cause of death in June Winslow's case was blunt force trauma to the back of the head, most likely due to a blow by a large flat object." She took a sip of her coffee, and instead of meeting his eyes, she looked at the floor and scrubbed an invisible spot with her toe. "Was that right?"

He laid his arm across the back of the sofa. "Partially, that's true. The strike to the back of the head definitely caused severe trauma—enough to knock her out, as indicated by the bruising and bleeding of the interior membrane— but my determination is that the fall, which broke her neck, actually killed her."

"I hadn't heard that." She drew her legs up and hugged her arms around her knees.

"What are you thinking?"

"Did you run a toxicology screen?"

"Of course. That's standard in a case like this. It was clean—no drugs, alcohol, nothing. Remember, she'd just left a meeting at the library."

"True, but . . . I was wondering if there was anything else, like an herbal substance, present in the blood or—"

"I'd need a sample of whatever it is you're thinking that she might have ingested."

"I need to get back into that house."

"What house?"

"June's."

"What are you thinking, that she was drugged by an herbal concoction?"

"It's possible, isn't it?" She rose to her feet and paced. "Although, why would someone drug her and take her in the utility building to kill her? They would have had to practically carry her from her car to the shed if the concoction did what I'm guessing it would, and that doesn't make sense, does it?" She stopped long enough to glance at him and see him shake his head. "Also, how would they get the tea into her in the parking lot so it could take effect?"

He stood up and moved toward her. "I think you've lost me. I have no idea what you're talking about."

She placed her hands on his shoulders. "Think about it. It doesn't make sense."

"No . . . it doesn't."

"I knew it." She swept past him and paced again. "The tea must have been used for another reason. If I can get a sample, could you see if she'd ever been given that infusion at any time before?"

"What are you talking about?"

She stared at him, and then broke out laughing. "God, I must sound like a crazy person."

"You're making me dizzy." He placed his hands on her shoulders. "Please sit, and then explain it to me."

She propped herself on the arm of the sofa. "Okay." She took a deep breath. "There's this map, showing a tunnel system under the town. I think, from what I've read in June's notes, that she thought, after going through archives, that there might be a buried treasure somewhere, but so did someone else. The only problem is they needed June's research for the book she wrote to find it, and they were prepared to kill her for it. Or," she said, pursing her lips, "it's not in her research, and only she knew about it, but she ended up dead, and they're still looking for it."

Simon blew out a deep breath into his cupped hands over his face and shook his head.

"Now do you see what I'm talking about?"

"Not really, but I guess . . ." He shrugged and sat down beside her.

She leapt up. "Here, I'll show you the map." She dug it out of her handbag. "Look at this. It's a map of the town showing pirates' smuggling tunnels that were constructed during the sixteen hundreds to the eighteen hundreds. Piracy was an important part of Harbor history."

He took it from her shaking hand. "Now we're talking about pirate treasures," he chuckled. "This is becoming even more fascinating." He squinted and looked at the map. "Where did you get this? Is it legitimate?" He looked up at her, his eyes seemingly pinning her to an imaginary board.

At her nod, he stood up and handed the map back to her. "The whole story sounds like something out of a novel, and I'm not sure how I can shed any light on your theory, but if you can get me a sample of whatever it is you think she took, it might add one more piece to this crazy puzzle you are trying to sort out."

She reached up and kissed him on the cheek. "Thank you, thank you, thank you."

He rubbed where she had kissed him and smiled. "Well, if my help leads to more of this, then I'll be a very helpful, happy man."

She laughed and swatted his arm. "Don't count on it. I was just lost in the—"

A cell phone rang. Addie checked her pocket.

"It's me," he said, retrieving his phone. "Hello, Dr. Emerson . . . Sorry, this is who? . . . Oh, hi Carolyn, yes, I'm on call tonight for Dr. Adams. . . . Where? . . . Why did they call the police station and not an ambulance? . . . Okay, I see . . . Yeah, tell them I'll be right there."

"An emergency?"

"Yes, do you want to come along?"

"What, with you to see a patient?"

"You said you wanted to get inside June's house again to look for this tea, if I'm not mistaken."

Her eyes widened.

"It seems Jeanie, who is currently staying in her mother's house until her belongings are packed up, stumbled and hit her head. A friend who's with her is a bit concerned, because

Jeanie appears to be confused now. So, here's your chance to get back in."

She grabbed her handbag and coat off the chair. "I'm ready. And before I forget, I think you owe Serena an apology, not just me." But her words were met with a silence that continued to hover between them as they made their way outside.

Chapter Nineteen

"You're right. I guess I do." His voice wavered and became strained as he opened the passenger door for her. "I'm just not sure what to say though."

"All you have to say is, 'I was a jerk, and I'm sorry I was rude to you.' That's it—no further explanation required."

His lips tightened, and he went around to his door. "So, me sharing with you what I did wasn't required." Buckling his seat belt, he glanced sideways.

"Not to her. I do appreciate you telling me about your ghosts, and it helped me understand what happened, but it's not a required part of an apology . . . unless it's meant as an ulterior motive?"

"No, it wasn't. I guess I just sensed that you have a few ghosts of your own and might understand."

She pursed her lips and stared out her side window, her cheeks growing warm. "This is a great little car. I can see why you bought it," she said, hoping the change of subject would send him a clear message.

"A self-indulgent treat, I'm afraid." He glanced sideways at her. "There's no real need for a car in New York City, but when I moved here and saw the endless miles of winding highways along the coastline, I couldn't resist."

"That's nice," she mumbled absently, her thoughts lost in what he had said about ghosts and in remembering the plans she and Marc had made for Founder's Day. She bit the inside of her cheek to keep her tears in check.

He pulled onto June's street and slowed down at the sight of a police cruiser parked in front of the house. Addie sucked in a deep breath, her eyes glued to the side of the patrol car as they passed to park in front of it. Number 001. It was Marc's. Her knees wavered as she stepped out onto the sidewalk. Simon retrieved his medical bag from the trunk. She locked her knees and strutted up the sidewalk behind him. There was no way she was going to let Marc see how his rejection had pained her. Left her numb. The door swung open, and a voice she dreaded to hear cut through the crisp night air.

"Hello. You must be Dr. Emerson. I'm Chief Chandler. You can call me Marc."

"It's a pleasure to meet you, but frankly, I'm surprised to find you here."

"How's that?"

"Does the police chief usually attend all medical emergencies in Greyborne Harbor?"

"Standard procedure, that's all, especially when a head trauma is called in. We're required to respond, assess and secure the scene before medical personnel can enter. Just to be safe, you know. And I happened to be the closest car, so here I am."

"Well, then, I feel we're in good hands." Simon stepped aside, revealing Addie's presence, placed his hand on the small of her back, and presented her before Marc like a prize. "Do you know my companion, Addison Greyborne?"

Marc's face crumbled when he looked from Simon's twinkling eyes to Addie's panic-stricken ones.

"Yes, we've had the pleasure. Good evening, Miss Greyborne." He tipped his cap and stepped aside.

"Good, then no further introductions are required. I'll be

off to see my patient, then." Simon swept them past Marc into the house.

Addie hesitated. She cast her gaze downward. She glanced up at Marc as they passed him, but his narrowed eyes appeared to be drilling holes into the back of Simon's head. She lifted her chin and strode into the hallway. The door thudded shut behind her, the sound vibrating in her chest. She glanced over her shoulder, but Marc hadn't followed them in.

Jeanie lay stretched out on the sofa in front of the window. Simon went immediately to her side. Addie stood in the doorway, shuffling from one foot to the other, torn between running outside and explaining to Marc why she was here with Simon or searching for the tea. Her right foot won. She turned and headed down the hallway to the kitchen. When she passed the bedroom door, it was slightly ajar. She peeked over her shoulder—all clear—and poked her head around the door. In front of the closet were shoeboxes, an old suitcase, and stacks of books tipped over, but it was the sight of an empty file box similar to the one Jeanie had given to her with June's research notes that drew her into the room.

She surveyed the ransacked heap at her feet, crouched, and pulled a tissue from her handbag. Shielding her fingerprints, she picked through the items. Pieces of a shattered teacup underneath one of the file boxes caught her eye. Clearing the debris covering it, she picked up the largest piece in her tissue-wrapped hand and rummaged through her bag for another tissue with her free hand, wrapped it, and slipped the package into her purse.

Addie stood up and scanned the room, noting a lamp stood intact on the bedside table. She was certain it was the same lamp she caught a glimpse of earlier through the doorway before Jeanie closed it behind her. She looked from the bed to where the shattered teacup lay. Her eyes followed the splatter marks up the wall and came to rest on a slight indentation at about her head height. The point of impact? She bit her lip. "Why did you throw a teacup, and who were you throwing it at?" she muttered and resurveyed the room, and then she remembered the black-haired man had exited this room not long after she'd heard the crash.

She pulled her cell out of her pocket, snapped photos of the clutter on the floor and the splatter pattern across the wall, checked the front hall, and dodged into the empty kitchen. A coffee maker hissed and gurgled on the counter; a teapot sat beside it. She peered around the dining room doorframe into the adjoining living room. Simon was bent over Jeanie, checking her pulse. Mildred, the owner of the Emporium on Main, sat on a chair across from them, sipping from a large mug with the words "I Love Coffee" written across it, and on the coffee table beside Joanie was a delicate teacup.

She went over to the teapot on the counter and wrapped her hands around it. Still warm. She lifted the lid, inhaled, cringed, and closed it. Behind the pot was a cellophane bag, clearly marked with a sticker that read, *SerenaTEA, Special Blend*. Addie undid the twist tie holding it shut, rummaged through the drawers until she found a sandwich bag, and then retrieved a tablespoon from another drawer. She transferred two heaping spoonfuls of tea leaves from the cellophane bag to the sandwich bag, which she zipped closed and tucked into her purse. She sealed the cellophane bag again with the twist tie and placed it back where she'd found it.

"Looking for something?"

She jumped and spun around. "Marc? No, well, yes, I was going to get more coffee for Mildred. Would you like some?" She pointed to the steaming carafe.

He shook his head slowly and said, stroking his jaw, "So, tell me, Addie, have you given up detective work and taken up nursing since I last saw you?"

"Why would you say that?"

"Why are you accompanying the good doctor on a house call? You play detective with me, and nurse with him. Are you a chameleon, changing color to please whoever you're with at the moment?" His narrowed eyes fixed on hers.

Her knees gave way at the stinging strike of his venomous tone. She grabbed behind her for the counter edge and hung on.

His top lip turned up at the corner of his mouth, and he spun on his heel out of the room.

She heaved out a breath and squeezed her stinging eyes shut to fight the tears back. Marc's voice echoed down the hall. She sprinted around the corner into the dining room.

He stood in the hall at the living room entrance. "Well, are you going to transport the patient or not?" His look turned to Addie. "I'm sure you're *anxious* to get on with your evening plans."

Simon removed his stethoscope from his ears, hung it around his neck, and turned to Marc. "To be honest, Chief, I'm not really clear on why you're still here. Obviously, these two lovely ladies are no threat to myself, nor to Miss Greyborne." He reached casually into his medical bag and pulled out a prescription pad.

"Standard procedure—but why am I explaining this to you? I'm sure it's the same wherever it is you come from."

"New York City—and yes, sometimes it is, when a call comes in where the patient could possibly cause harm to first responders. Or in the instances that it is a known crime scene. However, you did your due diligence in securing the scene before my arrival. I think your job here is done, because obviously those are not issues in this case." His eyes locked with Marc's unyielding glare. "Unless, of course, you have another motive for wanting to remain here?"

"Don't be ridiculous," Marc all but spat out. Addie flinched.

Simon scrawled something on the notepad and handed it

to Jeanie. "Remember, show this to the triage nurse when you arrive, and they'll page me right away. But if you start feeling sick to your stomach or the dizziness gets worse tonight, call an ambulance immediately. Don't wait till morning."

"Thank you so much, Doctor." She squeezed his hand.

"I really wish you would reconsider and let me take you in tonight. I'd like to run a few tests."

"No, I'm fine, and Mildred said she'd stay over and keep an eye on me, and I've been enough trouble to you already. Now, you and Addie go on and enjoy the rest of your evening."

"I'm glad to hear you're feeling better, Jeanie." Addie crossed the dining room into the living room, shooting Marc a piercing side glance as she walked by him, and clasped Jeanie's hand in hers. "Make sure you listen to the doctor and keep your appointment in the morning. Promise?"

"I promise, and I'm sure Mildred will make certain I do." She chuckled.

"Damn sure." Mildred stood up. "You can be stubborn, Jeanie, but I'm a match for you." She moved to the far end of the sofa at Jeanie's feet.

Simon packed up his bag. "Okay, ladies, I'll be off, then. If you promise me again that you'll be in first thing tomorrow?"

"I promise. Thank you so much, but I'm fine, so don't worry."

Mildred patted her foot. "I have first aid training, so she'll be okay. I'll keep a close eye on her."

"I'm counting on it, Mildred." He placed his hand on the small of Addie's back and escorted her around Marc, who was looming in the doorway. Simon sidestepped past him. Marc turned his full body, and their eyes locked, never wavering off each other's, like two bucks posturing to show dominance. Two *bullheaded* bucks was more like it. She grabbed Simon's wrist and tugged him out the door.

He opened the passenger door for her. "Well, based on what I overheard coming from the kitchen and that performance, I'd say we just visited one of your ghosts, if I'm not mistaken."

"You have no idea." She slid into her seat and let out a deep breath.

Simon got in and looked at her. "Are you okay? Do you want to talk about it?" She shook her head. "Okay, if you say so." He pulled out onto the road. "I'll be honest though, Carolyn told me that you and Marc worked closely together, but based on what happened just now, I'd say it was more than the working relationship she told me it was, am I right?"

She stared out her window at the blur of lights passing by her tear-filled eyes. "You and Carolyn seem to talk about me a lot. What's up with that?"

He let out a heavy sigh. "I saw you in the window of your shop one day and was intrigued and wanted to know—"

"Was that before or after the articles came out in the newspaper? Because I guess I must be a really intriguing sideshow now."

"It was before, and I wanted to know if you were single." She laughed.

"What's so funny about that?"

"I guess tonight you got your answer."

"Look, Addie, with whatever that was back there and the newspaper articles, if you ever need anyone to talk to, remember I'm a doctor, besides your new friend, and I'm here."

"What, you have a degree now in psychiatry, too?"

"It doesn't take a specialist in the area to see you are dealing with a lot lately." He glanced at her as he pulled up in front of her house. "Just remember I'm here if you need me, that's all."

"Thanks, I'll remember that." She flung the door open.

He clasped her arm. "Wait, aren't you forgetting something?"

"What?"

"The tea."

"Oh, yes!" She exclaimed. "I got it, plus a piece of a broken cup."

"Good work, Nancy Drew."

She smiled and pulled the packages out of her purse and handed them to him. "I hope it's enough to test."

"It looks like more than enough, thanks."

"No, thank you . . . you know, for indulging my grand crime-solving delusions."

"Anytime." He winked as she hopped out. "Wait, I thought we had a bonding moment tonight, so aren't you going to invite your partner in crime, me, in for a drink?" He leaned out the window, grinning like a schoolboy.

"Phffft, you're so transparent." She headed toward the door.

"No, not usually, keep pretty guarded actually," he called out the window as he made a U-turn in the drive, "but I'm starting to think you have X-ray vision and can see right through me."

"That's not hard to do." She laughed and shook her head.

He beeped his horn and slowed down in front of her. "That's a better look on your face." He smiled. "I'll call you tomorrow." He accompanied his goodbye with a wave and drove off.

Chapter Twenty

Addie broke into a grin as she spotted Catherine outside waiting for her to open. "Catherine, how nice to be greeted by you first thing in the morning." Addie smiled.

"Good morning." Catherine said. "I wanted to catch you before you got busy, and"—she produced a key from her pocket—"to give you this on behalf of Brian."

Addie retrieved the key dangling from Catherine's fingers. "He left my new door key with you?"

"He does apologize, but had another appointment and was running late, and since I was here waiting . . . I hope you don't mind?"

"No, not at all, and thank you. Come in." Addie opened the door. "Would you like to join me for some morning coffee before I start doing nothing for the day?"

"Oh dear. So business hasn't picked up then?"

Addie shook her head, tossing her purse on a shelf under the front counter.

"I'm truly sorry to hear that." Catherine slid onto a stool. "I really thought once the gossip column stuff settled down, people would move on and everything would return to normal."

"It seems they have very long memories." Addie plopped a pod in the coffee maker.

"Too long. Some are still fighting battles that happened generations ago."

"Yes." Addie's eyes narrowed. "I hear some can carry on for hundreds of years."

Catherine smiled, accepting the steaming cup Addie handed to her. "Well, I'm not sure about that but who knows? People can be strange."

"Some more so than others." She dropped another pod in the machine.

"So, the reason I'm here is the girls and I have decided we're going to move right along with the club meeting. Is tonight too early for you?"

"No." She stirred cream into her coffee and slipped onto the stool next to Catherine's. "Is Jeanie aware? After all, it was only yesterd—"

"Actually, it was her idea."

"Really?" Addie took a sip, watching Catherine's face over the rim. "Is she feeling up to it today, you know, after last night?"

"Why, what happened last night? Well, other than the tumble she told me that she took, but I'm sure she was just exhausted."

Addie reflected on the events that had occurred at June's house the night before and the odd-smelling tea sample she'd taken with her. "You're right." She shook her head. "She was probably just tired."

"She sounded fine when she called me first thing this morning and said it was time some normalcy returned to our lives and suggested having the book club meeting tonight."

"Well then, sure. That gives me all day to run out and pick up some snacks. What do the girls usually have at the meetings?"

"That's the wonderful thing. Jeanie said she has so much

food left over at her mother's house from yesterday and doesn't want it to go to waste, so she's bringing it. You don't have to do anything."

"Even better, but I really don't mind if it's part of the job as chair."

"We usually take turns anyway, bringing snacks and stuff, as long as you supply the coffee and tea."

"No problem. If Paige ever gets in, I'll run next door and pick up some tea."

"I saw Paige go into SerenaTEA when I was waiting out front."

"Really? That was over fifteen minutes ago. I wonder what's keeping her?"

"I best be off." Catherine stood up. "I'm supposed to be meeting Dorothy, one of the club members. You'll meet her tonight. We swim at the Y three times a week, and today is one of those days." She headed for the door and turned around. "By the way, I hear you and the very handsome new doctor make the loveliest couple." She winked.

Addie sputtered out her mouthful of coffee.

Catherine laughed.

Dabbing her chin, Addie said. "We're not a couple. We just met."

"Not according to Mildred."

"Mildred? What does she know about it?"

"She said there were lots of sparks between the two of you, and she guessed—"

"'Guessed' is right. We're just friends, new friends, that's all."

Catherine smiled. "I'd say the lady doth protest too much." With a laugh, she closed the door behind her.

Addie dropped her head on the cool countertop. "Just what I need—more rumors."

The door chimes rang, and she lifted her face to see a

sheepish Paige bolt in and head to the back storeroom. "Sorry I'm late," she called out.

Addie straightened her shoulders and stood up, following her into the back. "Is everything okay?" She leaned against the doorframe. Paige hung up her coat, and Addie noted she hadn't brought a take-out cup back with her. "Was the tea shop swamped this morning?"

"Yes." She looked at Addie and, with a flushed face, skirted past her to the front.

Addie watched Paige busy herself by straightening and rearranging bookshelves. She shrugged and went back to the counter to review yesterday's receipts. "I can see it was a good call to send you home early yesterday. Not one customer in all morning?" She looked over at Paige, who stood motionless in front of a bookshelf. "Paige? Did something happen? Are you okay?"

Paige shook her head and righted a book that had fallen on its side.

Addie's eyes narrowed as she studied the girl, obviously lost in her own thoughts. She closed out the receipt totals, or lack thereof, and checked to see if she had any consignment customers booked in today. She scanned the blank page and slammed the appointment book shut.

Her phone vibrated. She grabbed it from her pocket, and when she looked at the unknown number her heart sank. Secretly, she'd been hoping Marc would call today to apologize for his boorish behavior last night, but . . . She sighed. "Hello . . . Oh, good morning, Simon . . . Fine, thanks, and you? . . . Oh dear. No rest for the wicked, as they say." She laughed and tucked the phone closer to her ear. "Umm, tonight? No, I'm afraid I can't do dinner. I have a book club meeting at seven and doubt we'll be done by eight . . . Yes, Jeanie will be here, why? . . . Oh, I see. Sure, I understand, patient-doctor confid—" She frowned. "Okay, I guess it wouldn't hurt for you to sit in and observe . . . Sure . . . See you about eight, then." She set her phone on the counter and stared down at it. "I hope her test results this morning were okay."

The rest of the day plodded on in silence. Paige didn't have much to say and appeared to be avoiding Addie, or at least avoiding making eye contact with her, at any rate. To occupy her own mind, and to put Paige out of the misery of trying to avoid her at every step and turn, Addie set up shop in front of her blackboard in the back room. Her mind was racing with possibilities, and she knew she had to see them in black-and-white before any of it might even take on any semblance of sense.

She whisked the sheet covering from it and stood eye to eye with the last name she had written. *Lacey Davenport.* "Well." She picked up the brush and wiped the name off the board. "Not sure you're a murderer, but you're definitely guilty of something—" She stopped when she got to the side where she had written the notes about Lacey, then stood back, tapping her chin. *Used fictitious stories as a leg up* popped out at her. "Would she go as far as murder to create her own story? One that could potentially kick-start her failing career?" She circled her notes and wrote *LD* above them.

Addie stood back, crossed her arms, and tapped her foot, staring at the space across the top of the board. "Think, what *do* you know? Start with the facts, as Dad would say, and see where they lead." She wrote, *June Victim, Map, Tunnels, Research, Book,* and then paused, tapping her chalk on the board. "The book? The book's important, but the original research is more so, I think, so here's one link." She drew a line between them. "But something is missing." She scratched her head. "Oh my God, the original. That's it." She scrawled *original manuscript* and stabbed the chalk, drawing an exclamation mark. "Where is it, and what's in it that the town council didn't want published?" She drew a large question mark beside it.

"Okay, think, think, Addie." She stood back and studied the board. "What else do you know?" She could almost hear her father's voice. An idea hit her, and she wrote:

The salt-and-pepper-haired man?

The black-haired man with glasses?

Jeanie

She stood back, looking at the last name she'd written, her eyes narrowing. "Think, Addie, how does she fit into this? Well, the only thing I can see right now is that she's the link between the black-haired man and the salt-and-pepper-haired man, because I've seen her with both of them." She drew an arch between them. "Jeanie must know they are the same man. If I can see that she definitely couldn't miss it." Three question marks marched along behind Jeanie's name.

"Okay, now where?" She rapped the chalk piece on the board. "Talk to me, Dad, please." She took a deep breath. "Back to the victim. What do I know about June?"

Head librarian

Author

Dead from a shove or a fall

Murder weapon?

Purse

"Those all get check marks."

Cell phone

"Not with body. This gets an X."

"Addie, do you need anything before I go?"

Addie jumped. "Paige, you startled me." She placed a hand to her pounding chest.

Paige apologized but didn't make eye contact.

"Yes, one thing. Could you run next door and pick up a package of black tea for tonight, please?"

Paige nodded and turned.

"Just take the money out of petty cash," Addie called out. However, as per how the rest of the day had gone, there was no response from Paige except for the tinkling of the door chimes. Addie placed the chalk back on the tray and refitted the sheet over the board. She was at a complete loss as to what had made her assistant so distant today. It must be bad, really bad, and her heart ached to reach out to Paige.

The door chimes rang again, and "I'm off" was the only thing Paige said before there was complete silence in the store.

Addie made her way to the front to lock the door, noted the bag of tea on the counter, and peered out the window. Paige was on the sidewalk in front of SerenaTEA, chatting with Lacey. Her skin crawled at how friendly their conversation appeared, and then Lacey hugged her and kissed her cheek. Paige turned toward Main Street and spotted Addie. Her face went scarlet. She put her head down and marched past, her eyes focused straight ahead.

Chapter Twenty-One

"Enough, girl, you don't need any more drama in your life. What will be, will be," Addie said to herself, repeating her grandmother's favorite mantra. She turned from the window and eyed the configuration of the store, then began clearing and arranging an open space for six to eight people to sit comfortably. She dragged leather chairs from various reading spaces she had set up, and inch by inch, shuffled some of the smaller bookshelves out of the way, cursing herself for not thinking of this while Paige, another set of hands, was still here. When she had managed to set up a cozy meeting space, she stood back and smiled. "Not bad for a start." She cleared the counter of the books she had displayed there as sale items, making room for the food, and then retrieved a supply of paper cups from the back room.

The door chimes rang, and she turned as Catherine entered. "Hi, is it that time already?" Addie checked the clock.

"Don't mind us. We came a few minutes early to see if you needed help." Addie nodded at the tall woman accompanying Catherine. "I'm sorry, this is my swimming partner, Dorothy. She was June's assistant at the library and is a member of the town council."

Addie extended her hand. "I'm pleased to meet you."

"Likewise." Dorothy returned her handshake.

"June's assistant *and* a member of the town council?" Addie's PI radar zapped. "How long have you sat on the council?"

"I feel like I've been there for years." She laughed.

"You have." Catherine chuckled and gave her friend a shoulder nudge.

Dorothy's eyes sparkled as she scanned the bookstore. "I love your shop. I can't believe I haven't been in here yet."

"Thank you." Addie assessed the woman. Her height and wavy, mid-neck-length, white hair combined with a husky voice that matched her build reminded her of the actress Bea Arthur, who starred in *The Golden Girls*.

"I'd love to pick your brain about books another day, when we have more time."

"I see some books now that I remember from your aunt's extraordinary collection. This is exciting." Dorothy began reviewing titles on a bookshelf. "Yes, I most definitely will be back. I see some titles that the library doesn't have, and I would love to get my hands on them."

"Everything you see here is for sale, and if it's any of the rarer books I still have at the house, we might be able to arrange something. Although some of those I've promised to the Boston Public Library and a few museums. But," she added, smiling, "I could add the Greyborne Harbor Library to my distribution list, too, if you're really interested."

"Am I interested? Of course I am." She dug into her handbag. "Here's my card. Call me one day soon, and I'll come by and take a look to see what you have and are willing to part with. As closely as June and I worked, we did feel very differently about a few topics—local sources for library acquisitions being one of them." She glanced at Catherine. Addie couldn't help but notice the glaring look Catherine shot back at her.

"Well, we'd better finish setting up here," said Catherine quickly. "Although I see you've done most of it already."

"Yes." Addie's brow furrowed as she studied the two women, who were now walking in the direction of the seating area. "I wasn't sure how many people to expect, so I have the six leather chairs and three folding ones. I hope that's enough."

"It's just fine. There are seven of us, then eight with you, and then the one spare seat for good measure, in case an extra pops by."

"Actually, that was my thinking, too. Because Dr. Emerson mentioned he *might* come by after his shift. He's anxious to get to know people in town, and—"

"Dr. Emerson, hey?" Catherine winked.

Heat crept up Addie's neck, and she turned her flushing face away from the two women and the glint of amusement in their eyes.

The chimes rang and three more women Addie didn't recognize entered. She followed Catherine to the door. "Addie, this is Ida; she works at Fielding's. This is Connie; she's a judicial clerk at the courthouse. It's on the top floor of the police station, in case you weren't aware."

"No, I wasn't. Nice to meet you. All of you." She shook their hands.

"And this is Maggie. She's the owner of the real estate company on Main Street."

Addie nodded at the women.

"So," said Catherine, clasping her hands together, "we're just waiting for—"

The door flung open.

"—Gloria, our never-fails-to-be-tardy travel agent." Catherine laughed.

Gloria made a face at her, but her rosy, round cheeks couldn't hide her friendly grin. "Hi, Addie. I've seen you around, but I don't think we've spoken." She shook her hand.

Catherine looked at Addie. "I guess we're all here—well, except for Jeanie, and I'm sure she'll be along soon."

Addie motioned to the counter. "There's coffee and tea set out. Help yourselves, ladies, and make yourselves comfortable."

The women chatted as they each made their beverage of choice, then began perusing the shop. Addie smiled inwardly—this was the most people she'd had in here for over a week, and she crossed her fingers it might be the start of customers returning to her store.

She spotted Dorothy in the historical book section and made her way toward her. "You're a history buff like me."

"Yes." Dorothy glanced up from the book she held. "It's a passion I shared with June, too. That's one of the reasons we got along so well." Her eyes filled with tears.

Addie patted her arm. "I know her passing must have been hard on her friends." She gave her arm a light squeeze.

Dorothy placed the book back on the shelf and retrieved another one. "Oh, look! I know June borrowed this one from your aunt once. *The History of Pirates* by Dr. Angus Konstam."

"Are there any other books here you know of that she might have used in her research?" Addie scanned the shelf.

"I don't know if they're here, but I do know there were a number that your aunt loaned her over the course of her research. She told me she found your Aunt Anita's attic collection *extremely* helpful. She'd spend hours up there making notes on her laptop."

"Was that where she conducted most of her research, from my aunt's collection?"

"No, she also visited the Lighthouse Museum down in the harbor frequently, and then . . ." She shrugged. "There were some other museums, one in Boston and one closer. I can't remember where it was, but she went to that one regularly. She said their archives were more extensive than the one here."

"Interesting. If you can remember the name of it, please let me know."

Dorothy nodded.

"Did she ever mention which one of my aunt's books she found most helpful?"

"No, not really." She frowned, rubbing her forehead. "There was one she did remark on that was a very old, rare book. It was a collection of New England pirate journals, if I remember correctly. Yes, and your aunt wouldn't let her take it out of her house, which was why June had to read through it in the attic."

"But you don't know the name of it?"

Dorothy shook her head.

"I guess I have some more exploring to do in that attic." She looked at the book Dorothy held in her quivering hand. "Could I give you that one? To remind you of her?"

Dorothy took a deep breath and smiled at Addie, shaking her head. "Thanks anyway, dear, but it's not necessary." She replaced the book on the shelf. "New England pirates were June's speciality. Anything I need to learn about them I can find in her book now, I suppose." Addie noted the cutting edge to her voice.

"I assumed you'd worked on it with her, being her assistant and all."

Dorothy sucked in a sharp breath. "No, I didn't help her with her book." She bit her trembling lip. "Well, I did in the beginning, but then out of the blue she said she didn't need or want my help anymore. After that, she kept her research pretty close to her chest."

"Sorry, I guess I misunderstood."

Dorothy rested her hand the cover of the pirate history book. "I never even read any of her later notes." She straightened her shoulders. "My first reading was when the book was released."

"But weren't you on the town council when they rejected her first draft?"

"Yes, I was."

"But you never read it?"

She shook her head. "Only Blain Fielding—you know, part of the family that Fielding's Department store is named for. He was the council chairman back then, and Dean Davenport was the vice chair. They're the only two who read it."

"Dean Davenport?"

"Yes, Lacey's brother. He runs a charter boat business down in the harbor." Her eyes continued to scan the titles on the shelves.

"I didn't know she had a brother. So you never saw it? Did anyone aside from them?"

"Not as far as I know. Dean said that we should take their word for it, that it was garbage, and we had to reject it and her grant, pending a rewrite."

Addie's heart raced. "What was in the book that he objected to?"

"I have no idea."

Dorothy retrieved another book from the shelf. "I'm not sure if you knew, but Dean was pretty indebted to the Fielding family, who thought they ran this town, which is why he was selected to be on the town council in the first place. He was their yes-man. Ask Ida—she's worked as a sales clerk at Fielding's for over twenty years."

Addie tried to keep her voice level, unassuming, normal. "Do you know what happened to the original manuscript?"

"No idea. Jeanie might know though."

"Thanks, I'll check with her." Addie watched Dorothy's face as she ran her fingers over the spines of the books on the shelf in front of her. "I know you were very close to June and obviously shared her love of books."

Dorothy smiled and nodded.

"So I was surprised to hear that the two of you disagreed

on—was it acquisitions you mentioned? What did you mean by—"

"Pfftt." She waved her hand and moved along the shelf away from Addie. "That was nothing."

It was apparent that Dorothy wasn't going to disclose anything telling about her and June's friendship tonight. She'd have to grill Catherine about it later.

Addie was busying herself by straightening the bookshelf Dorothy had been browsing when the door chimed behind her. She heaved a sigh. Finally, she'd be able to ask Jeanie about a few of the burning questions she had. Like whether she'd come across the original manuscript since they first talked. And then she could try to get some information about the man of many disguises that she'd seen her with. Addie wanted that information before she told her the file box was missing. She was afraid if she mentioned it now Jeanie might get scared off and refuse to answer because she is somehow involved, or she would become angry with Addie for losing it, and then she'd be no further ahead in finding the answers to all the questions whirling around in her mind.

"Serena?" Catherine's voice gushed from the storefront. "How lovely of you to join us, and Lacey, too. This is a wonderful surprise."

Addie's heart plunged to the pit of her stomach.

Chapter Twenty-Two

"Hello, everyone." Lacey fluttered her fingers. "Isn't this a quaint little shop?" She dramatically waved her hands in the air, waltzing around the room, nodding and oohing as she glanced from the book section to the curios. "It's just delightful, isn't it?" The group murmured their agreement.

Addie bit the inside of her cheek and headed to the front. Her eyes fixed on the back of Lacey's head as she moved up beside her. "What are you doing here, Lacey?"

"Me?" she exclaimed loudly, drawing all eyes to her. "I can't believe I haven't made the time to come in here before, but you know how it is." She turned to the group. "I've been working so hard to help poor Serena in her shop."

"Yes." Catherine smiled at Serena, who shifted from one foot to the other, looking sheepishly at Addie. "And Serena should be so grateful for all your hard work. You've done a wonderful job there. Hasn't she, ladies?"

Through a round of applause and hails of congratulations, Addie gritted her teeth and whispered, "I could have sworn that you stopped by just the other day?" She hoped her smile still matched the fake one splashed across Lacey's face.

Lacey shrugged. "My bad. But then that day I wasn't

focused on anything or anyone except *my* Marc sitting at the counter." Her icy eyes flashed at Addie.

"Give me a break," Addie hissed through gritted teeth.

"Oh, I will, darling." She leaned closer to Addie and whispered. "When I have exactly what I want."

"And how adorable is this, everyone?" Lacey's voice rose as she made a showman's gesture, waving her arms in front of the Founder's Day decorations in the window then clutching her hands to her heart. "Our Addie is so talented." She beamed, looking at Addie, and the group murmured and nodded. But then she leaned toward her, lowering her voice. "Of course, Addie, your display isn't even close to being up to the same standards as the other merchants'. But I'm sure if you're lucky enough to still be here next year, you'll get the hang of how things are done around here and *always* have been. So back off."

The hair on the back of Addie's neck stood up so hard it hurt. Had Lacey just given herself away as the person who had sent the gift box with the dead rat in it? She raised her hand, wanting nothing more than to slap the smirk off Lacey's face, but remembered where she was, and that she was an adult, like it or not. She scratched at her tingling neck instead and averted her eyes from the tasteless wonder before her. Her gaze landed on the small car that pulled up in front of the door. She shook her head and let out a deep breath to release her tense jaw. "It looks like Jeanie's here."

"It's about time," Maggie muttered, fluffing her coiffured hair.

"Stop it," said Gloria, her already round cheeks puffing out. "She's had a rough week. I'm surprised she came at all."

"You're right. I wouldn't have blamed her if she hadn't," Ida added.

"Who's that guy driving her car?" Lacey said, standing on tiptoe, peering through the window display.

Addie ducked to see around her. It was the man from the church. "Why, do you know him?"

"I think I do." Lacey leaned forward, knocking over a nautical flag and tipping the pirate ship off its book perch.

Addie shook her head, reset the display, and stretched to see over Lacey. The black-haired man got out of the driver's side and walked around to Jeanie's, where he retrieved two large trays from the back seat, placed them in her outstretched arms, and then produced a third, setting it on top, kissed Jeanie's cheek, and got back in the car.

"Well, Lacey," Addie murmured, "don't keep me in suspense. Who is he?"

Lacey glanced back at her. "He looks like a reporter I worked with in LA." She shook her head. "No, Peter's blond. It couldn't be him. Although I must say, other than the glasses and dark hair, they could be twins." She swept past her and perched in the chair that had earlier been designated for Addie.

Addie's mouth opened, then snapped shut. She glanced back out the window. Jeanie stood at the closed door, struggling with the trays, her car and driver gone. Addie rushed to open the door, took the large covered trays from Jeanie's arms, and placed them on the counter.

Jeanie flopped down on a stool. "Thank you, they were heavier than I thought they'd be." She helped Addie spread the sandwich, fruit, and vegetable platters in a line across the countertop. "We'll probably eat later, so leave the covers on them, if you don't mind."

Addie nodded. "I'm surprised your ride didn't help you bring these in."

She waved off Addie's comment. "Steven had a business meeting this evening and was running late. I guess neither of us realized how awkward these platters would be. But they're here now, so no damage done." She turned her back on Addie, swiveled around on her stool to greet the book club members, and smiled when her gaze came to rest on Lacey. "How nice of you to join us, and Serena, too. I had no idea Mother's book would garner all this interest."

Lacey's pencil-sketched brows rose as she glanced up from her cell phone, smiled unseeing at Jeanie, and returned her focus to her screen. Addie was dying to ask Jeanie about the man who had dropped her off, but knew she had to deal with a more obvious problem at the moment. She walked nonchalantly over and stood behind Lacey's chair, glancing down at the woman's cell phone screen. Lacey snapped it off and looked up over her shoulder. "Can I help you?"

"It's just that I do believe you're sitting in my seat." Addie hoped the Cheshire grin she had learned to master when dealing with Lacey didn't falter now as their eyes locked.

Lacey stood up. The wave of a successful battle won rushed through Addie.

"No problem, my ride's here anyway." Lacey headed toward the door, waving her hand over her shoulder. "It's been a pleasure seeing you all again." She bounced out the door.

An uncomfortable silence gripped the room as all eyes witnessed Lacey hopping into Marc's patrol car. Addie glanced from one startled face to another. Serena's confused expression didn't go unnoticed by her, and she tried to ward off her own pain at Serena's obvious disappointment in Lacey's latest unexpected antics.

"I guess we should get started now." Addie sat in the chair still warm from Lacey's toxic residue. She looked from one hesitant face to the other and picked up her copy of *The Ghosts and Mysteries of Greyborne Harbor* from the table in front of her. "Who would like to begin?" They all opened their books but sat quietly as though they were waiting for Addie to begin a class lesson. She shifted in her chair. "Okay, I'll begin, then." She took a deep breath and flipped to the first page.

For the next hour, discussion centered around June's findings, which led to a debate on how an adjustment to the annual Founder's Day Eve ghost walk tour should include something about the pirate history of the Harbor. It was a unanimous decision that the Smuggler's Den Restaurant might be the perfect place to end the evening tour. They were all certain the restaurant would be more than happy to contribute to the town's event, as it would mean patrons would want to quench their thirst in the bar after an evening of local ghosts and legends.

Dorothy agreed to speak with the Den's manager and take the proposal to the Festival Committee later in the week. Dorothy and Connie had both confirmed that there was indeed a cavern beneath the centuries-old floorboards, although it was still undergoing renovations. Dorothy then promised to ask the manager to consider opening it, at least partially, for the ghost walk finale. Addie fought to contain her enthusiasm for the idea. This was exactly the opportunity she needed to explore what she believed could be the source of the extensive tunnel system shown on the map.

All in all, it was an interesting discussion as it continued around her, but Addie was disappointed that no one had any further information to add about June's research and the original draft that the town council had dismissed. She threw out a reference to the first version, but no one bit, not even Jeanie. Although she had told Addie previously she didn't know anything about the original manuscript, Addie kept hoping the animated conversation about her mother's book and the ghost walk would spark a forgotten memory in Jeanie's mind, but it hadn't. Maybe she really didn't know anything.

Addie studied each of the faces around the table, trying to determine which one of them June may have confided in. She was certain that someone at this table had information about the original work, but for whatever reason, wasn't talking.

There was Dorothy, who had worked as her assistant. Did she know more than she was saying? After all, it had slipped earlier that she and June had been in disagreement over at least one issue, which Addie intended to find more about later. She made a mental note to add Dorothy to the blackboard.

Seated next to her was Ida. Her small eyes darted around the room, which only enhanced her sharp, birdlike features. She had worked for Blain Fielding for over twenty years. Perhaps she'd had access to the manuscript when he was reading it for the town council. Then there was Gloria, the bubbly redheaded travel agent. Addie frowned. She really didn't know much about her or Maggie, the blond-haired real estate agent, who appeared as though this was a camera shoot for the *Million Dollar Listing* television show. She realized that she didn't know much about any of them. She'd have to try to get the inside scoop from Serena and Catherine later.

Something her father had once told her about investigations flooded her mind. *In the law, you wait. You listen, and you watch, and eventually everyone reveals him- or herself.* Her eyes met Jeanie's. She flushed and quickly averted her attention to Serena beside her.

Addie sighed and glanced at the wall clock behind the front desk. It was after eight, and Simon would be here any minute. She stretched out her stiff neck and shoulders and suggested it would be a good time to break for refreshments. The group members eagerly agreed and headed toward the counter. Addie remained in her seat, feigning interest in the book on her lap, and flipped through pages while she surreptitiously watched Jeanie incessantly check her watch. Addie closed the book and stood up. It had been clear to her that although Jeanie was indeed the distraught daughter, there was something else she knew or was hiding, and Addie just happened to have a few unanswered questions, so now was as good a time as any to try to get a few of them answered.

Addie moved toward Jeanie, who was standing at the end of the counter beside Ida. She reached between the two women for a sandwich. "These look so good. It was really thoughtful of you to supply the food, Jeanie. Too bad your companion couldn't have stayed. He doesn't know what he's missing." Addie smiled at her and reached for a napkin.

"As I told you earlier, he had a meeting to attend," Jeanie said without looking at Addie as she plopped a pod into the coffee maker.

"Oh, yes, I remember." Addie positioned herself between the women.

Ida stopped in mid-bite of her sandwich. "Funny, I thought he owned a travel agency in Chicago. What business meeting could he possibly have attended here?" Addie couldn't miss the piercing look Ida shot Jeanie.

"He's a travel agent—how nice." Addie glanced back at Gloria, who was deep in conversation with Catherine at one of the tables. "Does Gloria know him, too?"

"I doubt it." Jeanie's shoulders stiffened.

"I just thought that since they were in the same . . . never mind. What was his name—Peter, wasn't it?"

"Steven," mumbled Ida, pushing the last bit of her cheese and ham sandwich into her mouth. "His name is Steven."

"Right," said Addie. "Peter was Lacey's blond friend from LA, the one she said could be your friend's twin brother."

Jeanie flinched and stiffened.

"I was just wondering," Addie continued, shifting against the counter, "who was the salt-and-pepper-haired man you were speaking with the other day after you left my shop? He could have been Steven's brother, too." Addie met her startled look. "I just ask because it's so weird that three men all look remarkably similar. Does Steven have brothers?"

Ida glanced sideways at Addie.

Jeanie looked at Ida, then at Addie, spun on her heel, and walked toward Catherine. She bent forward and whispered something to Catherine, picked up her coat and purse, and left. Ida's eyes never left Jeanie's back until the door swung closed behind her.

She looked at Addie, grinning. "Well, looks like you struck a nerve."

Addie's mouth dropped open. "What just happened?"

Ida's eyes twinkled. "I've bit my tongue for weeks, waiting to get a shot in at her. Too bad she left. I was ready to jump in and give the knife a good twist."

"I just don't get it. I wasn't prying, just being chatty. Who is Steven, and what did I say that made her leave?"

"She doesn't like to talk about him."

"Why? You'd think she'd want to talk about him. He seems to be an important person in her life."

"He is, and before that, he was an important person in June's life, too."

Addie leaned closer to Ida. "What do you mean?"

"She *stole* her mother's boyfriend," Ida whispered, "and a few of us won't ever forgive her for that. Well, all except Dorothy there." Her head ticked in Dorothy's direction. "They're best friends."

"Who? Jeanie and Dorothy?"

Ida's birdlike head bobbed up and down.

"Really?"

"The whole mess broke June's heart." She wiped crumbs from her mouth, scrunched the napkin into a tight ball, and tossed it on the counter.

Chapter Twenty-Three

Addie finished wiping down the counter and looked at the clock. It was well past nine, and there had been no word from Simon. She stretched her stiff neck and shoulders, thankful the meeting had ended earlier than anticipated. If only she'd had more time to talk to Ida about the bombshell she'd dropped. Jeanie had become involved with her own mother's boyfriend? That revelation just moved Jeanie and the mysterious chameleon of a man, Steven, to the top of her list of suspects. This was something she needed to tell Marc. She pulled her cell out of her pocket, began dialing his cell number, and stopped. Her shoulders sank, and she slipped the phone into her pocket again, ignoring the pain in her heart.

She retrieved her purse and jacket, turned off the lights, and had begun setting the alarm at the back entrance when a pounding noise echoed through the building. Heart beating in her throat, she crept toward the rear entrance door.

"Addie, Addie, are you still in there?" an excited voice shouted from the other side.

"Simon?" She flung the door open, laughing. "I'm afraid you missed the book club, it was—"

He pulled the door open, wrenching it from her grasp, and stepped inside, banging it closed behind him.

"What is it?" She placed her hand on his arm. "You look shaken. What's happened?"

His eyes dropped, and he sucked in a deep breath and shook his head. When he raised his eyes, they held a tortured look that sent instant prickles rushing up Addie's spine. "What's happened?"

"I think I'd better take you directly home."

Her eyes narrowed, and she recoiled. "Why? What's happened?"

"There are people waiting for you." He looked at her, his face taut and pale. "I came to warn you."

"What people? You're not making sense."

"The police. If they're not there now, they will be shortly."

"The police? Why would they be at my house? Oh, God no." Her hand flew up to her gaping mouth "Have I been broken into again?"

He shook his head.

"Then what?" She sank onto a wooden storage crate and stared up at him. "What is it you're not telling me? Is it Serena? Has that witch Lacey—"

"No, it's that . . . it's, well . . ." He sat down beside her and took her hand in his. "I stopped by the police station on my way here to drop some dinner off for Carolyn. She'd forgotten hers at home, and her husband can't leave the kids alone, so . . ." He stroked the back of her hand. "Apparently, an anonymous tip had come in to the station." He took a deep breath. "Someone reported that you are in possession of the shovel believed to have killed June Winslow." He squeezed Addie's trembling fingers. Her mouth dropped. "Marc was in the midst of obtaining a search warrant when I bolted out of there and came directly here to warn you."

Addie couldn't move. She stared at Simon with unseeing eyes. "You're joking, right? Someone's pranking me?" She glanced around the room. "Who is it? Serena? Lacey? I bet it's Lacey." She stood up, her knees wobbling.

He leapt to his feet to steady her. "I'm afraid this is no prank, Addie." His hands gripped her shoulders. "Come on, I'll drive."

Addie gulped and willed her shaking legs to behave, but her knees rebelled and gave way. Simon looped his arm around her shoulders and escorted her into the front seat of his car. Her mind reeled, and her stomach churned. She sat forward in the passenger seat, her head between her knees. Simon stroked her back as she played out the evening in her head, trying to recall who had said and done what. Had she offended someone tonight? This had to be some kind of cruel joke, but there had to be a reason that had forced somebody to make such a claim. Had she gotten too close to the truth with her questions? She flashed over the names written on her blackboard. Was it someone on there who felt threatened? She bit her lip and came up with a mental list of people who would fit into the anonymous tip category. By the time they pulled down her driveway, she had a list to supply Marc with. Surely he would listen to her and see just how ridiculous this all was.

She stepped out into a barrage of blue and red flashing lights. Officers and dogs were scouring the estate grounds. Every light in the house and the garage beamed into the darkness. Her chest constricted. Simon supported her elbow as she marched up the stairs and across the porch and stood frozen in the open doorway. *Just breathe; keep breathing*, she repeated over and over in her mind, but then she spied the splintered doorframe, and indignation at the intrusion unleashed within her as she stepped inside.

"Where is Chief Chandler?" She glowered at a young officer in the foyer. "I want to see him *and* the search warrant immediately."

The young police officer nodded and headed down the corridor to the kitchen.

Addie glanced at Simon, who was standing silently beside

her. His focus appeared to be on the two officers conducting a search of the living room. Her shoulders tensed.

"Miss Greyborne." Marc's voice from the porch behind her cut through the airless foyer.

She spun around, greeted by a set of unyielding, dark eyes. Without ceremony or explanation, he handed her a tri-folded sheet of paper. She reached for it, but her trembling hand gave away the dread building inside her. Simon snatched it from Marc's fingers and scanned it. His eyes met hers, and regret waved across his face. "It—" He cleared his throat. "It seems to be in order."

Marc looked from Addie to Simon, then to Addie again. "Miss Greyborne, the search warrant also includes your vehicle. Where might my officers find it, in order that they may complete the property investigation?"

"It's still at my shop."

He tipped his cap and stood back, waving his arm in a motion for her to lead the way.

"What, no handcuffs?" she sneered sideways at him.

"Not at this point. Provided you cooperate." He escorted her to his patrol car.

"What about my house? I can't leave it unsecured." She looked back at the splintered doorframe. "You know, since you and your men decided to make such a grandiose entrance."

"I'll stay here," Simon called from the porch. "Call me later if you need anything."

She nodded back at him as Marc pushed down on the top of her head, guiding her into the back seat.

He went around and got into the front. Their eyes met as he glanced into the rearview mirror. She glared at him. Nothing was said between them on the drive to her shop. When they arrived, they were met by two officers in another patrol car.

Without a word, Marc reached over the back seat, his

palm open. Addie's lip curled up as she fished around in her purse and plunked her car keys into his outstretched hand. "Stay here" was all he barked before he joined the search team at the rear of her Mini Cooper.

Addie was numb. This couldn't be happening—and why was Marc treating her like a criminal? He knew her better, and this was an obvious setup. Why couldn't he see that, and why was he taking this whole stupid thing so seriously? She leaned forward, trying to see what was happening with her car. Marc returned, started the engine, and without a word, began driving down the alley, then turned on Main Street right into the police station's rear parking lot.

"Now what? Am I under arrest? Do I get booked, thrown in a cell?" She looked up at him as he swung her door open.

He still didn't utter a word as he took her by the arm and led her up the stairs and through the rear door into the station. "Marc, talk to me," she pleaded, but he only swept past the front counter into his office and shut the door.

"Have a seat, Miss Greyborne." He motioned to the chairs, went around behind his desk, and sat, his hands folded on the desktop.

She stood by the door, mouth gaping open. He motioned again. "Sit, please."

She edged her way to the closest chair and slumped into it.

"Thank you." He retrieved a file from his in-basket. "Now, it seems we have a bit of a problem."

"I don't think it's *we* that have a problem," she said with a tick of her head. "I'd say it's *you* that has the problem."

Marc tilted his head, a puzzled look in his eyes.

"I do believe that even with a search warrant, the police can't legally break into someone's home."

He lifted a brow, shuffling some papers on his desk, appearing amused by her statement.

"That's right, isn't it?"

"Not entirely." He chuckled and sat back in his chair. "The truth is according to the law if police have reason to believe that drugs or something else might be hidden on the property. In this case, it was possible evidence in a murder investigation. We only have to knock and announce our presence and then wait for a reasonable amount of time for the occupant to come to the door. Depending on the seriousness of the crime the wait period is generally less than a minute."

"What? You only give people that long to reply. What if it's a big house like mine?"

"We can't take the chance that the person or people inside might try to dispose of the evidence we're searching for before they answer. If we've followed the knock-and-announce rule, we then have the authority make a forced entry."

"You could have at least called and told me what was going on, and then I could have met you there and let you in." Her eyes flashed with outrage.

"What," he said, shaking his head chuckling, "and tip you off so you could get rid of anything you were trying to hide from us?"

"You can't be serious, Marc. This is me. I'm no criminal, and you know that."

He leaned forward, tapping his pen on the folder in front of him. "Actually, Miss Greyborne, I'm beginning to wonder how well I really did know you in the first place."

She jumped to her feet. "You can't be serious?"

"I am taking this very seriously. As one of my officers pointed out, this was a very sleepy town until you arrived, and now . . . well, let's just say it's not what it used to be."

"You can't really think that I . . ."

"Sit down." His lips twitched into a half smile. "Please."

She flopped into her chair and smoothed her clammy

palms on her knees, her mind whirling as she tried to get a grasp on what game was being played out here.

"Look." He leaned forward, resting his elbows on the desk, his eyes meeting hers. "We didn't find anything. Obviously, the lead was false and meant to scare you off and lead us down a different path of investigation. But it does concern me. Someone knows you're investigating, which is exactly what I told you not to do."

"But I haven't been, I promise."

"Nothing?"

"No. Well, aside from asking questions of a few people and keeping track of suspects on my board."

"Then I'm guessing one of those people thought you knew too much and was trying to take our—and by *our*, I mean the police—investigation in another direction so that should you stumble across anything, it would show a lack of credibility on your part and anything you found would be tossed out."

She slouched back in her chair. "I guess the good news is I must be close to discovering something."

He stood up and walked to the window behind the desk. "Too close. I tried to warn you to leave it alone."

"I know, but—"

"No buts, Addie." He spun around. "This is a cold-blooded murderer we're talking about, and now he has his sights on you. What's next?" He leaned his hands on the desk, glaring at her. "Do we have to get Serena or me or *Simon* to identify *your* body?"

She cringed and sank back.

"Seriously, Addie," he said, sitting down in his desk chair, "another thing I asked you was to bring any and all of your findings to me."

"Well . . . things haven't been exactly . . . that close be-tween us recently."

"No." He coughed, clearing his raspy throat. "No, they haven't, and I think that's for the best right now, considering . . ."

"Okay, if that's the way you want it, fine. We'll just keep things professional and both be happier."

He looked down at his notepad. "So, you were about to tell me," he began, looking up and holding her gaze, "what you have discovered that has made someone nervous enough to set up this wild-goose chase."

"I did find out that Dorothy and June, as close as they were, had some disagreements, and June basically fired her from working on the book, from what I can gather."

Marc pursed his lips.

"And that Jeanie's boyfriend was seeing June before her. As Ida said, Jeanie stole him from her. And that Lacey knew someone in LA who looked exactly like him." She edged to the front of her seat. "Except for the hair color. And I've seen him with both black and salt-and-pepper hair, so . . ."

Marc scribbled something in his notebook.

"And no one seems to know where June's original manuscript is, and I think it holds a clue to who the murderer is at least and why they wanted her dead and—"

"Wait, let's go back to this boyfriend of Jeanie's. What else do you know about him?"

In a rush of words, she began. "Only the changing hair color thing, and of course the fact that he was beside us at the restaurant that night and appeared a bit too interested in our conversation, if I say so. And Ida told me he was a travel agent, and Gloria is a travel agent, too, but when I asked Jeanie if they knew each other, she bolted from the meeting. So Gloria might be a lead, too, and Lacey's brother, Dean, because he was one of the only two council members known to have read the original book draft." She paused and took a deep breath.

"Anything else?"

She shook her head. "Wait, yes." She sat upright. "When we were at June's house after the service, I overheard the black-haired man—well, at least I think it was him—quarrelling with Jeanie in the bedroom. Oh, and the weird-smelling tea I found at June's, and the broken teacup."

He studied her, his pen creating a rapid staccato beat on the desk.

"I'd have to look at my board." She shook her head. "I know I'm missing some of the clues." She snapped her fingers. "Tonight Lacey almost admitted to being the one who sent the dead rat. She told me to back off—the exact wording in the note. Don't you think that's too much of a coincidence?"

His mouth pursed. She couldn't help but note that his jaw tensed. "One more question." He started writing in his notepad without looking up at her. "How does the good doctor, Simon Emerson, fit into all this?"

Addie's mouth dropped. "Probably the same way Lacey does."

"I doubt that." He shook his head and continued to write.

Her eyes narrowed as she studied his detached features. It was no good. He'd masked his tell, that thingy he did by tensing his jaw when he was trying to hide his true thoughts and feelings about something. This told her that he wasn't going to say anything else on the subject. She gripped the arms of the chair and stood. "Well, if that's all for tonight, then I'll let myself out." She looked hesitantly at him. He nodded without looking at her. She made her way to the door and glanced over her shoulder. He was still writing. She shrugged and stepped out into the main reception area. The desk sergeant, Carolyn's, eyes lit up when she saw her. She nodded her head toward the waiting room.

"Serena, have you come to bail me out?" she said with a laugh, striding across the room with her arms spread wide to hug her friend. Lacey popped up from the chair behind her and pushed Serena aside, her notebook in hand. Addie froze in mid-motion. "Lacey, what on earth—"

"Do you have a statement for the *Greyborne Harbor Daily News*?"

Addie frowned and shook her head. Serena grabbed her arm and ushered her toward the door.

"Don't you have anything to say about the search warrant issued and your arrest tonight?" Lacey called after her.

Addie spun on her heels, her nostrils flaring. Serena pushed her through the door.

"Chief Chandler. Perhaps you can make a statement about Miss Greyborne's arrest?"

Addie looked back over her shoulder and blinked. Lacey's bleached teeth flashed in the waiting room's fluorescent lighting. She swore she saw fangs and blinked again as Serena shoved her out into the cool night air.

Chapter Twenty-Four

"Why did you do that?" Addie tugged her arm from Serena's clutches.

"To stop another murder from happening, that's why."

"Then why did you bring her to the station with you?"

"I didn't." Serena led her around the side of the building to her older model Jeep Wrangler, parked in the visitors' area. "She just showed up, *after* I was there." She got in and unlocked the side door.

"How did she know about the warrant and me going to the station with Marc?" Addie settled into the passenger's seat.

"I have no idea," Serena said, buckling her seat belt, "but she arrived only minutes before you came out of Marc's office and was purring like a cat with a mouse the whole time she was there."

Addie stared out the side window. "How did you know I was there?"

"Simon called. He said he was on guard duty at your house, told me the whole story, and asked if I could swing by and drive you home when you were done there."

Addie glanced sideways at Serena, waiting for her to mention something snide about Simon calling on her behalf, but her friend focused on the road and said nothing.

Addie relaxed and sat back. "You know, we haven't had many chances to visit lately, since Lacey blew into town and ensnared both you and Marc in her web." She almost spat out the last words. "So why don't we stop somewhere for a quick drink and catch up before we head back?"

Serena shook her head. "Can't. Simon made me promise to bring you straight home. It sounds like he's cooking up a surprise for you."

"As in actual cooking or as in plotting?"

"You know him better than I do," she chuckled. "Speaking of which . . ." Here it was. The confrontation Addie had feared would happen. "He seems like a great guy. You're lucky. Did you know he even had Brian come around tonight and have your front door repaired?"

Addie's eye widened. "No, I didn't." So that was that. No heartache, no accusations from Serena about her stealing *her* love interest—just a genuine, friendly remark. Addie studied Serena as she maneuvered the car up the winding hill toward Addie's house.

"What?" Serena glanced sideways at her.

"It's just that, well, you seem to be taking my spending time with Simon better than I thought you would."

Serena waved her hand. "Forget it. Momentary fleeting crush. And besides, I've met someone."

"What? Who? Tell all."

"Remember that cute waiter from the Grey Gull . . . ?"

"You're kidding?"

"Nope, and he's wonderful," she sighed, pulling into Addie's driveway. "Zach Ludlow. And guess what? He's a descendant of *the* Roger Ludlow who helped establish the Connecticut colony back in the sixteen hundreds. Addie, he's just perfect."

"That's great news. I'm so happy for you. So what's he like? What does he do—you know, besides being one of *the* Ludlows?" She chuckled.

Serena snickered. "He said he's a distant relative from the poorer side of the family, which is why he's working his way through college."

"And?"

"And he's doing his third year of his four years of naturopathic medical school. These last two years are mostly hands-on, practical work, so he's just moved here from his college in Bridgeport, Connecticut, to work at the Essence Wellness Center down in the harbor with Dr. Lee." She squealed and then sighed. "He's kind and gentle, he loves my quirkiness, and he's just . . . just everything I've ever wanted in a man."

As they came to a full stop, Addie reached over and hugged her bubbling friend. "I'm so happy for you."

"And I want you to know," Serena said as she shut off the ignition and unbuckled her seat belt, "I may have fallen into Lacey's web, but tonight I wiggled myself free and am beginning to see what Marc's tried to tell me for years."

Addie reached over and patted her hand. "Welcome back from the dark side," she said, laughing. "Now, what's Marc's excuse? He knows better."

"Who knows?" She hopped out, but then popped her head back in. "You're right. He knows her better than anyone does. I wonder what she has on him."

"Or him on her." Addie scowled and headed for the front door. "Brian did a great job. I'm glad he added the metal door strip and lock plate. That should help deter the police the next time they want to use their battering ram." She opened the door and stepped inside.

The heady scents of garlic and lemon immediately enticed her senses, but most inviting was the comforting aroma of an oven-roasted chicken. "Wow, what has he been up to?" She tossed her purse and jacket on the side table and headed for the kitchen to explore the source of the banging and clattering that echoed through the main floor.

Simon was maneuvering the hot roasting pan from the oven. Her gaze settled on the island top, which was covered with stacks of mixing bowls, measuring cups, and an array of cooking utensils that Addie didn't even know she owned. She stood with her hand on the doorframe, cringing at the sight of his handiwork. Serena joined her and burst out laughing. Simon spun around, and the chicken slid out of the pan and splattered onto the counter.

He hung his head. "At least it didn't land on the floor." He used the lifter forks to place it on the platter. He stood back. "Voilà."

"And to what do I owe the honor of this culinary delight?" Addie smiled, walking over to the counter.

He shrugged. "I was bored and nervous waiting to hear from you. Which, by the way, why didn't you call?"

"I was sort of busy." She dipped her finger in the mashed potato bowl and licked off a clump. "I was hauled off to the police station, remember?"

"So, are you a free woman then?"

"She's very free." Serena winked at Addie and slid onto a stool at the island. "And now I'm not the only jailbird here," she chuckled. Addie nudged her with her shoulder.

"So, what do you need us to do?" Addie looked at the bowls of vegetables, the gravy boat, and the steaming chicken that were spread across the counter. "Everything looks so perfect."

"Thank you." He grinned, his eyes casting an enticing wave over her. A heated rush raced through her, and she felt as if she'd been thoroughly cooked, much like the chicken laying before her. "Nothing. The dining room is set out. You two can go ahead, and I'll bring the food in. Go." He waved his hand in a shooing motion.

"Are you sure we can't help?" Serena glanced at all the dishes to be carried in.

"Positive. Go." He looked at Addie hovering at the side of the island. "Both of you, now, scoot."

Dinner was delightful. Addie sat back, looking at her tablemates, and smiled. It was exciting having Serena back in her life to share her theories with again and to hear Simon's fresh insights from a medical professional's perspective. She relayed some of the points that she'd noted on her blackboard earlier and then told them about her conversation tonight with Dorothy and her thoughts about how Dorothy perhaps was upset about June moving forward without her. Serena confirmed that the two women had been childhood friends but said that as far as she knew, Dorothy had been happy for June's success. Then Addie tossed out the information she had received from Ida about how Dorothy was also good friends with Jeanie and supported her affair with Steven, too. Serena appeared taken aback by that tidbit but didn't say much. Addie went on to share her observations about Jeanie's reaction to her inquiring as to whether Gloria also knew Steven, since they were in the same industry, and how Jeanie abruptly left after that.

"Well, even with hearing all this local town gossip—and most of it is just that, I think—my money is on Lacey." Simon poured them another glass of wine, set the empty bottle down, and leaned forward on his elbows.

Serena stopped in mid-sip. "Really? Why do you think that?"

"Because I don't think the rest of it is consequential; just coincidental. Besides, I think that from what Addie's told us about Lacey's none-too-professional dealings in LA and the family feud that took place, she has the most to gain by murdering a woman who may have known the whereabouts of a pirated fortune. You know, avenging her family name while making a name for herself as an ace reporter." He took a sip and flicked a glance at Addie.

She leaned forward, matching his posture. "But do you really think she'd murder someone? If anything, she wants a story that will propel her back into the spotlight."

He nodded. "True, but perhaps it got out of hand, her trying to set it up and discredit you and the Greyborne name, and, well—"

"I've known her my whole life," said Serena. "I don't think she'd kill anyone. Although I wouldn't put it past her to be the anonymous tip caller."

"I agree." Simon raised his glass in a toast.

Addie sat back, tapping her fingers on the table. "She seems desperate and scared. Maybe Simon is onto something. It's worth considering, anyway."

"No." Serena fidgeted with her napkin. "She can be devious when she wants something, like how she hired Paige to work in my shop without even telling me about it, but—"

"She did what?" Addie's elbow sipped off the edge of the table.

Serena's freckles popped out as her face paled. "You didn't know." She looked down at her empty plate.

"No. So that's what was bothering Paige today." She shook her head. "I wonder when she was planning on telling me she was quitting."

"As far as I know, which isn't much these days. Since it seems *Lacey* has made herself the controlling partner of *my* tea shop." Serena leaned forward on her elbows. "My understanding is that Paige told her that she'd work for *her* only during our *newly* scheduled seven a.m. early opening time—Lacey's idea, not mine—to help out with the before-work rush and during her lunch break from your shop and that's it."

Simon cleared his throat. "As I was saying. My money is still on Lacey."

Addie bit her lip and looked at him. Her brow furrowed, and then she looked at Serena. "Tell me about her brother Dean."

"Her brother? What does he have to do with anything?"

"Well, I found out tonight that aside from the chairman of the town council, Dean was the only other person known to have read June's original manuscript, and I'm just curious, I guess."

"There's not much to say about him." Serena sat back. "He's a few years older than her, not too bright as far as I'm concerned, always looking for a get-rich-quick scheme. He worked at Fielding's Department Store for a while, or was more like their errand boy, and then he went out to live with Lacey last year in LA with high hopes of becoming a famous actor, but never even got an audition. When he came back, I heard someone loaned him some money, and he set up a small charter boat company." She took a sip of her wine. "There's nothing remarkable about him. He's the kind of person that's always chasing the dream or after those he thinks can lead him to it. But I really never knew him well." She shrugged. "I think he just considered me as one of the little girls who used to tag along after Lacey."

"What are you thinking, Addie?" Simon asked.

"Just wondering." She looked at Serena. "Did Lacey mention if her brother ever met Lacey's friend Peter when he was out there?"

"No, I don't think so." She shrugged. "Is it important?"

"Maybe."

"I can ask her, then."

"Please, but discreetly."

"Okay." Serena stood and began to clear the table. "Not sure what you're thinking with that. She's never mentioned anyone named Peter to me, so I don't think he would have been important to her."

"It's just a name she brought up tonight." Addie handed her plate to Serena. "And that on top of hearing she has a brother and he's spent time out on the West Coast and him being one of the only two people who read June's first draft, well . . ." She frowned. "Was his trip to the West Coast after he was on the town council?"

"Yes, I think it was. It was kind of sudden, too. He just up and left one day. He's only been back a couple of months. Do you think he's involved somehow?"

Addie shook her head. "I'm thinking out loud. Just ignore me. I'm still trying to put puzzle pieces together, and I'm tired, so maybe they're getting all jumbled up in my head."

"Well, I think you might be onto something with your suspicions as far as Lacey is concerned, at least." Simon rose and began removing serving dishes from the table. "I think this Lacey person sounds like a prime suspect."

"Simon, was the detail about the shovel being a suspected murder weapon ever released to the public?"

"No, I don't think it was, because although the blow to the head with the shovel probably caused the fall, it was the fall that actually killed her. Why?"

"Because . . . whoever called in the anonymous tip to the police knew about the suggestion of a shovel. How?"

"You're right." Serena almost dropped the chicken platter. "Who would have known about the autopsy report?"

Addie sat back, toying with her wineglass. "I wonder," she said slowly, her eyes set on the red liquid she was swirling around in her crystal goblet.

Chapter Twenty-Five

With the dinner dishes done and put away, and with no trace of Simon's gallant cooking event left in sight, Addie walked her zombielike guests to the front door. When they'd left, she collapsed against it. She rubbed the pounding spot at the base of her skull and glanced at the mantel clock over the fireplace in the living room. Past two a.m. No wonder she was exhausted and her head was spinning. She locked the door, set the alarm, and dragged her reluctant legs up the stairs toward her bed. Her foot hovered over the top step. She sighed, glancing woefully at her bedroom door as she passed by it, her focus now on the doorway at the end of the corridor.

She opened the door leading to the attic staircase and flipped on the light switch at the bottom. Her legs rebelled, but she pushed on and stood breathless at the top. She scoured her hands over her face and shook her head. What was she thinking? But something that Dorothy had said at the meeting nagged at her, and she knew she wouldn't be able to sleep until she had a quick look.

Addie skirted around stacks of books, wooden crates, and cardboard boxes that still screamed out for her attention. They were a reminder of how she'd felt that day when she first discovered this treasure trove of her great-aunt's possessions, but tonight her mind was focused only on the small door across the main attic room. This back room had been neglected in her previous attic adventures because she'd been overwhelmed by the sheer volume of sorting in the outer rooms. However, this evening when Dorothy mentioned June having worked up here, she had vaguely recalled seeing a small writing desk on that first day of exploration. Tonight, it wouldn't take long to confirm her suspicions as that being June's work space, and besides, maybe she'd get lucky and find the original manuscript in there.

Trace scents of dusty, stale air combined with aged leather nipped at her nose. With her hand, she explored the wall beside her for a light switch. Success. The small room filled with a glowing yellow hue, and there by the window was the ornately carved secretary's desk. On it was the very thing she had come to find.

She crossed the uncluttered room, heading directly for the bundle of handwritten and typed notepapers on the desktop, and glanced through them. From what she could tell through her overtired mind, they were some of June's notes for the first draft. Disheartened at not finding the completed manuscript, she scooped them up in her arms and then noticed the shelf-lined walls filled with aged leather-bound books. She made a mental note to investigate further on another day and headed for her bedroom.

Addie sat cross-legged on her bed, the notes in her lap. She searched through them, jotting down her own notes and separating pages she felt held vital clues as to what may have been in her original book. She squinted at the blurring text in front of her and rubbed her stinging eyes, but her determination increased with each page read. Marc had completely rejected her theory about a tunnel system underneath the town. He also had continued to remind her that *he* was the cop, not her, and to stay out of any future investigations unless invited. She would rise to his challenge. He'd left her with no alternative but to continue the search. No, she wasn't a cop, but *she* was the researcher, and she'd prove him wrong. If she happened to solve a mystery, or even a murder, at the same time, so be it.

Addie swept her hand at the buzzing sound in her ear, but it continued to torment her. She cracked one eye open, and shot upright, sending the notepapers scattered over her fluttering to the floor. The incessant buzzing persisted. She scanned the room, looking for its source. Her cell phone on the bedside table rang, and she jumped, fumbling it like a wet football before she managed to save it from clattering onto the hardwood floor.

"Hello . . . Simon? . . . Why, where are you? . . . At my front door . . . really? . . . Okay, I'll be right down."

She clicked off the call and stumbled half-awake down the stairs, aware the relentless buzzing noise had stopped. She shook her dull head. Of course—it had been the old-fashioned doorbell. She couldn't remember having heard it before, as most of her unexpected guests usually just broke in. She opened the door and stifled a yawn as a beaming-faced man swept past her into the foyer, carrying two cups of steaming brew. She snatched one of the cups from Simon's hand as he passed, took a sip, sighed, and smiled with satisfaction.

"Glad I caught you before you headed to your store. Paige told me you might still be here."

She squinted at him. "What on earth are you doing here at this time of day, and why is she at the store so early?"

"Early? It's past ten."

"What!" Addie scrubbed her hands over her face. "Not again," she moaned. "But I knew there was a reason why I hired Paige."

"Why? Because she's reliable, conscientious, a pure delight, a darn good salesperson, and loyal?"

"Yeah, everything I'm not apparently."

He ruffled her hair. "Don't beat yourself up, by the look of that rat's nest you're sporting on your head today. It looks like the bear you wrested last night already tried that," he said, laughing, and made himself comfortable on the sofa, in her spot. He scanned her from head to toe. "Please tell me why you're still wearing yesterday's clothes and looking like . . . well . . . how you do this morning? I'm thinking this might be a great story." His eyes flashed with amusement.

She ran her hand through her hair tangles and winced, but said nothing.

"Did you have company after we left?" He sipped his coffee, watching her over the rim of the cup.

Her face flushed. "No, I did not, and if I did, it would be none of your business, would it? Is that why you're here? Are you spying on me?"

He laughed and set his cup on the coffee table. "No, I have a few things to show you." He pulled some booklets and brochures from his jacket pocket and set them on the table beside his cup.

She crossed her arms and peered at them from the living room door. "What are those?"

"You'll have to come over here and see, won't you?" He sat back, a smug look on his face.

She huffed and walked to the table and picked up the top booklet. She turned it over in her hand and looked blankly at him. "What is this?"

"I have to admit that when you first told me your ideas, I was skeptical. Don't get me wrong, I love a good conspiracy theory as much as the next person, but hidden tunnels and pirate treasure all leading to the murder of a sweet librarian?" He grimaced. "Well, it seemed way too out there. Then, let's just say that after hearing the whole story last night over dinner, my curiosity was piqued, and I decided to make a stop at the Greyborne Harbor Lighthouse Museum first thing this

morning, and"—he waved his hand over the booklets—
"now, I'm intrigued."

"Well, I'm glad to hear that I finally got your attention."
She chuckled and picked up the rest of the booklets from
the table.

"You got my attention a long time ago." He winked.

Her cheeks grew hot, any witty comeback that should
have come to mind caught in her tight throat. Instead, she
studied the booklet in her hand.

"But seriously," he said, rising to his feet, "the reason I
came by was because I have a one o'clock meeting at the
DA's office in Salem this afternoon."

"Thanks for telling me, I guess." She cursed the blush
she couldn't suppress. It wouldn't be so bad, but it left her
blotchy. If only she were a pretty blusher, she thought rue-
fully as his lips spread into a tantalizing grin.

"I guess what I'm trying to say is, do you want to come
with me?"

"Why would I do that?"

"Because," he said, placing his hands on her shoulders,
"a couple of the best museums of pirate history in New
England are apparently located there."

"Oh, I see. So, you stop in at the museum here in town
and now you're suddenly an expert?"

"No, but it was the manager at the one here who told
me that."

"I wonder if that's the one Dorothy was taking about.
You know . . . I might just go with you. Just let me text Paige
and tell her I won't be in today." She pulled her phone
from her pocket, her fingers clicking across the keyboard.
She kept her eyes on the screen, waiting for a reply, aware
that he was watching her every move. "Okay, done." She
slipped the phone back into her pocket. "Come up to my
bedroom with me for a minute." She turned and headed for

the staircase, looking back at him from the bottom step. "Well, are you coming?"

He made his way to the stairs. "All right, if you insist, then, but just so you know," he said, his twinkling eyes capturing hers, "it usually takes a bit longer than a minute."

"No, not that." She swatted at him. "I have something to show you that I found in the attic last night after you guys left."

His face dropped, and she shook her head.

She led him to her bedroom. He hovered at the door.

"Come in—nothing in here will bite you."

"Well, that's disappointing." The corners of his mouth turned up in a faint smile.

"Men." She rolled her eyes, then pointed to the note-papers and bent down to retrieve those that had drifted to the floor. "These are June's earlier notes, preceding even the ones that Jeanie gave me that were stolen from my shop."

Simon took a pile of them from her hands. "What did you find out?" He glanced through them. "Any clues to a treasure or a possible murder suspect?"

"Not so far, but I have learned a lot of the early history of Greyborne Harbor that I wasn't aware of. Quite fascinating, actually." She sat down on the edge of the bed.

He sat beside her, scanning one of the pages in his hand. "This one talks about somebody named Gerald Greyborne?"

"Yes, he was my great-great-great-something grandfather, a merchant sea captain credited for starting the actual town of Greyborne Harbor."

"So he was the first person to settle here?" He looked back at the page.

"No, not the first, from what I could gather. When he brought his ship into our cove as a refuge from a hurricane, there were already a number of other ships here. You know, pirate ships and merchant ships. Apparently, this harbor had been used for over two hundred years before that as a safe haven from the Atlantic hurricanes and storms *and* the British navy patrol ships."

"Then how did it become known as Greyborne Harbor? Why not Smuggler's Cove or something?"

"Good point. I guess because he was the first to take it from a pirate and privateer haven and make it an actual town."

"Sounds intriguing and dangerous."

"Yes, it would have been in those early days. I find it interesting, as it seems Gerald saw potential here to start a legitimate business, gave up his days as a seafaring merchant, set up shop as a trader, and opened a mercantile store. It said on this page, I think"—she pointed to one on Simon's lap—"that there was always an abundance of sailors seeking refuge in the cove. Either they were here because it was off the British navy's radar, which was why the pirates frequented it, or because of a storm haven. They all needed supplies, and because of his shipping business, he had contacts in Boston, Salem, and along most of the East Coast, so he saw it as an untapped gold mine."

"So he wasn't the first settler, so to speak."

"No, not really, but he was the first to build a permanent home here."

"This house?"

"No, he built a small house on this site away from the squalor below, something more suitable for his wife and children back in England to move into. This house eventually replaced the original one as the family trading business flourished."

"Yeah, I can understand why he chose to build up here." Simon read the pages in front of him. "Pirates had a reputation for living a rough life, and if the harbor was teeming with sailors and pirates, it was probably not the place for a British merchant's wife and children."

"Definitely not, if all the stories are even half-true,"

she chuckled. "It sounds like it wasn't long after he made the move up here and brought his family over that other merchants from the docks followed, like Henry Davenport. Who worked with the pirates but had tried to pass himself off as a regular merchant by opening an ale house in the dock area."

"So that made your ancestor the first permanent resident of the Harbor, giving it the name. Amazing. I love digging into the past. I sometimes wonder if I should have been an archaeologist instead of a doctor."

Addie stretched her legs and looked at the bedside clock. "What time is your meeting again?"

Simon stood up and stacked the papers on the bedside table. "It's at one, so you'd better jump in the shower and get dressed . . . or at least maybe change clothes . . . so we have time to stop for lunch first."

"Okay." She grabbed her robe and headed to the bathroom. "Go ahead and make a coffee if you want one. I won't be long."

She bounced into the living room, freshly showered and wearing what she hoped was appropriate for spending an afternoon searching the archives of a small pirate museum. Simon took one look at her pink body-hugging V-neck tunic sweater and slim-fitting cropped jeans. The look in his eyes told her he approved of her fashion choice. It dawned on her that this was the first time he'd seen her out of her work attire, which usually consisted of a tunic blouse, boyfriend jacket, and slim-fit slacks that didn't hug her curves to this extent.

"Just let me text Paige and make sure all's well on the store front, and then we can be off." She pulled her cell out of her hobo-style handbag.

Simon settled back onto the sofa and flipped through the

Lighthouse Museum booklets and brochures. Addie watched him out of the corner of her eye as she messaged Paige and waited for her reply. When it came back, the color drained from her face, and she sat down on the arm of the sofa. Her heart pounded in her throat, and her eyes burned with the tears she fought back.

He looked up at her, his brow cocked. "You look worried. Is everything okay?"

She took a deep breath. "Well, as okay as it can be when no customers have been in yet."

He placed his hand on her knee and gave it a pat. "I'm sorry to hear that, but it's going to get better, don't worry."

"I doubt it." She snapped off her phone and shoved it into her jeans pocket. "At least not until the real killer is caught, because *apparently* there were more accusations made against me in Miss Newsy's column this morning."

"Oh, no." His face crumbled. "What was it this time?"

"The search warrant and me being taken into the police station, of course." She jumped up and walked toward the window. The early-morning fog had burned off, leaving the land to the sun's ownership. If only the fog in her life would vanish. For good. "She asked readers why the police would bother to issue one if they didn't suspect a fire to be burning where they'd found the smoke, or something just as ridiculous." Addie all but spat out her words.

"I guess you're not up for an adventure today, then?"

She straightened her shoulders, tilted her chin up, and turned on her heel. "Nope, it's just what I need—a reprieve from all that. And it gives me even more motivation to figure this whole mess out." She grabbed her bag and headed for the door. "Well, come on. We don't have all day."

Chapter Twenty-Six

Addie stretched out her long legs and marveled at the interior features of Simon's Telsa Roadster. The leather seat cradled her body like a custom-made glove. She snuggled in and looked forward to the thirty-minute drive to Salem as he guided the car effortlessly along the twists and turns of the coastal highway. She understood now why he had been tempted into such a luxury purchase.

She glanced down at her lap, where she still had the brochures that Simon had picked up from the Greyborne Harbor Lighthouse Museum, and began perusing them. Her heart raced. "Did you know that Dixie Bull was one of the first known New England pirates?" She jabbed a finger at the pamphlet. "It says here that in 1623, he started plundering trading vessels and attacking trading posts all along the New England coast, and then in 1633, he just disappeared, never to be heard from again."

Her eyes widened. Each brochure she held talked about the waters from off of Boston's North Shore all the way to Canada as being a favorite area for numerous pirates to roam. Better yet, they all hinted that since many of them were originally New Englanders and New Yorkers, they had buried the treasures they'd acquired, up and down the North East Coast, and it was still waiting to be dug up.

"Just think," she sighed wistfully, resting her forehead on the cool side window and looking out at the rugged coastline below them, "pirates like Dixie Bull, Black Sam Bellamy, Ned Low, William Kidd, and Jack Quelch used to roam these very waters."

"You're forgetting the most notorious of all."

"Who's that?"

"Blackbeard."

She laughed and looked down at the museum folder. "Yes, he was about as bad as they came. Did you know that in 1691, he buried a bunch of silver bars off of Portsmouth, New Hampshire, that've never been found?"

"I bet that you're thinking he wasn't the only one." Simon glanced sideways at her and laughed.

"Well, it is logical. They were wanted men, for the most part, unless they were registered as privateers for the British, and to be caught with a hold full of looted treasure would have meant death. Maybe Dixie Bull had stashes somewhere and that's what he retired on—you know, withdrawals from his cave bank accounts."

"I guess anything is possible."

"Yes, it is. And don't forget about Thomas Veal. It was mentioned in one of these that he stashed fortunes in more than one spot along this coast."

"I'm thinking you have a bit of treasure hunters' fever."

"Lord knows there are enough coves and caves. It must have made the pirates downright giddy," she said, her eyes following a small sailing craft dancing with the wind on the waters below.

When they arrived in Salem, Simon's adept driving skills came in handy as he maneuvered through the narrow streets with ease and grace. Addie's gape flitted from one attraction to the next as she tried to take in all the sites of the historical buildings and the Essex Street Pedestrian Mall. "Look, it's the Witch History Museum," she squealed, grinning.

"It's too bad I have to work this evening. Otherwise, we could do some sightseeing later. Maybe we'll have to come back another day." Simon smiled at her as he slipped neatly into a street-side parking spot.

"Or two." Addie wriggled in her seat and then stopped. "I didn't mean to imply an overnighter." She felt her cheeks burning.

Simon chuckled as he turned off the ignition. "A guy can always hope, but don't worry. I know what you meant. There's a lot to do here, and one day . . . or two days"—a slight smile pulled at the corner of his lip—"we'll explore it together. But first we just have enough time to eat before my appointment."

Lunch passed too quickly for Addie. She devoured her delicious meal while chatting aimlessly with Simon. Her attention focused on the decor and quaintness of the small, red, First Period–styled building of the restaurant. All too soon, it was over, and they were back in the car, making their way through the busy tourist traffic to one of the pirate museums.

"There's no parking spaces along here, so I'll drop you off out in front." Simon pulled over. "I'll pick you up somewhere out here. Hopefully, I'll be able to find a parking spot by then."

"No problem. I'll watch for you." Addie slipped open the door and stepped out.

"I shouldn't be much more than an hour. That should give you plenty of time; if not, I'll wait in the car. It'll give me a few minutes to catch up on some emails from the hospital, so don't rush because of me." Simon waved as he pulled back out into traffic.

Addie dashed to the sidewalk and hopped up on the curb, noting that the hem of her jeans had crawled up her calf. She stumbled forward, dancing on one foot as she tried to straighten it, and smacked right into a pair of navy blue trousers. She looked up. "Marc?"

"Addie? What are you doing here?"

"I could ask you the same."

"I'm following a lead, and you?"

"Me, too."

"I can see that. So that means you still haven't taken my advice on not investigating by yourself?"

"I don't think coming to a museum is placing me or anyone else in any jeopardy."

"Tell me, just what lead is it you're following?"

"You first." She crossed her arms. "I thought you said my theory of pirate treasures and hidden tunnels was just that . . . a theory and there couldn't possibly be any merit in it."

"Well, I still do, but let's just say I am still a little boy at heart, and I did find the prospect exciting, so I dropped into the Greyborne Harbor Lighthouse Museum first thing this morning to get some information there. They gave me what they could but then steered me here because it's more extensive."

"Oh." She studied his unusually reserved face—not even a tense jaw. He was getting good.

"Funny thing though. At the museum, they informed me I was the second person this morning to be asking the same questions." It was then that his jaw twitched, and she relaxed. He was still the same old Marc.

"Really? What a coincidence."

"Yes, it is, isn't it? So I naturally thought of you," he said, his dark brown eyes softening, "and asked the attendant if it was a young woman about five nine or ten, longish past-the-shoulder golden-brown hair with big, round, hazel-green eyes, that sometimes flashed in the sunlight with flecks of gold." His eyes held hers, and for a fleeting moment she saw in them what she used to see when he was going to kiss her, but then it vanished. "Imagine my surprise when the manager there told me no, it was a tall man, black wavy hair, squared jaw, clean shaven, looked to be a professional or something."

Her eyes darted down at the sidewalk, kicking a pebble with her toe.

"So you've enlisted the assistance of the good doctor now in your amateur sleuthing? Don't deny it. I saw you get out of his car."

Addie straightened her shoulders and met Marc's darkening gaze.

He tipped his cap. "Enjoy the rest of your day, Miss Greyborne." He turned and walked away.

Addie's heart lurched. She fought the urge to run after him. Why did this man have such an effect on her? It had hit her the day she'd met him, and then again the first time he'd kissed her. What was it that brought out emotions in her that she hadn't thought she'd ever be able to feel again? She straightened her back and lifted her head. Obviously none of that mattered now. She had done what she had, and as she just witnessed, he wouldn't ever be able to forgive her for it. She'd been right when she had told Serena she wasn't ready. The ghost of David was still too fresh in her mind.

She took a deep breath and turned sharply on her heel. "Oops, I'm sorry," she said, sidestepping a figure blocking her path. She snickered and glanced around for witnesses when she realized it was a life-sized pirate statue welcoming her to the museum. Still giggling, Addie nodded her head at the statue as she entered the museum. Her breath caught at the back of her throat. It was more than she'd hoped for, and she fumbled through her handbag for her wallet to pay the admission price. The place was packed with eager pirate enthusiasts. She'd had no idea that so many people still wanted to glean a glimpse of the romanticized notion of piracy.

She browsed through the displays, reading plaques, peering in at life-sized sets designed to show the spirit of life aboard a pirate's sailing ship, street scenes, local taverns, and even a gallows diorama, which showed what many of them saw on their final days. It was all fascinating, but it wasn't what she'd hoped to find after all. There were numerous displays of artifacts, swords, knives, flags of the various pirate captains, though, and reproductions of those were sold in the gift shop for tourists.

She approached the souvenir counter and purchased a small flag of pirate Captain Edward Teach—aka Blackbeard. It displayed a horned devil skeleton with a spear stabbing at a red heart. She smiled, thinking it would make a wonderful addition to her display window of June's book. She then asked the clerk if she might speak with the manager. She quickly assured him that it was only to make an inquiry about a common friend. He nodded and headed into a back room. Moments later, he reappeared with a tall, well-endowed woman, her silver hair pulled into a topknot. A flowing pirate shirt did little to mask her ample form.

"Hi, my name is Addison Greyborne."

The woman took her outstretched hand and squeezed it tightly. "You are?"

Addie flinched and nodded.

"I've heard so much about you." The woman vigorously continued shaking her hand.

"You have?" Addie's eyes widened.

"Yes, please come into my office. I can't believe my luck. I've been wanting to get in touch with you, but—"

"I don't understand." Addie followed the woman into the back and took the seat that she gestured toward.

"The book, of course." The woman gave a gap-toothed smile.

Addie frowned.

"Your aunt's?"

"I still don't understand."

"The key research source for June's book?" The woman tilted her head slightly. "*A General History of the Robberies and Murders of the Most Notorious Pyrates* by Captain Charles Johnson, published in 1724? It doesn't ring a bell?"

"Afraid not."

The woman slumped into a chair on the far side of a cluttered desk. "I guess I shouldn't have gotten my hopes up about that being why you were here."

"I'm sorry. Who are you? Did you know June and my aunt?"

The woman's mouth puckered, and then she burst into laughter.

Addie squirmed in her seat. Was this woman mad? She couldn't tell and eyed her distance from the door, trying to judge how many steps it would take her to make a dash for it.

"I'm so sorry. You must think I'm a lunatic," the woman sputtered between chortles of laughter. "I'm Hanna Wall, direct descendant of Rachel Wall, the only known woman pirate of New England." She puffed out her ample chest and tipped her hand in a salute.

Addie inched off the front of her chair and sat back, sucking in a sigh of relief. "It's nice to meet you, Hanna." She smiled at the woman. It wasn't hard to imagine her as a swashbuckling pirate herself. "So, you knew June Winslow and my aunt?"

"I knew June. She used to come in here a lot when she first started writing her book. Then after she discovered that book of your aunt's, plus a few others that were in her attic, she said that was the missing information she needed and stopped coming around so often."

"Did she mention what this information was, by chance?"

Hanna shook her head. "Only that the one book was worth its weight in gold to her." She leaned forward. "I did ask her to please inquire if your aunt would be willing to sell it to the museum here."

"What did she say?"

"I never heard back from her, so I assumed the answer was no. Then when you introduced yourself, I thought you were here to make a deal for it."

Addie glanced at the wall clock behind Hanna and jumped to her feet. "I really hate to leave without having a full tour, but my ride will be waiting. I'll take a look for that book, and if it's not a first edition, perhaps we can work something out, but if it is, I'm afraid the only place it will be going is to the Boston Public Library."

"I understand. Didn't figure I'd get too lucky with it, but I hoped." She shrugged and walked her to the front entrance. "Are you sure you can't stay longer? Maybe your ride could join you for a personalized, behind-the-scenes tour."

"I wish we could stay for that, but my friend works at the hospital, and he has to get back." Addie pressed her hands around Hanna's. "But thanks so much for the offer and we'll definitely take you up on it soon."

"Come back anytime." Hanna waved.

Addie waved back and stepped out onto the sidewalk. She winked at the pirate statue and walked toward Simon's car, which was parked halfway up the road. She pulled the door open and settled in as he started the ignition.

"Was the tour good? Did you get what you came for?" He checked for traffic over his shoulder and pulled out onto the road.

"No, not really. It was interesting, but I didn't have time for a full tour."

"I told you I'd wait. You should have stayed."

"It's okay. I'll make another trip soon so I can pick her brain more and maybe stop in at the other pirate museum. I did buy this though." She pulled the flag from her handbag, waving it in front of her face.

Simon glanced sideways at it and groaned

"I thought it would make my window display pop. It's so fitting for June's book and Founder's Day." She giggled and tucked it back into her purse. "But it was something the manager, Hanna, said that made me want to rush home."

"What was that? Did she tell you where to look for a pirate's treasure?" he snorted, stifling a laugh.

"No, it was a book that held the key to June's research."

"What book?"

"A book Dorothy mentioned, too, and apparently it might lie up in my attic somewhere—but who knows where. At least I have the title of it now." She laid back against the seat and groaned. "I guess I have another attic adventure to look forward to tonight."

"If you want some company, I'm not working tonight, so just let me know."

Addie smiled and studied Simon's chiseled profile. His eyes were set on the road in front of him as he weaved expertly in and out of traffic. Was he a friend or a suitor? She wasn't sure, but aside from a few jokes, he never acted like he wanted more from her than they had, or even asked her about Marc. Besides, she enjoyed his company, so maybe she'd keep him around. "Deal," she chuckled. "By the way, how did your meeting go?"

"Good. The DA just had some employment papers for me to sign and a few questions about June's murder." He pulled onto the highway toward Greyborne Harbor. "Say, does the name Jeff Wilson mean anything to you?"

"No, I don't think so. Why, is the DA following a lead there?"

"He is the DA, and he asked me if I'd met you yet."

"Me? Why?" She sat upright.

"That's what I wondered, so I played it cool and said I had and that I'd been in your shop a few times and asked him why."

"Did he say anything?"

"Nope. He only nodded his head."

"That's curious." Addie stared out the window. "I wonder how he knows my name."

"Well, from what I understand, you were pretty instrumental in solving the last murders in Greyborne Harbor. Maybe he wants to hire you as a consulting detective for his office."

"I doubt that. He probably wants to tell me to keep my nose out of police business."

Chapter Twenty-Seven

Simon parked in front of Beyond the Page, and Addie hopped out to check how Paige's day had gone. A rosy-cheeked girl stood behind the counter, elbow-deep in paperwork. A wide smile lit up her face at the sight of Addie.

"Looks like you survived another day without me." Addie scanned the papers spilling around Paige.

"It was a great day, actually. Busier than it's been in a while."

"Wonderful." Addie sat on a stool across from her and picked up a folder. "These are inventory balances?"

"Yeah, the historical fiction section is running a little lean after today. It seems everyone is getting into the Founder's Day spirit. The front display window is *now* also bare."

"Speaking of the display window, look what I found to add to it." Addie grinned, pulling the pirate flag from her bag and waving it.

Paige clapped her hands, squealing with delight. "Perfect."

"I thought so, too." Addie crinkled her nose and placed the flag on the counter. "Now, we just have to find some books to showcase along with it."

"I was just starting to cross reference the books in other

sections to see if they'd fit into the historical fiction category, and since June's book has sold out, I ordered more from the publisher in Boston. They'll be here tomorrow, so we can display those."

"It's only, too bad it took her death to rekindle such high interest in her book."

"Yeah, and that's what most people were interested in today or anything to do with the Revolutionary War *and* pirates, inspired of course by her book. This appears to have ignited a whole lot of pirate treasure enthusiasts. Go look—the historical aisles are almost empty."

"Then it's a good thing that I already had an evening of digging through the attic planned for tonight." Addie chuckled. "Maybe I'll get lucky and find some. Although I don't know if my aunt was a big collector of Revolutionary War novels, but who knows? Stranger things have been found up there. Since our inventory is so low, I guess I'd better get an early start on my search." Addie paused with her hand on the door handle, and she glanced over her shoulder at Paige, who had gone back to scanning the inventory lists. "Did you break for lunch today?"

"I did." She smiled. "I ran to the deli on Main Street, then came straight back. Can you believe that in those ten minutes, four people were already waiting outside?"

"Really, only ten minutes? So, you had no . . . other errands at noon, then?"

Paige shook her head and glanced down at the papers in her hand.

"Did you manage to open on time, too?"

Paige looked up, her cheeks flushed. "There's nothing to worry about, Addie. I love working here and don't plan on going anywhere else." A slight smile tugged at the corners of her lips. "Anything else *was* an extremely temporary whim."

Addie breathed a huge sigh and smiled. "Good. See you in the morning—and by the way, you're doing a great job.

Keep it up." She waved over her shoulder and headed for Simon's car, but when she heard familiar laughter behind her, she stopped short and turned. Lacey and Serena were coming out of SerenaTEA, their arms linked, giggling like a couple of schoolchildren. Heat crept up Addie's neck. So much for Serena escaping the dark side. She attempted an evasive dive into the front seat of Simon's car, but smacked her head on the upper doorframe and dropped to her knees.

Simon grabbed for her across the car. "Are you okay?" He reached for his door handle and started to get out.

"No, stay put; the less attention the better. Just give me a second."

"Oh no," Serena shrieked. "Addie, are you all right?" She rushed over and helped her to her feet. "Let me see that bump."

"I don't need your help." Addie brushed her away. "I'm fine, really." Addie set steely eyes on her, and Serena's face crumbled. A slight jerk of Serena's head made Addie stop and search her friend's expression.

"No, let me have a closer look. I insist." Serena grasped Addie's head, drawing it toward her, and whispered, "I'm on recon, remember?"

Addie withdrew and rubbed the growing goose egg on her forehead and gave her a return twitch of acknowledgment. "I must have stumbled over the curb."

Lacey's lips crooked into a half smile. "I see," she cooed. "I guess that's your story, and you're sticking to it—as usual, these days." Her icy eyes held steadfast on Addie like a cat about to strike.

Addie's blood cooled at the venomous tone dripping from her voice. "And what does that mean?" She crossed her arms, ignoring the pounding in her head.

Lacey matched Addie's pose. "You know it's a lie, just like all the lies you've told about June's disappearance and death. I'm a reporter, remember?"

Addie sucked in a quiet, deep breath, counted to ten, and squelched the urge to wring Lacey's giraffe-like neck.

"I'd say it was more like you were trying to avoid us. What's the matter? Jealous about Serena's friendship with her *soon*-to-be sister-in-law?" Lacey traced a poison-apple-red fingernail over her bottom lip, her calculating stare on Addie unwavering. Addie lifted her head high and met the frigid windows into Lacey's soul.

Lacey's lips slithered into a grin, and she glanced at Addie's storefront window. "I see your meager window display is decimated. I guess there's just no getting good help these days, is there? You know, someone *competent* who can look after things while you're off running up and down the coast playing cops and robbers."

"Lacey, enough." Serena glared at her. "What's gotten into you? Addie's just hurt herself, and you're babbling on about who knows what."

"It's okay, Serena." Addie returned her own frosty stare on Lacey. "I would suspect nothing less from her." She caught sight of Paige standing in the shop window. "She's referring to my staff member who she tried to steal out from under me, but who has shown more loyalty and respect for me than Lacey thought she would, and that's made your"—she fought to spit out her next words—"*soon*-to-be sister-in-law here resort to character assassination."

Lacey sucked in a sharp breath and sputtered something incoherent. It was the first time Addie had ever seen her speechless.

"Is that true, Lacey?" Serena stared at her. "Are you being this way because Paige said she wouldn't work for *you*?"

"Certainly not." Lacey glared at Addie. "She knows what I'm talking about." She wagged her finger in Addie's face. "You may have Marc and the DA's office fooled, but not me or Miss Newsy. One of us will get to the bottom of this. Consider yourself warned."

Addie's mouth dropped. "The DA? What on earth are you talking about?"

"Don't play innocent with me. I overheard Marc on the phone."

Addie's eyes widened.

"I think we'd better go." Serena grabbed Lacey's arm and then looked back at Addie. "Are you sure you're okay?"

"I'm fine." Addie slid into the passenger's seat, yanked the door shut, and then massaged her throbbing forehead.

Simon looked over at her. "Are you sure you're okay? Do you want me to take a look at it?"

"No, I'm fine, but playing this constant game with Lacey is getting hazardous to my health." She grimaced at the pain that shot down her forehead to her cheek.

"Well, I am going to give you a quick look-over anyway," he said as he pulled the car out into traffic.

She glanced sideways at him. "Well, there is one thing."

"Are you dizzy? Blurred vision, feel nauseated?"

"No, but Lacey makes me feel sick to my stomach. Is that a symptom of anything?"

"Yes, but I'm not sure I have the cure for that. I will say that you handled yourself pretty well back there, though, head injury and all. What's up with Serena? I thought she'd learned her lesson." He pulled the Tesla down her driveway.

"It's all okay. She sent a coded message. Apparently, she's working undercover."

"That's good. I'd hate to think she was back to trusting *my* number one suspect," he said, shifting the car into park.

Addie hopped out, and her eyes were immediately drawn to a reflection on the chair beside the front door. She frowned, narrowed her gaze, and made a direct line toward it. When she reached the bottom porch step, she froze.

Simon, following close behind, bumped into her and sent her stumbling forward. He grabbed her in mid-motion and righted her before she crashed onto the steps. "Whoa, what just happened?"

"Look—that box on the chair."

He dashed up the stairs toward it.

"What are you doing? Don't touch it," Addie shrieked. "Call the police."

He looked at her, his brow creased. "Because of a gift someone left you? Don't be silly." He picked up the box and shook it, still wearing his leather driving gloves. "It's not ticking and definitely not heavy enough to be a bomb. Aren't you curious?"

"No, I'm not."

He slid the silver ribbon from around the tall red foil box.

"Stop, don't open it. It's not a gift—"

Simon pulled off the lid. His eyes widened. "If it is, someone's pretty warped."

"Is it another dead rat?" she choked.

He shook his head and looked at her. The pain in his eyes stabbed at her heart. "What is it?" She crept up the steps toward him.

"I don't think you want to know, and yes, we'd better call the police."

Addie cringed. "What's in it? Let me see." She stood on tiptoe and peeked inside the box. "What the . . ." She recoiled.

He closed the box, set it back down on the chair, and dialed 911.

She slid into the other wicker porch chair.

Simon moved around behind her, removed his gloves and began rubbing her shoulders. "I'm sorry. I wasn't thinking."

"No, you weren't, and you weren't listening. I tried to tell you. It looks just like the other one I received."

"I know, I know, but I forgot and hoped it would be something to brighten your day. I remembered the rat box too late." His hands rested on her shoulders, and he gave them a light squeeze. "Forgive me?"

"Why? You didn't send it. Did you?" She looked up at him.

His eyes dulled, and hurt reflected back at her. "Of course not. I've been with you all day."

"You didn't happen to put it there this morning when you arrived, did you?"

He pulled his hands away, walked over to the top step, and slumped down onto it. "What, just so I could have an alibi for when you suddenly saw it when we pulled up, since I somehow managed to camouflage it when we left this morning so you didn't see it then?"

"No, of course not." She slumped back in her chair. "Besides, that dagger is a replica of ones in the museum and is stuck through the heart on the exact same flag that I bought there today."

"I know. That's what scares me. Someone was watching you today, and the knife through the heart is a pretty strong warning for you to stay out of all of this."

"I can see that." She knew her voice held a biting edge to it, but she didn't care. The psychological message behind the contents of this box messed with her mind more than the blatant warning she'd received with the dead rat. She drew her knees up to her chest resting her chin on them. "I'm sorry I said what I did. I'm just so fed up with all this and tired of trying to figure out who has it in for me and why. Obviously, I've gotten too close to something for some-one's liking."

"Just remember, I'm one of the good guys."

She nodded.

"Here they come." He rose to his feet.

"Finally." She willed her shaking legs to support her as she stood. "Glad a murderer wasn't sticking that knife into my real heart right now."

Chapter Twenty-Eight

Addie had already become somewhat accustomed to Marc's aloofness and RoboCop demeanor when he was investigating anything to do with her calamities. But this evening, he presented an even colder detachment. She wanted to slap his face whenever he set his callous, dark eyes on her or Simon during questioning. He'd become outright rude, to not only her, but to her new friend, and she wanted to remind Marc that Simon was also the county coroner and a colleague.

Was he actually jealous of Simon? She shifted her weight from foot to foot as he snapped his notebook closed. How could he be? He'd walked out on her without giving her time to explain and then headed straight to Lacey's seductive arms. A soft growl escaped the back of her throat, and Simon glanced at her. She pasted a smile on her face. "So, *Chief*, are we done here?"

Simon rested his hand on the small of Addie's back. "Yes, can we let Miss Greyborne finally get some rest now?"

This slight gesture didn't go unnoticed by Marc. His eyes traveled from Simon's arm placement up to his face, and Simon returned the fixed stare. Addie stepped between them and turned to Marc. "Well, thank you for your time, Chief.

If we're done, I think I'll make some coffee. Would either of you like a cup?" Passing between them to the kitchen, she could feel the tension as neither man had blinked. She shook her head and plopped a pod into the coffee maker. "Men."

"I have one more thing to add, Miss Greyborne." Addie jumped at Marc's voice. Simon swept past him and came to stand beside her.

"What is it, Chief?"

His gaze went from her to Simon. She noted his jaw flinch as he took a step toward her. "May I remind you of a conversation we had just this very day? If I might quote, I told you not to investigate by yourself, and you replied, 'I don't think coming to a museum is placing me or anyone else in any jeopardy.'"

"Well, well, I—"

His eyes narrowed. "You said in your report that the dagger looks like one of the replicas sold at the museum, and, I might add, was stuck through a flag just like the one you purchased today at that very museum. So"—he paused and stroked his jaw—"it stands to reason even an innocent adventure to a museum *is* a danger to you and everyone else."

"That's not fair, Chief." Simon again placed a protective hand at the small of her back.

Marc's head jerked toward Simon. "I'll tell you what's not fair. Do you want to be performing an autopsy on Miss Amateur Sleuth here?"

Simon shook his head.

"That's more like it." Marc regained his earlier stance.

"I'm a certified amateur sleuth," Addie whispered, stifling a giggle.

Marc's eyes shot darts at her. "You don't seem to understand, do you? The force with which the dagger was thrust through that flag shows an extreme tendency toward pure hatred and rage. So much so it pierced through the bottom of the box."

Addie wilted back against the counter. "Have you asked Lacey where she was today?"

Marc ignored her and straightened his shoulders. "I hope this sees the end of it, and you stop your solitary sleuthing adventures. You've rattled someone, and who knows what's coming next."

"That's exactly why I shouldn't give up now." She stepped forward. "Marc, we're onto something. Something big. And we have to keep rattling and see what falls out."

Marc scrubbed his hands over his face. "Damn, you're incorrigible."

"You know her well," Simon snorted, suppressing a chuckle. Marc glared at him. "Well, you must admit, Chief, she does have a valid point about Lacey. I was witness to a conversation today that took place between the two women where *your* Lacey mentioned the fact that Addie was off up and down the coast playing cops and robbers. How did she know Miss Greyborne was out of town for the day? Where was *she* all day?"

Marc's jaw tensed. He nodded at Addie and left.

Addie took a long hard look at Simon.

"What?" He shrugged.

"You really thrust *your* knife deep into the heart of that one, didn't you?"

"This whole charade of his is ridiculous." Addie's head jerked. "Look, I don't know what happened between you and him, and I don't care to. But the fact of the matter is he's with her now. So why is he blinded by possessive jealousy over you spending time with me and not remaining open to clues or hints that could lead him to the real person responsible for all this?"

"I'm really not sure." So Simon sensed the jealousy from Marc, too. It wasn't all in her mind.

"Well, he'd better start seeing what's right under his own

nose. After her performance today and what she said to you, any doubts about her that I might have had are gone."

"I'm starting to agree." She looked to the front door that Marc had slammed behind him. "But I'm starving. Let's make some sandwiches and head up to the attic for a less exciting adventure."

"Have you heard from Serena?"

"No, not tonight, why?"

"Just wondering." Simon took a plate of cold chicken out of the fridge. "Hope you don't mind." His boyish grin melted some of her stress away.

She chuckled. "No, make yourself at home. It must be hard living in a room at the inn."

" You have no idea how much I've missed having my own kitchen, of all things." He retrieved a loaf of bread from the pantry.

Addie bit into her sandwich and moaned. "You're an artist in the kitchen."

"It's just a matter of getting all the ingredient proportions just right."

"Well, this is the best chicken salad sandwich I've ever had. Ever consider a career change?" She took another bite.

He shook his head and swallowed. "Not recently, no. Although . . . if I had a kitchen like this one, I might be persuaded." He winked at her across the island.

She set her sandwich on the plate. "Speaking of ingredients, have you received the analysis back on the tea yet?"

He stopped in mid-bite. "Didn't you know?"

"Know what?"

"I sent the preliminary to Marc's office." He pushed his plate away. "He didn't tell you?"

"Do we appear to be on friendly terms?"

"I guess not. Why would he share that? Anyway, they're

not conclusive yet. I still need more time. There's something the equipment isn't picking up on, and I just can't pinpoint it. It would sure help if I had an idea of what I'm looking for. Organics and natural products are hard to analyze unless"— he held up his thumb and index finger, squeezing them together—"you have an eensy-weensy idea of what you're looking for. It's a fairly broad spectrum."

"Natural and organic?" She looked at him. "Serena's new boyfriend, Zach, is a naturopathic medical student studying with Dr. Lee down in the Harbor district. Maybe he can help? And he works part-time at your temporary home, the Grey Gull Inn, in the dining room."

"There you go. I should have just asked you in the first place."

She blushed and popped the last bit of her sandwich into her mouth. "Okay, it's past eight, and I'd like to get to work in the attic." She rinsed her plate and set it in the dishwasher. "That is, if you're still up to it?"

"Of course—any reason to spend more time with you."

A warm flush crept up her neck to her cheeks. "Look, Simon I'm not sure what you know about my past, but . . ."

"I heard about David. If that's what you were going to tell me." She stared at him, question filling her eyes. "People talk." He placed his hands on her shoulders. "I get it. Grieving takes its own time. Just promise you'll give me a shot when you decide that you are ready." At her nod, he grinned. "Good, let's get to work."

They stood at the top of the attic stairs. Simon placed his hands on his hips and whistled. "Wow, where do we begin?"

"That's exactly how I feel every time I come up here, but follow me. Tonight, I think I can narrow it down a wee bit. Here is the back room. I've determined this is where June did most of her research, so we might as well start in here." She flipped on the overhead light and stood back.

He poked his head inside and nodded. "Okay, this looks more manageable. What am I looking for?"

"Anything to do with the American Revolution and pirates. I'll start with this wall of books. I noticed there were a lot of older leather-bound books in the mix yesterday, and I'll need to check titles and publishing dates. If you don't mind, you can work over there on that wall. They look newer, but still might be important."

He saluted and began scanning the shelves on the far wall. "This is quite the collection your aunt had. There's even some books from the Magic Tree House series for kids, including *Revolutionary War on Wednesday* and *American Revolution: A Nonfiction Companion to Revolutionary War on Wednesday*, and *Pilgrims: A Nonfiction Companion to Thanksgiving on Thursday* by Mary Pope Osborne and Sal Murdocca. There are even some duplicates on this shelf." He slipped a book from another shelf. "Here's *Johnny Tremain*, by Esther Forbes, published in 1943."

"You're kidding. That book won the Newbury in 1944." She rushed to his side. "Jackpot! Any other children's or young adult books? They're exactly what we need right now at the store."

"Well then, gold star for me."

"Yes, another one. Your star sheet is filling up fast."

"Good to know, because there's lots for adult readers, too. Look at this." He held up a copy of *Oliver Wiswell* by Kenneth Roberts.

She flipped it open to the title page. "And it's a 1940 edition. This is perfect."

"I saw a near-empty crate in the outer room. I'll go get it and start packing these up."

"Thanks, Simon."

She couldn't help but notice how his muscles rippled across his broad back as he walked out the door. Addie shook her head and moaned. "Just bad timing for me, I guess," she muttered to herself as she headed back to the wall of books that had caught her interest yesterday.

Simon worked on sorting the fiction books from the actual history books, and Addie browsed her designated area.

"How are you making out over there?" Simon stood up and stretched out his back.

"Good. I can't believe how many books my aunt had on piracy. It's amazing. Like this one. It's a 1996 copy of *The Pirates of New England Coast 1630–1730* by George Francis Dow and John Henry Edmonds, and this 2005 edition of *Buried Treasures of New England* by W. C. Jameson. There's so many like this. I had no idea she was such a pirate buff."

"Maybe she knew about the rumored treasure buried under the town and was hoping to find clues to its whereabouts."

"Maybe. Here's another good one for the box. *Lost Loot: Ghostly New England Treasure Tales* by Patricia Hughes. It will be perfect to display alongside June's."

"I'll have to go find another crate. This one's full."

He returned and began packing up the books she'd pulled out and stacked on the floor in front of the shelves.

"Now I'm getting somewhere," she cried. "Here are the ones I noticed yesterday. See all the calfskin bindings? This means they are probably older, if not first editions. Today a leather book is generally made of cheaper bonded leather."

He peered over her shoulder. "Is the book Dorothy and the museum manager mentioned there?"

Her fingers ran over the titles on the spines. She pulled a few off the shelf that didn't have spine imprints and read the publisher's page. "No, not yet, but this shelf stretches the whole length of the wall."

She tapped her fingers across the books as she made her way down the line. The last few books on the shelf made her heart leap. "Here it is—*A General History of the Robberies and Murders of the Most Notorious Pyrates* by Captain Charles Johnson. Did you know that since this book was first published it was widely speculated that Charles Johnson was a pseudonym for one of London's most prolific writers of that time, Daniel Defoe? He wrote *Robinson Crusoe*." She flipped to the publisher's page. "And it's a 1724 first edition. Look. Here are two other later volumes that were printed by another printer, Thomas Woodward. His first one was released in 1726, and the second volume came out in 1728. This particular one includes some additional notorious pirates not mentioned in the initial books—like William Kidd, Samuel Bellamy, and William Fly."

"You sure know your pirate history. Guess it's something in your family genes." He looked over his shoulder at the book she held open in her hands.

She smiled, "I suppose it is. And guess what I read at the museum today?"

"I have no idea."

She pulled her phone from her jeans pocket and scrolled through her pictures. "Here, read this."

He squinted and looked at the image, expanding it to get a better look. "You do have treasure hunters' fever, don't you? Okay, 'Where's Captain Kidd's Treasure? It's thought that Pirate Chief William Kidd buried his treasures throughout the world, including a large stockpile of treasures in the New England area . . .'" Simon groaned. "You aren't thinking that—"

"That's exactly what I'm thinking, and you know as well as I do that I'm not the only one, and that's what's behind June's murder." She snapped off her phone.

He looked at the two books she juggled in her hands. "Well, it's a start to figuring out this mystery. Too bad you didn't find June's original manuscript though."

She examined the bookshelf, walked to the door, closed her left eye, and scanned the alignment of the shelf. Measuring the depth of the wall with her hands and arms, she compared it to the actual bookshelf and smiled. "Not so fast.

Help me take this row of books down." She removed books from the shelf where she'd discovered Johnson's first edition and stacked them on the floor.

Simon brushed his hands on his pant legs. "Okay, all down. Now what?"

She began to tap the back of the shelf from the door to the far end, stopped, and pressed on the back of the shelf panel. A drawer slid out.

She looked over her shoulder and flashed him a grin as she brandished a tri-clipped bundle of papers.

"Well, I'll be. You really are a certified amateur sleuth, aren't you?" He chuckled and tucked a strand of hair behind her ear.

"Some would say certifiable." She turned to him and winked.

Chapter Twenty-Nine

"Good morning, Paige!" Addie shouted from the back door.

"Morning." A cheery voice greeted her from the front of the shop.

"If you're not busy, could you come and help me back here with some boxes I need to carry in?" Addie hovered in the back door, waiting for Paige's reply.

"Need help?"

"Marc? What are you doing here?"

His shoulders twitched with a slight shrug, and his trademark flinch of the jawline betrayed some inner turmoil.

"Never mind." She waved off her question. "Yes, I could use any help I can get, thanks."

"You can say that again," he muttered under his breath and slid past her out the door.

She huffed and glared at the back of his head. "They're in the back," she snapped.

He turned and looked at her. "Really? I never would have guessed." He opened the back hatch, pulled the first crate out, and made his way to the door.

"Wait, you'll hurt yourself . . . Those are heavy."

He set it on the floor of the storeroom and skirted past her, retrieving the second box of books and placed it beside the first. "Is that it?" He brushed off his hands. "Or do you have more in that van-sized vehicle you drive?"

She slammed the shop door closed. "Thank you. It wasn't quite so easy getting them in there."

He leaned against the doorframe, his eyes fixed on hers. "Didn't your new doctor friend help?"

She shook her head and walked over to the desk. "What brings you in today?" She flung her purse down and removed her jacket, tossing it on top.

He took a deep breath and straightened his stance. "We need to talk."

Her head cocked to the side as she flipped through the mail Paige had left on the back room desk for her. "Go ahead, I'm listening."

"I mean really talk." He took a step toward her.

She sliced open an envelope with a letter opener. "That's priceless. I've wanted to talk for a while now, and you weren't interested in hearing what I had to say."

"It's different now. It's gone on far too long, and to be honest, it's tearing me up to see you with Simon."

She set the letter down and narrowed her eyes at him. "He's a friend, just like Lacey is a friend to you." She spat out her words and returned to sorting the mail. "By the way, it amazed me at how quickly you fled from my arms to Lacey's."

"I didn't flee to Lacey's arms."

"That's the not the same picture I've witnessed or she's been painting."

"Addie, when you whispered David's name, it cut through my heart like a knife."

She gripped the desk edge. "It just slipped out . . . I didn't mean—"

"I know, I know." He walked toward her and spun her around, placing his hands on her shoulders. "That night, I stood back and studied your face and knew right then that what you'd been saying all along was true."

"What's that?" Her bottom lip began to quiver.

"That you weren't ready."

"But—"

"Shush." He placed his finger over her lips. "I knew you needed more time to grieve the loss of David. You tried to tell me that from the beginning, and I wouldn't listen, but when you said what you did . . . Well, I knew then that I had to give you some space. The only way I knew how to do that was to try to distance myself emotionally from you, but I guess I did a pretty bad job of it, didn't I?"

"You sure did. I couldn't believe how cold and mean you got."

"I'm sorry, really I am, but it was hard to turn off the feelings I was developing for you."

"If that's true, why did you run straight into Lacey's arms?"

"I didn't."

"But I saw you and her the very next day."

"That was business."

"Did she know that?" Addie crossed her arms.

"I never led her on. What she thought, I have no control over."

"What kind of business?"

"You said that you had suspicions about her, and I wanted to find out if any of them were founded. I thought you saw that."

She hung her head and peered at him through her eyelashes. "So she was a suspect?"

"She *is* a suspect. Not a friend."

Her head jerked up. "A suspect." She couldn't contain the saucy grin spreading across her lips. "Finally, you've seen the light?"

"I always did."

Addie tried to hide her surprise, but her eyes betrayed her.

He tucked a strand of wayward hair behind her ear.

She pulled back and stood upright. "So you suspect her of committing the murder." She turned toward the covered crime board.

"No, I don't think she's a murderer, but I do suspect her of something. Look, we both needed time to come to terms with our past ghosts. Unfortunately, she's mine, and I have some suspicions about her, just like you do. I wanted—no, needed—to follow through on them. The only way was to regain her trust, and it's paying off."

"I wish you'd shared that tidbit with me."

"How could I? The knife wound in my heart was too fresh, and the look in your eyes when I left has haunted me every night since. But just a minute." He lifted her chin and stared into her eyes. "Speaking of filling spaces quickly, what's with you and the doctor?"

She felt a flush rise up onto her cheeks. "Nothing. It's strictly business."

"Are you sure?" His eyes narrowed.

"Well . . . you'll just have to wait and see, won't you?" She turned and yanked the drop cloth from the board. "What do you have?" She stood waiting, the tip of the chalk beside the letters *LD*.

Marc heaved a deep sigh behind her.

She looked over her shoulder at him. "Well? What have you got?"

He sat on the desk edge and crossed his arms. "What I *can* share with you at this point is that I suspected Lacey either to be Miss Newsy or to have a direct line to her and be passing on information."

"And?"

"And she *is* Miss Newsy as a side job, in addition to being a reporter for the paper."

"Aha, I knew it." Addie wrote *Miss Newsy* on the board. "Anything else?"

"Yeah." He cleared his throat. "I'm kind of up against it with the DA's office. They're really pressuring me to close this, and I could use all the help I can get."

She studied him and saw the tic of his jaw. Her stomach fluttered, but she refused to acknowledge it.

"Actually, they've demanded that I try and work with you on a few of the stumbling blocks in the case."

She leaned against the board and crossed her arms, her eyes not wavering from his.

"Your expertise in books and past training as an appraisal expert prove that you have a keen eye for detail. Since this case now appears to be about a dead author and a book, the DA insisted, after he ran a background check on you, that I should utilize your expertise as a consultant, and . . ."

"Go on." She struggled to squelch the flutter building in her stomach.

"And the DA feels it would be in the Greyborne Harbor Police Department's best interest if you were officially read into any book-related portions of this murder case."

She sucked in a sharp breath.

He stood up and placed his hands on her shoulders. "As a *temporary* consultant and only because the order came from the DA's office. He asked me to tell you that this service would also come with a small honorarium."

She nodded, fighting to contain her excitement.

"I tried arguing with them and told them it was dangerous, especially now after the latest gift box incident."

She nodded.

"But they insisted we give it a go—a trial run, that's all. You understand, right?"

"I—"

"Am I interrupting?" Serena stood in the doorway, looking from Addie to Marc.

Addie searched Marc's face, which had turned to stone as he flashed a warning glance at her. "Not at all. Great to see you." Addie walked over and hugged her friend. "What brings you in?"

Serena glanced from Marc's detached expression to Addie's flushed cheeks and shook her head. "I was taking a quick lunch and thought I'd better drop in and explain about yesterday."

"No need. I got your message loud and clear." Addie smiled. "My, my, is it lunchtime already? Where does the time go?" She glanced at Marc.

Serena made her way over to a crate and sat down, her eyes flitting from Marc to Addie. "I hope you got the message. I didn't want you to think that I'd fallen back into the spiderweb." Her eyes seemed to drill into Marc's.

Addie noted Serena's expression. "I knew that, deep down."

"Anyway." Serena crossed her legs and leaned back on her hands. "I got a few tidbits for you to add to that board." She looked up at it. "Oh, I see you already have one of them up there."

Marc pointed to the *Miss Newsy* line. "You mean this one?"

Serena nodded. "You knew?"

"Yup. Part of police business."

"Is that what you've really been up to?" She locked eyes with her brother. "Spying on Lacey?"

"And what's your excuse, little miss puppy dog?" He stared down his nose at her.

"Yeah, but—"

He stood up. "No 'yeah, buts.'"

She hung her head. "Okay. But only because Addie's gut feelings are contagious."

"I've caught the same disease, too." He winked at Addie.

"Well." Addie flopped down on the crate beside Serena. "My dad always said that sometimes you just have to forget about the facts and evidence, stop following it, and go with your gut."

"My gut got really churned up when you asked me if Lacey's brother, Dean, had met her reporter friend while he was in LA last year."

"And?" Addie stared at her.

"He did, and apparently they spent a lot of time together." Serena smiled smugly. "What I did know about Dean and then hearing what you asked got me thinking, so I discreetly asked Lacey, and she spilled how the two were inseparable for awhile. Peter was leading him on apparently about some get-rich-quick scheme, but it didn't seem to happen, and Dean abruptly left LA and came back here."

"Maybe it did happen or is still happening." Addie dashed to the board and began frantically writing. "Did Lacey mention what kind of reporter this Peter is, any stories he was working on?"

"No, not really. I can try and get more from her if my cover's not blown." Serena glanced at Marc.

"I expect mine to stay intact, too." His eyes bored into hers. Serena nodded.

Addie scribbled on the board and then turned around, beaming. "Ta-da!" She pointed in her game-show-host fashion.

Marc leaned forward. His eyes scanned the board, murmurs escaping from his throat. Serena did the same. They looked at Addie in unison.

"Makes sense, doesn't it?" Addie grinned.

Marc scratched his head. "So you really think this Peter fellow, from LA, is the same guy as the salt-and-pepper man and the black-haired man you've seen with Jeanie?"

Addie nodded smugly.

His brow furrowed. "Why would he go to all that trouble, and for what?"

Addie heaved a sigh and pointed to the board, tapping the line where she'd written *original manuscript*.

"I'm lost." Serena shook her head.

Addie threw her hands up. "Okay, in black and white. Dean was one of only two people to read June's original manuscript—which I found in the attic last night, by the way. In a hidden wall compartment, I might add." She looked at Marc.

"You found it? Is it still there?" Marc's eyes lit up.

"No, it's safely tucked away in my aunt's other hiding place—you know, the floor thing." His gaze nearly undid her. "Anyway," she ground out, "the only other person to read it was Blain, the chairman of the town council at the time and the one who squelched the publication of the original. Dean then went to LA, and as soon as he returned Blain apparently financed his charter boat business. My question was always—why would he do that? Dean was a flake according to some people. So maybe . . . Dean found out something on the West Coast that would benefit Blain?" She looked from Serena's blank face to Marc's.

She shook her head when no epiphany flickered in either of their eyes. "It states in the town bylaws that all major town decisions regarding funding of programs has to be initially reviewed by at least two committee members, the chair and a member of his choosing, before it is taken to the entire committee for a vote. Just to save everyone's time, I guess." She shrugged. "So why wasn't Dorothy selected? After all, she was June's friend and original research partner. Because Dean was Blain's errand boy, and someone he trusted wouldn't turn against him. He must have had a quick review of the original and seen some fairly precise information about hidden treasure right under his feet and couldn't risk it being published and becoming general knowledge."

Serena's eyes widened. "You've read the original? It confirms there is a treasure?"

"I haven't found absolute proof yet, so I'm still surmising at this point, but it makes sense that there is."

Marc coughed. "Someone has treasure hunters' fever."

"Maybe, but I've read enough lately to know that it's a strong possibility." She turned back to the board. "And you're not the first to tell me that. So, as I was saying, Blain, who was chairman at the time, selected someone he knew he could trust, or persuade, or buy off, not to reveal what it contained as the other initial reviewing committee member."

"Okay," Marc said, stroking his chin, "but how does this Peter fit into it?"

"Not sure, exactly. Maybe he had further information or was the main funder in the operation. Maybe they were planning on digging up the town, or it may have been coincidence or timing. Perhaps it was something Lacey had mentioned to her brother about a story Peter was working on. I don't know, maybe the story was about treasure hunters—"

Marc looked up at her, a boyish gleam in his eyes. "I'm guessing you know all this because Peter contacted you for his story? Are you a treasure hunter in disguise?"

She pressed her lips tight. "No. I was going to say that Lacey might have arranged for the two of them to meet so Dean could talk to Peter about June's book for his story."

"Sounds pretty far-fetched to me." Serena sat back down on the crate. "That means Lacey orchestrated whatever it is that transpired, and I don't think she would, because she's too focused on herself."

"True," injected Marc, "but she is ambitious and maybe saw a future news story there."

"The initial meeting and why and where remain a question mark, but I think these are all links and are a major key to what's been happening and June's murder," Addie said, circling *original manuscript*, *Peter a.k.a. Steven?? Dean, Lacey,* and *Jeanie*, and then stabbing the chalk onto the board for emphasis.

"Why Jeanie? Her mother was murdered. They had their issues like in any mother-daughter relationship, but to be a part of her death?" Serena shook her head. "I can't buy that."

"I'm not saying she had anything to do with the actual murder, but she must have known the salt-and-pepper-haired man and the black-haired guy she calls Steven are the same man. Even I saw that."

"You're right." Marc rose to his feet. "She knows more than she's telling."

"Yeah, and she thinks he's a travel agent from Chicago, so she doesn't know he might also be Peter, a reporter from LA." Serena studied the board.

Addie looked at the names she'd circled. "I've got to talk to Gloria. She can find out easily enough."

"I'm sorry. Did I miss the party invitation?"

"Simon?" Addie spun around to face the voice that issued from the doorway. "No, of course not, come in. We were just discussing—"

"Addie's gut feelings," laughed Serena.

Marc rose to his feet and eyed Simon as he made his way into the crowded back room.

"Well, I know she's certainly made a believer out of me." Simon's gaze seemed to caress Addie.

She felt that familiar blush rise up her collar whenever Simon set his eyes on her. "What? You've just now come to the realization that I might know a thing or two?" She fluttered her lashes, aware Marc's attention was completely focused on their verbal banter.

Chapter Thirty

Simon stood back, studying the board. "I see you've made some headway since we last worked on this."

Marc turned away from Simon and stroked his neck, eyes fixed on the blackboard. "Yes, Miss Greyborne was just sharing some rather insightful information. Although, as a man of science, I'm not sure you'd catch the involutions of it, since most is speculation at this point and not black-and-white like science is." He turned back and fixed his gaze on Simon.

"I've become well versed in the manner in which Miss Greyborne theorizes an investigation," Simon responded, his eyes narrowed. "Which has led me to become a true believer in her abilities to see what others often miss because they are far too focused on facts and the reality of what they *think* they see as opposed to what really is right in front of them."

"You're a philosopher now, too?" Marc smirked.

Simon took a step forward. "I don't need to be to know what she is capable of. Do you know?"

"Okay, let's all take a break." Addie stepped between the two men for the second time in two days. "A time-out for coffee, anyone?"

Marc held his position, as did Simon. She shook her head and looked at a snickering Serena. "What?"

"Nothing," Serena chuckled.

Marc puffed out his chest, adjusted his holster belt, and rocked back on his heels. Simon appeared ready to explode with laughter. Marc grunted and took a step past Simon toward the door. "Wait, Chief," Simon said, "you might want to stay to hear what I found out this morning." His eyes twinkled with the spark of a mischievous child.

Marc's face held a flat expression.

"I'm curious," said Addie.

"Me, too," echoed Serena.

Simon turned his back on the unyielding human statue planted firmly by the doorway. "I made an early visit to your friend Zach." He nodded at Serena, who broke out into a grin. "The restaurant told me he only worked the evenings and said I'd be able to find him at the wellness clinic most days, so I dropped in."

"And? How is he today? I haven't spoken to him yet."

"He's just fine and asked me to say hello from him, and that he'd catch you later."

Serena brought her hands to her heart and moaned.

Addie couldn't resist an eye roll.

"He really is a very nice person. You've done well for yourself." Simon winked at her.

"Blah, blah, blah. What did he say about the tea?" Addie asked.

"Really? No niceties? All work with you?"

"Sorry, but the suspense is killing me." Addie pouted.

Simon sat down on a crate, casually examining her work on the blackboard.

"Simon," she growled.

"Give me a minute." He raised his hand. "It's the scientist in me." He glanced sideways at Marc, still looming by the door. "I'm studying your links here. Aha, there it is."

"There what is?" she cried in exasperation.

"That gut feeling of yours." He grinned up at her.

She looked at the board, then back at him. "I don't understand."

"Me, neither." Serena slid onto the crate next to him.

"See there, where you have Jeanie's name and tea with a question mark."

"Yes." Addie motioned with her hands.

"Well, you can write tea beside June's name, too. No question mark."

Addie clapped her hands. "You got the results back on the tea?"

"Yes, once I found out what I was looking for. And we have Serena's friend and his profession to thank for that."

Serena blushed and grinned.

"Actually, Zach wasn't positive when I handed him the baggie to smell. He thought it might contain valerian root, which is what gave it that foul, dirt-like aroma. So, he asked his mentor, Dr. Lee, to figure it out. Dr. Lee agreed with him, but he also taste-tested a small sample and said it had a slightly bitter, nutlike under-note to it and surmised it also contained ground *Strychnos nux-vomica*, which is a plant found commonly in India, Sri Lanka, and the East Indies, as well as Australia."

"And what does that mean?" Addie hovered over him.

"Strychnine," gasped Serena.

"Bingo." Simon pointed to her. "She gets a gold star."

Addie looked at Marc, who had edged closer to the group. "Did you rerun June's autopsy blood sample?"

"Yes. I've just concluded it contained valerian root, an herbal relaxant. The synthetic version of it is Valium, which has similar effects to those of the plant. There are also traces of strychnine."

"What about Jeanie's blood work you took the other day?"

"Not yet. I'll run it again this afternoon."

Marc drew his notepad from his jacket pocket and began to write.

Addie studied the board, tapping the chalk piece on her chin. Serena leapt up and wiped the chalk beard from her friend's face. Addie pushed her hand away, laughing.

Serena's cell vibrated. "I don't believe this."

"What?" Addie peered over her shoulder.

"The nerve of her." She looked at Addie, her eyes blazing. "It's from Lacey. She's just arrived and *demands* to know why SerenaTEA is closed at lunchtime, and then in all caps she writes, 'WHERE ARE YOU? IS MARC WITH YOU? I SEE HIS CAR OUT FRONT!!!'"

Without looking up from his notepad, Marc grunted, "It sounds like you've got some explaining to do if you don't want your cover blown."

"So do you, mister." She shoved her phone back into her jeans pocket and stomped past him out the door.

Simon looked questioningly at Addie.

"I'll explain it to you later," she mouthed.

He nodded.

Marc snapped his notepad closed and put it in his pocket. "I'd better be off, too. Think I've got everything I need from you today." He smiled at Addie.

She liked the way the corners of his eyes crinkled when he smiled, and that familiar flutter in her chest made her knees quiver. He stopped in the door, tapped his hand on the frame, and turned around. "I assume we're still on for Founder's Day Eve?"

She felt Simon's eyes bore into her.

"I'll catch you later." He double tapped the frame, his lips turning up at the corners when he glanced at Simon, and then left.

Simon sat silent, staring at the floor. Addie wanted to say something, to explain, but his body language told her no words could take away what he had just heard. He stood up and walked toward the door.

"Simon, wait. Let me explain."

He waved his hands in the air without turning around. "No need. I got the message loud and clear."

"It's not what you think."

"Isn't it?" He spun toward her. "I asked you to give me a shot when you decided you were ready, and it seems you are. Guess I'll just take a number and stand in line."

"No, don't go!" Her words fell on the empty space between them as he walked out the door.

She stamped her foot, fighting back tears. She knew there was something between her and Marc, something she couldn't understand and never had. But there was something between Simon and her, too. What it was, she didn't know. She only knew she couldn't let it end like this. She bolted toward the door and slammed right into him.

He grabbed her shoulders and steadied her. "We really have to quit meeting like this."

She struggled to fill her burning lungs. "You didn't leave?" she gasped.

He shook his head and tilted her chin up, his eyes as calming as a still summer morning sky, and her breathing came easier. "I decided that you were worth fighting for, and if I have to take a number and stand in line, I'm willing to wait out your rebound to Marc."

"What makes you think Marc's a rebound?"

"Let's just say I'm banking on studied patterns of human behavior. If I'm wrong, then so be it. You'll have made your choice, and all I want is for you to be truly happy. You deserve it."

"Simon. I'm sorry. None of this has gone the way I expected. I thought Marc and I were done, and then he said that about Founder's Day Eve and . . . I just don't know what's going on anymore." She gave a quivering smile. "But I guess you don't want to hear that, do you?"

"I will admit that the less I hear about him the better."

"Okay." She nodded. "You and I have what we have, and that's all that matters when we're together. His name, in future, will be unmentionable."

"Considering the circumstances, with him being the chief of police and you working as a *certified* amateur sleuth, and, well, me being the county coroner, that might prove harder than it sounds."

"We'll make it work. It has so far." She smiled up at him. Her cheeks warmed with that familiar flush she couldn't hide when she looked into his eyes.

"That's the Addie I know." He kissed the tip of her nose. "But I have to run. I'm already late for my afternoon shift. Chat soon." He dashed off, waving at her over his head.

Addie watched his long strides take him out the door. The chimes over his head rang in her ears like a heavenly melody, and she smiled, sighing. She glanced at Paige, who quickly averted her eyes to the books in front of her on the counter. The undeniable smirk on her face told Addie she had witnessed the entire scene with Simon.

Addie straightened her shoulders, held her head high, and did her best to impersonate a professional adult business-woman while fighting the flip-flops her heart was doing in her chest. She took a deep breath and strode to the counter. "It's past lunchtime. Did you eat?"

"Yes, I dashed next door to grab a sandwich."

"From the bakery?"

"Yeah, I didn't want to close, since there were customers, but I was starving, so I just popped out. It was the fastest choice I could see. I hope that's okay."

Addie thought for a moment, then nodded. "Sure, I guess. After all, I was here. It's not like the store was left unat-tended or anything."

"I knew you were busy in the back, and I didn't want to interrupt . . . especially when . . . well, the meeting size grew." Her rosy cheeks darkened, and she grabbed a marking pen from under the counter.

Addie pursed her lips and nodded. "Glad you managed to eat. By the looks of the empty shelves, you've been busier than I thought. You should have poked your head in and asked for help."

"I started to once, but it didn't look like a good time to interrupt, so, well, I managed."

"Was your mother there? In the bakery when you popped in?"

Paige nodded. "She started grilling me about you and why the police had been here all morning. Needless to say, I was back in minutes, but on the upside, my sandwich was free. So I have money to buy Emma a treat after dinner tonight."

"Who's Emma?"

Paige looked down at the book she held in her hand. "My daughter."

So it wasn't a rumor. "You never told me you have a daughter." Addie was completely taken aback, but more so, she was a little hurt. "Why wouldn't you say something about that after all this time?"

"I wasn't sure you'd understand or approve because . . . I'm not married."

"I'm certainly not the one to judge anyone else. I live in a glass house, too, as most people do. How old is she?"

"She's just about two."

"A handful, I expect."

"You have no idea." Paige laughed. "The day care tells me she's a holy terror there, too."

"No wonder that some days you look like you haven't had a wink of sleep. Now I know why." Addie reached over and patted her hand. "If there's anything I can do to help you and Emma out, let me know."

"I will, thanks."

"Good. Well, we do have some work in the back since there's a lull in walk-in traffic. I found some books to fill all those empty shelves with when you get some time."

"Now would be a great time." She grabbed an empty book cart from beside the counter and rolled it toward the back room.

Addie watched her young assistant. She certainly was a go-getter, and it made her proud. After hearing she was also juggling the responsibilities of single parenting, her heart went out to her. She remembered how hard it had been on her father. She wished she could do more to help ease the burden. A raise was out of the question right now. Cash flow in the store had become too erratic lately. She turned toward the empty book display window, sure she'd come up with something.

"Paige," she called, "do we have an expected time of delivery for June's books from the printer yet?"

Paige's head popped out the back room door. "The courier's here now."

"Perfect, I'll start working on this." She went to the back of the sales counter and plucked the pirate flag from the bottom storage shelf. She shook out the creases and stood back. Her eye went immediately to the spear stabbing at the heart. A vision of what lay at the bottom of the box that had been left on her porch raced through her mind, and she dropped the flag on the counter.

"Are you okay?"

She took a deep breath and nodded at Paige. "Fine."

"Here's six copies of the book. Do you think that's enough for the window?"

"It should be fine." Addie glanced at the flag and shivered. "There's some other books about pirate ghosts and hauntings in the crates. Grab a few of those, and we'll piggyback them in the display with these."

"Sounds good."

"And here." She handed Paige the flag. "Try to find a piece of cardboard or something to mount this on so I can stand it up behind the books."

Paige nodded, grabbed the flag, and headed to the back.

Addie gripped the counter. She took a deep breath to calm the queasiness still churning in the pit of her stomach from seeing the flag again. Picking up the books Paige had brought up, she studied the empty window and tried to distract her mind from how the flag appeared to her in the box. She tapped her finger to her chin, refocusing on the ghostly pirate images she wanted to create with the books, but the fixed image of a death threat directed toward her was all that emerged.

She gasped and leaned forward into the bay window. The black-haired man, Steven, stood across the street in front of the park. A silver sedan pulled up, a tall, blond-haired man jumped out, and the car pulled away. Steven looked at his watch and turned into the park. The fair-haired man checked both ways over his shoulders and followed behind him.

"Here are the books you wanted." Paige rolled the cart up beside Addie.

"Paige, see that blond guy going into the park?"

Paige stood on tiptoe and peered out. "Yes. Why?"

"Do you know who he is?"

She squinted. "It looks like Dean Davenport, why?"

"Interesting."

Chapter Thirty-One

Addie's PI radar was running in overdrive. She glanced over her shoulder at Paige, who was busy restocking the empty historical fiction section, and looked back at the park. "While you're doing that, I'm going to run out for a minute." She dashed through the door and nearly knocked Gloria, from the book club, off her feet. "Sorry, sorry." Addie gripped her shoulders, steadying her.

Gloria patted her heaving chest, laughing.

"Gloria! I'm just mortified, I hope you're—"

"Never mind. No harm done." She waved off Addie. "I'm just glad I caught you, or you me," she giggled, "before you were gone."

Addie glanced over Gloria's head to the park, frowned, and then eyed the furry bundle in Gloria's arms. "Is that your dog?"

"Yes." She gave the small dog tucked under her arm a poochy-smooch. "This is Pippi, my Yorkie-poo and best friend."

"Pippi? What a cute name, and such an adorable dog." Addie raised her hand to pat its head and stopped. "Does it like strangers?"

"Oh, yes, she goes everywhere with me, don't you,

Pippi?" She kissed the dog's nose, and it licked her face. "I named her after my favorite book character from when I was a child. Pippi Longstocking."

"I loved that series, and you aren't going to believe this, but we have the whole collection inside."

"You do? I'm afraid I still only have one or two, and I do miss reading them so much. I should buy some, and then I could read them to my own Pippi." She snuggled the dog and kissed its head again.

"Tell you what, why don't I take Pippi for a short walk in the park? You go in and have a look at the collection, and I'll be right back so you can see if Pippi agrees with your book choices."

"Wonderful idea. She's in need of her constitutional anyway. Here, you'll need this." Gloria produced an unused doggy doo-doo bag from her pocket.

Addie took Pippi from Gloria's outstretched arms and dashed across the street to the park entrance. She set the little dog down and clasped the leash tight. "Okay, doggy, you look after your business, and I'll look after mine." With a yip from Pippi and a deep breath from Addie, they headed off in the same direction that the two men had gone in.

Addie's jaunt proved to be frustrating, to say the least. When she wanted to turn left, the dog became distracted by a scent and veered right. It became a constant battle of wills between the two alpha females, but finally Addie was successful. The two reached an understanding that she was in charge, and Pippi soon trotted along obediently at her side. After she could focus her attention on her mission, it didn't take long for her to spot the two men standing shoulder to shoulder beside the utility shed at the rear of the library, deep in conversation.

Addie quickly turned away and led Pippi to a tree trunk to investigate the new and wonderful scents that she might find at its base, all the while keeping an eye over her shoulder on the men. She fished her cell out of her jeans pocket. Stretchy skinny jeans might look and feel good, but they were too hard to dig a cell phone out of some days. She strained and then almost dropped it when it did come free. She eyed the men and snapped some photos over her shoulder before Pippi yanked on the leash, tangling it around the tree trunk.

When she had untangled Pippi, she looked back just in time to see the men shake hands and the black-haired man head off toward the library. The fair-haired one who Paige identified as Dean Davenport turned and began walking in her direction. She pulled Pippi around the back side of the large maple tree, circling around it as he moved past them. When all was clear, she stepped out and hurried to the street to catch a glimpse of which direction he had headed in. Too late. Pippi had decided it was time for her constitutional and couldn't be budged.

By the time Pippi had finished her business and she was done cleaning it up, there was no sign of Dean on the road. She picked Pippi up in her arms and headed back into her shop, where Gloria greeted her.

"Addie, you are a saint. Thank you so much." She took the little dog from her. "I hope she behaved. You did, didn't you?" She kissed and tickled the dog while it excitedly lapped at her face.

"Yes, she was wonderful. We had fun."

"And look what I've found." Gloria swept her hand over the stack of books on the counter. "All twenty Pippi Long-stocking publications. You weren't joking when you said you had the entire collection," she laughed. "Some of these I've never seen before."

"I'm just glad you found something of interest."

"Did I ever," she cried. "I've hit the jackpot. I'll take them all."

Addie smiled. "Great, I'll just ring them up for you."

"I forgot in my excitement why I came in here today."

"I'm guessing it wasn't to add to your home library," she chuckled.

"No. Dorothy asked me to pop in and see if you had received the copies of June's book from the printer yet. And darling Paige here told me they came in just today."

"Yes. Did she want some of them for the library?"

"Well, yes, she wants some, but not for the library. They're for the Smuggler's Den restaurant."

"Have they agreed to host the finale to the ghost walk?"

"Yes." Gloria beamed. "And they want one to display for advertising the event, then thought maybe a dozen or so to sell on the side."

"Tell you what. I'm happy to donate the one for advertising, since it's for the town, and then another twelve, providing all proceeds from the sales are used as fundraising for the library."

"Perfect." She clapped her hands. "Dorothy will be tickled."

"Paige—"

"I'm on it." Paige made her way over to the book cart and scooped up an armful of books she hadn't shelved yet and placed a dozen copies of *The Ghosts and Mysteries of Greyborne Harbor* on the counter beside Gloria's other purchases. "Will you be taking all of these with you today?"

Addie jumped when her cell vibrated in her jeans pocket. "Sorry." She looked at Gloria and chuckled. "I forgot it was there, and it tickled." She smiled when she saw it was from Simon. So, all was forgotten and forgiven after all. She read the message, stopped, and then read it again.

> *Jeanie's blood work was positive for mixture.*
> *Called her to tell her not to drink any more of the tea.*
> *Just said it might be contaminated. Did not tell her*
> *with what. She is furious with Serena for selling bad*
> *tea and on her way over there. Just thought I should*
> *warn you.*

"Oh, no." Addie looked out the window just as Jeanie stomped past.

"I hope it's not bad news?" Gloria followed her gaze to the window.

"No, just unexpected. Paige, will you finish up here? I have to go for a minute. Thanks again, Gloria. Loved meeting Pippi. See you at the next book club meeting." She waved as she dashed out the door.

Addie flung Serena's tea shop door open and stepped inside. She heard Jeanie's raised voice before her eyes adjusted to the change of light and she saw her at the back counter, wagging her finger in Serena's face. Addie made her way toward them across the (thankfully empty) shop, but a movement out of the corner of her eye when she passed by the storeroom doorway caught her attention. Lacey was counting out what looked like hundred-dollar bills and placing them in Dean's outstretched hand. She looked at her friend whose face was crumbling further with every word Jeanie shouted at her. She glanced back at Lacey, who appeared oblivious to what was happening in the front. She'd deal with Lacey later. As nonchalantly as possible, she slid onto a stool beside Jeanie where she was standing at the counter.

"Have you come for an afternoon pick-me-up tea, too, Jeanie?" Addie tucked a wayward strand of hair behind her ear and looked up at the daily blackboard special on the wall. "I think I'll have a Heavenly Delight." She smiled and looked at Jeanie, whose temple veins pulsated with anger.

Jeanie snapped her mouth closed and glared at Serena. "I'm not finished with you yet. I'll make sure you are put out of business by the health department."

Serena looked at Addie, her eyes filled with tears.

"Is there a problem, Jeanie?" Addie's brow creased as she looked at her and then at Serena.

"You might say that. This child playing with all of her

roots and herbs has sold me tea that is contaminated. It could have killed me, I'm sure."

"We can't have that. Is that true, Serena?"

Serena's eyes widened, and she looked in horror at Addie and shook her head.

"Are you certain the tea came from Serena's shop? After all, there are other tea merchants in the county."

"It had her label on it." Jeanie crossed her arms and glared at Serena.

Serena wilted and shuffled backward.

"So you bought it here. I guess that proves its origins." Addie looked at Serena, then glanced at Jeanie while toying with a napkin on the counter.

"No, I didn't."

"Oh?" Addie looked at her. "Who did, then?"

"I don't know. I found it at Mother's."

"I see." Addie stroked her neck. "So, June bought it?"

"Well, I assume so." She looked down her nose at Addie, tapping her foot.

Addie turned to Serena. "Didn't you tell me that a man with salt-and-pepper-colored hair came in and bought that special blend of tea as a gift for a woman friend of his who was having trouble sleeping?"

A wave of understanding crossed Serena's face, and she nodded. "Yes—he was quite insistent that he wanted a special tea for the special woman in his life, and he even had me put it in a silver gift box for her."

"Wrapped with a blue satin ribbon, wasn't it?" Addie added.

Jeanie's face dropped.

"Perhaps he gave it to June and knows how it became contaminated after it left Serena's shop?" Addie twisted the napkin in her hand. "Do you still have his contact info in your records, Serena? Maybe we could track him down and find out if he accidentally spilled it in the dirt before he could give it to her, or maybe a pet cat got into it when he had it at his home, or something." She shrugged her shoulders. "That might explain a lot. It's worth checking out. I really hate to think that Serena sold a tainted product."

Jeanie's reddened face turned ashen. She spun on her heel and fled out the door.

"Can I have my tea now?" She winked at Serena.

Dean rushed into the front of the store and headed out the door. Lacey appeared in the storeroom doorway, looked at Addie sitting at the counter, and then looked at Serena's grinning face. "What's *she* doing in here?"

"Excuse me?" Serena looked at her.

"Riffraff," she muttered. "Well, at least she won't be around for much longer." She turned back into the storeroom and slammed the door.

"I see your cover's still intact," Addie whispered and rolled her eyes.

A devious smile crept across Serena's face. "And I've decided to tell her this shop isn't big enough for the two of us, and it's time she—"

Lacey burst through the storeroom door and headed for the main entrance. "Marc's here. I'm gone for the rest of the day." The door banged behind her.

"Finally," Serena moaned, slumping onto her stool behind the counter.

Addie shook her head. "I guess Marc managed to salvage his cover, too?" She fought the flush just speaking his name brought to her cheeks.

Serena nodded. "She thinks so little of you that she can't conceive of you being a threat to what she has with him or me. Although I can't help feeling guilty about what I'm doing. She was my friend."

"Was she? Ever?" Addie growled. "You know the real her now."

"Speaking of what I'm doing, I wish you'd given me a

heads-up with that whole Jeanie thing. It took me long enough to see what you were up to. I was furious with you, thinking you had taken her side."

"I really couldn't have warned you, could I? She was in accusation mode when I walked in. I needed to act fast and then plant a few poisonous seeds of my own before she ruined your business."

"Whatever you said sure stopped her."

"Yes, I think Steven will have some explaining to do now," she chuckled. "I'd better text Marc and tell him to call me later. He should know about this, and about what I saw in the park today."

"What's that?" Serena offered Addie a scone from the covered tray on the counter.

She shook her head. "Let's just say that there is no question that Dean knows Steven—aka Peter, if we're right about Steven's true identity. They had a meeting by the utility shed, of all places, this afternoon."

"Really?" Serena took a bite of her scone.

"Speaking of Dean, if you're going to fire Lacey, check your till and back room safe first."

"Why?"

"When Jeanie was ripping into you, I saw Lacey hand him a large amount of money."

Serena reached over to her till and pressed the No Sale button. The drawer popped open. Empty.

"When's the last time you made a bank deposit?"

"Not for a few weeks, but I don't really know. Lacey's been looking after the finances lately."

"You're kidding, right?"

"No . . . but that's when I thought she was a trusted friend. Oh God." She dashed into the storeroom and returned moments later, clutching a note in her hand, her face sheet-white.

Chapter Thirty-Two

Addie took off her work wear and slipped into her black, cropped yoga pants, a sports bra, and a green tank top. She cat-stretched and moaned. Good God, it felt great to finally be in comfortable clothes. It had been a long day, and a quiet evening reviewing June's manuscript was the perfect way to end it.

She grabbed her phone from the bedside table, trotted down the stairs to the kitchen to make some coffee, and headed to the living room to retrieve June's book draft and the first-edition pirate book from her hiding place under the floor-boards by her aunt's desk. Cross-legged on the sofa, she breathed a sigh of relief and settled back into the comfy cushions. After quickly checking her cell, hoping to find a returned message from Marc, she frowned, tossed her phone on the sofa beside her, pulled the manuscript onto her lap, and began reading.

She skimmed through the early chapters, since they were mainly a recap of the town history and its strong roots in the pirate trade, similar to what had been published in the book. However, she paused when she came to a more detailed account of the Greyborne-Davenport family feud. Apparently, when Henry Davenport trudged to the gallows, he turned toward Gerald Greyborne where he was standing among the crowd, looked him in the eye, and cursed him and the Greyborne family name for eternity. A shiver ran through her, and she wrapped her arms around her knees.

She instantly thought about Lacey and her behavior toward her; it was similar to the attitude that Martha'd had since the first day Addie had introduced herself. Perhaps there was another branch of the Davenport family she wasn't aware of? When the doorbell buzzed, she jumped and looked at the mantel clock. Eight o'clock. She tried to remember if she was expecting anyone. Then she laughed—in all the time she'd lived here, only one person had used the antiquated door ringer. She smiled as she opened the door and was greeted by Simon's schoolboy grin.

"I hope you don't mind my stopping by. I was in the area."

"I'm not buying that, since it's a dead-end road, but come in." She stood back, allowing him to enter. "I was just reading June's manuscript and need a break anyway. Can I get you something?"

"Yes, that would be perfect. It was a busy shift."

"Anything interesting?"

"Not unless you find patients vomiting on your shoes of interest." He stepped past her into the living room.

"What?"

"Stomach flu is sweeping through the town." He laid his overcoat on the chair at the far end of the sofa, making it clear he had no intention of sitting in the chair this time.

"What you would like? It sounds like there's a need for something stronger than coffee." She headed to the liquor cart.

"Scotch neat, if you have it?"

"The neat I can do, the Scotch? . . . Umm . . ." She searched the second shelf of the cart.

"Smart-ass." He made himself comfortable on the sofa. "Anything you have will do."

"Never mind. I found some Scotch," she said and proceeded to pour two glasses.

He reached his hand out to take the drink from her over the back of the sofa. "Thank you. Now show me what else you found."

"It's all here on the cart if you want something else."

"I meant the manuscript." He grinned and missed his mouth with the drink. "Looks like I have a hole in my lip."

She set her drink down on the desk, pulled a clean tissue from the box beside it and handed it to him.

"Thanks." He wiped his chin and blotted his shirtfront. "I hope I don't get any calls tonight. It's not good for a doctor to show up stinking of Scotch."

"I can well imagine." She called over her shoulder as she went into the front hall to retrieve the book she'd dropped on the table when she'd answered the door. "It certainly wouldn't instill much confidence with your patients," she said from the living room doorway.

"Especially if they required surgery." He stretched his long legs out under the table, and settled back, watching her as she flipped through the pages of the manuscript.

Addie quivered under his unwavering gaze and presented the pages to him. His eyes locked with hers. "Do you want me to come all the way over there to get them?"

She dropped her eyes. If she looked up at him now, she'd give away the silly, teenage-girl-style infatuation that stirred inside her whenever he set eyes on her. Then it hit her. That was it. Marc, like David, masked his emotions and rarely gave away what he was really thinking, but was strong, solid, dependable, and safe, with just enough of a hint of danger surrounding him to make it exciting. Simon was open about his emotions, candid about what was on his mind. He was outgoing and impetuous, constantly moving her out of her comfort zone, which was scary and thrilling at the same time.

She slid into the spot he patted beside him. She handed him the manuscript without looking at him and sat back, her hands on her lap, aware that his eyes were still on her.

He sighed, looked down at the page she indicated, and began reading. "So, you're cursed?" He looked sideways at her. "I always knew there was something off about you."

She opened her mouth to speak but snapped it shut when he turned and winked at her . . . and there it was again. That sea-blue wave that washed over her, consuming her, and she leapt to her feet. "Ready for another drink, or is coffee on the menu now?" She moved toward the desk and picked up her drink, untouched, and set it on the liquor cart. "You know, in case you get called out."

"No, I'm good, but thanks."

She remained at the liquor cart, toying with her glass.

He began reading again and then looked at her over the back of the sofa. "Is everything okay?"

She nodded.

"I'm sensing that it's not. Want to talk about it?"

She rubbed her hands over her face. Where would she start? How could she tell him how confused he made her feel? Instead, she bit her tongue, changed her line of thought, and took a deep breath. "I guess it's the whole curse thing."

"You really don't believe in them, do you?"

"No, I don't, but curses come from the power that those who do believe in them have. What if Lacey is aware of this, and that's what's driving her in her quest to destroy me?" She stood in front of him. "Maybe it has nothing to do with her trying to win Marc back, but has everything to do with her attempt to destroy a Greyborne, because . . . because of that." She pointed to the book.

"Maybe." He stroked his chin. "But I still think that she is trying to create a news story that will propel her failed career into the spotlight again, and she thinks she's found one, or has created one herself. She needed someone with a recognizable name behind them to achieve that. I mean, if she'd gone after, let's say, someone like Martha, then outside Greyborne Harbor, no one would be interested. But accusing one of the members of a town's founding family—well, that's big news everywhere."

Addie spun around and walked toward the window. "Maybe you're right. It just gave me a couple of other things to consider."

"Like what?"

"You mentioned Martha." She turned toward him. "She's a perfect example. She's disliked me from the very second I introduced myself to her. Why?"

"Could be lots of reasons—she was in a bad mood, you reminded her of someone else she had a falling-out with?" He shrugged. "It could be any number of things going on with her."

"Yes, but . . . maybe she's a Davenport."

"It could be. Stringer is her married name, isn't it?"

"Most likely." She bit her lip. "I'll ask Paige tomorrow."

"You'll be discreet. I hope. You don't need to start rumors of curses and feuds with her, too."

"Of course I will."

"Good. Shall we get back to the *facts* of the manuscript and see what else we can come up with?" He opened it to the next page and began reading.

She shook her head, began pulling the window curtains closed, and froze in mid-motion. Marc was walking toward the front door. She looked back at Simon, still focused on reading. This was exactly what she didn't need tonight— another showdown. She managed to count to five before the dreaded knock came. Simon glanced up at her. She shrugged her shoulders, feigning ignorance, and went to the door with him close on her heels.

"Marc," she said, her tone as surprised as she could manage, considering the churning bile in her stomach, "what brings you here tonight?"

He looked past her to Simon. "You texted me and said you needed to tell me something."

"That was hours ago, sorry. I forgot. Come in, please. We were just having a drink and going through June's manuscript. Can I get you anything?"

He shook his head and stepped into the foyer, his eyes fixed on Simon.

"We're here in the living room. Please have a seat." She motioned to a seat on the sofa closest to the door.

He walked past Simon and sat where she had designated. She took a seat on the end of the sofa closest to the chair by the fireplace, removed Simon's coat from it, and patted the chair seat gesturing to Simon that was his place when he entered behind Marc. There was no way she was going to let these two sit on the same sofa. "There, nice and cozy. Are you sure you won't join us in a drink?"

"No, I'm on duty till midnight. Had a guy go off sick." His eyes never wavered from Simon's.

"Well, Simon was just telling me that the stomach flu seems to be going around."

"Yeah, that's probably it." He took a deep breath and placed his cap on the coffee table. "So, what is it you needed to tell me?"

She proceeded with her tale of witnessing Dean and Steven's meeting at the park behind the utility shed. She also summarized Jeanie's verbal assault on Serena about her selling tainted tea, and her own part in saving Serena from Jeanie's threats to have the health department close the tea shop. Even in the retelling, she still couldn't figure out Jeanie's strange reaction and immediate departure. She went on to tell them about her seeing Lacey hand Dean a large sum of money and how Serena then discovered after Lacey left with him—those words caught in her throat—that the till and storeroom safe had been emptied out except for a note that simply said, *Thanks for the loan.*

Marc leaned forward, resting his elbows on his knees. "I guess, since I've been ordered to read you into this—"

Simon sat upright in the chair. "Since when?"

Marc glared at him.

"I forgot to tell you, Simon," Addie said. "Remember when you had the meeting with the DA in Salem?"

Simon nodded, returning Marc's eye daggers.

"It seems your friend Jeff Wilson called Marc and asked him to take me on this case as a consultant. So it appears I'm *temporarily*"—she smiled at Marc—"working with the Greyborne Harbor Police Department."

"Wonderful news." Simon clapped his hands. "That means we're all colleagues now." He locked eyes with Marc.

"I guess we are." Addie grinned at Marc.

Marc shook his head, grabbed his hat from the table, and stood up. He tossed it back on the table and sat down again. Simon flinched and looked blankly at Addie. She shrugged and shook her head.

Marc looked down at the floor, then at Addie and Simon. "You're right. We're all colleagues and adults. So, from here on in, we all share information with each other freely, and I, as the police officer, will follow any leads we find. Deal?"

"Deal." Addie barely kept herself from squealing with excitement.

"Deal," Simon murmured.

"Okay, I'll track down the background on this Steven fellow and dig up more information on Dean's last trip to LA. You, Doc, look into the tainted tea and possible suppliers, and, Addie . . . do what you do best. Research that manuscript to see if we can find out exactly what it is we're dealing with here, but most of all, stay safe and out of the line of fire. I have a feeling this is a powder keg ready to explode."

She took a deep breath and nodded.

Marc headed for the door then turned back. "I forgot. I also came here to tell you about something you might be faced with in the morning, Addie."

"What?"

He leaned against the doorframe, fumbling with his cap. "I suspected Lacey of being Miss Newsy, as I told you, but never had the exact proof I needed to call her on it."

"I thought you had it?"

"Only what I've gleaned from conversations we've had and a few side comments her editor, Max Hunter, had made. Before I confront her, I want to catch her red-handed."

"Okay? Not sure what you mean though. How?"

He straightened his shoulders. "I planted some false information with her today. I told her we were on the verge of making an arrest in June's murder and kind of hinted that you might be involved, but we were still in the process of following a lead on that."

"You did what?"

"I know, I know, I should have left you out of it."

"Darn right you should have." Simon stormed across the room toward Marc. "Do you have any idea what that will do to her already tarnished reputation?"

"Think about it. Lacey can't do any more damage than she already has." Marc planted his feet, looking down his nose at Simon.

"But why?" Addie joined Simon.

"Because sometimes in the investigation business, you have to feed some people manure just to see what comes back to you. No one else in the station can corroborate it, because it's not true. Which makes me her only source. So, if she prints anything in that column tomorrow, I can nail her on it and prove to the DA that there is no leak within the department, just an underhanded reporter willing to do and say anything for a story."

Simon crossed his arms. "Well, you do realize, don't you, that Addie's going to be the one to pay the price?"

Marc looked at Addie. "It's no worse than it's already been, and this is a chance to stop her without you having to continue worrying about what she's going to print in the paper every day."

Simon opened his mouth. Addie placed her hand over it. "No, Simon, he's right. This is nothing different than she's already said about me. Except this time, we're in control of what it is."

Marc relaxed his stance. Simon scoured his hands through his hair and walked back to the sofa.

"Talk to you tomorrow." Marc's finger traced the outline of her jaw, and she shivered.

When he left, she went back into the living room. Simon stared out the window into the blackness. She took a seat beside him on the sofa. He didn't say a word.

She picked up her laptop and volume I of the 1724 pirate book and began reading. He sighed, took the manuscript from the tabletop, and settled back into the sofa.

Chapter Thirty-Three

Addie stretched out her neck and arms. Over an hour ago, Marc had dropped his bombshell, then left and Simon had yet to utter a word to her. She glanced sideways at him. A faint smile graced her lips. He was tucked up in the far corner of the sofa, one leg, folded loosely under the other, propped up the manuscript. His other knee was drawn up, balancing a notepad. His eyes moved unwavering between the two.

She went to the kitchen, returned with two steaming cups of coffee in hand, and waved one under his nose. Without looking up at her, he accepted and returned to scribbling. She pressed her lips together and plopped down on the sofa, sighing noisily. "Are you okay? Are we okay?" She tilted her head, waiting for a reply.

He went back to scribbling and then tapped his pen on the notebook. "Everything's fine, and we're fine. I'm just trying to help you comply with the commanding officer's orders."

"The commanding officer?"

"You heard him. You were given your orders and I mine, so I figure two heads are better than one, and the sooner we comply, the faster this can all be solved then we can move

on to a life without living under the scrutiny of the chief."
He all but spat out his words.

"Okay, then, I guess I'd better get back to work." She
looked down at her laptop but watched him out of the corner
of her eye.

He went back to his reading and then looked back at her
and closed the manuscript on his knee. "I'm sorry. I know
Marc means something to you, and obviously you and your
safety are important to him. I'll try and be a little more
sensitive . . . or a little less, whatever . . . in the future."

"Thank you." She set her laptop on the coffee table. "I
know all this is hard, and there is too much drama, but
please try and understand. I've never been in this situation
before, and I'm not sure—"

"Me neither." He smiled.

Her gaze lingered on him for a second or two, only breaking off when heat began to creep up her cheeks.

Simon coughed, breaking the spell between them. "Have
you found anything of use?" his voice a raspy whisper.

"Not really, but it's interesting. I can see why June used
this book as a resource."

"So no pirate treasures pinpointed, then?"

"No, lots of history and a few maps, like this one." She
pulled a map out of the pages. "Not sure it's actually part of
the book, but it's a woodcut engraved plate map of the east-
ern coastline of the United States. There's an X, which I'm
guessing, by the looks of it, is Greyborne Harbor, although
it's not named on here. What about you?"

"I think I have."

"Ooh, tell me." She drew her legs up and hugged her
knees.

"Well, I've been comparing June's original notes to the
map you found in the notes Jeanie gave you, and it seems
she was under the impression that the dotted line showing a
tunnel system under the town wasn't one continuous tunnel

but a series of shafts built under the marked landmarks. The dotted line wasn't indicating a tunnel, only the landmarks' proximity to each other for easier tracking."

"And what do these shafts represent?"

"The hiding places for pirate loot and contraband, it seems."

She edged closer, looking at the map Simon held in his hand.

"See here—the dotted lines. This map was drawn to represent where each of these shafts was located."

"That makes more sense, because there's a lot of bedrock, and I have been trying to figure out exactly how an entire tunnel system could have been dug back then with only hand tools."

"Exactly. That's what June figured, too. These lines are like navigational lines to show where these shafts and caverns were located, like a grid."

"And this one is a solid line. See where it comes from the coast, where the cave entrance is, and goes here to under the Smuggler's Den restaurant."

"Yes, that was obviously an actual tunnel. But didn't you say the British found that one and blasted it?"

"Yes. I was told there are signs of cannonballs having been used."

"Right, so after that, it appears the pirates took their stores more inland and used a series of smaller shafts and caverns to hide their loot farther away from the eyes of the British and people like Gerald Greyborne. It's all kind of like criminals today using multiple offshore bank accounts to evade authorities."

"So, according to this and what you read in her notes, there's a cavern under the big rock, which Serena told me is the site of the hospital now, and then this one here where Fielding's Department Store is. And then what's this one here, by the playground?"

"That's an interesting one." He looked at her, his eyes sparkling, and stabbed his finger on the X by the playground location. "This is where Henry Davenport's original house stood."

"Really?"

"Yes, it seems when he brought his wife and children over from England, he followed in the footsteps of Gerald and built a home for them above the harbor to keep them away from the riffraff of the sailors and pirates down below."

"And what happened to the house?"

"When he was arrested, his property was confiscated and burned by the British because it had been gained by criminal activity."

"So his house was burned down?"

Simon nodded. "His house . . . but not the tavern in the harbor—or the small house he'd built beside the tavern to live in before his family came over, which he later ran as a lucrative brothel, adding to his business portfolio."

"So why didn't the British burn those?"

"Because they were in place before property in the Harbor was registered, and they didn't know they were his."

"What happened to his family?"

"They were turned out on the streets, which was typical of that time, as wife and family were seen only as an extension of a man's property."

"Well, obviously since Lacey and Dean are still here to carry on the family name, they must have survived."

"Oh, yes. Henry's wife, Lillian, was a woman of resourcefulness, and rather than live on the streets, begging, she soon took over the tavern. The family lived upstairs, and her six children went to work downstairs in the tavern, and . . . she ran the brothel next door."

"What? She became a madam?"

He smirked. "It seems our little Miss Lacey isn't the only

Davenport woman to do whatever she can to survive and create a future for herself."

"That must be part of the reason Blain and Dean didn't want this first version of the book published. Today, that's probably not common knowledge."

"It did take me some digging. When the family, under Lillian's guidance, got back on their feet, she built the house where Lacey grew up in the area on the other side of Oak Street from where the original house stood, and the family were then seen, once again, as upstanding members of the community. Lots of new folks had moved to town, and they weren't aware of the family's shady past."

"That is, all except the Greybornes and a few others that had come before."

"So the infamous Madam Lilly departed, and the Harbor saw an emergence of the gracious Lillian Davenport in town, Fear of her past being discovered was something that Lillian apparently took with her to her deathbed."

"And her family has carried on her charade these past three hundred years. Interesting." She stood up and stretched, then spun around. "You said one of the spots marked was at the site of the original Davenport house?"

"Yes, why?"

"Maybe Lillian found a treasure Henry had buried under it, which also helped finance her new life?"

"Maybe, but that would have been a long time ago. No trace would be left now."

"But what if there is more treasure hidden under the other marked shafts? Maybe ones under the hospital or Fielding's Department Store that are just waiting for someone who knows they are there. I mean, if there was treasure in the Smuggler's Den cavern, the British probably took that before they blew it up. They'd be fools not to."

"Could be. And Dean did read this manuscript, so he knows all the shaft locations."

"Yes, and what if Dean is already working on digging some of them out—you know, after he read this first draft when June submitted it to the town council?"

"That was over two years ago, wasn't it"

"Yeah, but it would take planning and financing first, wouldn't it?"

"That's a lot of what-ifs."

"Yes, and there's only one way to find out."

He slowly shook his head. "No. You can't be thinking what I think you are."

"Yes, let's go."

"At this time of night? It's almost eleven."

"I'm wide awake." Her eyes pleaded.

"Where do we start? We can't just go digging around in the basement of the hospital or Fielding's. Or start hacking up the playground."

"The utility shed. The tunnel in it links up with the hospital at the far end, which is where the large rock on the map used to be located."

"That's a long shot, and I have no intention of doing any digging tonight."

"No, just looking, that's all. No digging. I promise."

"And just how are we going to get access to the utility shed? It's a highly secured area, remember?"

"I'll figure that out. Let's just go look and see if the whole idea is feasible first. Maybe there is no way it can be, and it's only my wild imagination taking over."

"That I tend to agree with." He chuckled.

"What? You're not supposed to agree with me."

He looked down at her. "You, my friend, must have been a witch in another life."

Her eyes widened, and her mouth dropped open.

"I'm not sure what spell you've cast on me, but let's go before my wit and good sense come back and I have second thoughts."

Chapter Thirty-Four

"What is going on down here?" Simon's eyes darted from one side of Main Street to the other.

"I forgot. Tomorrow's the first day of the weekend festival. They're setting up."

"That's tonight? I'm supposed to be volunteering. Well," he said as he turned down her shop street and pulled into a parking spot in front of the park, "at least we'll be inconspicuous in our quest."

"Yeah, we'll just pretend to be working."

"Now I feel guilty that we aren't here to help, especially since I'm on a list somewhere." He joined her on the sidewalk and they made their way into the park, heading in the direction of the utility shed.

"Look at it this way. We *are* helping the town, in a roundabout sense, if my hunches pay off."

"I'll try." He weaved around groups of people and their collection of ladders, stringing lights in the park. "Just a minute, you said festival weekend? Does that mean I volunteered for two days?"

"I doubt it. You most likely volunteered just for the setup."

"I hope so. I'm on call all weekend."

"Don't worry, there are other committees that look after everything else."

"Like what?"

"Well, like the ghost walk tour of historical sites in the harbor area, held after the park festival tomorrow night, and then the Sunday-morning minutemen parade, and after that the day-long sailing regatta, followed by a family dance and fireworks."

"It sounds like fun. Are you going? I could meet you if I'm not work—"

Her hand flung out to the side and smacked across his stomach. "What?"

"Look, there's Gloria by the shed. Who's that she's speaking with?"

"I'm guessing by his white hard hat and that utility company truck parked over there"—he pointed to the library parking lot—"that he works for the utility company."

"I can see that, but why is he here?"

"Not everything's a mystery. Maybe they needed an extra power boost for all the lights they're hanging."

"Could be." She bit her lip. "Hi, Gloria." She smiled, sliding up beside her. "Power trouble?"

The utility worker tipped his helmet and turned toward the shed door.

"Hi, Addie." Gloria put her hand on her arm. "I'm not sure. There seems to have been a power surge, and I called them in to inspect. I'd hate to think we're overloading anything."

"What happened?"

"Well," she said, juggling Pippi under her arm, "we started to set up about ten. You know, after the restaurants closed, so as not to interfere with their businesses. When I came at nine to set up the volunteer station down in the hospital parking lot, there was a weird humming sound, and I noticed flashing coming from the library, so I walked down to investigate. We hadn't started plugging anything in yet, so

I didn't know what to make of it." Pippi squirmed excitedly under her arm, yelping to get to Addie. "Looks like you've made a friend, Addie," she laughed.

Addie patted the small dog. "I guess I have."

"That makes me feel better," said Simon from behind her. He grinned at her scowl. "Well, you know, the whole witch thing," he chuckled. "Do dogs take to witches like that?" He patted Pippi's head, and she snapped at his hand.

"Maybe I'm not the one who should be questioned about my past life?" Addie rolled her eyes and gave the little fur ball another well-deserved pet.

"I'm sorry, Doctor. She's usually so friendly to everyone." Gloria wagged her fingers in Pippi's face, scolding her. "Now you say you're sorry, Pippi." She held the dog up, thrusting her in Simon's face.

"Maybe she just senses the hospital smell on me and thinks I'm a vet." He took the growling dog from her. He caressed Pippi and stroked her head. In no time, Pippi settled into the crook of his arm, panting. She eyed Addie with a look that screamed, *Look at my new friend*, and her puppy face appeared to be smiling.

Addie chuckled and locked gazes with Simon. "They are so human sometimes, aren't they?" Realizing she'd been staring, she cleared her throat. "So, Gloria, what did the utility guy find?"

"He didn't arrive until just now. It seems there was a power problem out on the road to the Smuggler's Den earlier, and they were working out there, so it took a while to respond here. So I don't really know. But I did run into Dorothy, and she said"—Gloria leaned in close to Addie and whispered—"the night that June disappeared, she saw exactly the same thing happening a little while after the book club meeting ended and most of us had left."

"Interesting. Did they figure out then what caused it?"

"No, but they did report it as a power surge, and Dorothy

thinks tonight it's just all the lights being hung that have overloaded the circuits."

"Did you tell her this was before the volunteers started working?"

"I tried, but she saw Jeanie and was off and running." Gloria looked at the workers on the street and in the park. "There's so much to do. I think we'll be here all night by the looks of it." She clucked her tongue. "I guess I'd better wait here though and see what the power company says. I certainly hope we don't have to shut down. It would ruin the festival."

"I'm sure it'll be fine." Simon handed Pippi back to Gloria.

"Yes . . . why don't Simon and I stay here and wait for them to finish their inspection, then we can report back to you."

"That would be wonderful. Thank you so much, both of you."

Addie elbowed Simon. "Yes." He jerked and smiled at Gloria. "We'll wait here."

"Excellent." She headed off, shouting orders at a volunteer hanging lights around the pavilion behind the police station.

Simon crossed his arms. "Now what?"

She glanced sideways at him. "Now we wait to see what they say."

"Addie." Serena ran toward her across the library parking lot. "I didn't expect to see you here. Hi, Simon." She waved and reached them, her breath coming in short bursts. "I can't believe the volunteer turnout this year. I guess people are buzzing about the festival though, since the ghost walk is going to end with a bang this year."

Addie glanced at the utility shed and shivered. "Let's hope it's not an actual bang."

Serena frowned and then looked at Simon, who shrugged

his shoulders. Paige ran over, grinning at them. "Addie, glad you could make it."

"Why is everyone so shocked that I came? This is my town, too."

"Not shocked," said Serena, "just surprised. I saw Simon's name on the volunteer list, but didn't see your name. I figured this wasn't your kind of thing."

"What, helping out in my community?"

Serena looked at Simon, and then at Addie. "Helping your community, really? Okay, whatever you say."

Addie glanced sideways at Simon, who was grinning like a cat who'd just swallowed a bird. "I'll have you know we are on special assignment, sanctioned by Gloria."

Serena slid in beside Addie and whispered in her ear. "It's just that we all know you, and I'm pretty sure hanging lights isn't on your agenda tonight." Serena nudged her friend and laughed.

"Darn, there's my mom by the pavilion." Paige moaned. "I'd better hide, or she'll start grilling me about you again, and why I didn't take the job with Lacey." She turned to go.

"Wait, Paige." Addie stepped toward her. "I know this in none of my business, but . . ."

"Yes?"

She looked back at Simon, then at Paige. "What was your mother's maiden name?"

"What? Why?"

"Just curious. I've been reading up on the history of families in Greyborne Harbor. You know, ones that are mentioned in June's book. And your mother seems to be so well established. I was only wondering if Stringer was one of the founding families."

Simon coughed and cleared his throat behind her.

"No, my dad was from Boston. Her name was Davenport."

"Really?" Addie's mouth twitched.

"Yes, Lacey's my cousin. Her father was my mother's brother."

Addie didn't say anything. Serena stabbed her elbow into Addie's side. "Thanks." Addie spoke as normally as possible. "I was just curious."

"Yeah, because she's family, Mom thinks I should have jumped at the chance to work for her and Serena." She bit her lip. "Okay, well this is me hiding from my mother like a naughty ten-year-old." She ran toward Main Street.

"I thought you were going to be discreet about finding out Martha's name?" Simon said, stepping up beside her.

"Well," she said, shrugging her shoulders, "I thought I *was* being . . . discreet."

"Real smooth. There wasn't exactly a lead-up to it in natural conversation." He shook his head. "You're like a dog with a bone, aren't you?"

"That's exactly what I was thinking." Serena spun around, looking at her. "What difference does it make what Martha's last name was?"

"She thinks she has a curse on her incanted by the Davenports some three hundred years ago." Simon rolled his eyes at Serena.

"Well . . . don't you find it even a wee bit interesting that Martha took an instant dislike to me when I introduced myself the first day I opened, and since then, she's gone out of her way to spread gossip and discredit me around town? This confirms that she is a Davenport." She stuck her tongue out at Simon, mocking him.

"You're too much." Serena smirked. "I think this whole Founder's Day thing has gone to your head. First, it's pirates and treasure, now it's witches and curses—what's next, ghosts?"

"Hey, you know I'm onto something." She looked from one tentative face to the other. "I have a method to my madness."

"Madness is right," Simon chuckled.

"It's that madness that I love." Serena wrapped her arms around Addie's neck and hugged her.

Addie looked at Simon over Serena's head. He grinned, then his eyes flickered behind her and she spun around, facing the utility worker. "Hi. So what did you find?"

"Where's Gloria, the woman who called in the power surge complaint?"

"She's busy right now with the volunteers, but she left us here to wait for you so we can report back to her."

He looked at the three expectant faces and frowned. "I really can't . . ." He shuffled from one booted foot to the other.

"Look, I've got to go anyway. I left Mildred with the ladder and a string of lights in front of the library and told her I'd be right back. If I don't show up soon, there'll be another catfight tonight."

"A catfight?" Addie looked at Serena.

"Yeah, Dorothy and Jeanie just had a huge argument in the middle of Main Street."

"Did you hear what it was about?"

"No. I think it's because people are just tired, and it's late, and there's still so much work to do." She looked at the utility worker. "You're not going to shut us down, are you?"

"That's not for me to say."

Serena shrugged. "Okay then, I guess we'll keep at it until we hear otherwise. See you later, I hope."

Addie jumped when Marc's voice boomed from behind her. "Hi, Jim. You wanted to see me?"

"Hi, Chief. Yes, we need to talk." Jim motioned with his head for Marc to follow him.

Addie stepped in behind the two as they headed toward the shed. Jim stopped and looked at her.

"That's okay. She's cleared." Marc motioned to Simon. "And this is the county coroner, he's"—Marc coughed—"part of the team, too, apparently."

"We found something interesting with the main electrical panel and in the tunnel. Actually, it's probably easier if I show you." Jim headed onto the platform that led to the ladder-like stairs.

The trio followed close on his heels and descended into the main utility chamber. Jim walked over to the wall-sized electrical box and pointed. "See, the cover appears to have been pried open, and more than once, I'd say, by the look of these faint scrapes. They're hard to see in this light— that may be why they've never been reported before." He shone his flashlight directly on the area he'd indicated. "See them now?"

Marc leaned forward, eyed the dent and scratch marks along the access panel door, and nodded. Addie took out her cell phone and began snapping pictures.

"What else?" Marc looked at Jim. "You said you found something in the tunnel?"

"Yeah, that's where I found another mystery. Follow me." He led them down the utility corridor past where the library would be and stopped at what Addie surmised to be under the police station. "See?" He pointed to an industrial extension cord. "That's not one of ours. It's one that can easily be picked up from any hardware store."

Marc stood back and rocked on his heels, scrutinizing the cord as Addie took another picture. "And what's at the other end?"

"Nothing. It goes for about another hundred feet or so, then nothing. Just the female plug end."

Addie surveyed the tunnel, her eyes following the length of the cord. "So, someone was working down here, packed up in a hurry, and forgot a section of their extension cord?"

Jim shrugged. "I guess. I can't think what else it's doing here, and if they were piggybacking off the main box, it would be the reason for the power surge and flashing lights."

"What's at the far end?" She looked at him.

"Just a dead end at the ramp up to the hospital."

"A ramp? No stairs?"

"No, the hospital used to use it as a loading ramp for heavy equipment, CAT scan machines and stuff, but they have an actual loading dock now. The old utility elevator up to the street has been closed off for years. Although, there's still a diesel forklift parked against the back wall."

"What's on the other side of the wall?" She looked at him, then to Marc.

"Nothing. It's just a brick wall."

"Addie," Marc said, frowning at her, "what are you thinking?"

She ignored him and turned back to Jim. "Can you show us?"

"Yeah, come on."

Marc groaned.

Addie snapped a photo of the far end of the extension cord and followed Jim as he continued up the wide hallway toward the hospital. When they reached the ramp leading up to the hospital basement, Addie inspected the steel access door and eyed the old, rusted forklift stored against the dead-end wall beside the ramp. She surveyed the cement tunnel floor and walked to the side of the lift, then nodded and went back to the three men watching her, questions filling their eyes.

"I think we'd better move that forklift away from the wall and see what's hiding behind it," she announced.

Jim was the first to speak. "It hasn't been moved for years. I don't even know if there's still a key to start it up so we could."

Marc's gaze flicked from the forklift to her. "What are you thinking?"

She crossed her arms and met the skeptical look in his eyes. "It's been moved, recently, and regularly, I'd say. You can tell by the marks etched into the cement floor, not to mention the trail of disturbed dust around it."

Simon looked up at the ceiling of the tunnel. "Where was the big rock located from here?"

Marc scanned the corridor and followed Simon's gaze to the ceiling. "Probably right above us."

Simon pressed his lips tight and glanced sideways at Addie.

Addie looked up, then looked over at the brick wall behind the forklift. "Marc, can we talk about my theories now?"

Chapter Thirty-Five

It didn't take long before the tunnel was filled with crime scene investigators. Addie had to dodge more than one officer snapping pictures and dusting for prints. "Hey, Chief," Jerry called from the front of the forklift, "come look at this."

"What do you have?" Marc crouched down beside him, looking at the front frame.

"These marks on here, see? It looks like a winch has been attached."

Marc scanned the markings and looked behind him, then at the frame again. "I guess that explains how the forklift was moved." He stood up, brushing dust off his trousers. "Okay, we're going to have to get this out of here."

"Want me to get the winch from the SWAT truck?" Jerry stood up.

"No, the forklift isn't that big. I think we've got enough manpower now to drag it out."

Jerry called for assistance, and soon six officers had the antiquated forklift pulled away from the wall. Addie stood on tiptoes to see past them, her eyes set on the brickwork behind it. "Look."

Simon whistled. Marc shook his head. "I don't know how you do that."

"What?" She looked up at him.

He shook his head again and walked toward the gaping hole in the brick wall. "You must be a witch or something," he muttered.

Simon stifled a laugh. "Told you."

"What are you talking about?" She slid up beside Marc.

"You have this uncanny way of knowing what's going on before there's any proof." He gave her a sidelong glance. "Okay, Jerry, Dave, take a look and see what we've found."

The two officers pulled out their flashlights and crawled through the three-by-three-foot opening in the wall. Jerry's head popped out of the hole. "Chief, you'd better come see this."

Marc flipped on his flashlight and entered. Addie turned on her phone light and followed close behind him. Marc stopped halfway through and glanced back at her, frowning. She smiled demurely at him. He grunted, held out his hand, and assisted her to her feet on the other side. Jim and Simon followed closely behind. She shone her light across the dirt walls to the earthen ceiling and stopped. "Jim, there's old lumber boards across this portion. What's above them?"

He shone his light up at the cavern roof and squinted in the dim light.

"There definitely appears to have been recent visitors in here," Jerry said behind her. "Here, Chief, these boot marks in the dust cover every inch of this cave."

A rumbling sound from above sent chunks of earth falling to the cavern floor. They all flinched and looked up. "My best guess," said Jim, "is we're right under the new loading dock. It's not safe in here. A truck backing into the dock is disturbing the ground and—" A piece of dirt thudded off his hard hat.

"Okay, everyone, back to the main corridor as fast as you can. Jerry, you make some footprint molds. Everyone else don't disturb the ground any more than we have. Let's go, now."

"But, Marc—" Addie turned toward him.

"No buts. We can't risk a cave-in or contaminating the evidence any more than we already have before Jerry gets the plaster molds or we'll lose them under this falling dirt."

Her shoulders slumped, but she obeyed orders, and they crawled back through the brick wall opening. She dusted herself off and looked at Marc as he climbed out. "I needed more time in there. How can I make certain that it's a pirate hideout?"

His eyes bored into hers. "That's your problem, Addie. You have the instincts, but not the wherewithal to know when you're in danger, which makes you even more dangerous to yourself," he snapped, turned away and crouched down in the opening. "Jerry. You done yet?"

"Almost, give me a minute."

"Hurry, I don't want this to cave in on you."

"I doubt that would happen," she said over Marc's head. "It's been here for a few hundred years already and—"

He looked up at her. "Are you questioning my orders and concern for my officers?"

"No, I was just making a *factual* point."

"Here's another *factual* point for you. The loading dock has only been here about ten years, so the vibration of the heavy trucks above is something new and is obviously stressing the integrity of this grotto."

"Come on, Addie." Simon tugged on her sleeve. "Let the police do their job." He pulled her away.

"But, Simon," she said, shaking off his hand, "I need to know what's in there."

He leaned toward her. "Will these help?" He grinned and opened the photos on his cell phone.

She gasped. "Yes, I could kiss you right now."

"Well, I always did like your thank-yous." He winked.

She playfully slapped his arm and glared at Marc's back as he crouched in the entrance waiting for Jerry to emerge. "Come on. Let's go back to my shop and have a good look at these."

"I can't believe that find. Wow!" Simon puffed as they jogged across the lawn out of the park, attempting to avoid a run-in with Gloria in case she tried to recruit their volunteer services.

"I know," Addie panted. "Obviously the pirates covered the shaft opening with the lumber beams and dirt to hide it."

"And it's exactly where it was marked on June's map."

"Yeah, and when they built the hospital, they just paved over it, and no one was any the wiser to what lay underneath."

"That's why whoever's been excavating had to go in from the utility tunnel."

"Yes, digging up the parking lot would have drawn attention." She unlocked the front door, made her way through the dark to the back room, and turned off the alarm. She threw her handbag on the desk, pulled up her rickety old office chair, and patted a crate next to it. "Come on, show me what you got." Simon grinned. She shook her head. He plopped down beside her and pulled out his phone.

They scanned the pictures for several seconds before Addie broke the silence. "Look at these old barrels. They're crushed. These clay wine casks are all broken, too, and there doesn't appear to be much else in there."

"So why would the pirates dig the shaft and cave to store rum and wine? It doesn't make sense."

"Yeah, they look like they've been like that for years, and I don't see any sign of a chest or crate that might hold a buried treasure."

"Unless whoever broke through the wall did find what they came for and they have it now."

She shook her head. "I'm no archaeologist, but by the

looks of these photos, I'd say this cave was looted years ago." Simon glanced sideways at her.

"I'm just thinking that June may have found evidence that there once was treasure buried under Greyborne Harbor, but my guess is that it's long gone."

"You're probably right." Simon shifted on the crate. "After all, the British destroyed the cave on the coast, and this one under the big rock appears to have been cleared out years ago. We can't go digging up the playground to search the cavern below the old Davenport homestead."

"My thought is that Lillian probably cleared that out about three hundred years ago, anyway."

"So now what?"

"We need to focus on who killed June. It must have been someone who still believes treasure is here and is so bent on finding a buried treasure they'd stop at nothing to achieve that."

"But where do we start?"

"Let's start with all the major players." She glanced at the names on the blackboard. Her eyes flashed from one name to the next, running each of their relationships with June past Simon. The name that kept popping up was Steven, aka Peter. Addie went to her computer and searched the names of staff members in the news department at Lacey's old network.

"Here, look. Peter Jacobson, news reporter known for his two years' worth of investigations into to America's lost treasures. That's it. He was researching buried treasure and, probably through Dean, when he was in LA, heard about June's book. He has to be this mysterious Steven character."

"Okay, how do we prove it?"

"We need to talk to Jeanie."

"She might still be setting up at the park."

"Let's go." She grabbed her bag.

Simon walked up one side of Main Street and Addie the other. They met up at the loading ramp behind the hospital.

"Maybe she's working in the park." She glanced back at the loading ramp as they headed toward the twinkling fairy lights in the park behind the municipal buildings.

Addie spotted Dorothy at the pavilion speaking with a group of volunteers and turned in that direction, tugging Simon along with her. "Hi, Dorothy, looks like you guys are nearly done. Great job." She stood back and admired the lights hung throughout the festival area.

"Yes, almost there. Some of the vendors are done setting up their booths and stalls already, and the last of the lights have just gone up." Dorothy smiled, and relief swept across her face.

"It's magical." Addie beamed, looking around her.

Dorothy looked at Simon. "Were you two working on Main Street?"

"You might say that." Simon coughed.

"Have you seen Jeanie?" Addie stood on her tiptoes, scanning the thinning crowd.

"She left a few hours ago. Steven came—in a foul mood he was, too—and swept her out of here in a flash." Dorothy clucked her tongue. "Trouble in paradise, I assume."

"That's too bad," Addie said. "How did Jeanie and he end up together when he was dating June first, anyway?" Simon elbowed Addie's arm. She glanced at him, her top lip twitching.

"He's a travel agent from Chicago and apparently had read June's book and emailed her saying he wanted to arrange to bring tours down here—you know, to explore the pirate sites she talked about in the book. So, he came down and that was that. June fell immediately in love. Her husband passed away over twenty years ago, you see. She's been pretty lonely."

"I didn't know that. But Steven looks so much younger than what June would have been."

"Well, when he first arrived, his hair was gray, and he did

look and dress much older, very conservatively, but after he and Jeanie got together, he started changing and began using that men's shampoo that slowly covers the gray."

"I guess dating a younger woman like Jeanie brought out a more youthful side of him," Addie chuckled.

"Well, he is younger than June was, but I don't think by too much, and he's not much older than Jeanie. Perhaps he was just at the age where he was bored by June's sudden need to turn in by eight or nine at night, as she'd always been such a go-getter before, and still was when they first met."

"I wonder what caused the change in her?"

Dorothy shook her head. "I just know what Jeanie told me, and that was he soon got tired of sitting around the house all evening by himself. She felt sorry for him, not realizing her mother had suddenly become so old and frail."

"How old was June?"

"She was a very young, active seventy-year-old. We swam at the Y together, went hiking. She liked a good party as much as anyone. She was fun and lived life to the fullest."

"Then she suddenly changed?"

"Yes, it started to happen almost right after Steven arrived. It was weird, but we all thought perhaps he just wore her out, if you know what I mean." She nudged Addie's arm. "Anyway, Jeanie, just being friendly to her mother's boyfriend, took him out to a couple of local clubs and such, and well, one thing led to another, and they fell in love."

"Really?"

Dorothy gasped. "Just look at that guy over there. Does no one these days have any common sense? Hey, Albert," she shouted, marching off toward a small balding man, "are you trying to pull all the strings of lights down on purpose? Who taught you how to carry a ladder?"

Simon's eyes widened. "Wow, remind me to never get on her bad side."

Addie studied Dorothy berating the poor volunteer and nodded. "So, what do you think?"

"About that bullying?"

"No—well that, too." Addie looked back at Dorothy and shook her head. "But I mean about the sudden change in June's disposition."

"I'd say, as we suspected after analyzing the tea, that Steven had been drugging her."

"Yeah, maybe so he could use it as an excuse to get close to Jeanie, who he thought might be more help to him." Her eyes narrowed.

"What are you thinking?"

"What if—and this is a big what-if, based purely on speculation . . ."

"Okay, I'm following you."

"What if Steven had read the book and heard through Dean about the original manuscript and knew there was nothing about the pirate hiding places in her published book and was searching for the original Dean had told him about?"

"I see where you're going with this."

"You do?" Her eyes lit up.

"Yeah, and he started drugging her so she'd go to bed early and he could search her house for it."

"Exactly!" she cried, clapping her hands. "That's it, and when he didn't find it, he thought Jeanie might know where it was and—"

"Started working on her, thinking she could lead him to it? Maybe your theory isn't as far-fetched as you thought?"

"No it's not, and that could be why they had the argument in front of my bookstore that day after she dropped off June's notes to me. He thought she'd given the original away. I wonder if Jeanie knows."

"It could be possible that after the confrontation with Serena in her store and your planting the seeds of doubt about him, she started to figure it all out. You did say she bolted when you told her about the man who bought the tea."

Addie's eyes widened. "Yes, and her life could be in danger if she confronts him about it."

Simon's cell phone sent off a foghorn sound alert. "That's my emergency ring tone," he explained apologetically and pulled it from his jacket pocket. He read the message. "I've got to go."

"Please don't say it's about Jeanie?"

"I don't know. I hope not." He spun on his heel, stopped, and turned. "Here—you'll need these to get home, I might be hours." He tossed his car keys to her and dashed off toward the hospital.

Chapter Thirty-Six

Addie pulled her car into the parking stall in the alley behind Beyond the Page, tapping her fingers on the steering wheel in time with the music playing through the speakers. She turned off the ignition, hopped out and took a deep breath of the fresh, sea salt–filled morning air and smiled, still humming the tune that had just played.

Serena's back door burst open. Her red head popped around the corner, and her eyes locked with Addie's. She tossed a bundle of paper at Addie's feet, retreated, and closed her door. Addie looked down at the elastic-bound roll at her feet. *The Greyborne Harbor Daily News* banner glowered up at her. She tucked it under her arm and entered the back room of her store.

Paige looked up from the book crate she was unpacking and stopped in mid-motion. She grabbed an armful of books and darted into the main shop.

"Umm, good morning?" Addie called after her, but her greeting was met with silence.

She shrugged and tossed her purse on the desk, the newspaper beside it, and took off her coat. She started for the door and paused, her hand against the doorframe. She glanced over her shoulder at the newspaper, sucked in a deep breath, went back, removed the elastic band from around it and laid it flat on the desk. The top story headline jumped out at her.

Area-wide Manhunt Under Way

Greyborne Harbor Police has issued an area-wide warrant for Dean Davenport, who has been reported as being a person of interest in the brutal attack on an area resident who was discovered unconscious last night in a local garage. If anyone has information about Davenport's whereabouts, they are urged to contact the police department immediately.

"Wow." Addie drummed her fingers on the page and reread the news alert. "Dean, what are you up to now?" she muttered, thumbing through the paper. She stopped at page five and blinked. "Got you now," she smirked, fist bumping the page. "It looks like there's more than one snake in the family."

Paige's head poked around the doorframe. "Every . . ." She cleared her throat. "Is everything okay in here?"

Addie looked over at her, a wide grin across her face. "Yup, it's a great day."

"Okay?" Paige grimaced. Her eyes went to the paper, then back to Addie. "Dorothy's on the phone and wants to know if she can pick up some more copies of June's book for the Smuggler's Den."

"How many do we have left in stock?"

"A couple of dozen, I think."

Addie whistled. "Is that all? We just got fifty in."

Paige nodded. "They've been flying off the shelves, same as the books you brought in to restock the historical fiction section with."

"Good news all around, I guess."

Paige glanced back at the paper, frowning. "Yes, good news?" She looked at Addie. "So, what do you want me to tell her?"

"Tell her we can give her another dozen, but then they'll have to wait for us to reorder if they want any more copies after tonight."

Paige double tapped the doorframe and returned to the front.

Addie looked down at Miss Newsy's latest rant and smiled.

I have it on good authority that police are ready to make an arrest for the murder of local librarian June Winslow. It has also been reported that due to excessive police activity in and around the Beyond the Page bookshop and at the home of area resident Addison Greyborne, she may know more than she's saying in regard to this matter.

She walked into the main shop, winding her way down the aisles, making mental notes of which book genres she'd have to concentrate on restocking. Paige was right; the historical fiction section was nearly empty again. She went to the cash register, input the code to bring up the weekly sales reports, and smiled. The door chimes rang and she looked up.

"Dorothy? Good morning. I see you're out and about early."

She nodded and slumped onto a stool. "I haven't had any sleep either."

"That's not good. Trouble with the setup?"

She shook her head. "No, we were just finishing up when you left, and then I got a call from a rather hysterical Jeanie. They'd just taken Steven to the hospital."

Addie's mind flashed to the text Simon had received. "I read about an attack in the paper. Was that him?"

Dorothy nodded.

"Is he okay now?"

"He's in critical condition, but stable. Jeanie's a wreck though."

"Understandable."

"I had to get some work finished up for the festival, and, well, have just left her with Mildred in the waiting room of the hospital." She shook her head. "It's so uncalled-for, this random violence."

"So, it's being considered a random act?" Addie plopped a pod into the coffee maker.

"They have a suspect. Jeanie said she and Steven were at home, and he got a call from Dean Davenport out of the blue, demanding to meet him out back. He went out to the garage without another word to her."

"Did he know Dean? Were they friends or . . . business partners?" Addie handed the steaming cup to Dorothy.

"Not as far as Jeanie knew, but she said he may have run into him sometime around town." She clasped the cup Addie presented to her and took a sip of her coffee. "It just doesn't make any sense. Why would Dean attack someone he didn't know—at least not very well, if he did?"

The tip of Addie's tongue burned to speak out, but she ran it over the inside of her cheek and shook her head. She spied calluses on Dorothy's hands, and her brain began whirling.

"Your hands look sore, like you've been chopping wood for a month straight."

Dorothy jerked her hands to her lap. "Not quite. Just been hanging lights and hauling stage risers and booth lumber for the past few days."

"I have some cream in the back that might help."

"No, I'm fine. They'll heal when all this manual labor is done."

A cell phone rang. Addie glanced at her silent phone on the counter. "Dorothy. Dorothy? That must be yours."

Dorothy's head jerked. "Sorry, I must be half-asleep." She fished around in her bag of books, withdrawing a phone. "Hello . . . hello?" The ringing persisted. She frowned, turned the phone over in her hand and shook her head, dropping the pink pearl tortoiseshell phone back into her bag and withdrawing a plain white one instead.

The fine hairs at the back of Addie's neck stood up.

"Hello? . . . Yes . . . Okay," she sighed. "I'll be right there." She clicked off. "I have to go. There's an issue with the fire department regulations over in the park."

"You have two phones?"

Dorothy waved her hand. "I keep forgetting to give Jeanie June's phone. She left it at the last meeting at the library. That night she . . . she"—Dorothy looked down at her bag—"disappeared. I picked it up to return it to her later, and then, well, with everything that happened, it's just slipped my mind, I guess. Well, I'm off." She turned directly into Marc's path.

He caught her arm. "Morning, Dorothy."

"Morning, Chief," she muttered and dashed past him.

Marc slid onto a stool. "She's in a hurry today. The fire chief's doing his inspection of the lights." His mischievous grin had her lips dancing in a return move.

"I think it might be more than that."

"How so?" He set his cap on the counter.

"Did you know that she has June's missing cell phone?"

"No, how do you know that?"

"She just tried to answer it and realized she'd pulled the wrong phone out of her bag."

"Interesting." Marc spun around on his stool and looked out the window toward the park. "We've been looking for that."

"I kind of thought you may have been." She leaned her elbows on the counter, cupping her chin in her hand, and toyed with his cap. "She said June forgot it at the library the night she disappeared, so Dorothy picked it up to return it to her when she saw her again."

"I need to go and get it from her. We want to check the call history." His eyes watched her finger as it traced the bill of his cap. He cleared his throat. "I came in to tell you that I won't be able to take you on the ghost walk tour tonight, after all." He traced his finger down one of hers as he retrieved his cap. "I want to, but with the manhunt on for Dean . . . I'm sure you read about it this morning?"

"Yeah, I . . ." But no words would squeak past her tight throat.

"And now with the phone discovery . . ." He looked at his cap, which he was twisting in his hands, looked at a pile of books she'd yet to shelve, but didn't make eye contact with her. "I'll try to catch up with you later tonight, but can't promise. I'll text you though." He turned to go and stopped, without turning around. "And the Lacey issue's been resolved, too. There shouldn't be any more Miss Newsy articles written." He straightened his shoulders and walked out the door, the chimes ringing behind him.

Addie slid onto a stool and took a deep breath.

"Here are the books Dorothy wanted." Paige dropped them on the counter. "Is she coming back for them?"

Addie looked blankly at her, and then shook her head. "I think she'll be busy with the festival. Maybe you could run them over to the Smuggler's Den, if you don't mind?"

"Sure. I'll see if I can borrow Mom's car."

"No, take mine. I know you're trying to avoid her."

"Not anymore." She beamed. "She finally cornered me last night at the park, and we had a long talk. Everything's good now. She even said Emma and I could move into her house. She's there alone now since all us kids have moved out. There's lots of room, and she seems lonely, so . . ." She shrugged. "I guess all's well."

"I'm so happy for you. I know it's been hard. And if, for some reason, it doesn't work out . . . I was thinking . . . that I have a two-bedroom suite above my garage. It hasn't been lived in for years, by the looks of it, but it's in good condition, and, well, with a good cleaning, you could move in there if you wanted to. Rent free. I'd love to have some company on that property."

"Thanks." Paige smiled at her. "It makes it easier knowing I have a backup plan in case it doesn't work out. You know my mother." She laughed.

"Yup, a plan B is always good to have." She winked. "My keys are in my purse on the back desk."

"Okay, be back soon." Paige put the books in a paper sack and waved as she left.

Addie started straightening bookshelves. The door chimes rang behind her, and she spun around. "Simon," she said with a grin, walking toward him, and then frowned. "Have you had any sleep? Want a cup of coffee?"

"No, thanks. Carolyn's out front. She's off duty now and is going to drive me to your place to pick up my car. Then I need to go back to the inn and try and get at least a few hours of sleep."

"Did you work all night?"

"Yeah," he yawned. "Feel like I'm back in my residency days. Think I'm getting too old to pull an all-nighter in the operating room. My feet are killing me."

"Was it Steven?"

He nodded. "He's pretty smashed up—shattered orbital bone, ruptured spleen. It was touch-and-go for a while, but he's stable now, I think."

"It said on the news that an area-wide manhunt is on for Dean. Did you hear that?"

"No, haven't heard the news all day." He leaned against a bookcase. "If it was him, he sure did some serious damage. There was a lot of rage in those blows."

"His fists?"

"Fists, probably a shovel, too."

"Really?"

He nodded, yawning again.

"Is Jeanie still there?"

"Yeah, she was in the intensive care waiting room with Mildred when I left."

"No Dorothy?"

"Nope." He stretched out his arms and shoulders. "I haven't seen her at all."

"Interesting. I'll get your keys."

"That would be great." His dark, hollowed-out eyes attempted a crinkled smile, but even that seemed to take too much effort. When she returned, she found him slumped onto a stool, his hand propping up his chin.

"Here." She dangled the key ring in front of his closed eyes.

He jerked awake and smiled sheepishly. Without a word, he stumbled out the door and into his sister's awaiting Ford F-150.

The day flew by. Addie and Paige were both kept busy taking orders for out-of-stock books and ringing in sales. At four o'clock, Addie flipped the door sign and pressed her back against the cool glass. "That's it. We're done."

"So early?" Paige looked at her from across the counter.

"Yup, we're sold out of the American Revolution, pilgrims, and anything to do with local history, and we have a festival to go to."

"Are you wearing a costume?"

"I wasn't aware it was a dress-up event."

Paige looked her. "Of course, it's Founder's Day, everyone dresses up."

"I never thought of that. What are you going as?"

"I found the perfect Martha Washington dress, complete with bonnet, and then came across a child's minuteman outfit and wig for Emma."

"That sounds so cute. I can't wait to see it."

"I know Emma will fight me on wearing it. She's at that stage. But I know I'll eventually win."

"Well, if you have a two-year-old to wrestle, then you'd better head off now."

"I won't argue." She grabbed her purse from under the counter and scooted out the door.

Addie stood in the window. A group of minutemen marched past her door, crossed the road, and headed into the park. She laughed, looking over the collection of costumed people on the street who were heading into the park. There was a combination of pirates, minutemen, and a few Paul Reveres, Martha Washingtons, and Betsy Rosses. Even a couple of brave souls dressed as redcoats. She mentally ran through her own closet at home. "I got nothing."

She closed out the cash register and walked to the back room, grabbed her purse and jacket, raised her arm to press the alarm on the panel, and stopped at the sound of a banging noise coming from the alley. She opened the door a crack, peered out, and gasped.

"Lacey, let me in, damn it," Dean yelled, his fist repeatedly smashing against the door.

She ducked back in and then heard the sound of tires spinning on gravel. She peeked out through a narrow crack in time to see a silver sedan speed off toward Birch Road. Her hand shaking, she dialed Marc's number.

Chapter Thirty-Seven

By the time Addie had turned off the lights, set the alarm, and stepped out onto the front street, the sound of sirens could already be heard heading down Birch Road. She locked the door and took a deep breath. The aroma of cooking food tickled at her nostrils. Following her nose, she traipsed across the street to the park.

The fairy lights were breathtaking against the backdrop of the darkening sky. She made her way past a face-painting station and the haystack maze and started to make a beeline to the scents of fresh barbecue, but got momentarily distracted at the bake sale table. She withdrew a dollar from her wallet, purchased a giant chocolate chip cookie, and munched happily on it as she wove her way through the crowds of costumes.

In front of the bobbing for cannonballs booth, she laughed when she saw a familiar redhead sputtering water, trying to catch one of the floating black plastic balls in her teeth. Carnival games of every kind blocked her passage to the food court, and even though her stomach growled in anticipation, she couldn't help but smile at the antics of the revelers, and she noted a giant cannonball-toss tournament in session. Squeals of laughter filled her ears as eager participants flung bowling balls in a testament to their strength. She stood on tiptoe, searching out her target. There it was: the food court.

After several minutes of jostling and squeezing through a boisterous group of Minutemen, she sank her teeth into her hamburger. She was in the middle of a moan of appreciation when her hair was twisted into a ponytail and lightly tugged on. She spun around and came face-to-face with a smiling pirate wench who still held a lock of Addie's hair gripped in her hand. Her friend's own, still wet, hair was pulled up into a loose topknot.

"I heard you laughing at me." Serena crossed her arms and faked a frown.

Addie laughed and glanced at the man standing beside her, who was also wearing a swashbuckling pirate costume.

Serena's face glowed as she latched onto her fellow pirate's bicep. "Addie, this is my good friend Zach, and Zach, this is Addie, my best friend."

Addie shook his hand and smiled. "Nice to meet you. I was starting think you were a figment of her imagination." She winked at Serena.

Serena's mouth dropped open. Zach chuckled and wrapped his arm around Serena, drawing her close into his side, and kissed the top of her head. "No, I'm very real."

Addie felt a tug at her heart as she watched the two of them, and she smiled.

"Oh, oh, oh!" Serena jumped excitedly. "Did you hear?"

"Hear what?"

"About Lacey?"

Addie shook her head.

"You're going to love this, then." She leaned closer to Addie. "I went out to grab a pizza roll from Martha's at noon, and when I got back there was a note from her saying she left for a job with a major television network in New York City."

Addie's eyes widened. "No! You're kidding, right?"

"Scout's honor and all that."

"Just like that?"

Serena nodded.

"But what about her mother? I thought she was"—Addie dropped her voice—"dying."

"Seems not. And actually Betty was shocked to hear the reason why everyone had been offering her sympathy looks and support. She said she did have a cold a while back but had recovered well. She had no idea how the rumor got started about her impending demise."

Addie heaved a deep breath. "So just like that, she was gone? She couldn't even wait until you got back from picking up lunch to say goodbye?"

"Nope, it's just like last time, when she headed off to LA. One day she was here, the next day . . ." She shrugged.

"Did she repay the money she took?"

"Nope, didn't even mention it. I'm not even sure how I'm going to pay this month's bills."

Addie reached out and clasped Serena's hand, giving it a light squeeze. "You know that I'll help you with whatever you need. So don't worry about it."

"But your shop doesn't make any more than mine does most of the time." Serena sniffed, her eyes clearly fighting back tears.

"No, but I have the money in my personal accounts, so don't worry. I'll be fine."

"Yeah but—"

"No yeah buts. I don't want to use my aunt's inheritance to keep the doors of the bookstore open, but using some of it to help a friend in her time of need is different."

"Thanks, I promise I'll pay you back."

"I know you will," Addie said, patting Serena's hand. "When you can, so don't worry. It'll be okay."

Serena pursed her lips tight and nodded. "You know. I just don't get it. Lacey knows my shop only makes enough to survive on. How could she possibly have thought that she was entitled to that money? Did she think when she wormed her way into my business that she should be paid for it? I thought she was helping me out, as a friend?" Serena's bottom lip quivered.

"Oh no, Serena," Addie cried, leaping to her feet, wrapping her friend in her arms. "She *was* probably in the beginning, but then something might have changed for her to do what she did." Addie tightened her hug. The memory of seeing Lacey hand money to Dean and the fact that he was now on the run rushed back to Addie, and what Marc had said this morning about Lacey not being a problem anymore flashed through her mind, too.

Serena nodded and pulled away, a forced smile on her lips. "Well," she choked, taking a deep breath. "We're off to watch the talent show before the ghost walk starts. You should join us when you're done eating."

"I might do that, thanks."

"Okay, see you there." Serena smiled, and when this one reached her eyes, Addie knew her friend would be all right.

"Yup. See you soon." She waved, took her seat and stuffed the last cold pieces of burger into her mouth, then gulped down her lukewarm coffee and dropped her trash in the can. When she turned toward the main aisle between the vendors, she spotted Dorothy talking to Ida beside the cannonball toss and made her way through the crowd toward them. By the time she got there, Dorothy was gone.

"Hi, Ida." She rested her hand on the petite woman's shoulder.

"Addie, nice to see you."

"Are you enjoying your evening?"

She groaned. "I guess as much as anyone can who has a dictator for a boss."

Addie's brow creased.

"Dorothy seems to have taken over from Gloria as volunteer coordinator today and is barking orders at everyone."

"She's probably just tired. I heard she was at the hospital all night with Jeanie after she left here."

Ida stared up at her. "No, I went at noon to give Mildred a break so she could eat. She told me that Jeanie called Dorothy last night, but she never showed up. Mildred's been alone with her since they took Steven in."

Addie flinched. "My mistake, I guess."

"I'd better get back to work. We're setting up for the talent show and best costume contest. They'll be held before the ghost walk tour starts at around eleven. Are you coming?"

"I'll probably go on the tour, but think I'll pass on the rest. There's something I have to do first."

"Okay, see you down in the harbor. It starts at the museum parking lot." She waved as she made her way through the crowd.

Addie turned and darted through the crowds, the sounds of musicians tuning up for the talent show screeching through the air behind her. She had just swept past a family group when a hand reached out and grabbed her wrist. "Hey, where are you off to in such a hurry?"

The force of the stop spun Addie right around, and she came face-to-face with sea-blue eyes. "Simon?"

He looked questioningly at her. "What's the rush?"

"I have to find someone."

"Okay. But by the look on your flushed face, I'd say you better rest a minute."

"I'm fine, really. I have to go."

"Is something wrong?" Carolyn stepped up beside them, a wiggling three-year-old boy in tow.

"I just have to find Marc. Do you know where he is, by any chance?"

"I don't, but I can check. I've got my police radio." She flipped it open and turned up the scanner volume.

Simon placed his hands on Addie's shoulders. "What's happened?"

"Dean's still in town, and Marc took off after him, and before that he was looking for Dorothy because I found out she has June's cell phone, and Dorothy told me she was at the hospital all night with Jeanie but she wasn't. I just saw her and—"

"Slow down." His fingers pressed into her shoulders. "Take a deep breath. You're not making any sense."

Carolyn leaned toward them. "Marc's combing the harbor in his patrol car. I'll let him know that you're looking for him."

"No." Addie placed her hand over the radio. "I'll find him, thanks." She turned and stepped away.

"Addie, wait, I'll go with you," Simon called.

"Uncle Simon's going to take me to the cannonball bobbing thingy," giggled a curly-headed six-year-old girl, looking up at her with big blue eyes.

Addie looked from Simon to Carolyn and sucked a breath in through her teeth. "No, you go and have fun with your family."

The little girl jumped up and down excitedly. "Come on, Uncle Simon." She tugged on his hand. "I want to win a prize."

He shrugged in a helpless gesture.

Addie smiled and dashed off toward the park entrance. She raced across the road, through her shop, and out the back door into her car. At the turn onto Birch Road, she headed down toward the harbor.

She scanned every back alley and side street she passed but in the fading daylight, it was difficult to make much out. See did notice a large police presence in the area. Their cruisers weren't hard to miss with the street lights reflecting off the roof-mounted blue and red light bars. Unfortunately, none of them was number 001. Addie pulled over to the side at the south end of Marine Drive. Her hands, white-knuckled, gripped the steering wheel. Was this all for nothing? Why was it so important for her to see Marc right now? She could just call him and tell him her suspicions about Dorothy, but the truth was . . . she missed him. She missed sharing her theories and having him refute them as just that. She missed their teasing banter, but most of all she missed how she felt when . . . Addie shook her head and pulled out onto the road.

Marine Drive teemed with people making their way down the hill from Town Square. She glanced at her console clock. The festival in the park would be winding down soon, which meant the ghost walk tour would be shortly underway.

She hesitated at the intersection that would keep her in the harbor, where she might be lucky enough to find a parking spot and go ahead on the tour with the others as planned, or follow the road straight out of town leading to Smuggler's Den, where the finale would take place. She gripped the wheel and went straight.

When Addie pulled into the parking lot, she was amazed to see the number of cars already there. Apparently, she wasn't the only one who had opted to take a shortcut to the refreshment part of the evening. She made her way to the front door and noted that strings of lights now hung along the pathway she and Paige had explored down to the beach. She guessed it was to allow safer access up from the beach for the ghost tour participants.

At the door, a man dressed in full Blackbeard regalia greeted her, and she immediately recognized him as being the manager who had assisted her and Paige after their run-in with the falling rocks.

His eyes lit up when he saw her. "Hello! So you've finally decided to take me up on that offer of a free meal." He clasped her hand in his, shaking it.

"Well, yes and no. I'm actually here for the ghost walk tour finale, but I see"—her eyes scanned the dining room and bar—"that I'm not the only one who skipped the tour and came here directly."

The manager's black beard shivered with his laughter.

"Actually, judging by the looks of the number of people attending the tour, you're going to run out of room in here fairly quickly. Have you thought about serving refreshments outside, too?"

His eyes widened. "No, I didn't realize there would be so much interest. I'll get my staff on that right away. Thanks for the heads-up." He pulled back his lacy cuff sleeve and checked his watch. "There's just enough time left, I think." He waved a server over, whispered in his ear, and smiled when the young man scooted off toward a group of staff members setting up behind the bar.

He clapped his hands together. "That's taken care of. And now for introductions, so I may tell my staff the name of our most favored patron, not only for tonight, but for every visit hereafter." He bowed and kissed the back of her hand as though she were royalty. She blushed and pulled her hand away.

She dropped in a curtsy. "Addison Greyborne, at your service."

He stood straight up. "Addison Greyborne? I've heard a lot about you."

"Well, I guess you have, like everyone else, given the newspapers lately."

His eyes dropped, a slight smile tugging at the corners of his moustached lip. "Not completely true—I also know you are the owner of the Beyond the Page bookstore, and the wonderful young woman who most generously donated the books for us to sell on behalf of the library fundraiser." He held out his hand. "I'm very pleased to meet you." He clicked his heels together. "Phillip Madison, proprietor, at your service." He bowed his head. "So, what is your pleasure as you wait for this event to get started? A drink at the bar? Dinner in the dining room? You name it; everything for you will always be on the house."

"That's very nice, but completely unnecessary."

"Nonsense; it's my place. I can do what I want for whomever I want. Just name your poison."

"You know what I'd like right now?"

"Just name it."

"I'd like a tour of the cavern you're revealing tonight— you know, before all the ghost walk tour participants arrive."

"That's all?"

She nodded.

"No problem. Your wish is my command. Follow me." He gestured her forward with a low, sweeping bow.

A young serving girl came over to them and whispered in Phillip's ear. He frowned. "I'm sorry, Miss Greyborne, as we are still scrambling to set up, there appears to be a minor issue that demands my attention."

"That's fine, I understand. I'll wait and have my tour with everyone else."

He shook his head. "I promised you anything you want. If I show you the access, you could go down by yourself and wander around. We've strung lights all through the main parts of the tunnel system, except for a couple of small off-shoots, which are marked as hazardous still. I don't recommend anyone entering those. Our guides will stand beside those areas on the main tour. However, as long as you're aware beforehand and promise me not to go down them."

"Deal."

"Okay. I do apologize again." He led her to the back wall and pulled open two wide wooden plank doors. "These were designed to look like part of the facade in the dining room, but what lies behind them is another world that we discovered during refurbishing. I've kept them closed while renovations were underway."

"I've eaten here twice," she said, eyeing the doors, "and just thought they were part of the wall decor."

He smiled. "That's exactly what we wanted people to think."

She followed him into a well-lit, small grotto—in the center of which was a gaping hole. The top rungs of a ladder protruded from the rim.

"It's an easy climb down to the bottom, and there you will enter the world of Blackbeard, Captain Kidd, and William Fly, just to mention a few of our most notorious earlier inhabitants. Enjoy."

"Is there anyone else down there now?" She walked to the edge. "Staff or renovation workers?"

"No workers at this time of night, and I'm keeping the staff busy up here putting the final touches on the event."

"Thanks. Just wanted to know what to expect."

"See you later, but I do have to run now." He turned and disappeared back into the main part of the restaurant.

She peered into the hole. It wasn't that far down. She took a deep breath and began the short descent to the bottom.

A huge grotto opened up before her. She scanned the oak barrels, arranged from the floor to the ceiling, interspersed with ceramic wine casks. In the center of the cavern sat chairs around a long, rough timber table, laid out with pewter mugs, plates, and serving jugs. It appeared tonight just as it may have during the golden years of piracy, although this setting was most likely tidier than it might have been a few hundred years ago. She walked through the cavern to the lighted passageway she spotted on the back wall.

The passage gradually narrowed and descended into a tunnel, its walls lined with rough-hewn bunk beds covered with straw sleeping pallets. She passed by three smaller side passage openings that were all blocked off by wooden barriers and "No Entry" signs. When she reached the end of the main tunnel, she scanned the boulder-clad wall and figured the other side would be the beach cave that the British had blocked with their cannon blasts.

If burying treasure was really a pirate thing, it would have been buried, not stored in a well-established hideaway. This cave appeared to be a hideout, a haven, and not the kind of place where someone stashed their treasures. She headed back to the main grotto, but stopped in mid-step.

A scuffling sound echoed out from the barricaded passage on her right. She cocked her head and listened harder, slowly making her way over to the entrance. The scuffling continued, then a pinging noise like metal striking rock echoed down the blackened passage. A light flicked in the distance, and she squinted. "Is someone there?" She leaned into the tunnel mouth. "Hello, is anyone there?"

She dropped her handbag and climbed over the wooden barrier, pulling her cell phone out of her pocket. She turned on the flashlight app and crept toward the source of the light and sound. "Hello," she called again. "I think all work is supposed to stop. A tour will be coming through soon."

All went silent, and the far light snapped out. She cocked her head, listening for any sounds of movement. A chill rippled across her shoulders. She flipped off her light and turned toward the main tunnel. "Stupid, stupid, stupid me," she muttered and picked up her pace.

"Yes, you are," a husky voice hissed from behind her.

A hot, sharp pain slammed into the right side of Addie's head. She started to drop to her knees, but fingers gripped the back of her hair and yanked up hard. In the faint light from the main tunnel, out of the corner of her eye, she caught sight of a whizzing blur aimed directly for her head. She grabbed her hair at the roots to help fight off the searing pain in her scalp and dropped down as far as her hair would allow her to. The swing swooshed inches above her head.

She reached behind her and grabbed hold of the sides of her attacker's head and yanked hard, smashing it into the back of hers. The grip on her was lost, and she stumbled forward. Arms grabbed her around the knees, and she plummeted, face-first, onto the bedrock ground. Blinding pain seared across her face. An unseen arm flipped her onto her back. Hot breath wafted across her cheek, and the chill of cold steel pressed against her skin.

She fought the pulsating pain that seized her and struggled to open her eyes. "You?" she wheezed, the knife blade pressing hard against her throat.

Chapter Thirty-Eight

A cold, calloused hand gripped the back of Addie's neck and yanked her to her feet, the blade edge biting into her skin. Dorothy's pungent breath wafted across her face when she thrust Addie against the tunnel wall.

"I'm not going to let you," Dorothy growled, pressing on the blade, "or anyone else, stand in the way of me getting what I worked hard for." She jolted Addie's head against the wall. "No one. Do you hear me?" she shouted, spraying droplets on Addie's face.

The razor-sharp blade had already sent a warm, oozing sensation trickling down her neck. Even if she wanted to respond, she didn't dare move.

"Addie, are you down here?" a voice called from the main tunnel.

Her eyes darted to the entrance, and Dorothy's hand clamped hard over her mouth. "Shhh," she whispered, "don't say a word, or . . ." The blade nipped at her throat.

"Addie?" The voice grew louder. "Addie, it's me, Simon. Are you down here?"

Dorothy pinned her with wild eyes. Addie kicked out hard against Dorothy's shin, sending her reeling backward.

"Simon!" Addie screamed. "Hurry, she has a knife." His silhouette raced toward her. She gasped a sigh of relief.

Out of the dark, a shape leapt up and tackled Simon to the ground. Addie pulled her phone from her pocket, brandished it over her head and smashed it hard across the side of Dorothy's head. She slumped forward onto Simon. With her foot, Addie rolled her to the side and pressed her boot down across Dorothy's neck to hold her still. She reached down to help Simon to his feet, and a bloodied hand grasped at hers. He cried out in pain and slowly made his way to his feet, cradling his hand.

"Oh my God, Simon, you're hurt." She scanned the ground for her cell phone, which she'd dropped in the force of striking her target.

He wavered on his feet and slumped against the tunnel wall. "I'll be okay," he gasped. "Don't take your foot off her. I'll call 911." He retrieved his phone from his pocket and slid down the wall to the bedrock floor.

Addie rocked back and forth in her chair. The tight gauze and tape applied to her throat was a reminder of having just lived through her worst anxiety dream come to life. She shivered and focused on the swirling gray patterns of the waiting room floor. The sight of a pair of black boots broke her concentration, and she looked up.

"Marc?" She leapt to her feet. "Thank you for coming so quickly after Simon phoned. I don't know what I would have done if you had come any later."

"It's a good thing I was just outside the Den doing crowd control." He held out her purse. "Here, I thought you might want this back."

"How did you get that?" She looked at it and then at him, taking it from his hand.

"From Simon, I guess he went looking for you when you

didn't show up at the ghost walk. So he went to Smuggler's Den on the off chance that you were already there. The manager told him the last time he saw you, was at the tunnel entrance. You must have dropped it outside the barricade. That's how Simon knew where you were in the shaft." He held her out at arm's length, his eyes wide, and studied her face warily. "Are you okay?"

She sniffed and looked down at her feet. "Yeah, I will be. The cuts aren't too deep, and the doctor said they should heal up nicely. I might get lucky and not even have much of a scar."

Marc tucked a strand of hair behind her ear. "That's good." He smiled. "Come here." He held his arms open.

"No, I'm fine. I don't need a . . . sympathy hug."

"Come here." His arms remained open and waiting.

She nestled into his chest and took a deep breath. The heady scent of his cologne overran her erratic thoughts. His closeness felt so good and right—how had they ever come to the place where they were now? "I was going crazy. I couldn't check Simon's stab wound, so I didn't know how bad it was, because I had to keep my foot on Dorothy's throat, in case she attacked again or ran."

"You did just fine," he whispered into her hair.

"Any word on Simon yet?"

His arms stiffened. "Not that I've heard lately." He pulled away.

She jerked, the spell broken. "It's just that his hands are so important to his work. What if he can't perform surgery anymore?"

"Don't worry about the what-ifs."

"I can't help but worry. You should have seen the blood, it was everywhere, and they won't tell me anything because I'm not family. The only information I have is through Carolyn, and she's barely left his side." Tears pooled in her eyes.

"They won't even let me in to see him. Oh, Marc." A single tear rolled down her cheek. "His work is his whole life."

"Let me see if I have any better luck getting information." He patted her shoulder and headed to the nursing station.

"Look who I have here?" Carolyn's voice rang out behind her. Addie spun around on her heel.

"Simon," she squealed. "Oh my God." She threw her arms around his neck and hugged him. "Thank you, thank you, thank you for finding me when you did." She grinned at him and wiped a rogue tear off her cheek.

He smiled up at her from the wheelchair. "I always did like your thank-yous." His smile widened.

"So, what did the doctor say? When will you be released?"

He looked up at her, her throat catching at his searching gaze. "I guess no one told you, but . . . as soon as my chauffeur here"—he motioned his head behind him to Carolyn—"wheels me out that door"—he nodded toward the emergency entrance—"I'm a free man."

Addie's mouth dropped open. "You're kidding, right?" He shook his head.

"Isn't that wonderful?" Carolyn beamed.

"So, no damage done by the knife wound?"

He shook his head. "I got real lucky. No tendons or ligaments touched; just a clean through-and-through stab." He held up his gauze-wrapped hand. "I'll be back in the operating room in no time." He smiled, and then a shadow swept across his face. "Sorry to disappoint you, Chief, if you dropped by to offer Carolyn your condolences on my demise."

Marc snorted above Addie's shoulder. "I came to check up on my"—he cleared his throat—"*team*, wondering if I was going to have to replace the both of you."

Addie glared at him. He stood rigid, adjusting his holster belt, and then grinned at Simon.

Addie laughed and slapped his arm. Carolyn and Simon chuckled.

"Glad to see you in such high spirits, Doc, but so you know, I do expect a full report on your medical treatment of Steven and what happened this evening on my desk by morning."

Addie's eyes widened. "But it is morning. Look out the window."

"Well then, he'd better get to work right away." His teeth flashed in a smile.

"The only work he'll be doing right now is getting comfortable in my spare bedroom, I'm afraid, Chief. So I'd better get him to bed now before the kids wake up and find out he's there and don't give him a minute of peace and quiet." Carolyn whisked him past Marc and Addie. "Say good night, Simon," she ordered.

"Good night." He waved over his shoulder.

Addie yawned. Her hand immediately shot to her throat. "Ouch, that pulled." She rubbed at the gauze.

"Hands off." Marc pulled her hand away. "Those butterfly strips are there to keep the wound from opening, so you don't need stitches."

"But they itch."

"Better than the alternative."

"I guess." She pouted.

"Good. Now it's time to get you home, little lady. You're turning into a two-year-old."

"No." She scrubbed her hands over her face. "I'm too wound up for that. Think I need a cup of coffee though. How about you?"

"Yeah, I could go for one. It's been a long night."

She followed him over to the vending machine, where he produced a steaming cup and held it out to her, then dropped some more coins in the machine and waited for his. They made their way over to a quiet corner of the waiting room and slumped down into two chairs. He leaned his elbow on the chair arm, scrubbing his hand over his face.

"Were you interrogating Dorothy all night?"

"And Dean."

"You caught him?"

"Yup." Marc stretched and leaned back, his fingers interlocked behind his head. "Jerry picked him up out on the highway headed toward Boston."

"And?"

"And," he said, pressing his lips tight, "he wasn't Steven's assailant."

"What?"

Marc nodded. "He's guilty of conspiring to commit a crime, among a few other smaller things, like sending the last threatening gift box to you, but—"

"Wait, he sent the flag and knife?"

"Apparently, he saw you having lunch with Simon," he said, dropping his eyes, "and he followed you to the museum."

"He could have. I didn't know who Dean was then and wouldn't have recognized him. What about the first one, the one with the rat?"

"That was Steven. He knew you had some of June's notes and was afraid you'd start searching for the treasure yourself and wanted to scare you off."

"Okay then, who was it that attacked Steven? Don't tell me his attacker was Jeanie?"

"Nope."

"Who, then? Come on," she said, grasping his arm, "I'm too tired to play right now."

His eyes crinkled at the corners, and he glanced sideways at her. "Dorothy."

She gasped. "She beat up Steven?"

"Well, you know her strength."

Addie's hand went to her throat. She shifted on the hard chair. "I don't get it."

"I don't doubt it. The whole thing gets a little complicated. It took us a while to sort through it all, but we did, eventually, because I kept remembering the . . . theories, you shared."

She snorted, stifling a laugh and glanced around the empty waiting room. "Okay, then spill."

He chuckled and leaned forward, his elbows on his knees. "You're going to make me say it, aren't you?"

She nodded, her eyes twinkling.

"Well," he said, yawning, "most of it is as you suspected all along, and I was too pigheaded to listen." He sat back and crossed his arms. "It seems Dean and Steven, aka Peter Jacobson, did meet up in LA through an introduction by Lacey." Addie nodded and mentally checked that clue off her blackboard. "Dean told him about June's book, and they concocted a plan to search for the buried treasure that June thought might still be hidden in Greyborne Harbor. Peter created the false identity of Steven, including dying his hair."

"I bet he thought changing it from blond would disguise him enough in case someone recognized him. I guess he hadn't counted on that someone being Lacey, who had worked closely with him and spotted the similarities right off, which is what really got my radar buzzing."

"Yeah, he was definitely trying to hide his true identity. First, he made himself appear older for June, but when he got nowhere with her. He gradually went straight black to make himself more attractive to the younger Jeanie. In the hope he could dupe at least one of them into giving him access to the original manuscript, because Dean couldn't remember all the details after his one and only read of it. As you know, it's far more detailed than the published version was, so they needed it to move forward with their plan."

She leaned forward, her eyes set on his.

"It seems that Steven *was* drugging June in order to knock her out so that when she slept, he could search through her house for it. When that didn't work, he started an affair with Jeanie, continuing to drug June, so he and Jeanie could spend time together in the hope that she might reveal where the original was."

"But she didn't know where it was."

"No, she didn't. Anyway, while all this was going on, Dean and Steven were also working on excavating the utility tunnel, because Dean thought, from what he could remember of the manuscript, that was the most likely location of this supposed treasure."

"But when they finally broke through, they found it empty, right?"

"Right. Dean was furious, as he had invested all his money into the project and was left empty-handed."

"So he had a fight with Steven that night in the garage. But I thought you said he wasn't Steven's attacker?"

"I did, and they did, but just a few punches were exchanged. Dean swears that when he left, Steven was fine."

"So how does Dorothy fit into all this? Was she a partner, too?"

He shook his head. "She wasn't part of their scheme, but she did catch on to it. She was already furious with June for dismissing her from working on the book; she felt like June ignored her and wouldn't share credit for the success of the book. She found another way to make sure she got payment for the research work she'd helped June with in the beginning."

"From the first day I met Dorothy, I had a gut feeling she was involved somehow and hiding something. I should have known better and followed my instincts."

"But you did as soon as you had proof, like Dorothy having June's phone and her lying about being with Jeanie at the hospital. And you acted on them—you let me know."

"And look where it got me." She pointed to her neck.

"There were just so many puzzle pieces I was missing. No wonder I couldn't put them together."

"But you had most of them. Just think, if you hadn't been asked to join that book club, we wouldn't know half of what we do. So I figure that because of your intuition, we are miles ahead in unraveling all those pieces you're whining about." He took her hand, rubbing his thumb in small circles over the back of it. Her skin quivered under his touch, and she pulled her hand away.

"Anyway, getting back to another one of those missing pieces." He took a deep breath. "Apparently, when June and Dorothy were leaving the book club meeting, they noticed the utility shed door wasn't quite secured. As I understand it, Dean and Steven were working down there, and a pebble had probably gotten stuck in the doorjamb, so it hadn't latched behind them."

"Pretty sloppy on their part."

"Well, neither man showed much smarts through this whole thing anyway. Except when Dean had a good friend who worked for the utility company and he managed to make a copy of the shed key that his friend had."

"Maybe he was smarter than I thought." She looked down at her hand in her lap and wished she hadn't pulled it away from him. She needed his warmth, his touch.

"June was curious as to why the door wasn't secured and went in. Dorothy had already started to put things together about what Steven was really up to with June, so she followed her in. When she saw the extension cord and a tool kit she'd seen once in the trunk of his car when he drove her home after a book club meeting, it confirmed it for her. She had never told June about the tools or her suspicions, so when June wanted to call the police because things didn't appear right in the shed, they had an argument."

"And I'm guessing that since Dorothy was already furious with June for cutting her out of the book deal, she wasn't going to let her cut her out of an opportunity to get her hands on a piece of the treasure, too?"

"Exactly. She said she wasn't thinking straight, saw a shovel by the door, and, well . . ."

"Wow." Addie sat back. "Dorothy was the killer all along." She shook her head. "I didn't see that one coming. Was it her, then, who called in the report about me having the shovel?"

"No. That was Lacey trying drive a deeper wedge between you and me, and to keep her news stories going."

"It all really does come down to something my dad always said."

"What's that?"

"The motive behind every murder is love, jealousy, or money. It seems this one had all three."

He shifted on his chair. "I think your dad was onto something with that."

"Did she say why she hung onto June's cell phone?"

"There are lots of nasty emails and text exchanges between them, and she didn't want anyone to see them."

Addie rubbed the sides of her neck.

"Stop that." Marc pulled her hand away and helped her to her feet. "Come on, let's go. We both need sleep."

She shook her head and flopped back into the chair.

He kneeled beside her. "Now what?"

"I was just thinking . . ."

"Oh no," he groaned and laid his head on the armrest.

"You stop it." She looked at his hair, just inches away from her hand. How her fingers itched to feel the softness. "You know what the really sad part of all of this is—aside, of course, from so many people getting hurt by it? Is that any treasure's been gone for years, and I think June tried to tell people that after she found the British navy's document on their exploits here. The only real treasures left to discover were the first editions of *A General History of the*

Robberies and Murders of the Most Notorious Pyrates in my aunt's attic."

"How much are they worth?" Marc lifted his head off the armrest and studied her.

"Well, not a fortune—only about fifteen to twenty thousand all together—but these copies are in a remarkably good condition so might get a little more on the open market."

"So what's your plan with them?"

She shrugged. "Not sure. I think I'll probably donate them. Maybe take them to Boston to see if the library or maybe the Marine Museum will be interested. After all, you have to consider how many works of classic literature this set inspired. *Treasure Island* by Robert Louis Stevenson, to name only one."

"So, after all this, June did find a treasure." Marc smiled. "Well, I'm sure one of them will be interested." He stood up again and assisted her to her feet.

She held on to his hands longer than necessary. "Yeah, I'll think on it and maybe take a drive down there and see what they say."

"Okay, but first, you sleep." He placed his hand on the small of her back and escorted her out the door.

Addie quickly showered and dressed, then dabbed some makeup on to hide the dark circles that no sleep brings out. She hopped in her car, opting to take the scenic coastal highway to Salem, after the events of the night. She needed the serenity of it to calm herself down. Her plan setting out was then to cut over to a route, just past Salem that would lead her to the interstate. Addie crossed her fingers that her nerves and lack of sleep wouldn't catch up to her before she hit the crazy traffic into Boston. She estimated that the round-trip should take less than two hours, including her stop and then *nothing* was going to keep her from her warm, comfy bed. That was the mental carrot she dangled in front of herself as she turned onto the highway.

On the drive, she was still torn between which one she should approach first: the library or the museum. Addie hesitated for a moment when she came to an overhead sign indicating an exit ramp, at the last minute. She cut hard to the right and sailed into the early-morning traffic. She pulled up in front of the museum, parked, grabbed her bag from the seat, and headed through the entrance. There was no one at the desk by the door, so she walked over to the back counter.

A silver-haired woman looked up from the paperwork spread out in front of her. "Addie, great to see you again."

"Hi, Hanna." She grinned. "I have something for you." She pulled the original 1724 version, and the 1726 and 1728 volumes printed by Thomas Woodward of *A General History of the Robberies and Murders of the Most Notorious Pyrates* out of her bag and laid them on the countertop.

"What?" Hanna patted her chest. "You're kidding?"

"Nope, they're all yours to display in the museum."

Hanna stroked the calfskin binding. "How much are you selling them for? They must be worth—"

"No, I'm donating them."

"You can't be serious." Her mouth dropped open.

"I am," Addie said, smiling, "in my aunt's name and in memory of June. I can't think of a better home for them than with the descendant of a real pirate queen who is working at something that she was obviously born to do."

"I don't know what to say." She looked down at the books and caressed the soft leather with her fingers.

"Have a great day." Addie turned and headed out the door.

"Thank . . . thank you," Hanna called out.

Addie stopped on the step. She looked up at the pirate statue, winked, and shook her head. "Pirate books, treasure maps, and ghosts—what next, a band of rogue elves out to destroy Christmas?" She chuckled and headed to her car.

Please turn the page for
an exciting sneak peek of
Lauren Elliott's next
Beyond the Page Bookstore Mystery,

MURDER IN THE FIRST EDITION,

coming soon wherever
print and eBooks are sold!

Addison Groyborne's eyes glistened with the reflection of the glimmering snowflakes hanging from the delicate fairy lights she'd retrieved from her aunt's attic. They were perfect. Both of her shop's bay windows resembled a winter wonderland of lights. She wrapped her arms around her middle and crossed her fingers. Hopefully, the holiday glow would beckon passersby.

"Morning, Addie," a stocky woman called as she passed along the sidewalk.

"Good morning, Carol." Addie smiled and waved.

Had it really only been just over a year since she'd established Beyond the Page, her book and curio shop? It was hard to believe given the bumps and bruises she'd endured along the way, but now, she was truly a part of this town that she'd grown to love.

"Good morning, Addie," another passerby called out.

"Morning," she said, smiling.

"Your displays are looking good."

"Thanks." Addie grinned and took a step back to get a clearer view of both windows. The display of books in the right one caught her attention.

She pressed her face to the cold glass, wiped off the

condensation from her warm breath, and peered at the small tree in the center, colorfully decorated with antique ornaments. But it was still missing something. Tinsel! That's what it needed, and the book sets she'd wrapped with holiday ribbon and displayed like gifts on a red tree skirt beneath it needed an extra splash of sparkle to make it all just perfect. She made a mental note to buy tinsel and added another package of artificial snow to her shopping list. Outdoor inspection complete, she opened the door to her store and drew in a deep breath.

The crisp smell of the New England sea air combined with the scent of old books and leather tickled at her nose, but this morning she also detected the hint of a new aroma. It appeared that Paige Stringer, her shop assistant, had placed small, festive bowls and baskets of apple-cinnamon potpourri on bookshelves throughout the shop.

The fragrance stirred warm memories of her childhood home and her family, now all since passed, including her beloved David. They were to have been married by now and should have been celebrating the season together, but he . . . A tear slid down her cheek. She swatted at it and forced that memory back into its box in her mind as she headed for the coffee maker on the far end of the long antique Victorian bar she used for a sales counter.

Paige poked her blond, curly head out of the storeroom, grinned, waved, and disappeared back inside. Addie shook her head and tossed her purse and red wool coat on the counter. Dropping a coffee pod into the machine, she sorted through the previous day's receipts as the aroma of fresh brewing coffee taunted her. Paige reappeared, wearing an "I ♥ the Cook" apron and carrying two steaming mugs in her hands.

"What are you up to?"

"Well?" Paige waved a mug under Addie's nose. "What do you think?"

"I think I smell my grandmother's Christmas apple-spiced punch?" Addie clasped the cup and waved the fragrance toward her. She took a sip. "Yes, perfect." She beamed over the rim.

"Good." Paige gave a toothy grin. "After you told me yesterday that your grandmother's punch was one of your fondest Christmas memories, I worked most of the night perfecting the recipe you gave me."

Addie took another sip. "You've done well, thank you."

"I brought in a small hot plate so I can prepare it in the back room and a large coffee urn that we can refill as needed. I thought it might be a good idea to have it up here on the counter for customers. You know as an alternative to coffee for the holidays. What do you think?"

"I think," Addie said, setting her mug down, crossing her arms, and looking hard at Paige, "that you come up with some . . ."

Paige sucked in a sharp breath.

". . . of the most . . . outstanding ideas."

Paige's cheeks flushed with a rosy glow. "You always get me."

"Just keeping you on your toes." Addie winked, grinning. "I don't want all your brilliant ideas going to your head."

"No risk of that happening with you as my boss." Paige returned an exaggerated wink. "I'll fill the urn and set it up." She swung on her heel and headed to the back room, straightening bookshelves as she went.

Addie smiled at her protégé. She really had turned out to be the perfect employee, despite her best friend, and the local tea merchant, Serena's, initial misgivings as to where Paige's loyalties might lie. Would they be with Addie, her employer, or the tyrant baker next door, Martha, her mother?

But time proved Paige most adept at finding a balance between the two of them.

Addie scanned the store. A large wreath and a few more lighted green garlands to wrap around the pillar posts would complete the holiday ensemble. Now to only find time to shop. When she glanced past the window, she spotted a man dressed in a black trench coat and black hat with the brim pulled down covering his features. He stood across the street, seemingly staring at her shop. A shiver traveled up her spine. She moved closer to the window for a better look, but a large delivery van pulled up, blocking her view of the man.

The courier driver hopped down from his truck and scurried to her front door, yanking it open. The door chimes protested with a merry tinkle. Within thirty seconds, he had delivered a package, asked for a signature, and left with the same force, the chimes still echoing from the first time. She peered across the street after Mr. Speedy screeched away. The man in black was gone.

Addie shrugged and glanced at the large envelope. From Boston. With a smile, she placed it on a shelf under the front counter. The door chimes rang. She looked up, a welcoming smile forming on her lips. The color drained from her face, and the smile faded. The man in black removed his hat, ran a leather-gloved hand over his silver hair, and stood silently staring at her.

She grasped the counter edge to keep her wobbly knees in check. "Jonathan?"

"Hi, Addie." A smile tickled the corners of his mouth.

She swallowed hard to release the lump growing in the back of her throat.

He shuffled his weight from one foot to the other. "Maybe I should have called first?"

"No." She shook her head and walked around the end of the counter. "You just surprised me. That's all. Come in;

please have a seat." She motioned to a counter stool. "Would you like some coffee, or hot spiced Christmas punch?"

He shook his head and slid onto a stool. "Coffee's fine. Just a quick warm-up and I'll be on my way." He pulled off his gloves.

"You're leaving?" She glanced over her shoulder from where she stood at the coffee maker. "But you just got here."

"Afraid so. There's a big storm coming tonight or tomorrow, and I'd like to get past it before the highways are closed. But I'd heard you'd moved to Greyborne Harbor, and, well . . . just stopped to say hello."

"Five sugars, right?" She grimaced, wondering how he didn't go into instant sugar shock as she passed him his coffee. "This is hardly on the interstate running to and from anywhere, is it?"

He nodded, lifting the cup to his lips. "Exactly what I needed, thanks." He set it down. "No, it's not, but I'm on my way home from a business meeting in Boston and am living north of Albany now. So, before the forecast changed, I'd already decided on a short detour to drop in to wish you a merry Christmas." He reached over and clasped her hand, guiding her to the stool beside him. "But now it appears it's going to have to be a shorter visit than I first planned."

"I'm glad you stopped by anyway." Her throat tightened. "It's wonderful to see you again." She released her hand from his.

Paige coughed and placed the large urn on the end of the counter, glancing at the stranger.

"Paige, this is—"

The chimes over the door jangled. "Morning, Addie." Catherine Lewis swept toward the counter. She pulled off her gloves and slid onto a stool.

"Good morning, Catherine." Addie rose to her feet. "You're out and about early today."

"Yes, lots of shopping to do, and my car's in the garage. So I'm on foot today and have a lot of ground to cover. I thought I'd better get an early start and headed right here for one of your delicious fresh brewed coffees to get me going." She nodded at the silver-haired man seated beside her.

"Paige, Catherine, I'd like you both to meet my . . . umm, David's father. Jonathan Hemingway."

"Hemingway?" Paige's brow creased. "I thought David's last name was Armstrong or something?"

Addie nudged Paige with her elbow.

"Yes." Jonathan cleared his throat. "His name *was* Hemingway. His mother and I divorced when he was quite young, and she remarried."

"You're a relative of Addie's?" Catherine turned to him, her hand outstretched. "How wonderful."

His eyes and hand held fast with hers. "I must say, your husband is a very lucky man."

"I'm . . . I'm not married." Her porcelain complexion turned a shade of peach.

"Jonathan, this is Catherine Lewis. She's a good friend of mine and was also a close friend of my father's."

"It truly is a pleasure to meet you, Catherine." He brought her delicate hand to his lips and kissed the back of it. "Any friend of Addie's and the late Michael Greyborne's is a friend of mine, too."

"Hemingway, like the author?" she all but purred when his thumb began stroking the back of her hand.

Paige looked at Addie, who was in the midst of an involuntary eye roll.

"Yes, he's a distant relative and may be the reason my son had such a fascination with books and women who love books." He glanced at Addie, but then caressed Catherine with another gaze. "Do you love books, too, Catherine?"

Catherine let out a breathy sigh and pulled her hand away.

Her already flushed cheeks brightened with an intense, fiery hue. She straightened wayward strands of her brown, shoulder-cropped hair, slid off her stool, and backed toward the door. A shy smile graced her lips. "It . . . ah . . . was wonderful to meet you. I hope . . ." She swallowed. "I hope I run into you again, Jonathan, before you leave." She studied the tips of her toes before bolting out the door.

Addie looked at Jonathan from under a creased brow. "I see you haven't changed at all." She clucked her tongue.

He tossed his head back and released a barrel-chested laugh. Addie gave Paige a dismissive head tilt, and after the girl retreated with the book cart into the back room, Addie glowered at him.

He smirked. "What?"

"I see you're still up to your same old tricks. I thought you promised David that was all in the past."

He looked up at her and set his cup down. "And I see you have carried on the same grudge my son held against me for years. He forgave me in the end, Addie. Why can't you?"

She threw her hands in the air. "I did, and I tried, for David's sake, but what do you expect after that seduction I just witnessed?"

"Really? Just exactly what did you see? Me being kind to an attractive woman? I didn't see her complaining. Did you?"

"I saw the same thing I saw for the five years David and I were together. Something he'd lived with his entire life."

His eyes narrowed. "And just what was that?"

"Every time you dropped in out of the blue, there was a different woman on your arm. You'd deposit her on our doorstep and disappear, leaving us to entertain your flavor of the month and then not return for hours, acting all nonchalant like you'd just popped down to get something from your car." Her knuckles whitened when she gripped the edge of the counter. "You never showed any regard for the emotional havoc those visits created, leaving me to try to put him back together after you'd disappear again for months without another word."

"I didn't realize that my family visits were such an imposition on you." His lip twitched.

"They wouldn't have been except for the fact that you never spent any time with your son, and left us to make small talk with your . . . your . . ." Her whole body vibrated.

He shrugged. "They were all in a similar line of work as you were in, and there were even a few who were in David's line. So, you had something in common with them." His hand clasped hers. "Look, I was busy. Working."

"Working?" Her eyes widened. "The visits were just a cover for having us babysit your latest piece of arm candy?"

"Addie." He squeezed her hand. "David eventually came to understand the hours my work demanded, and he didn't let it stand in the way of our relationship the last few years." She yanked her hand out of his. "Why can't you let the past go, too?"

Her chin jutted out. "Because you kept lying to him, and it broke my heart."

Jonathan's shoulders stiffened. "I never lied to my son."

"But you did, every time you'd tell him that this wasn't like the old days, that this woman was serious. But it never was, because he saw the same old revolving door of your women friends, just like he had his whole life. Then you'd promise him that the next visit would be longer, and you'd spend more time with him." Her eyes flashed. "Did you know that after one of your later visits, he started to become withdrawn? He seemed worried and wouldn't even talk to me about you anymore."

"I see." He stood up and collected his hat and gloves from the counter. "Just remember that everything is not always as it appears. David came to know that." He placed his hat on his head and nodded, pulling one glove on.

"Look, Jonathan, we're like family, and I want to believe in you, but Catherine is a good woman. A nice woman. But she's emotionally fragile, because she's been hurt more than she ever should have been during her life. Stay away from her, please. She doesn't need you and your old philandering ways, only to have her heart broken again."

He tilted his head. One corner of his mouth twitched. "Give me more credit than that, will you?"

"I know you, Jonathan."

He leaned over the counter, fixing his steel-gray eyes on hers. "Do you?"

She crossed her arms and nodded. "I just saw it with my own eyes."

He straightened and pulled on his other glove. "Don't worry about Catherine. I'm pretty sure she's a big girl and is capable of making her own decisions." His brow rose, and he smirked. "I have a lunch date, so if you'll excuse me."

"I'm warning you. Stay away from her, please. For me. I don't want to have to clean up another mess in the wake of your visit."

To her surprise, he smiled just a little, revealing a suggestion of dimples in both of his cheeks. Addie wavered. Everything about his features reminded her of David, from the set of his jaw to his magnetic gray eyes and the way he held his head. David had looked exactly like a younger version of him.

"Don't worry," he said, his throaty voice softening, "I'm not about to go chasing down the street after Catherine. My luncheon is with an old friend who lives in Greyborne Harbor now."

"Who's that? Another friend of mine I'll have to warn about becoming involved with you?" She searched his face for a moment. "Although if she knew you before, I'm pretty sure she knows what you're all about."

His eyes twinkled with a hint of mischievousness. "She does, don't worry. Teresa Lang is very familiar with my ways."

"Teresa Lang." Her eyes flashed.

His lips turned up at the corners.

"You don't mean the same Teresa who's the charity fund-raising coordinator for the Hospital Foundation, do you?"

"Yes, why, do you know her?"

"I have an appointment with her today after lunch about the Christmas Charity Auction."

"Then you'd better not plan on her being there until at least mid-afternoon. You know, in case our lunch date goes as per usual." He gave her a sly wink and then added, "Merry Christmas." The door closed behind him, the overhead chimes seemingly singing with joy at his departure.